WATER AND WIND

ASH FITZSIMMONS

WATER

AND

WIND

THE CROSSING

3

WATER AND WIND. Copyright © 2023 by Ash Fitzsimmons.

Print Edition ISBN: 978-1-949861-59-4

Cover design by MiblArt.

www.ashfitzsimmons.com

CHAPTER 1

The gods demand truth.

Once upon a time, in the kingdom of Daril, there lived a well-beloved king, Jaanarel, one of the most successful of the long Fulquir line to sit the throne in Deoni. Handsome, skilled at arms, and blessed with roguish charm, he could have chosen any lady in the kingdom—or in any of the human realms of Kopaat, for that matter—but he wooed and won Callo Tolva, a beautiful lady who'd caught his eye at a summer party. Callo was no one of particular prominence, the fourth daughter of a minor nobleman, but she was clever, and once she saw the effect she had upon the young king, she worked it to her advantage. When the two were married, Daril feasted for three days in their honor.

But the king and queen's happiness was marred by the silent reproach of the empty palace nursery. Try as they did to conceive, they remained childless. Thrice Callo found herself pregnant, and thrice the gods took the child from her before birth. In the midst of the queen's struggles, the king's advisors quietly suggested that he look beyond their marriage bed for an heir. His firstborn would rule after him, no matter who the child's mother might be. Indeed, there was precedent—Jaanarel's own grandfather was the son of a junior palace cook, and though the queen had railed against the unfairness of her own sons not inheriting the throne, the law was clear about the succession. But Jaanarel loved Callo too much to be unfaithful to her, and so he continued to go to her bed and pray for a miracle.

Finally, the gods granted his request. Callo brought forth their firstborn child, a dark-haired, blue-eyed daughter. The little princess was perfect, a pudgy, rosy-cheeked baby with *very* healthy lungs, and her overjoyed parents named her Erianthe.

The crown princess would be her parents' only child. All attempts to produce a sibling ended in failure, and too soon, the royal midwife told Callo that her days of childbearing were behind her. Thus, it should come as no surprise that Erianthe was the darling of her parents' eye, loved, coddled, and more than a little spoiled.

As far as Jaanarel was concerned, his precious girl could do no wrong, and no request was too great. It fell to Callo to civilize Erianthe, insisting that she pay attention to her lessons and learn to act in a manner befitting her station. Callo appointed masters for etiquette and dancing, history and politics, penmanship and needlecraft, poetry and painting. By the age of ten, Erianthe was fluent in both New Kopaati and Common, the language favored in Daril's trading posts in distant Ga'besh. She could ride a chiquiw as well as any well-bred child, and while she was no great student, her academic progress satisfied the masters. She'd even shown the rudiments of talent. Though humans in general could do very little with magic, Erianthe's position gave her access to Aen crystals, which she learned to use to amplify her ability. With proper concentration, she could call objects to herself from across a room or dim or brighten the lanterns, but what she most frequently accomplished with her power was a temporary deadening of the gnawing in her stomach. Unlike her mother, who'd been girlishly thin all her life, Erianthe still bore her baby fat, and Callo carefully monitored her daughter's diet.

Erianthe's looks weren't the only matter on the queen's mind. Noting the young men who circled at the periphery of the court, even though the princess was more than a decade from majority, Callo decided to nip their jockeying in the bud and went to Jaanarel with a proposal: they should betroth her to a suitable man and secure an advantageous marriage for their daughter before she grew old enough to allow her eyes to lead her astray. At first, Jaanarel wasn't thrilled with the idea—he'd appreciated having the freedom to choose his own bride—but he warmed to the plan when Callo named a suitable candidate: Narod Terol, a young prince of Cirivant. As his parents' fourth child, Narod was almost guaranteed never to sit his father's throne, but he was sufficiently highborn for a Darili princess. Plus, Callo explained, if their families were so joined, then surely Cirivant, the wealthiest human kingdom in Ga'besh, would be willing to employ its peerless navy to assist when Daril's trading posts were attacked by pirates.

Duly convinced, Jaanarel sent word to the Cirivanti crown through the maladetas resident in their respective courts. The prospective groom's parents were delighted with the idea and easily saw the benefit to both sides: Daril would receive protection, while Cirivant's prominence would rise beyond Ga'besh when a ruler of Terol blood took the Darili throne. Erianthe was only about a year older than Narod, so they could marry soon after she reached majority. To the parents, it seemed like a perfect plan.

Erianthe, however, had her doubts. At ten, she wasn't thrilled with boys in general, much less the idea of being betrothed to one of them. But when she balked, Callo grew firm with her. Erianthe wasn't just a child—she was the crown princess, and as such, she had a duty to her people to marry well and produce an heir to the throne. Narod was an excellent match for her. And while the decision to agree to the betrothal was ultimately Erianthe's, Callo informed her daughter that there would be *consequences* should she refuse to sign the contract.

The princess was young, but she wasn't stupid, and she knew quite well how far she could push her parents. Thus, shortly before her eleventh birthday, her parents received from a courier one of the two signed copies of the betrothal treaty. Erianthe considered Narod's signature and tried to discern something of him from the red loops and swirls, but he remained a cipher.

Thus, though engaged to be married, she put thoughts of her distant nuptials aside and returned to the far more engaging business of entertaining herself in the castle's garden. Designed by her grandfather's grandfather, the garden was an exquisite oasis in the heart of the stone fortress, complete with an arbor, fruiting bushes, and manicured flowerbeds. As the castle had been built along the Falova River's banks, the garden's architect had even pulled a bit of the river into his plan, digging a meandering channel through which the water might flow. A pair of thick grates at the river's entry points through the outer and inner walls blocked access to anything larger than a fish, and so the king and queen paid little mind when Erianthe went down to the garden to play. Safe within the walls, she was protected from the world beyond the castle, and no one could reach her without their knowledge.

Or so they thought.

Erianthe tried to love Narod. That was how marriages worked in the stories she read as a young woman—two people loved each other against all odds, perfectly, passionately. She wanted to feel that fire when her thoughts turned toward him, that fluttering in her belly heralding desires of a more carnal nature.

Instead, she felt dread.

The Cirivanti royals visited when she was sixteen, perpetually hungry but laced into a deep blue gown with a dainty waist and a neckline cut low enough to hint at her burgeoning womanhood. She had hoped to find a strapping young man in her intended, the sort with corded muscles and a square jaw and good hair, a man who would literally sweep her off her feet and slay monsters in her honor. In that respect, Narod had been an utter disappointment. Erianthe was of average height, and Narod was barely a head taller—that is, when he straightened up. His brown eyes were pretty enough but myopic, leaving him with a perpetual squint into the distance. His interests skewed more scholastic than martial, which was probably a good thing, given his slim build— Erianthe noted with dismay that he was barely heavier than she was. But worst of all, he was reserved, almost shy, content to sit at the table by his parents with his pimpled face and floppy brown hair and constant squint, listening but saying little unless manners demanded a response.

That was to be her husband. That gawky boy who probably couldn't have slain a rat.

But their marriage had been arranged by treaty, and they had both agreed, though they'd been children at the time. Barring some great catastrophe, there was no way to avoid her fate, so Erianthe tried to make the best of it. She dutifully sent Narod letters and hoped to find romance in his replies. As they matured, he did seem to try to woo her, writing letters filled with interesting little stories from Cirivant and amateur but apparently heartfelt poetry. Narod had little interest in politics or dancing, or even the breeding of chiquiws, but he could write pages to her about the newest ships in their navy, and so Erianthe gamely attempted to feign interest in hulls and sails.

She would have to bed this man. Birth his children. Rule with him sitting by her side, squinting at her people. And to Erianthe, who dreamed of a mighty warrior, or at least a man with half her father's wit and humor, the future seemed utterly depressing.

Finally, her parents gave her the news that a date was closer to being set. She would turn twenty-two during the long dry season. When the rains came that year and travel from the tunnels between their worlds grew less hazardous, they would invite Narod to Daril for the wedding. True, he would be freshly twenty-one, but he would be a man by the Cirivanti reckoning, though slightly underage in Daril. The priests would bless their union all the same.

Seeing her fate flying toward her like one of Narod's precious ships at full sail, Erianthe quietly despaired. The young ladies of the court twittered around her, talking up the wedding and her betrothed as if Erianthe were to wed a god. To distract herself, she retreated with growing frequency to the castle garden, where she could sit beside the shallow river and read or paint in peace.

It was there, while she was sketching a tree late one afternoon shortly after her twenty-first birthday, that she met the elemental.

That the Falova River was inhabited by a water elemental was common knowledge. He was generally content to leave the river traffic unmolested, taking issue only when ships dumped concentrated effluvia into the depths or took to piracy and attacked innocents. Most of the river merchants who traded between Daril and Ti'cal had their own small rituals before departure, asking him to let them pass without trouble, but he was seldom seen, nor did he speak to sailors without cause.

Thus, Erianthe cried out in alarm and fell off her chair when a watery form began to rise from the garden stream. It reached out a hand—or what she thought was a hand, given its bizarre form—as she tumbled, and she heard an unfamiliar but concerned voice in her mind: *Oh, no, are you hurt, Erianthe? I apologize.*

As she picked herself up, she realized she was in the presence of the elemental and stared at him in wonder. Only a torso had emerged above the surface, a head and chest with a pair of arms, human in form if not substance. His body was entirely composed of water—in the fading light, she could make out a confused fish swimming in the area where his stomach might have been—and though his face lacked full definition, she could discern the folds and valleys of his features.

"Who are you?" she asked.

His head tilted slightly as he considered her. *I am myself.*

"He of the Falova?"

The same.

"How do you know my name?"

At that, she could almost feel his smile.

He had observed her for years as she occupied herself alone in the garden. There was, he admitted, something beautiful about her—something within, he clarified. Of late, however, he had sensed her sadness, and he enquired as to the cause.

Falova was gentle, and he seemed sincere, so before she knew it, Erianthe found herself sitting on the grassy bank, confessing her dread at her impending marriage. The elemental listened in silence as she told him of her unhappiness at the thought of a life with Narod, then asked a simple question: why not reject him? *Your life is brief,* he told Erianthe. *Too brief to be spent anchored to someone you do not love. Why condemn yourself?*

It wasn't that simple, she told him. There was a treaty to consider. Duty. The dishonor to Daril if she failed to uphold her end of the bargain.

But as night fell and Erianthe brushed off her dress in anticipation of dinner, she asked Falova if she might see him again. He agreed to meet her whenever she liked.

He kept his promise, evening after evening, night after night, telling her tales of the river and of his kind—lessons not even her most learned masters could have shared with her.

And Erianthe, though a young woman, was wise enough to visit him only in secret.

Erianthe did not love Falova—not precisely, and certainly not at first. He was peculiar, a being unlike any she had known, and far from the men of her fantasies. But unlike the rest of her circle, Falova accepted that she had no desire to marry Narod and never tried to coax her into loving the prince. Quite the contrary—as the months passed, Falova continued to encourage her to break the treaty and end the engagement if she truly had no desire to be bound to the Cirivanti.

Half a year into their acquaintance, during a winter storm that howled around the castle walls and even rimed the river's edge, Jaanarel took sick and died in his sleep. His was a peaceful death, a fitting end to a peaceful reign, but his passing sent Erianthe spinning. Though still a few months underage, she was crowned queen hours after her father's death, with the understanding that Callo would serve as queen regent until the summer.

Erianthe had prepared for this moment since earliest childhood, but she flailed at first. Young, overwhelmed by the gravity of her responsibility, and paranoid about the nobles who came to her seeking favors, she worked long hours and slept little. Narod sent word as soon as he heard the news, offering to come early and assist her, but Erianthe gently declined. Moreover, she informed him that their scheduled autumn wedding would need to be pushed back, as she simply did not have time to find her footing as queen and plan the ceremony. Narod agreed, though he reiterated his offer to travel to Daril if his fiancée desired his company.

Stressed and quietly grieving, Erianthe slipped off to the garden whenever she could, and Falova was always waiting to lend an ear. He could offer her neither political advice nor easy solutions to the problems of the realm, but he listened without asking anything in return.

One night that spring, after unburdening herself in the moonlight, Erianthe laughed softly and told Falova that he was the only person in her life willing to speak with her without seeking riches or power in return.

His response was simple: *I love you, Erianthe. I will always be here if you want me. And if you do not or cannot love me in turn, that is of no consequence.*

The young queen was shocked by his declaration, but as she considered it that night in her bed, she found that she felt something for Falova. Perhaps not love, but her infatuation could not be denied. Narod was a distant disappointment, but Falova was *there*, constant and uncritical, demanding nothing of her—not even reciprocation of his feelings.

A few weeks later, on a warm summer night, Erianthe slipped from the castle, past the guards her mother had placed on duty near her chamber, and hid herself in the shadows of the garden. When Falova rose from the river to greet her, she murmured, "Have you ever made love to a woman?"

No, he had not, he admitted, but he knew something of the procedure.

Erianthe gave herself to him in the river, buoyed by his power as he brought her to shuddering release.

No, she did not love Falova, but she craved the way he made her body sing. Once satiated on those nights, she could sneak back into her bed and sleep deeply, worn out from her exertions in the garden but satisfied on a primal level.

And then her bleeding ceased.

As the weather turned cold and wet, Erianthe told herself that she was simply overtired. Fatigue could make a woman's time come late or not at all, and she'd been exhausted for months. She gained a little weight, which she blamed on her irregular meals, and loosened her dresses just enough that her mother wouldn't chide her for overindulging. Slipping down to the garden to be with Falova in the way she desired had grown impossible as the season turned to winter, and she told herself that her moodiness would abate once the water was warm enough for her to join him again.

But then Erianthe felt the movement within her—not indigestion, she realized with horror, but the stirring of a child.

Panicking, she broke down and confessed all to her mother. Though Callo was furious with Erianthe's carelessness, she comforted the girl and promised she would fix the problem.

The simplest solution, and Erianthe's choice, would have been to end the pregnancy. Any good midwife in Daril knew the techniques to prevent an unwanted birth, if the price was right. But while Callo trusted the royal midwife to tend to her needs, she knew she could not trust her with a secret of this magnitude. Given Callo's own difficulty in keeping a pregnancy, she doubted that the midwife would even treat Erianthe—after all, the child the queen was carrying would be the next crown prince or princess as soon as it drew breath.

Instead, Callo sent Erianthe into her room with a single servant, a half-blind and slightly doddering old woman, and informed the queen's ministers that she had taken sick with a particular fever known for its long duration. Having lost its king only a year prior, Daril sent up prayers for Erianthe's speedy recovery while Callo managed affairs in her stead.

The kingdom also sent up prayers of a different kind. Inexplicably, although the river flowed as mightily as ever, it ceased to support life. The water stank, the fish disappeared or floated to the surface, and the vegetation on the banks began to brown. Assuming the elemental had died, an almost unimaginable event, the people importuned their gods to send a replacement to restore the river.

That summer, a few days after Erianthe's twenty-second birthday and the end of Callo's regency, the queen mother knew that her daughter's confinement was drawing to an end. With the aid of six of her most trusted guards, she spirited Erianthe out of the castle and into a carriage, an extravagance purchased from a dwarven craftsman but scaled for human comfort, and had them flown to the tunnel's mouth in the wilderness beyond the kingdom's borders. Seeing no lights of an oncoming carriage in the distance, the guards piloted the little craft into the tunnel and flew away from Kopaat toward the Crossing, the space to which the passages between the worlds of the Aen was anchored.

The cavern at the center of the Crossing was large enough for the carriage to park out of the way of potential traffic. Giving Erianthe a small lantern, Callo told her to leave them and climb the staircase leading to the surface. Erianthe knew well the task ahead of her, as Callo had made plain her instructions before their departure: find a quiet place on the strange world beyond the Aen, deliver the child, and kill it.

Though contractions gripped her body, she managed to stagger out of the tunnels, then found herself in a wood at twilight. She wanted nothing more than to sink down in the soil and push, but Callo had stressed that she needed to put distance between herself and the tunnel before an Outsider, one of the ravenous beasts from beyond the Aen, emerged and found her. Quietly crying with pain, Erianthe dragged herself through the trees until she spotted the glint of a lake. Her masters had said that the world on which the tunnels was anchored lacked elementals, and she didn't worry about being discovered by one at the water's edge, but Erianthe decided she had gone as far as she could. She stopped in a small clearing, spread a blanket on the ground, then readied herself for the inevitable.

Terrified and alone in a distant world, Erianthe delivered her firstborn child that night—a daughter, she saw by the lantern's light, an ordinary-looking child with a soft whorl of dark hair and eyes that stared uncomprehendingly at nothing. Once she was delivered of the afterbirth, Erianthe left the baby alone on the blanket and hobbled down to the lake, where she gingerly washed herself off.

The sound of the baby's cries drew her back to the blanket, and she looked down at the newborn with unease. This might be the most difficult part, Callo had warned her, as the wails of a distressed infant could tug on even the hardest heart. All she had to do was smother the child, Erianthe told herself. Or she could toss her in the lake and let her drown, or hit her in the head with a convenient tree limb…

But the baby cried pitifully, and Erianthe's resolve waivered. Carefully, touching the child as little as possible, she deposited the girl on the ground and folded up her bloodied blanket. Erianthe saw no lights of nearby habitation, nor any sign of a path—surely the baby would die on its own without needing her hand to administer the fatal blow.

She didn't look back as she made her slow way into the tunnels, and she lied to her mother about the princess's fate. After all, the girl was as good as dead.

As were the guards, though they suspected nothing at the time. Once back at the castle, Callo called them to her private dining room to personally thank them for their service with food and wine. The wine, however, was poisoned, and when the men fell, foaming at the mouth, Callo called for other guards and explained that she had caught her victims plotting against the queen. Naturally, Erianthe pardoned her for taking matters into her own hands.

Truly, a mother's love knew no bounds.

Two months later, despite the difficult travel of the dry season, Erianthe married Narod in a splendid ceremony in Deoni. The groom's appearance was a pleasant surprise to the bride. While Narod hadn't grown any taller, his complexion had cleared, his hair was less greasy than it had been, and he had put on muscle—not enough to make him seem well-built, but muscle sufficient to fill out a tunic. He was courteous to Erianthe, quick to smile and more self-assured than he had been on his last visit, and she decided that she didn't *hate* the man.

They held one of their more intimate receptions in the castle garden. By then, to keep out the dead river's stench, Erianthe had ordered the grates replaced by heavy masonry at both walls. The decorative course through which the river had run had evaporated by the time of the wedding, and the gardeners had filled it with gravel, turning it into a walkway among the trees. Within the outer courtyard, a bridge still covered the dry channel where the river had flowed into the castle grounds—once an easy source of water and the occasional fish, now an unsightly ditch.

Over the years, though Narod doted on her, Erianthe never truly grew to love her husband. She took comfort in his familiarity, and she appreciated his willingness to stand by her side in all things, but he inspired no passion in her. Still, Erianthe did her duty as queen and brought forth three children from their union: the crown prince, Edes, followed by another son, Jerrcoa, and a daughter, Zadi. Cognizant of how close she had come to disaster, Erianthe never strayed from Narod, nor did she confess to him the secret of her first pregnancy. When Callo died, with her went the knowledge of Erianthe's shame, and the queen breathed a sigh of relief.

That is, until I showed up with a dwarven princess, a half-elven prince, my half-tekorish best friend, and a cursed sword and asked for help.

It was understandable that Erianthe was pissed to find me, Susan Cole, in her throne room. As the hapless human recently drafted as the Watcher, I was meant to be guarding the Crossing, luring Outsiders to me with the Aen crystals in the sword's hilt and killing them. With me on the run in the four realms, the Crossing was unguarded, and the monsters had eschewed Earth and followed the traces of Aen through the longer tunnels into worlds like Kopaat. Darili subjects had died, towns had been destroyed, and the queen's first impulse was to lay the blame on my head instead of, say, considering the injustice inherent in a system that trapped someone into fighting ravenous creatures every night for the rest of her life.

In light of my youth, however, she reconsidered her initial impulse to execute me and visited me in my tower cell that night to offer me an alternative: return to the Crossing and do my duty, and I'd be allowed to live. But then she caught me playing with my newfound talent, tossing around a ball of water I'd pulled from the washtub. She pressed me for details of my family, and I told her how I'd been abandoned in the woods at birth.

And she *knew*.

I had no clue, of course, and Erianthe didn't come clean. Instead, she told me a half-truth about a princess of Daril, an elemental, and the shame inherent in my existence. She'd meant to convince me that my selection as the Watcher was fated—I could return to my post, work off my mother's sins, and never trouble Daril again.

Instead, I pushed back and asked for my parents' names.

She never told me, and she left that night unsure whether she would be banishing or executing me in the morning. Instead, she was awakened in the dark hours to the news that all four of us had escaped, with some of the men swearing that we'd jumped off a tower roof.

Erianthe slept uneasily in the nights that followed, wondering if I would trouble her again and castigating herself for saying too much. A few weeks later, however, she received wonderful news from the maladeta in her court: the Watcher was going Outside to try to destroy the monsters once and for all. No one had ever retuned after such an attempt, so Erianthe allowed herself to rest easily.

And then, having returned to Kopaat victorious, down

one magic sword, and with scores to settle, I crashed my little brother's engagement party.

The gods demand truth.

That was the refrain Erianthe and I heard all day following my surprise declaration of maternity—a declaration I had made before the royal court, the assembled nobility of Daril, and Edes's fiancée's family. I knew damn well that my existence was a massive problem for Erianthe, so I'd followed the strong suggestion of the maladetas in my life to make a public pronouncement, something that couldn't be easily ignored. Moreover, thanks to the maladetas' PR campaign and a convenient recording of me leading the charge against the biggest Outsider of them all, I was a certified *hero*, and Erianthe wouldn't be able to casually execute me.

The feasting ended abruptly that afternoon. Priests were called, then human adepts skilled in manipulating the Aen, who could determine the truth of my claim to the throne with a single drop of blood from each of us. They ran their spells five times, just to be certain, before announcing that I was indisputably the queen's daughter—Susan Fulquir now, part of that ancient royal line.

This left the highborn of Daril in a tizzy. The law was clear: I was the crown princess by right, even if I was a rogue elemental. Though I had the ability to be understood without a translator, anyone who watched my lips could tell that I didn't speak a word of New Kopaati. I knew very little of Daril's history and virtually nothing of its culture. I bore a prominent scar on one cheek and wore *trousers*, of all things, scandalous for a Darili woman in most contexts. But I was also the princess who'd destroyed the monsters and restored the Falova River, and so the nobles quietly tried to make the best of the awkward situation.

But then there was the slight matter of the broken treaty.

I felt for Narod, who was a victim in all of this. He was blindsided by his wife's infidelity, as a betrothal like theirs was practically as good as a marriage, and he had never cheated on her. Worse still, Erianthe couldn't fulfill the terms of the treaty with Cirivant because I took priority over Narod's children in the succession. And within days of my arrival, Edes's engagement fell apart—the Eranegi princess had contracted to marry the heir to Daril, not an ordinary prince.

They should have hated me. Erianthe, at least, suggested between fits of furious tears that I leave them alone and go throw myself off the edge of the world. But Narod insisted that the law was the law, and as I had done such a service for the kingdom, let alone the four worlds, I would remain in Deoni and begin my remedial education.

And so, satisfied that I was safe for the moment, my entourage departed. Terj, the air elemental I'd freed from the Watcher's sword, offered to carry Fanakel, Anji, and Mia across the vast wasteland between Deoni and the tunnel entrance, while the maladetas returned to their settlement by the sea, though not before making arrangements. The maladeta stationed in Deoni, Tonnera, gave me an update a few days later: sisters of hers in other clans had been waiting at the tunnel mouths in Honslia and Ildon for my friends to emerge, and they had made their way home safely—all but Mia, who'd abandoned our hometown to run back to Blackhorn Mountain with Anji. I wasn't sure what the other dwarven nobles would think about Anji's new training partner—or girlfriend, as the case might be—but I trusted that Mia wouldn't be abused in Heartfast. As for Fanakel, Tonnera reported that he had been welcomed, if not enthusiastically, then at least with gratitude by his father and aunt, the king and queen of Nokan'ti. In truth, I worried about him—it couldn't be easy to be half human in a society that prized elven blood above all else—but Tonnera told me that he'd finally been removed from the royal guards after seventy-four years of service and elevated to a minor council position.

While I missed my friends, I wasn't alone in Deoni. Terj returned from ferry duty and stuck by my side, but as the days passed, I began to dread the day when he, too, would leave me. Elementals born to air never stayed long in any one place, and Terj had been bound for centuries. He proved strangely reluctant to take off on his own, however, and though I wanted him to live his best life, I was grateful for his company. At least *someone* in the damn castle got my jokes.

But as the hot, dry summer gave way to the wet chill of winter, I began to hear whispers of plans in the making.

One way or another, it seemed, my disgraced mother was going to keep her end of the bargain with Cirivant.

CHAPTER 2

I was making miserably slow progress through a book of Darili children's poetry when a servant knocked. "Your Highness?" she said, peeking into the room. "The prince consort wishes to speak with you."

Grateful for the interruption, I stretched and stuck a makeshift bookmark at my place as I rose from my desk, an antique wooden piece nearly the size of my old dining room table back in Cole's Crossing. I would never have chosen it, but the last six months had been a touchy time, to say the least, and I didn't want to make matters worse by complaining about the furniture in my suite. The fireplace certainly worked well enough, and that cold day, the comfortable heat overcame the shortcomings of my apartment's interior design. "Is he upset?" I asked, heading for the door.

The servant gave me a quick once-over but kept her opinions to herself. Erianthe could swan around in gowns all she liked, but I'd be damned if I let myself be laced into a dress just to sit alone and struggle with New Kopaati. "He didn't seem to be, ma'am," she replied. "He wasn't shouting."

"He seldom shouts," I reminded her.

She cracked a faint smile. "He did not raise his voice, then."

Nor had he done so yet when talking to me. That Narod was deeply hurt by Erianthe's actions was no secret to anyone with half a toe in court life, but to my great surprise, he didn't take it out on me. I'd expected sullenness at best from the prince consort, but Narod had taken it upon himself to appoint masters to teach me what I needed to know, and he remained a kind, if somewhat melancholy, presence in my new life. My mother ignored me as if I might simply vanish if she pretended I wasn't there, but her husband had stepped up in her stead.

"My feelings don't matter in this," he'd told me a few weeks after my notorious debut. "You are the heir to the throne, I swore to protect Daril when I married your mother, and part of that protection includes ensuring that the next person to wear the crown does so competently. You cannot help what you are and where you come from," he'd added, folding his arms. "Some of those choices were made for you."

"I really won't be offended if you don't want anything to do with me," I'd begun, but he'd shaken his head.

"In all honesty, were I in your position, I would be *furious*," he'd murmured. "And...I might do much the same as you have done. You're merely reclaiming your birthright."

"That doesn't mean you're not allowed to be furious, too."

His smile had been brief and strained. "That's a matter for the queen and me to work through. Worry about your studies, Susan—that's far more important."

Part of me had rebelled at the idea of forced education. I'd already received my bachelor's degree, after all, and college had been my choice, an adventure I'd enjoyed. But I understood the importance of acquainting myself with the kingdom I was born to rule, and even if the masters droned and the lessons were tedious, I had Terj at my side to make the days bearable.

It took two weeks for anyone in the castle to recognize that I was seldom alone. Terj generally stayed invisible, finding it unnecessary to bend the air around him into a sort of body, so he could hide in plain sight. Moreover, as elementals relied upon mental instead of vocal communication, he and I could carry on conversations whenever we liked with no one the wiser. The family's reaction to the news that I had a silent, often unseen companion varied. Erianthe ordered Terj out—I laughed in her face at that—but Narod took it in stride, just one more quirk about his wife's slightly feral offspring.

He was in his study that afternoon, a quiet space halfway up a little-used tower, and he smiled and put his book aside as the servant announced me and departed. "Ah, Susan."

"Your Highness," I replied with a nod. "You wanted to see me?"

"I do. Are we alone?"

"We are." Unburdened by needy, sensitive flesh, Terj had set off in the chill to explore that morning, a plan I'd heartily encouraged. As much as I'd come to enjoy his presence, I wanted him to be happy, and that meant nudging him along the path toward independence.

Narod smiled again. "Come in, please. No need to stand in the doorway." He waited while I took a seat in the chair beside him, and then his expression shifted toward a teasing grin. "Stealing from your brother's trunks again, I see."

I glanced down at my slouchwear—my old leggings, a long green tunic Edes had outgrown, and an oversized knit sweater thrown over top—and smirked back at him. "It was a gift, not theft."

"Somehow, I don't doubt that." Sitting back in his leather chair, he crossed his legs and held my gaze. As closely as we were positioned, he might have been able to see me well enough with straining his weak eyes, but he'd resorted to his glasses within the privacy of his rooms, a pair of thick lenses in a gold frame that pinched the bridge of his nose. His pride never let him sport them in public, and I'd been around long enough by then to have learned not to mention them. "How are your studies proceeding?" he asked.

"Well enough, I think. Except language," I muttered. "I've never been great at picking them up. Master Slighn is doing his best."

"I remember studying New Kopaati as a boy. *Hated* every minute of it."

"You're fluent now, right?"

"I am, but that's the work of years and practice. Which I would encourage, incidentally," he added, looking at me over his lenses.

As usual, I spoke English without a second thought, trusting the strange gift—well, *one* of the strange gifts—of my elemental heritage to translate for me. "Unless you'd like to sit here and listen to me fumble all afternoon..."

"Another time, perhaps." He steepled his fingers and cleared his throat. "I *have* received complaints from Master Vantosh. Again."

I sighed and rolled my eyes to the stone ceiling. "He can complain all he likes, but I'm not going to sit there and take notes when what he's teaching me is blatantly wrong."

"Such as?"

"Well, yesterday, he tried to lecture me about how lightning is flashes of divine power, proof that storms are created by the gods."

The crown prince nodded slowly. "That would be within the purview of a science master..."

"Except it's bullshit. Thunderstorms form from the confluence of warm, moist air and colder air. Lightning is just an electrostatic discharge, sometimes within a cloud or between a cloud and the ground. It's the scaled-up, scary version of what happens when you shuffle your socks across the carpet and touch metal. Look, I took a survey class in meteorology a few years ago—that's the science of forecasting the weather," I explained as Narod's expression shifted toward bemusement. "It's not gods at work—it's a highly energetic storm system."

He seemed unconvinced. "Perhaps things are different beyond the Aen."

"Not *that* different. Trust me," I said, "I've created thunderstorms here. If there were gods involved, I'd have noticed."

Narod's eyes widened behind his glasses. "You've *created* storms?"

"Twice. I can manipulate a *lot* of water, but it takes time, and it's exhausting at that level. Anyway, I can try not to be rude to Master Vantosh," I offered, "but he's not doing me any good."

Cole's Crossing, my hometown, might have been an unremarkable hamlet in an inauspicious corner of eastern Kentucky, but my public school education was still centuries ahead of the "science" taught in Daril. The humans whose ancestors had found their way into the worlds of the Aen had focused on ways to use that magical potential, while those left behind on Earth had mostly given up on magic in favor of the promise of technological advancement. I'd tried to explain this to Narod, and while he'd been politely receptive to the idea that, say, stars were enormous balls of fusing gasses, I got the sense that he didn't entirely believe me.

There were, I'd quickly realized, certain drawbacks to my new home—the dearth of electricity, computers, and cars, for starters. The palace in which Anji had grown up had figured out sanitation through the use of dwarven forging, but the royal seat of Daril lacked amenities like flush toilets. True, compared to the average Darili, I had *zero* room to complain—for God's sake, I was a damn princess—but after six months in Deoni, I'd have paid dearly for a few hours with my old cell phone and some decent Wi-Fi.

"I will speak with Master Vantosh," said Narod. "Perhaps his talents would be better used elsewhere. Now," he continued, "I do have a request."

I winced. "Whatever the masters are telling you, I *have* been doing my lessons."

"Oh, I have no doubt of that," he reassured me.

"No—your mother and I would like for you to dine with us tonight."

That surprised me. "Is something wrong?"

"Not at all. But she has some matters to discuss with you, and we thought it best if the three of us did so together." His smile seemed genuine in its warmth. "Perhaps you could consider something slightly more formal for the occasion, hmm?"

Sensing the end of the audience, I rose and tugged down my sweater. "If it'll make everyone happy."

I was almost to the door when Narod said, "Adjusting to a new place is always difficult, Susan. I had my own set of…cultural missteps, shall we say, when I came here. But I'm confident that you'll find your way in time."

I grinned at him over my shoulder. "Until then, the leggings stay."

He sighed but followed it with a soft chuckle. "Do try to keep the scandals to a minimum, Princess, won't you?"

I saw myself out and latched the heavy door behind me, then turned and caught my breath when Edes, who'd been waiting in a window near the spiral staircase, startled me. "Sorry," he said, sliding down from his perch on the stone ledge. "I saw you going up to Father. Is everything all right?"

"Fine, aside from the heart attack you just gave me," I replied, and joined him. We began to descend together, and as Edes stayed two steps ahead of me, we seemed almost of a height. My half brother was about six feet tall, I estimated, with broad shoulders and long limbs. Like me, he wasn't exactly thin, but whereas my body clung to fat, his converted most of the extra weight to muscle. Our hair was the same shade of brown, though his was far straighter than mine, and he wore it almost constantly in a low ponytail. We both had Erianthe's eyes, at least in shape, though Edes's were brown like his father's, while mine were somehow green. Frankly, I had no true idea how I *existed*, and so minor issues like working out my eye color from my parents'—Erianthe's blue, Falova's incorporeal—went unanswered.

That he had anything to do with me had come as a pleasant surprise. Of all the Fulquirs, after Erianthe, Edes had suffered the most following my arrival in Daril. Within two days of my appearance, he'd been knocked back a place in the line of succession, losing the throne for which he'd been preparing all his life, and with it, lost his fiancée. I wouldn't have blamed him had he refused to speak to me.

In truth, Edes was *delighted*.

My brother loved hunting. He enjoyed sports of all kinds, watching and participating, and he shared Narod's fascination with ships, though the offerings were less impressive along the river in Deoni than they'd been in the seaside city where Narod grew up. Unlike his father, however, Edes wasn't a great reader, nor did he have much patience for the endless meetings and councils that clogged Erianthe's schedule. While he very much enjoyed the perks of royal birth, he had no desire whatsoever to rule. Erianthe refused to hear of this, and when Edes "hypothetically" floated to Narod the notion of removing himself from the succession in favor of his siblings, his father had discouraged it. Jerrcoa, about three years Edes's junior, was a quiet, studious teenager, but a childhood illness had ravaged his body and left him paralyzed from the waist down, and Daril wasn't ready for a chair-bound king—particularly not one who wasn't expected to survive middle age. Zadi, five years younger than Jerrcoa, was only fourteen, a pretty girl with her father's poor vision and her mother's artistic sensibilities. She was a gifted painter, and her needlecraft was impeccable, but Zadi shied away from anything approximating a spotlight. Anyone who spent a few hours in her presence knew that she'd be miserable wearing a crown.

This left Edes without any good options. Worse, as a major part of the monarch's duties was to produce children, he would need to take a wife. Erianthe had arranged for his betrothal to the Eranegi princess, which would have been a smart political move for Daril, but Edes had despaired at the news. Erianthe couldn't understand why. Curin of Eraneg was gorgeous, a tall, slim beauty with golden-brown skin, thick black hair, and large round eyes of deep amber. She could dance and sing, play the harp with virtuosic skill, and speak four languages. Any man should count himself fortunate to marry such a woman, Erianthe chided her son as he moped.

The problem, which Erianthe refused to acknowledge, was that Edes was gay.

Initially, based on previous reports, I'd imagined that my brother would be the worst kind of sexist asshole. Anji had told me about his behavior when he and his parents visited her father three years before. He'd made so many inappropriate comments to the female servants that two of Anji's sisters had threatened to pulverize him if he didn't stop—and since dwarven princesses were taught to fight alongside their brothers, I had no doubt that they could have made good on the threat. But the Edes I saw in my first days in Deoni was far removed from that jerk, loud and talkative but not a walking sexual harassment lawsuit.

His behavior in Heartfast had been an act, he confessed when I finally brought it up. Rumors had begun to spread among their servants and guards that Edes had certain *unnatural* proclivities, and he, with the brilliance of a teenager, had tried to silence those whispers by acting like an overconfident frat boy. His performance had worked— after all, any human man horny enough to proposition a bearded female dwarf must be desperately in need of a woman—but once such a woman was promised to him via marriage treaty, Edes had quietly freaked out.

While the monarch had to marry and procreate, his or her siblings were somewhat off the hook. For ending his betrothal, if nothing else, Edes had welcomed me into the family.

My other two half siblings had been hesitant at first, then curious, and they soon followed their brother's lead. Jerrcoa, almost twenty but with the demeanor of a world-weary graduate student, was often to be found in the castle's library—useful for me, as he was my first stop when my lessons didn't quite compute. He spoke little unless addressed, and as he was so quiet, people tended to forget he was there. But after my first week in Deoni, when Edes invited me to join the three of them with a bottle of wine, Jerrcoa had a couple drinks and spilled the dirt on nearly everyone of note, and I decided then and there to try to stay on his good side. As for Zadi, the baby with two older brothers, she seemed pleased to have a sister, even if I was nine years her senior and preferred the sort of ensembles that would make a stylish Darili woman gasp in horror. We sat around that night and got acquainted, and as Edes opened a second bottle, Jerrcoa asked me if the things he'd been hearing about our mother were true.

The official line was heavily sanitized: yes, Erianthe had fallen pregnant by an elemental, a youthful indiscretion, but it was the queen mother who had ordered that I be left beyond the Crossing. In private, Erianthe had at first tried to pin the blame for my abandonment on her mother, saying she was a scared young girl who only did what she was told, but I hadn't bought it, and neither had Narod—especially considering her willingness to execute me on my previous trip to Deoni. Still, Narod had thrown his mother-in-law under the bus as a way to restore some of Erianthe's standing before the Darili nobility, though her reputation had been irreversibly tarnished.

But despite her polished public admissions, rumors of the *rest* of Erianthe's confession had spread in the castle. I'd been reluctant to confirm or deny, especially with Zadi sitting there, nibbling her lip as she watched me, but Edes had heard the full account, and he told them everything he'd learned. I filled in the gaps and added to the story, telling them about my life beyond the Crossing, my adopted family, and my brief stint as the Watcher, which had almost ended with Erianthe executing me. I didn't mention Falova—that part remained between Erianthe and me—but the damage was done. Zadi looked stunned when I finished, but Jerrcoa, who had an excellent poker face, clenched and unclenched his fists atop the arms of his wheelchair.

Relations between Erianthe and her children had turned frosty from that point, and months later, there was no sign of a thaw. After all, if she could so cavalierly sentence me to death, then what protection did the rest of them have? Moreover, the three of them loved their father, and anyone who saw Narod when he wasn't in front of a crowd knew how badly he'd been hurt. In public, he spoke of mistakes and forgiveness, and he remained a smiling presence at the queen's side, but in private, the two of them maintained separate routines within the castle.

"Father has always loved Mother more than she loves him," Jerrcoa confided in me one evening over a late dinner and my inscrutable reading assignment. "He dotes, she tolerates. It's not a great secret. But of late, considering what she did to you…"

"He's cooled toward her?" I asked.

"Oh, he still loves her, but he's horrified."

The one member of the family with whom I'd yet to make peace was my mother. I'd publicly humiliated Erianthe, and her solution going forward appeared to be ignoring my existence to the greatest extent possible. But during those hectic first days, between solemn meetings with the priests and visits to the adepts, I had quietly made known to her that I knew *exactly* what had happened to Falova. "You paid for his murder," I'd told her in a lonely chamber while we'd waited for the latest bunch of adepts to arrive. "He told me about the three men who ripped him from the river and brought him into the wilderness to die. They're the ones who took pity and tossed him in a pond instead of killing him outright, and they were smart enough to flee."

Her eyes had bored into mine, unblinking but frightened. "You have no proof."

"I have all the proof I need. But for some reason, Falova still loves you enough to let bygones be bygones." Leaning toward her, I'd added, "He's the *only* one. Don't try me."

And she hadn't. Our relationship was as cold as a Siberian winter, but we'd survived half a year in the same castle by pretending the other didn't exist.

This made Narod's request all the stranger.

"Your father wants me to have dinner with him and Mother tonight," I told Edes as we headed for the bottom of the tower.

He looked over his shoulder, his face scrunched. "*Why?*"

"Beats me. Think I should hire a taste-tester?"

"Surely she wouldn't try to poison you."

"I don't know, man. *Her* mother resorted to poison."

Edes grunted. "Fair. Bring Terj along, eh? In case you sicken, perhaps he could go for help."

"I'd invite him if he were around," I said, "but he's gone off for the day."

"Poor timing, that," Edes replied, reaching the landing. "Can you not contact him?"

I stopped on the wide stair and closed my eyes for a moment, then opened them again and shook my head. "Nope. I can't feel him close by. I mean, if there were an emergency, I suppose I could ask Falova if he's seen him...but this is just dinner, right? What's the worst that can happen at dinner?"

The look of incredulity my half brother shot me spoke volumes. "King Selener, our great-great-great...uh...add a few more generations, grandfather—yes?"

"Um..."

"His closest advisors invited him to an intimate dinner.

Just before dessert, when he was half-drunk off fortified wine, they grabbed the daggers they'd been hiding and stabbed him to death."

"*Shit*, Edes."

"Yeah. They thought his son would be a better king. And he was, to be fair, but the first thing he did was have all of them executed for treason." With that, he started downward again. "I'm not suggesting that you should expect an ambush tonight, but…you know, perhaps you shouldn't tempt the gods."

"Noted," I muttered, losing my appetite with every step.

One of the queen's servants came to escort me to dinner that evening, and I swept through the halls of the castle in a forest green confection of thin wool and satin. It wasn't a *bad* gown, as gowns went, but the laced bodices so popular in Darili women's fashion were a pain in the ass—or in my back, really, as the combination of the tight laces and the boning forced me to maintain excellent posture. My maid had done what she could to keep me happy by leaving the laces just loose enough to allow moderately deep breaths, but she couldn't work miracles.

As I was announced at the dining room, I stepped inside and found the queen and prince consort already seated at a round table that might have comfortably fit four. It had been set for three, with the two of them partially facing the door, leaving me the empty seat at the focal point of their stares.

"Mother," I said, nodding to Erianthe, then nodded to Narod. "Your Highness."

"Susan," Erianthe murmured. "Sit."

As soon as I smoothed my napkin into my lap, the servants arrived with a decanter of kirit, a white wine made of local berries, followed quickly by fragrant bowls of fish chowder. I tucked in and was making steady progress on my soup course when the queen pointedly cleared her throat. "Were you planning to *finish* that?" she asked in a withering tone.

I lowered my spoon and cocked an eyebrow. "Yes?"

"In *your* condition?"

"It's good," I said, noting that she'd barely made a dent in her portion, "and I'm hungry, so yes, I intend to eat this."

"Honestly, girl," she muttered. "Show a little restraint."

I took a sip of wine as she tutted. "You know, I'm not actually fat. I'm fairly average for my height, especially since I've been working out with Edes—"

"Working where?" Narod interrupted.

"Sorry, uh...conditioning. Exercising," I explained, and his face smoothed with comprehension. "He's a good sparring partner."

"Hardly a ladylike pursuit," Erianthe snapped.

I shrugged. "Says you. I've found it remarkably useful in the last year. Anyway, I've lost some weight, I'm toning, and I'm going to eat the damn soup," I told her. "I can't help it if your perception of what a normal body looks like is skewed."

My mother was a decently pretty woman, albeit pinched in the face from her years of carefully monitoring every bite she put in her mouth. Her chestnut waves, styled into a braided updo, were what mine could have been with an hour of work from a team of skilled maidservants. Honestly, I lacked the patience for more than a ponytail most days. She'd left off the tiara that evening, but as usual, she sported a heavy golden necklace set with a blue-green Aen crystal the size of a quarter, and her cream-colored gown was laced to the point that I worried about the condition of her ribcage.

"'Normal,' she says," Erianthe remarked, glancing at Narod, who continued to eat in silence. "That's ridiculous. You've allowed your body to swell, and—"

"There is nothing wrong with my body," I interrupted,

and glared at her when she looked back my way. "It's perfectly functional, and I dare say it's stronger than yours. So why don't you worry about your waistline and let me worry about mine, hmm?"

"Your mother's simply looking out for your best interest," said Narod, trying once again to play the conciliator.

I held her stare and smirked as I raised my glass. "First time for everything, I guess. Now, if I'm not supposed to be eating, why did you ask me to come to dinner tonight?"

Erianthe and Narod shared a brief look, and she proceeded. "We asked you here to inform you that your betrothal has been arranged."

I almost spat my wine across the table in my shock. Forcing myself to swallow, I managed to say, "*Excuse* me?"

"You're of age, Susan," Narod explained, "and we've located an appropriate young man—"

"Was someone planning to run this by me first?" I demanded, glaring at them both. "At what point have I mentioned anything about wanting to get married? And who is this perfect guy that I'm sure to love, sight unseen?"

Erianthe remained unruffled in the face of my sarcasm. "*Love* has nothing to do with it. For the highborn, marriages are tools of dynastic alliance. We have found a suitable match for you, and you will marry him."

"Oh?" I retorted. "And if I say no...what, you'll lock me in a tower again? Dump me back at the Crossing?"

She reddened but didn't take the bait. "Your arrival here upset a very important treaty—"

"Do *not* blame me for that. You're the one who upset that damn treaty. I just happened to be born."

"Blame whomever you like," said Erianthe with practiced calm, "but the result is the same. The treaty has been broken, and Cirivant is *greatly* displeased. Daril needs their navy if our Ga'beshi settlements are to withstand pirate attacks. Without it, our people are virtually defenseless. Now," she continued, turning to Narod, "despite the recent unpleasantness, their king is willing to amend the treaty."

"My oldest brother," Narod offered. "He's a good man, Susan."

"Most understanding," Erianthe concurred. "He has a son of appropriate age who has agreed to overlook your glaring deficiencies and marry you."

"My *what?*" I said, fighting the urge to fling the rest of my soup in her face.

Erianthe cocked her head and faintly smirked. "A princess of nearly twenty-four who is unmarried would inspire caution in any worthy man. You are untutored, you can't even speak the language of the country you intend to rule—"

"And whose fault is *that*, Mother?"

"I'm not the one arguing with the masters, am I?" she countered. "Let's see…you're no great beauty, Susan, especially with that hideous thing on your face."

I resisted the urge to run my fingers over the long, puckered scar running from the corner of my left eye to my mouth. Six months of treatment by the questionable royal medical practitioners had done little to smooth my cheek, and I'd vehemently refused the suggestion that I wear a partial mask so as not to disturb people.

"An Outsider did this to me," I said through gritted teeth. "You think I ripped my face open for fun?"

"Regardless of the cause, it's ugly."

"And I'd never have acquired it had you done the bare minimum for me," I snapped. "But let's move on. Please continue—I'd love to know the rest of my *deficiencies*."

Narod softly coughed. "Well…and I'm not saying this is a deficiency, as such, but it does give people pause—"

"You're not even human," Erianthe spat.

"Uh…*half*," I replied, folding my arms over my tight bodice. "And once again, not my fault."

She stared at me for an uncomfortably silent moment,

then said, "You see, Susan, that's the problem with you. *Nothing* is ever your fault. You're entitled to whatever you desire because of the *tenuous* claim you make on me. So be it. You're the crown princess now—you've pushed our son out of his rightful inheritance. Well done," she said dryly. "But that inheritance comes with duties. Responsibilities. Sacrifices…which you would know little about, as you've been nothing but a spoiled child since the night we met. Now, you *will* hear me, girl," she said, leaning forward in her chair. "Daril needs Cirivant. You are the reason that our alliance has been jeopardized, so you will solve the problem. Because this isn't about *you*. It's not about your wants, your desires, whatever girlish dreams of romance you've conjured up—it's about Darili subjects who will die if left without assistance." When I didn't immediately argue with her, she added, "Of course, given your absolute callousness when you allowed Outsiders to invade this world, I shouldn't expect you to understand your duty to ensure the people's good—"

"Fuck you," I said, and pushed back from the table. "Thanks for the half bowl of soup, Mother. A pleasure to see you, as always."

As I opened the door, Narod called, "Susan?"

I turned back, glaring, but I was probably too far away by then for him to see the details of my expression.

"My brother is a good man," he said softly. "I'm sure his son would treat you well. Consider this, yes?"

"I'm not here to fix *her* mistakes," I said, pointing to the queen.

"No," he replied, "but your mother is not wrong. If Cirivant withdraws its protection, our colonies will be attacked, and people will die. This marriage could help ensure their safety."

I didn't answer him, and I slammed the door behind me, my guts roiling as I marched back to my room to free myself from the prison of my gown.

While I hadn't been an adult long in the grand scheme of things, I'd recognized late in adolescence the necessity of the adultier adult—someone to whom I could turn who knew how to do more than flail in times of crisis. My dad had occupied that role at first, a man blessed with common sense, an even temper, and the fortitude to run a small town. When I was twenty-one and Dad's heart gave out, his brother, Uncle Malachi, had done his best to fill Dad's shoes. Since Malachi, then the Watcher, had much bigger problems to worry about than my college affairs, the fact that he kept up with my drama was a testament to his kindness. But he'd been gone almost nine months by that point, and as my longtime neighbor now lived miles away with her maladetan clan—Ardith Quince to me, Ardielta of the Taln'een to the rest of Kopaat—I turned to the one "real" adult left in my life that night.

My relationship with my biological father was...well, unusual. Having grown up in a single-parent home, I'd been a daddy's girl by default, and part of me still insisted I was being disloyal to Dad's memory by getting to know Falova. I'd tried to keep those feelings to myself, but my father had picked up on them all the same—there was, I'd discovered, very little I could hide from him. To my relief, he wasn't offended. Falova appreciated that Dad had been my parent when I truly needed one, and while he was glad to find a place in my life, he didn't push. All the same, I never doubted that he loved me. Something in me recognized our kinship, and if I felt that, then surely he felt it at least as strongly as I did.

I climbed onto a quiet battlement, comfortable once more in my leggings and sweater but still queasy with anxiety, and stared down at the wide river as it flowed along the castle's foundation in the starlight. *Father?*

He didn't rise from the water—with me that far from the bank, there was no need to expend the energy—but I heard him all the same: *Soul of my soul, you are troubled.*

I sighed and took a seat in a crenel. *Erianthe and Narod*

told me tonight that they want to marry me off.

To whom?

One of Narod's nephews. Someone about my age. Since my arrival blew up the treaty with Cirivant, they want me to marry a Terol to make it up to Narod's family.

I could sense his unease as he considered that. *Is this what you want?*

I don't think so, no. Never even met the guy.

Then why would you agree to this plan?

Tucking my feet onto the stone, I pulled my knees to my chest and hugged them against the damp chill. *Because it's the only way that Cirivant will keep using its navy to protect Daril's outposts in Ga'besh. They want someone from the Terol line on the throne here.*

It seems I have heard this before, Falova replied.

Familiar, isn't it? And maybe this guy's great. Narod's certainly not a monster, so maybe his nephew is a nice person. But...

But?

But whenever I've thought about getting married, it's never been to a stranger. Resting my cheek on my knees, I stared out at the night and the rippling water below. *Perhaps I could make this work.*

How so? he asked.

Well...rogues are immortal, right?

I have never heard of one who was not.

Okay. So say I marry this guy. He's around maybe another seventy years, we have a child with Terol blood, and the treaty's fulfilled.

Not precisely.

I frowned down at the river as if I could see Falova's face in the dark depths. *How so?*

If I understand you, Cirivant's goal is to put one of its sons or daughters on the throne of Daril. That would only happen once you were no longer queen.

And if I'm truly immortal, I finished as the pieces fell into place, *that could be a long time coming.*

Exactly. The only way you will satisfy Cirivant is for you to marry, procreate, and then either abdicate or die.

Groaning softly, I tried to find the holes in his logic. *Or—hear me out—I could marry, procreate, and leave the rest of the treaty fulfillment as a problem for myself seventy years from now.*

This is true, but in the interim, do you <u>want</u> to be married to this person? To bear his children? While I have never known of a rogue to die of natural causes, I cannot tell you that you would be impervious to the risks of childbirth, soul of my soul.

I don't want to marry him, I replied, *but if I don't, Darilis will die.*

Falova let me sit with that for a moment before he spoke again. *This is not a problem of your creation.*

Eh...kind of?

Erianthe bears far more blame for this than you do.

I'm not saying you're wrong, but if I'm going to rule Daril someday, don't I need to do the best thing for its people?

Again, he fell quiet for a moment, then murmured, *Is there someone you would prefer?*

I said nothing, trying to hold my thoughts to myself.

You can tell me, Falova insisted. *I wish only to give you good counsel, Susan.*

Though torn, I relented after a few long seconds and opened my thoughts to him.

Ah, he said, his tone both satisfied and unsurprised. *Does he know?*

I haven't said anything.

Perhaps you should speak plainly with him before you commit yourself to this Cirivanti boy.

No, I replied, and pushed myself out of my perch. *It wouldn't be fair to him.*

Because you will require a consort?

Because I won't try to tie him down. That's not right.

Have you considered that he might not be opposed to such a bind?

He needs his freedom, I told Falova. *I'm not going to take that from him.* Rubbing my arms against the wind, I said, *Goodnight. I'm going in before I freeze.*

Goodnight, soul of my soul, he replied. *A word of advice?*

Sure.

Be honest with Terj. I will say nothing of this to him, he added, *but before you pledge yourself to Erianthe's choice…*

Falova left the thought unfinished, but I plainly saw where it was heading. *I'll think about it*, I told him, and started down the staircase toward the warmth of my apartment.

Nothing needed to be decided that night, I told myself. I could sleep on this mess.

Besides, Terj was still away. I had time to stew over this brewing disaster without complicating matters with my heart.

CHAPTER 3

Looking back, I can't pinpoint the exact moments at which my feelings toward Terj began to shift from camaraderie to true friendship, and then to something more.

I'd met him at his lowest, most desperate point: imprisoned in a sword for five centuries, trapped in constant agony by the way the spells holding the sword together drew upon him as a power source, unable to communicate, and mourning my uncle, to whose side he'd been attached for almost forty years. Thus damned by the maladetas who didn't realize they'd left him alive in the first place, he'd been forced to condemn a new Watcher every few decades, ruining a string of human lives but helpless to do more than wait until time or an Outsider ended the sword wielder's tenure.

To say that Terj was a little bitter about his fate would be a gross understatement.

For nine generations in a row, he chose a member of the Cole family to assume the role of Watcher, which left them stuck within about a ten-mile radius of the opening to the Crossing and gifted with a sword they couldn't shake—a sword set with Aen crystals strong enough to draw an unending stream of monstrosities to them to be dispatched. I was the tenth Cole to inherit the sword, the last member of the family left in town. Dad and Malachi had reassured themselves that I'd avoid the family curse because I was a Cole by adoption, though Malachi had still begged the sword to spare me. But while neither they nor I knew what I truly was, Terj had sensed the elemental in me, and in his desperation, he'd chosen me as his best hope of salvation.

Once I brought him back within the Aen and he was able to speak to me, I felt his storm of emotions: anger over his mistreatment and the horrors the spells forced him to commit, guilt and remorse for surrendering to the spells and choosing Watcher after Watcher, weariness from his torture, despair at the idea of spending the rest of his unending life in his personal hell...but also a flicker of hope. I offered him what forgiveness I could, and he began to open to me, showing me glimpses of the personality behind the pain. Despite the way in which we'd come to be attached, I cared about him, and I knew the same was true on his end.

When the sword was destroyed, Terj was free to go, but he approached his liberation with baby steps. He helped me save Falova and carried my friends back across the wasteland to send them on their way out of Kopaat, but instead of flying off to explore in the manner of other air elementals, he returned to me in Deoni. Simply put, having been imprisoned young, and then having spent most of his life around humans, he wasn't ready to go off on his own just yet.

In truth, I didn't mind at all. Alone in a new town, a new country—hell, a new world—I appreciated his familiar presence. Terj didn't whisper about me like the servants did or try to mold me into a proper Darili princess. He knew Cole's Crossing well, and when homesickness threatened to overwhelm me, he came through with stories about the old place and people long dead. He had a keen memory for the members of the Cole clan, and in his retelling of family stories, they seemed almost alive. Terj's was usually the first voice I heard in the morning and the last at night, and even when he opted not to be seen, I could feel his presence nearby like a hand I could reach out and grab for comfort.

And though Terj insisted that he was a terrible judge of human aesthetics, he somehow made me feel beautiful. Maybe it was the simple fact that I never caught him staring at my scarred cheek or tutting about my rumpled clothes and mussed hair. He'd offer an opinion if asked, but he never sought to alter me, which was a refreshing change of pace in the castle.

Somewhere in that long winter, as I tried to cram in the years of Darili education I'd missed and Terj started venturing out into the city, I realized that what I felt for him was no longer simply platonic. I *wanted* his company, and I missed him when he was away. He swore that he always faced the window when I was dressing, but part of me wished he'd turn around and appreciate what he saw, hold me in my wide bed instead of just bidding me goodnight...

...and I knew it couldn't happen. Terj needed to be free, and trying to chain him down would be cruel.

So I said nothing. I continued on as though we were friends and I'd never imagined what his impossibly light touch might feel like on my lips, and I applauded him for his forays into the wide world beyond the castle walls. Terj had jokingly called himself an injured bird at a rehabilitation center, but there was more truth to that comparison than he acknowledged. After hopping around for so long, he was rediscovering his wings and learning to trust himself again. Soon enough, he wouldn't need me...and then he would go.

As it should be.

My tutors had provided me minimal information on the nature of elementals, either because they didn't have any answers or they wrongly assumed I knew everything already. What little I'd gleaned from my reading was that elementals were creatures of energy, sustained by the Aen but able to survive without it, and that they could not be tamed. Elementals inhabited oceans, volcanoes, and cliffs, or if they were born to air, they rode tempests for the sheer joy of it. Though I'd been born into a physical body, I could do incredible things with water if I put my mind to it—beautiful things, powerful things.

Deadly things.

I refrained from exhibiting my abilities in front of audiences. My siblings had pressed me until I'd given them a mild demonstration, and the Darili highborn had seen the recording of my fight with the Great One of Unara, in which I'd thrown around an acidic lake, but I tried not to remind people of what I could do unless absolutely necessary. Folks never looked at you the same way once they understood that you could weaponize a glass of water. The local adepts who'd developed skill with the Aen had fairly standard limits, but I was an unknown quantity, a monstrous potential in human form. Then again, pissed-off water elementals had been known to drag entire ships down to the depths, so my talents shouldn't have come as such a shock.

But I was, at least in part, born to water, unanchored to a stream of my own but still firmly grounded. Terj, born to air, had his own power—and unlike me, he was designed to go and see and do, never resting in one place for long. Air elementals preferred the wild places, free from the choking fumes and congestion of the cities of physical beings, and when the winds whipped around the castle at night, I could sense Terj perking like a dog hearing footsteps coming up the walk. Maybe he wasn't ready to be alone just yet, but he was approaching that point, growing stronger and more confident.

Wild things aren't meant to be caged. Terj had spent half a millennium shackled, and now, he was learning what freedom felt like. And so, even though a little piece of my heart worried that he wouldn't return every time he flew off, I cheered him on and hid my feelings from him. If I loved Terj, I told myself, the kindest thing I could do would be to let him live the way he was intended to live, unencumbered and unattached.

I couldn't go with him. My place was in Daril, learning about the people I'd been born to govern…and I owed those people my loyalty.

Didn't I?

I awoke to the sound of the first bell clanging in the courtyard, the castle's version of a wakeup call, and groaned as I tried to bond on a molecular level with my sheets. My mattress wasn't great, a feather-stuffed affair that tended to sag, but I was cold, and I had no desire to be vertical that morning.

Rough night?

Hey. When did you get back? I asked Terj.

Maybe an hour ago. You've been mumbling in your sleep.

"Nng," I croaked in agreement.

Susan? Were you planning to open your eyes today?

"Nng."

I felt the blankets lift at the edge of the bed, not enough to bare my legs but a tease to let me know Terj was doing his part to rouse me. Clutching the covers more tightly around my chin, I grumbled and pulled my knees in close.

Are you feeling all right? Bad dreams?

Though Terj never slept, he'd witnessed sleep long enough to recognize the common ways in which a night could go wrong.

I pried my eyelids apart and blinked at the gumminess in my vision. While winter's grip on Deoni was beginning to loosen, the sun still rose late, and the only light in my room came from the lantern left burning on the hook by the privacy screen, a helpful glow in case I needed to stumble to the chamber pot in the dark. I couldn't see Terj, but the sensation of a slight settling at the foot of the bed told me where he was lurking.

Weird dreams, I told him. *I tossed and turned.*

I can tell. Half your blankets are on the floor.

I squinted at the rug as a wadded shape rose, smoothed itself into a rectangle, and settled over me. *Guess that explains the chill.*

Well, that, plus the shitty insulation in this building. The glass in your window is doing you no favors. He paused, then said, *You're troubled. What's on your mind?*

While I had no desire to have this conversation before breakfast, I knew Terj well enough to guarantee that he wouldn't let the matter drop. One of the spells on the sword that had bonded us—for all I knew of magic, maybe the one that had left the design on the hilt branded into my right palm—had kept us particularly attuned to the other's moods. Sure, Falova could pick up on my state of mind because he literally recognized himself in me, but Terj's intuition was superb.

I sighed and forced myself to sit up in bed, though my bare arms wished I'd reconsidered. *Erianthe and Narod had a proposal for me last night.*

Oh? Send you into exile and pretend none of this ever happened? he replied, only somewhat in jest.

Marry me off to Narod's nephew.

Terj's shock radiated from him like heat from the blistering great fireplace in the castle kitchen. *Why?*

Because Erianthe fell through on her end of her marriage treaty, Daril's Ga'beshi settlements need protection, and Cirivant has agreed that a second Fulquir–Terol union would make it up to them. I shrugged in the darkness. *Since I'm conveniently single and of marriageable age, and since Narod's brother has a son who satisfies the same criteria, the powers that be think this is a great idea.*

You told them no, didn't you? When I didn't immediately confirm it, Terj's agitation swelled. *Didn't you, Susan?*

I'm still thinking it over. Hence the sleepless night.

You can't marry someone you've never even met! he protested. *What's he like, is he kind, is he intelligent, is he at all appealing to you?*

No clue, I replied. *All that matters for political purposes is that he's male, a Terol, and a prince.*

Is that what matters to you? A prince?

Of course not! I don't want to tie myself to this guy just because he's a damn prince. I mean, I don't want to tie myself to him at all.

Terj's hackles, which had shot up in the last moments, began to fall.

But it's been made clear to me, I continued, *that if I reject this plan and Daril can't fulfill its end of the treaty, then Cirivant will withdraw its protection of our colonies. You know about the piracy problem in Ga'besh. The Central Sea is lousy with them.*

That may be, but it's not your *problem.*

Except it is. Crown princess, right? I'm supposed to do what's best for Daril...and that may mean biting the bullet and marrying this dude so Darilis in Ga'besh don't die.

With the initial surprise wearing off, Terj was calming somewhat, though he still seemed perturbed. *Again, this is a mess of Erianthe's making. She's the one who broke the treaty, she's the one who fucking left you to die in the woods...let her work something out with Cirivant. Surely Daril can pay for protection.*

Cirivant is the wealthiest human settlement in Ga'besh by a wide *margin,* I replied. *They don't need Daril's money—they want clout.*

Then let Erianthe find a way to make it up to them. You shouldn't be a trophy she can give away as needed. It's not like she ever did anything to earn you, he grumbled.

Father pointed out another problem—

Wait, Terj interrupted, *is* he *in favor of this madness?*

I don't think so, no. But he noted that if the goal is to get a Terol on the throne, and if I turn out to be immortal...

Exactly! How many generations of your family would be left waiting for you to die or step aside? And what if someone from Cirivant decided that it was time for you to make good on the deal, hmm? An assassin wouldn't be too great an expense for one desperate to take the throne. Look, Susan...

In the dim light, I could barely tell that he was materializing as a figure of swirling air until he gripped my hands.

Marry, if that's what you want, said Terj. *If it will make you happy, fulfill you...hell, scratch an itch...then get married.* Someday.

To someone who loves you as more than a ticket to a throne. Someone you genuinely want to be with.

I clamped down on my mind, hoping he couldn't pick up on my thoughts about him.

But don't marry a Cirivanti prince you've never met just because it's the most convenient solution to Erianthe's problem. You don't owe her convenience.

I know, I said, and squeezed his hands in turn. *But I also realize there's a solid chance that people will die if I don't go along with this plan.*

This may sound cold, but people will die no matter what you do. Such is the nature of mortals.

Huffing a sigh, I said, *People will die prematurely, if you prefer. And since my choices have already left corpses on the four worlds and Unara…*

Because I forced you to take up that sword! he exclaimed. *Susan, if there's blood on anyone's hands, let it be mine.*

You didn't force me to leave the Crossing, I reminded him. *That was my choice. And once Outsiders started coming through—*

A small repayment of the debt deferred for five centuries. Don't do this to yourself.

I sat there on my bed for a time, collecting my thoughts and taking comfort in the steady pressure of Terj's hands holding mine, then told him, *I just don't want to make things worse. I don't want to be the reason that some little kid loses her family, you know?*

I…understand that, he allowed. *I do. But don't rush into this. Think about it—this is your life Erianthe's trying to sell. Your freedom. She has no right to make such claims on you, and whatever Cirivant offers in trade, they'd receive the far better deal.*

Before I could think better of it, I leaned forward until I felt the faint resistance of his face, then kissed his cheek. Registering his surprise and pleasure, I said, *You're sweet. I think I'm going to have a word with Edes.*

Want me to rouse him? If I don't, you won't see him before midday.

I glanced over my shoulder at the twilight beyond the

glass, then grunted. *If you don't mind. He'll forgive me eventually.*

Perhaps thinking it would help his cause, Terj didn't stop with waking Edes. An hour later, I met all three of my siblings in Jerrcoa's apartment. The delay had been at Edes's insistence that he not be required to think on an empty stomach, and so a servant had laid breakfast at Jerrcoa's table.

That we'd ended up in his quarters was no accident: because of his mobility issues, Jerrcoa needed to be carried between the floors of the castle, as the old complex couldn't be properly retrofitted for his wheelchair. Thus, whenever any of Jerrcoa's siblings wanted to meet with him, it was usually done in a place accessible to him without the help of the staff. Jerrcoa bore his frequent manhandling with good humor, but even I could tell that it chafed at him to be lugged around in his burly valet's arms, so none of us grumbled about the trip to his corner of the castle.

By the time I arrived, Edes had made himself a heaping plate, Zadi had perched on the padded windowsill in her dressing gown with a cup of the bitter tisane Erianthe favored, and Jerrcoa was waiting at the table, cocking an eyebrow as I closed the door. "All right, I'm listening," he said while Edes choked down a mouthful of eggs. "What's so important that it couldn't wait for daylight? And good morning, Terj," he said as his eyes flicked to the slight disturbance to my left. "You'll forgive the screaming, I trust."

"Screaming?" I asked.

Terj sounded embarrassed when he answered me. *I couldn't very well light the lamps before I woke him…*

"And you might imagine why being shaken awake by an invisible hand in a nearly dark room is somewhat disconcerting if one isn't anticipating such," said Jerrcoa. "Anyway, I think I smacked you at some point. My apologies."

No harm done. I'll stand back next time. But on to the important matter—tell them, Susan.

With a long, slow exhalation, I settled into the chair across from Jerrcoa and poured myself a cup of tea, which I liberally sweetened. At least honeybees had found their way into the four worlds. While Zadi joined us, I recounted my dinner with Erianthe and Narod and the announcement that I was to be engaged.

If Terj had expected an indignant outcry from my siblings, however, he was sorely disappointed.

"It might seem sudden, but you're of the right age," said Edes through the thick slice of buttered bread he'd crammed in his mouth. He paused, took a sip of juice to clear the works, and continued. "Most highborn girls are betrothed or married by their mid-twenties at the latest."

"Some of my friends are betrothed already," Zadi offered. "Mother says she wants to wait until I'm a little older," she added with a heaved sigh, "but if she waits too much longer, all the best boys will be *taken*."

Jerrcoa, at least, seemed to understand why I might be upset. "It's unfortunate that they didn't consult you before announcing this plan," he said, cutting his sausage into smaller pieces. "But Edes is correct—marriage at your age is nothing unusual. Is this not the custom beyond the Crossing?"

"I mean, some people from my hometown get married in their early twenties," I replied, "but it's always to someone they know and choose. I'm being set up with a *stranger*."

"Which isn't uncommon among the highest of the highborn. Royal marriages are seldom love matches, Susan. They're prayers and parties attached to treaties. Look at Edes's betrothal," he added, jutting his thumb toward our bottomless pit of a brother. "Mother and Father arranged that one, and you see how much care they took to find a spouse to his liking."

"She *was* very pretty," said Zadi between sips of tea.

Edes shot her a warning look, then turned to me. "Believe me, I didn't want that marriage, but the heir to the throne *needs* to marry, and politically, it was a good match. I was told to marry her, and so I intended to do my duty."

"Until I stole your happiness and ruined everything," I joked.

He reached around the table to slap me on the back. "I knew I liked you."

But surely you see the flaws with this plan, Terj protested, agitation rippling from the window seat he'd stolen from Zadi. *If nothing else, after what Susan did for our worlds, she deserves the right to choose her own spouse.*

"Were ours a perfectly fair world, I might agree," said Jerrcoa, glancing over his shoulder in Terj's direction. "But it's not. Susan could do worse than…which prince was it? Gerinet is married, is he not?"

I shrugged and poured myself a cup of tea. "They didn't tell me, just said it was one of the king's sons."

Jerrcoa and Edes traded looks. "Uncle Fetull has two sons and six daughters," Edes replied. "Since Gerinet is the crown prince, your intended has to be Makou. He's a year or two older than me, so you're of an age or close."

"Age isn't the problem," Jerrcoa murmured, and held Edes's gaze. "I know it's been years since we saw them, but don't you think that Makou—"

"He's said nothing to me on the subject, and I won't speculate," Edes interrupted, shutting down the line of enquiry.

But Jerrcoa had made his suspicion clear: Makou might be just as unenthusiastic about marrying me as Edes was about his princess, and it had nothing to do with my looks. "Great," I muttered. "That's just *perfect.*"

"I may be completely mistaken," Jerrcoa hastily backpedaled. "Again, it's been years, and people change as they mature…"

Still, the future at which he'd hinted rolled out before me in my mind's eye: decades of loveless marriage to someone who bound himself to me only out of duty, who might never voluntarily touch me—hell, who might be repulsed at the thought.

I groaned into my teacup and knocked back the brew.

For the next three days, I stewed over the decision. To my siblings, there really was no choice—Mother had made up her mind, and that was that. To Terj, there was also no choice to be made—Erianthe was using me as a quick fix and perhaps trying to help her people forget the previous year's *unpleasantness* with a royal wedding. Falova didn't offer me unsolicited advice, but I could feel him whenever I approached the river side of the castle, silent but present if I wanted to talk.

I slept poorly for two nights, waking to cold arms and the covers in a wad or cascading off my bed. But on the third, I found myself in one of the most vivid dreams I'd ever had.

I was flying—not so unusual for a dream—across a shadowy world toward a red glow on the horizon. As I neared it, I recognized the village I'd found aflame and under attack by Outsiders during my first trip across Daril. Frantic to save it, I landed and ran toward the conflagration, only to discover that there were no monsters this time, and I was unarmed. But I saw the furious villagers all the same: the men with knives and hoes and scythes, the wailing women, the wide-eyed children with sooty faces and bare feet.

I had to help them. Their village would burn to the ground if I didn't take action…

Water. They needed to put out the blaze. I could do that…

Except I couldn't. In the dream, I couldn't even *feel* the nearby water, much less draw it toward me. It was as if the last year of my life had never happened, and I was just Susan Cole again—college graduate, store owner, unremarkable human.

"Help us!" one of the villagers demanded.

I remembered him too well, the ringleader who'd learned while interrogating us that he'd lost his wife. I would never forget his rage and despair.

"You're supposed to be back there! Protecting us! Where were you? Our homes! Our livelihoods! All of it, gone!"

His lament had changed in the dream, but not its tenor. "You're supposed to protect us!" the dream version cried. "Where were you?"

Looking around, I realized that the landscape had shifted. Gone were the Darili hinterlands, replaced by a bloody, corpse-strewn shore and an angry sea at my back. I spotted a ship anchored nearby, an incongruous wooden galleon out of my imagination that was somehow flying the Jolly Roger.

Dream logic is a funny thing, I guess.

When I turned back to the angry crowd, the man had fallen silent, and his son Kerul, the teenage priest, stepped forward. His red robe flapped in the sea wind, and a crimson gem glinted in the middle of his necklace like a drop of blood. "You did this," he said, pointing to me. "Selfish girl, this is all your fault."

"I didn't ask for this!" I protested. "I never wanted to be the Watcher!"

Kerul's eyes narrowed. "You wanted to be our princess, didn't you? And now you've left us to die."

"This is *Erianthe's* fault!"

"But you could have stopped it."

I stamped my foot in the sand. "Don't blame me for her mistakes!"

The priest's stony expression didn't waver. "You *are* her mistake made manifest, now brought forth to curse us all. What do you *want*, Susan? If you won't defend us, then why won't you leave us alone?"

As the waves lapped at my feet, I said, "I'm sorry—"

"That won't bring my mother back," he snapped. "None of our mothers, our fathers, our sisters and brothers, our children…" He turned, shaking his head in disgust. "The gods have spoken. Let the sea take her."

"Wait, please," I begged, but a dozen invisible hands suddenly wrapped around my neck and waist and legs, pinning my limbs and dragging me into the ocean. "Wait!" I screamed. "I can fix this—"

Cold brine washed over me, blinding me and filling my lungs. I sputtered, trying to draw breath, but the arms kept pulling me down until the burning town was just a dim red glow above me, and panic clawed at my ribs because I couldn't breathe, I couldn't *breathe*…

I awoke with a gasp, kicking and flailing until I remembered I was in my bed. My legs were tangled in the blankets, and I straightened the covers while my heart slowed and I tried to push the wave of guilt back into the corner of my mind where it usually lived.

That wasn't my first dream of the town and its angry, bereaved inhabitants. I'd been plagued by occasional nocturnal visits in the eight months since stumbling upon the destruction. After I'd had a quiet word with the priest who ministered to Erianthe, he had consulted the records and bloodlines until he found the information I sought: Kerul Gaffang, now seventeen, lived in a hamlet of no consequence called Tinnafil. Armed with that knowledge, I'd bypassed my mother to ask Narod for help, and he'd agreed to send a few wagons of rebuilding supplies. It wasn't much—and since the townsfolk had dragged my friends and me to Deoni to be executed, I knew it wasn't enough to settle the score in their eyes—but I thought the gesture might assuage some of my guilt.

I was wrong, and the dreams continued, a little something to make matters worse whenever my anxiety spiked.

That morning, as I caught my breath in the cold

predawn darkness, I felt Terj dart to my side and brush my hair from my face. *Susan? Are you all right?*

Bad dream, I told him.

Tinnafil again?

Yeah, except I drowned this time.

His incredulity swept across my mind. *Somehow, I find that unlikely.*

But possible. This body needs oxygen, remember. Grounded once more, I flopped back onto my pillows and groaned. "Shit."

I'm sorry. Dreaming seems like it would be a fairly unpleasant experience.

It's hit and miss, I'll give you that. However, since the alternative right now is sitting up until dawn...

Get your rest. The blankets finished tidying themselves as Terj tucked me in, and I sighed as I rolled over to face the wall.

Goodnight, I told him.

I'll be here if you need me, he replied, and I felt his presence dim as he moved away from the bed— presumably toward one of the windows, where he often camped.

As I lay still, I didn't know if I would be able to get back to sleep, but I *did* know that my subconscious had answered one question for me.

Like it or not, I would agree to Erianthe's terms.

My mother sounded peeved when one of her maidservants announced me the next morning. To be fair, the sun was barely up, and she was still half dressed in her boudoir, a combination walk-in closet and dressing room the size of Uncle Malachi's cabin. A quartet of servants was attending to her toilette as I walked in: one taming her hair, one applying her face, one lacing up her bodice, and the fourth, who'd stopped to answer my knock, polishing her shoes. Erianthe cracked an eye only long enough to verify my identity before she closed it again and let her makeup artist resume work on her foundation.

"Uh…hi," I began.

"Susan." She followed the murmured request to lift her chin.

I'd accepted that hoping for warmth from my mother would be roughly on par with hoping for world peace in terms of likelihood, but an actual greeting shouldn't have been too much to ask for. Still, I chose not to start a fight. "Can we talk?"

"We're doing so now, are we not?" Her maidservants tittered, and Erianthe smiled slightly at her own joke.

I rolled my eyes. "Perhaps I was unclear. Could we talk *alone*?"

"Who," she countered, "you, me, and your shadow?"

The name I'd suggested for Terj was the New Kopaati term for "shadow," a spur-of-the-moment idea taken from the various names used for the sword that had imprisoned him. Erianthe knew damn well that it was a name, not a descriptor, but to the greatest extent possible, she refused to acknowledge Terj's existence. I wasn't sure whether she disliked him because he was an elemental or because he had no qualms about calling her out on her bullshit regarding me, but in any case, there was no love lost between the two.

"Terj has gone out this morning," I replied. "So I was thinking you and me."

She heaved a sigh that any teenage girl would be proud of, then ordered her team, "Go into the corridor for a few minutes. This won't take long."

The maidservants dropped what they were doing and slipped out, closing the door behind them. As the latch clicked, I turned to Erianthe and folded my arms. "All right, I'll do it. I'll marry Makou."

Her eyebrows rose in surprise for an instant, but she quickly composed her expression. "I don't recall giving you his name…"

"Process of elimination. We assumed you wouldn't be marrying me off to the Cirivanti heir apparent."

She chuckled incredulously. "*No*. But your deduction was sound—the marriage treaty includes Makou." Pausing, she considered me for a moment, then said, "I admit, this is unexpected."

"Oh?"

"That you would do anything in the interest of someone other than yourself. Perhaps my children are serving as a positive influence on you."

Biting back a reference to glass houses—the phrase would have required explanation in translation, anyway—I said, "I don't agree with this stupid plan of yours, and quite frankly, it's not my responsibility to clean up your messes. But this is bigger than both of us, and if marrying me off is what it'll take to save our outposts in Ga'besh, then so be it."

"*My* messes?" she retorted. "If you—"

"My existence is not a problem for me to solve," I snapped. "Nor is the fact that your people now know you're a goddamn liar anything I need to correct. I'm doing this for the good of our people, not for you."

As I turned to go, Erianthe said, "They're not your people. They never will be."

"Maybe not," I replied, not even looking back, "but I've done more for them in the last year than you've done in your petty, miserable life."

Sure, slamming the door was an empty gesture, but it felt so satisfying in the moment. "She's all yours," I told the cluster of wide-eyed maidservants, then stormed off to my apartment to begin my lessons for the day.

Shortly after lunch, Terj returned and found me back at work with my much-despised children's poetry. "Hey," I said, glancing up when I felt him sweep into the room like a breeze. *Did you have a nice time out there?*

The temple bells have been ringing half the day.

I frowned, surprised by the agitation in his thought. *Yeah, they started up a few hours ago.* After the first twenty minutes, I'd more or less tuned them out, though their melodic pealing was muffled only slightly by the thin window glass.

I stopped there to learn the cause, Terj continued. *A priest was proclaiming it as I came in. Something about your betrothal?*

I couldn't very well lie to him. *It's what's best for Daril. I accepted this morning, and Tonnera passed word to the maladeta in, uh...* Pausing as I recognized the gap in my knowledge, I huffed, then added, *In whatever the Cirivanti capital is called. I should probably look into that, shouldn't I?*

Susan... Terj drew closer to me, then pulled the air around him into his quasi-physical form. *Don't do this. Please. You don't want this, do you?*

No, I don't, I concurred, *but this is one of those times when I have to think about what's in the best interest of the country. If this marriage is the only way they'll keep protecting our people, then what choice do I have?*

You have every choice. Susan—

He had grabbed my hands as he spoke, and I looked down at them together, mine pale with winter, his nearly transparent.

This problem is not of your making, he said. *You don't owe Erianthe or anyone else your life.*

But if I don't do this and people die because of me, I'll never be able to live with myself.

Terj made no reply for a long moment, but finally, his grip on my hands loosened, and he backed away. *If you're resolved to marry him, then I wish you every happiness.*

I didn't think I was imagining the sense of deep resignation in his voice.

And I believe it's time that I was on my way, he continued. *I've troubled you long enough—*

You haven't troubled me, I protested, surprised at the sudden declaration. *You're welcome here, but...*

But what? Wasn't the goal to get Terj back to the life that had been stolen from him? He'd learned to walk again, and now he was ready to fly...and that was what *he* needed. If I gave a damn about him, I had to do the right thing.

Even if my heart clenched at the thought.

But if you're ready to go, I told him, forcing a smile, *that's great. I'm happy for you. There's a wide world out there. Four of them, really,* I added with a little chuckle. *And you know how miserable it can be around here in the summer, so if you want to find a better place to explore, I don't blame you.*

Thank you, he said, and headed for the window.

Will I see you again?

Terj paused and turned back to me. *Is that what you want?*

What I wanted was for his to be the first voice I heard every morning and the last at night for the rest of my life. What I wanted was to hold him and never let go. But how could I condemn him to live like that—my often invisible companion, stuck in Deoni, alone in a castle full of humans?

Should your travels bring you back this way, I would love to see you, I said. *Hear about the craziest things you've found out there.* I hesitated, then quietly told him, *I'm sorry we never made it to the Grand Canyon.*

Neither did Malachi. He'd understand, Terj replied. A little gust of wind opened the latch, and the window swung wide on a crescendo of temple bells. *I'll miss you, Susan. Be well.*

Clenching my jaw so that I wouldn't start crying, I joined him at the window. *I hope you find everything you could want out there. Please take care of yourself.*

As I closed my eyes against the pricking, he cupped one hand over my scarred cheek, and then, ever so softly, I felt something brush against my forehead.

He'd kissed me.

But by the time my eyes shot open, he'd already

withdrawn and dematerialized. "Terj," I began, stepping toward the window, "I—"

I'll see you again, he promised, and then he was gone.

CHAPTER 4

One thing could be said for Erianthe: when she made up her mind, she didn't dawdle.

My wedding was set for a mere forty days from the time I affixed my shaky New Kopaati signature to the betrothal treaty, perhaps as insurance against second thoughts. As for the event itself, there was little I needed to do besides show up and keep breathing. Erianthe knew as well as any highborn Darili how royal weddings were supposed to run, and she immediately tasked her staff with attending to the details: the priests, the musicians, the flowers, the food, the parties and receptions before and after the ceremony itself. Invitations went out practically before the ink on the treaty was dry, While Erianthe wrote the guest list herself, including as was customary the heads of state with whom Daril maintained diplomatic relations, I did insist on four additions, each of whom received a separate invitation: Ms. Quince, who would surely come with Ganeel, the clan mother of the Taln'een maladetas, Fanakel, who might otherwise be left at home in Caritulo in favor of his more esteemed half siblings, and Anji and Mia. While I suspected that Rokund had sense enough to include Anji in his party, I didn't want to take any chances, and I *definitely* wanted to be sure that my best friend had her own invitation. Asking Mia to be a bridesmaid was out of the question—honestly, I wasn't sure if Darili weddings included bridesmaids at all—but at the very least, I wanted her there that day.

When I wasn't haggling with my mother over

invitations, I faced the disdain of her personal designer, who announced with a deep sigh that there was no way the queen's wedding gown could be repurposed for me. I was simply too big to squeeze myself into that constrictive bodice, and even if I starved myself in the weeks before the wedding, too much of my bulk was muscle. This left the royal tailors working overtime, as all six of us would require multiple ensembles for the event. Edes and Jerrcoa didn't particularly care, and Narod swore he had enough in his wardrobes to make himself presentable for a month of parties, but Erianthe demanded new gowns for herself and for Zadi, and I needed new *everything*. Two days after I agreed to this nonsense, I found myself standing in the designer's quarters, holding up pieces of blue and green fabric as she tucked and pinned and tutted about my waistline. Per tradition, my wedding gown would reflect the colors of the Darili flag—not a horrible combination on me, but not exactly the white wedding I'd imagined as a little girl.

In light of my impending nuptials, my tutors took my lessons in new directions, focusing on the ancient text of the wedding ritual—which was in Upper Kopaati, to my dismay, a language bearing about as much relation to the New Kopaati I'd been studying as did Anglo-Saxon to modern English—and on the conversational basics of Common, the language preferred in Cirivant, a blend of Upper Kopaati and Common Elvish that seemed to have more exceptions than rules. Thus it was that Jerrcoa caught me in the library late one night about a week after my betrothal, muttering to myself as I tried to keep three languages straight in my frazzled brain.

"Not *aa*," he said, mimicking my short *a* as he wheeled toward my table and the pool of lanternlight. "It's more like *ay*."

I looked up and groaned. "You speak Common, too?"

"Conversationally, if not fluently. It's often taught, and Father insisted, anyway. But what are you worried about?"

he asked, pulling up across from me. "You're a walking translator, sister. If one or two things are lost in translation, I suspect you won't cause offense."

"Any more offense than usual, you mean?"

He dipped his head in acknowledgement. "Once Makou spends a season or two here, I'm sure he'll acclimate to any...idiosyncrasies."

"I'm weird. You can say it," I muttered, closing my book. "And you'll never guess what the tailors have put together for me."

"A dress or two, I trust."

"Oh, more than that." Reaching into my satchel, I pulled out a folded piece of silky beige fabric from which two thin strings dangled. I slipped it into position over the left side of my face, centered the eyehole, and tied it behind my head. "Ta-da! So that my intended doesn't run screaming when he gets a look at me."

My brother scowled. "Take that thing off."

"Gladly." I wadded it up and shoved it back in my bag. "Not sure how I'm supposed to eat in that. One splash, and it's ruined. Then again, since Mother doesn't like me eating at the best of times..."

"If Mother had her way, I'd sit tucked in at a table during all events, lest someone realize I can't stand alone. Sometimes, it's best to nod, then ignore her." He paused, glancing around the library, then asked, "Where's Terj tonight?"

"He left a few days ago," I replied, trying to keep my tone neutral. "Said it was time for him to go on his way."

Jerrcoa's expression softened. "*Ah.* I'd wondered."

"Wondered what?"

"Well, I mean, it can't be easy to stand back and watch someone you love marry another person."

I laughed weakly. "What are you talking about?"

"Susan." Had he been wearing glasses, he'd have been staring at me over the lenses. "Come on."

"Terj doesn't *love* me—"

"You can't believe that."

I straightened in my chair, taken aback. "I do."

"Then you're the only one. Look," he said, folding his arms, "I may be crippled, but I'm not blind. I watch. I listen. And I'm telling you there's no explanation for why an air elemental, freed after so long, would linger *here*, of all places, if he wasn't desperately in love with you."

After a few seconds of silence, I realized that my mouth was hanging slightly agape.

"So yes, I'm not surprised that he's departed," Jerrcoa continued. "Even if he understands that he's not a fit consort for you, that knowledge alone probably has done nothing to quench whatever he feels."

I sat there for another moment, processing and fighting the sick churning in my gut, but before I could speak, Jerrcoa murmured, "And I know you love him, too."

When I cut my eyes to a spot over his shoulder as if he could see through them into my soul, he softly chuckled. "Believe me, I know there are reasons why you might not be honest with yourself," he said, "but I've watched you two interact for months. The way you look at him, that little smile you get when the two of you speak privately…it's blatant, at least to me."

"Who else knows?" I asked quietly.

He shrugged. "I've spoken to no one of this, and if Mother and Father have their suspicions, they've not shared them with me."

Sighing, I said, "You're…not wrong. About me."

"Have you not told him?"

"I can't," I protested. "He needs his freedom. He *deserves* it. Even if…if things were different, and we could be together, I couldn't do that to him."

Jerrcoa leaned back against his chair and drummed his fingers on the armrests. "You know, freedom can mean different things. Freedom to move about, to leave this place, to see the world beyond Daril…or maybe freedom to choose your own path. Perhaps, given his druthers, Terj would see choosing you as exercising that freedom. Of course, he's no fool," he added, "so since that option is unavailable to him, he's done the next best thing. I wouldn't want to suffer through a wedding like that, either."

"So what do you want me to do?" I asked, propping my arms on the table. "Ask my father to keep an eye out for him and see if he can send Terj back this way for a heart-to-heart chat?"

His head tilted in query. "Would Falova do that?"

"Probably, if I asked him. But what would that accomplish? What am I supposed to tell Terj? 'Hi, nice to see you. By the way, I'm in love with you, but I'm still going to marry the Cirivanti guy. Tough luck!'"

Smirking at my poor acting, Jerrcoa replied, "You're right, I don't see anything to gain there. Unless you're reconsidering your betrothal…"

I shook my head. "We need their navy, don't we? This is the only way, so I'll do my duty."

To my surprise, Jerrcoa reached across the table and took my hand. "I'm sorry," he said softly. "I didn't mean to grieve you."

"It is what it is, but, uh…thanks," I said, and gave his hand a quick squeeze before releasing him. Grabbing my bag and the lantern, I muttered, "Not going to master Common tonight. Walk you back to your apartment?"

"If you'd be so kind," he replied, and waited until I'd illuminated the path to the exit before pushing himself along the woven runner. "And if you're looking for a bit of good news, how about this?" he asked as I held the door open. "At least you're worth a marital alliance. I doubt that Mother could pay a princess to accept me."

"Jerrcoa…"

"I'm serious. What do I bring to a union? Third child, won't live long, probably can't father children of my own…who wants to be stuck with that, eh?"

He didn't sound self-pitying, but rather resigned.

"You know, you're worth more than your ability to marry and procreate," I told him.

At that, Jerrcoa turned and smirked at me over his shoulder. "You're new to royal life, aren't you?"

My final month of unmarried freedom passed far too quickly. Seven days before the main event, my intended and his family made it to Deoni.

As with every other aspect of my wedding, Erianthe had choreographed this moment with precision. She received our guests in the throne room, one of the most impressive spaces in the castle. Tall stone walls dotted with arched windows rose to the wooden ceiling, which I'd always liked: it was painted like the sky, with sunset by the doors at the start of the long lilac runner, a star-strewn sky above the middle of the room, and sunrise over the monarch's and consort's gilded thrones atop the dais at the other end. Instead of settling for mere portraits, Darili monarchs commissioned statues of themselves in brightly colored clothing, which lined the walls in the spaces between the windows. Erianthe's had yet to join them, but her father's and mother's statues faced each other in the places nearest her throne.

That afternoon, a smaller throne had been added to the pair for me, and I sat to my mother's left, tightly laced into a violet gown, as the Cirivanti royal family was announced.

First down the aisle—well, first behind a pair of pages bearing the Cirivanti standard, a red ship's wheel on a blue field—walked Narod's eldest brother, Fetull. Like Narod, the king was a thin man, but he held his back straight, and his gaze seemed sharp as he took in Erianthe's collection of guards and servants. His hair, once dark brown, had grayed at the temples and begun to recede. Beside and ever so slightly behind him walked a plump blonde in a loose green dress—the queen, Cofali. She had a nice smile, I thought, and I've have traded gowns with her in a heartbeat. While I couldn't speak to the fashions in Perem—the Cirivanti capital, I'd finally learned—if Cofali's wardrobe was on trend, then I'd be doing what I could to import my dresses.

The king and queen's eight children walked behind them, some with spouses of their own. The crown prince was easy to pick out of the crowd—blond like his mother, Gerinet was a bit shorter than the king but otherwise looked like a solid pick for a football player—and his wife, a redhead, had the sort of face that was begging to be photographed. In the middle of the pack, after a few of his sisters, walked a lone man in a dove-gray tunic and trousers accented with silver braiding. He was at least as tall as his father, brown-haired and brown-eyed, and though thinner than Gerinet, he seemed sturdy—the kind of specimen who could make riding up with a fluttering cape look manly as hell. As he neared, I tried to absorb the details of his face: olive complexion, square jaw, three-day scruff, thick but groomed eyebrows. His hair fell loose over his shoulders, and when he caught me staring at him, one corner of his mouth turned up in a secret little smile.

Shit. Makou Terol was *gorgeous*.

My face heated as I wondered what he thought about me. Mother had sent some of her maidservants to do their worst, and I'd been tucked, laced, pinned, and painted to their satisfaction, but I still didn't hold a candle to Gerinet's lovely bride. On top of that, I'd caved to maternal nagging and allowed the servants to tie my half-mask in place, ostensibly so as not to frighten the Cirivantis.

Surely someone had warned Makou about my scar, I told myself. Surely he wouldn't catch a glimpse of my puckered cheek and recoil in disgust.

Finally, Narod could take it no longer. He rose, beaming, and threw his arms open wide as he descended the dais, and Fetull broke ranks to march past the pages and embrace him. Between the hearty back slaps, I could make out their brief conversation in Common, though my talent translated it for me: a welcome, jokes about the wasteland they'd just crossed, comments about how much Fetull's children had grown up. Narod kissed Cofali's hand, then seemed to recall that his wife was still seated and waiting, and cleared his throat. "Be welcome, brother," he said in New Kopaati. "Erianthe, dear?"

After a few seconds' hesitation, she rose and accepted his hand as she made her way to the floor. "Fetull, Cofali," she said, nodding to each. "Your presence honors us."

"The honor is ours," the king replied, though I suspected there was more politeness than gratitude in the sentiment. "And this must be Susan," he said, gesturing to me.

Since we'd already strayed from the planned order of reception, I rose and joined the others. "Your Majesty," I said, dropping a practiced curtsy to Fetull, then a second one for Cofali. "Pleasure to meet you."

Cofali extended two fingers and held them beneath my chin, gently raising my head as she examined me. "I see much of your mother in you," she murmured as she released me.

I cut my eyes to Erianthe, then back at Cofali. "I'm fortunate to have her looks."

"And this?" she asked, tapping her bare cheek in reflection of me.

"This," I replied, brushing my fingertips over the cloth mask, "is for your comfort."

"Mm. May I?"

Without waiting for my answer, she gently turned me around, then loosened the knot holding the mask in place and pulled it away. When I pivoted back to her, uncovered, she smiled. "Much better. There's a healthy glow to your cheeks, dear—it would be a pity to hide it."

"That is *very* gracious of you, Cofali," Erianthe hastily cut in, "but there's no need—"

"To hide anything," Fetull finished, and gave me a

sharp nod of approval. "Our court maladeta showed us the recording of your deeds Outside," he said to me. "Miraculous thing, that, but what we witnessed…"

"Damn impressive," Gerinet interjected.

His father chuckled. "Just as my son said. And as I am well acquainted with the images of Daril's…rogue daughter, there is no cause for veiling your face." Looking over his shoulder, he called, "Makou! Come meet your bride."

The crowd of princesses parted, and Makou slipped between his parents. He was no harder on the eyes up close, and I sincerely hoped he shared the elder Terols' sentiments about my looks.

"Your Highness," he said, executing a formal bow.

I curtsied in turn, praying I could remember my Common. "Your Highness," I replied, rolling the unfamiliar syllables on my tongue. My accent, according to my siblings, remained a work in progress. "Welcome to Deoni."

He smiled at my attempt, though it never quite reached his dark eyes.

"You must be weary," Erianthe interrupted. "We've had chambers prepared for all of you, should you desire to rest or refresh yourselves before dinner."

That suggestion was met with firm approval from the Cirivanti party, and within a few minutes, servants had led the last of them off. I watched as Makou followed his brother, but though I certainly didn't mind the view, I was disappointed when he didn't look back.

I'd hoped for a chance to say more than a few words to the man I was meant to marry, but that night's banquet never presented an opportunity. Erianthe and Narod sat at one end of the table across from Fetull and Cofali, where the brothers kept up a lively conversation, while the rest of us were left to claim whatever places we liked. My siblings threw themselves into the mix, and before I'd grabbed a chair, Edes and Gerinet had flanked Makou, with a husband of one of the Terol daughters taking the seat opposite him. Even Jerrcoa had been slotted in nearby. Deciding that it would look a little pathetic to shoehorn myself into their conversation when they clearly hadn't planned to save me a place, I took a chair near the far end of the table, where I chatted with several of the princesses about their trip and the planned festivities.

Eventually, catching my glances toward the knot around Makou, his eldest sister, Velia, said, "Be patient with my brother. He's somewhat reserved, particularly around new people. Give him a chance to know you."

"He doesn't seem eager to get that process started," I mumbled into my salad.

She patted my shoulder. "This is a night for family. We've not seen our little cousins in years—look at Father and Uncle Narod," she added, nodding down the table. "Tonight is for reacquaintance, and tomorrow, I'm sure he'll turn to the business of making yours."

"Mm." I glanced his way again and found him bent over his plate, laughing with Edes. "Tell me something. Is he…at all excited about this?"

Velia lifted her fork and chuckled. "Nervous, I think. As was Gerinet, as was I." Her married sisters nodded emphatically. "But he'll come around. Let him open up to you, and I suspect you two will make fine partners."

"Maybe, but if he's not happy…"

She laughed in earnest, then bent toward my ear. "Susan, darling, he'll be prince consort of Daril someday. He'll *find* his happiness."

Yeah, I wanted to ask, *but will he find it with me?* Instead, I ate my dinner and smiled, and tried to ignore my mother's glares every time I lifted a bite to my mouth.

The next day was given over to taking the visiting royals

on a tour of the city. Shortly after breakfast, they were bundled into carriages, with Narod, Erianthe, Edes, and Zadi accompanying them. I was left behind, ostensibly so that I could practice my lines for the wedding ceremony, and I was muttering my script into the mirror when I heard a knock at my apartment door.

Jerrcoa awaited on the threshold, smiling grimly. "May I speak with you?"

"Uh…sure," I said, and nodded to his valet, who remained in the corridor.

That Jerrcoa had come to me was no small thing, considering the stairs between his quarters and mine, and I hastily cleared a path for his chair toward my sitting area. "What's up?" I asked as he maneuvered through the mess of books and boxes. "Sorry, between my tutors and the deliveries from the tailors, this place is a disaster…"

"I didn't come to criticize," he replied, and parked near the loveseat. "Just to pass on information."

"Good of you," I said, sitting beside him.

He grinned. "Well, I mean, you *are* my favorite half sister, so…"

"Fierce competition, there. What do I need to know?"

Propping his elbows on the armrests, Jerrcoa leaned back and steepled his fingers. "Do you recall when I suggested that Makou might share certain…similarities…with Edes?"

My heart sank. "Yeah…"

"Edes and I discussed it late last night. We're not completely convinced—the topic never arose, obviously—but unfortunately, I think my suspicions are correct."

I slumped against the cushion and groaned. "*Great*. And here I was hoping it might just be the scar putting him off."

"I don't believe your scar is the issue. Now, that said, he was perfectly pleasant last night. His New Kopaati is close to fluent, and he laughed easily. We talked about books after dinner—he's a bit like Father in that regard.

Superficially, there's nothing objectionable about him."

"Except for the part where he has zero interest in me," I said.

Jerrcoa briefly grimaced in agreement. "That's true, but I'd be shocked if he shamed you in public. I can't speak to how these things work on the other side of the Crossing, of course, but here, men like Makou and our brother...they learn to maintain appearances. Even if they act on their desires, they do so with discretion. Makou is no fool, and he'll do his duty by you."

Just what every woman wanted: a husband who'd force himself to be intimate with her only enough to produce a kid.

"Thanks for the update," I told Jerrcoa. "Guess it could be worse..." Pushing my script aside, I said, "We're to have dinner alone tonight. Do you think he'll deny it if I ask him?"

He shrugged. "Difficult to say. I mean, there's a treaty now, so his desires are immaterial at this point. But he truly doesn't seem like a bad person," he reassured me. "I understand that this isn't ideal, but perhaps you'll grow to enjoy each other's company."

My brother meant well, but he didn't manage to raise my spirits. By dinnertime, I was both starving and too nervous to think about putting food on my stomach, and I approached the meal with all the anticipation I might muster for a colonoscopy.

Mother had arranged for Makou and me to dine alone in an intimate space—well, by castle standards. The dining room could have easily fit a table for twelve, but it had been arranged nicely for a couple's dinner: a square wooden table draped with a white cloth, a sidebar laden with covered dishes, plenty of candlelight, and even a few small arrangements of dried flowers. I found Makou waiting when I arrived, and he rose and smiled as I entered. My dress, a dark brown number, was laced so tightly that I feared for the integrity of the strings holding the bodice together, and I eased myself into the other chair as a servant poured water and glasses of kirit. With that accomplished, I looked up at the man and nodded. "Thank you, we can take it from here."

The servant frowned. "Your Highness, are you certain? The queen said—"

"I'm sure Makou and I are more than capable of filling our own plates," I told him. "If you'd be so kind as to leave the pitchers on the sideboard, that will do."

Though he seemed troubled by the request, the servant did as I asked and departed, and I locked the door after him. "Well," I said, eying the soup tureen, "I'm up. Are you hungry?"

Makou's mouth quirked. "Honestly?"

"Me, neither." Settling back into my chair, I took a long drink of room-temperature wine, letting the alcohol warm me on the way down. "So."

He drank in turn, then sighed. "So."

"I need you to be honest with me, all right?"

"I...will try," he allowed. "What do you want to know?"

"If you had to marry a Fulquir, and you had your choice, would you choose Edes?"

Makou's dark eyes widened, and he cleared his throat as he mulled over his response. "I, um...well...that is..."

"I wouldn't blame you. He's a good-looking fellow, and he's very much into guys. Didn't shed a tear when I screwed up his betrothal a few months back." When Makou continued to hem and haw, I said, "We love who we love. I get it. And I'm going to assume that this marriage wasn't your choice, either."

At that, he paused and considered my face. "You do not wish to marry me?"

"I think you're very handsome," I replied, "and I've heard good things about you, but this was not my idea, *especially* if you're not even attracted to me."

His expression softened. "You are a pretty woman,

Susan—"

I snorted and waved that off with my wine glass.

"No, you are," he insisted. "And were I of a mind to take a wife, I believe I could do far worse than one such as you. Your deeds Outside were remarkable."

I smirked. "But?"

"But," he echoed. "You are not mistaken in your assessment of me."

We drank again, and Makou rose to get us a refill.

"So where does this leave us?" I asked him. "I have no desire to force you into a marriage you don't want. By the way, you don't have to speak New Kopaati. I'm not fluent."

"So Edes mentioned," he replied in Common. "And while I appreciate your concern, the decision was made for me. Wine?" I held out my glass, and he topped it up before taking his seat. "Frankly, I thought my parents weren't going to force me to marry. This is all rather sudden."

"Oh?"

He nodded and drank. "I have had a, uh…a companion. Since we were fifteen," he murmured. "He's very dear to me. My parents aren't delighted about this, but they seemed to have accepted it, especially with Gerinet married off. And then Father came to me a few weeks ago and announced that I was to marry you, so…"

I waited while he drained his glass, then said, "I'm not a monster, Makou. If we're…doing this…then I want you to be as happy as you can be under the circumstances. Invite him here, this companion of yours. What is he, anyway?"

Makou's eyebrows rose. "A junior clerk."

"I'm sure we could find a place for him. If you're going to relocate to Deoni, you might as well bring a friend, right?"

He peered at me over the flowers and candles. "You wouldn't protest?"

"Look, one of us ought to be with the person they truly love, and since I'm the reason the original treaty fell apart..."

He grunted and poured again. "How is my uncle, anyway?"

"Heartbroken, I think, but he fakes it well. He's been nothing but kind to me. His wife is another matter, now, but..." I drank. "She never wanted to be my mother in the first place, so I shouldn't really expect much from her."

"Hm. You know, this betrothal may be her way of trying to help you," he suggested.

"How so? I mean, sure, men aren't tripping over themselves to get with *this*," I said, pointing to my scar.

He chuckled. "Our marriage was your mother's idea."

"Yeah, I understand. It pushes back that whole 'Terol on the throne' agreement by a generation, but I'm glad your father went along with it. No offense," I told Makou, lifting my glass to my lips, "but the only reason I agreed to this is so that Cirivant's navy keeps protecting our interests in Ga'besh."

"No offense taken. I was told I'd be drafted into said navy if I didn't consent," Makou replied.

"Your family really wants a toehold in Daril, huh?"

He spread his hands. "It's not a bad thing to have. Father's not obsessed with the idea, now, but since your mother countered his proposal with this offer, he decided it was fair."

I frowned, perplexed. "Countered? What do you mean?"

Makou frowned back at me. "You don't know?"

"Know what?"

"Well"—he paused for another sip of wine—"when word reached Father of the broken treaty, he suggested that Erianthe could give him something equal in value to our continued protection, as she obviously could no longer deliver the throne to someone in our bloodline. His thought was that necklace she's been wearing since we arrived—you know the one, gold, large Aen crystal?"

I blinked, unable to do more as my brain struggled to

process *that*. "Wait—are you saying that your father *didn't* insist on this marriage? He just wanted her necklace?"

Makou nodded. "It's an expensive piece, I'm sure. An Aen crystal of that size and quality must cost a fortune. But I suppose Erianthe didn't want to part with it, so here we are." He raised his half-empty glass and smiled bitterly. "The backup plan."

I wanted to rage. To throw my glass against the wall and scream.

She'd lied to me. That bitch in a tiara had *lied* to me, had sold me off to be married rather than part with a stupid necklace.

I meant less to my own mother than that damn bauble.

Of course she hated me—I'd upended her carefully constructed house of falsehoods—but to guilt me into a loveless marriage just so she could keep a piece of jewelry...

Maybe it wasn't too late, I thought, my mind racing. I'd held on to the Aen crystals that had fallen from the Watcher's sword, and I kept them hidden beneath my lingerie, something I could sell if times grew desperate. If all Fetull wanted was a big crystal, surely I could satisfy *that*.

But invitations had gone out weeks ago, both to the Darili highborn and to heads of state across the four worlds. People were traversing the tunnels and crossing the desert to Daril even as I sat there and stared into the candle flame. If I backed out of the wedding now, with all the planning that had taken place, all the money spent on travel and clothing and food and entertainment...well, think of the *waste*.

Besides, I told myself, what was my alternative? Turn down Makou and sit around the palace, waiting for Erianthe to marry me off to someone else? The one person I truly wanted was gone.

At least Terj got his freedom in the end. If he could endure centuries of torture, I could put up with a few decades of a sham marriage.

"Susan?" Makou asked, drawing me back from my spiraling thoughts. "Are you all right?"

"Fine," I said, and forced a smile as I lifted my glass with his. "Here's to us."

CHAPTER 5

The foreign dignitaries began to trickle in over the next few days, arriving mostly in chiquiw-drawn carriages.

The four worlds' answer to the horse was a quadrupedal beast, but with a few differences: three-toed paws instead of hooves, a pair of short, curving horns atop their heads, and the sort of sharp teeth indicative of an omnivorous diet. While the original stock were domesticated by ogres, a race of secretive creatures native to Honslia, chiquiws had been bred for a number of uses. The most common around Daril were slightly smaller than their wild ancestors, with shaggy coats against the harsh dry season and elevated drought tolerance approaching that of a camel. The chiquiws preferred by elves were tall and sleek-coated—pretty, but not nearly as hearty as the ones popular among Kopaati humans.

Dwarves also bred chiquiws, having miniaturized them to the size of ponies, but I saw none of them from my window as the visitors approached the castle. Masters of forging—creating items with magical properties—dwarves traveled in carriages of a rather different sort, flying craft that could easily hit four times the top speed of a chiquiw team. Moreover, since the path across the wasteland was closer to a suggestion than a marked trail, the dwarven guests arrived earlier and in far better shape than did those of other races.

Occupied as I was with last-minute preparations and meetings with the priests, the tailors, and my future in-laws, however, I saw none of the dignitaries until the grand reception two nights before my wedding.

Mother had selected a large ballroom for the event, a space with a vaulted ceiling and tall windows in which people could mingle or leave as they chose. The servants had decorated the room with more dried flowers—a necessity, given the season—and dozens of candelabra and lanterns banished the shadows to the far corners. A balcony beyond one wall offered an escape, should anyone require a breath of air, but the action was otherwise contained within the room: laden buffet tables, servants carrying pitchers of wine and juices, and a sextet of musicians set up on a low stage out of the way.

Unsure of the protocol, I hung out with Makou as the guests entered and made beelines for Mother or Fetull. Having armed ourselves with glasses of wine, we tried to discern the newcomers' identities, and playing the part of the happy couple, we smiled and made polite conversation with any who approached us.

About twenty minutes into the festivities, I nudged Makou in the arm as an elven group entered the room. "See them?" I whispered.

He nodded. "Who are they?"

From a distance, the two I'd pointed out could have been identical: a couple inches under six feet tall, thin, and pale, with long, dark brown hair and brown eyes. They wore matching green floor-length robes cinched with golden belts, and each sported a braided golden circlet on their brow, resting above their pointed ears. They were beautiful in an androgynous sort of way, and only because I'd seen them up close did I know they were actually brother and sister.

"The Twins of Nokan'ti," I told Makou. "King and queen. Those other elves with them are probably their kids—"

"Not *their* children, surely."

I glanced up at him and grinned at his horrified expression. Rumors of elven…*proclivities* abounded in the four worlds. "His children or her children," I clarified. "They don't share any. And…ah, excuse me."

Leaving my fiancé, I hurried across the floor as I saw the last of the group arrive, a redheaded, green-eyed elf slightly taller than his father and aunt. While he shared his half siblings' and cousins' complexion, he looked little like the rest of them, and he'd opted for a less opulent blue tunic over trousers. He'd pulled his hair back into a low ponytail, and as he noticed my approach, his face broke into a wide grin.

Though we hadn't spoken to or seen each other in seven months, Fanakel hastened to greet me like an old friend. "You look lovely," he said before I could get a word out, then caught me around the waist, lifted me off my feet, and spun me around.

I laughed in surprise and hugged him, then leaned toward his ear. "So glad to see you."

"I've missed you madwomen," he replied, and released me. Affecting a more formal air, he said, "Daughter of Daril."

"Son of Nokan'ti," I answered in kind—or approximated, at least. Between my inherent abilities and his translator ring, we had no trouble communicating. "Thank you for making the journey. I hope it wasn't too difficult."

"Oh, saddle sores for days, but it's worth it to be part of your happiness." A pointed throat clearing to my right made him cut his eyes in that direction, and he straightened. "Uh…Father, you remember—"

"Your Highness," said Enoul with a nod to me, distinguishable from his twin by the low timbre of his voice.

I dropped a curtsy, though part of me wanted to slap the king across his beautiful face. "Your Serene Majesty. A pleasure to see you again."

"Yes," Fanakel quipped, "since no one's ending up in a cell this time." His father shot him a sharp look, and he shrugged. "What? I speak the truth."

"We need not revisit our previous meeting tonight," the king muttered, then turned and headed for Erianthe.

Once he was out of earshot, I snorted to disguise my laughter, and Fanakel grinned. "How have you been?" he asked, leading me toward the nearest server with a tray of glasses. "Tell me everything. And who is this fiancé of yours? How did you meet?"

I'd barely begun to fill him in on Makou's pedigree when I heard a shout across the room: an exuberant, "*Suze!*"

Fanakel and I wheeled around to see the party from Blackhorn Mountain enter. I hadn't known whether to expect a delegation—though the tunnel from Ildon was located on the edge of the dwarven kingdom's territory, the journey was still a trek. Moreover, Daril had closer ties with Nokan'ti than with Blackhorn Mountain, and while both the Twins and Rokund Elf-Bane had signed the treaty to end the fifteen-year War of the True Children, the two nations had yet to establish cordial relations. But the dwarves were not to be outdone, and Rokund had arrived in style.

The under-king of Blackhorn Mountain was quite tall for a dwarf, just a little shy of five feet, with deep-set golden-brown eyes and silver-threaded brown hair. While he showed his age more so than did the elven Twins, he was in excellent shape for a man of nearly five hundred— middle-aged by dwarven standards. As at our first meeting, he dressed simply in a black tunic over dark trousers and matching boots, but the ornate belt around his waist had to be silver, just like the ornaments braided into the triple strands of his thick beard and the heavy circlet on his head. Rokund might have kept things simple, but that didn't mean he went *cheap*.

Six dwarves accompanied him, though it took me a quick count of dresses versus pants to guess at the genders of his party from a distance. Male and female dwarves were built much alike—short and sturdy, with full beards—and I was certainly no expert at identifying the subtleties of their everyday attire that set them apart. At least two of the members of the under-king's group had worn gowns, which made matters simpler.

But it was the woman with them who had called my name, a stunning blue-eyed platinum blonde who towered a head and a half above Rokund. Her dress was simple enough, a soft purple number with flowing sleeves and a glint around the collar suggestive of silver embroidery, but it hugged her generous curves like a second skin and dipped low enough at the front to show more than a mere hint of cleavage. Her thick hair was partially braided back, but the rest fell over her shoulders in bouncy waves. She was, without question, the most beautiful creature in the room—probably in all of Daril that night—and I sincerely hoped that the elves' superiority complex took a bruising in her presence.

The dwarf by her side was a foot and a half shorter, with dark blonde hair, a well-manicured beard, and Rokund's eyes. While she'd opted for a tunic and trousers like her father that night, I'd have recognized her anywhere.

"Mia! Anji!" I cried, and ran across the room to greet them.

Mia squealed and darted past the dwarves to crash into me, her hug stronger than the lacing on my gown. "Oh, my God, I've *missed* you," she said, her English a most welcome sound to my brain after months of constant translation.

I said nothing for a moment, instead squeezing her more tightly. Though I hadn't begrudged Mia's decision to go home with Anji—hell, I was the one who'd upended her life in the first place—I was thrilled to see my best friend again.

I'd barely released Mia when Anji said, "Come here, lass," and hugged me in turn—nothing as intense as Mia's greeting, but still warm. "Congratulations. And thank you for the invitation," she said as we parted. "Father said he would have brought me anyway, but I'm honored all the same."

"And you *know* I wouldn't miss your wedding," said Mia, beaming, then glanced behind me and laughed. "Hey, you!"

Fanakel approached, now carefully carrying two extra glasses of wine. "Thirsty?" he asked, angling one of the fresh pair toward her.

"Won't say no." She accepted it and took a sip, then cut her eyes to Anji.

The princess stared up at the prince, her arms folded across her chest. "Elf."

"Dwarf."

They held their composure for only a second before the twinkle in Anji's eyes gave the game away. "Good to see you," she said as he handed her a glass, then raised her drink. "To the bride."

"Cheers," said Mia, and sipped before she realized I was empty-handed. "Shit, Suze doesn't have anything to drink—"

"I'm fine," I assured her. "Nowhere for it to go in this dress, anyway…"

I fell silent as Anji's father approached and gave our little knot an appraising stare. "Uh…Your Excellency," I said, hoping I'd chosen the proper salutation as I curtsied. "Thank you for coming."

"I believe it is I who owe *you* thanks, Watcher," he replied, "which I have yet to convey."

"We couldn't have done it without Anji," I told him.

Fanakel, who'd been awkwardly standing by, cleared his throat. "Her performance was…*most* adequate."

The under-king looked up at him with a little smile playing at the corners of his mouth. "Is that so?"

"More adequate than mine, let's say."

He nodded, satisfied, then patted his daughter on the

shoulder as she rolled her eyes. "Well, I'll let the young people enjoy themselves. Congratulations, Princess," he told me, "and may the High Queen bless your marriage."

As Rokund headed off to greet Fetull, Anji mimed wiping her brow, and Fanakel smiled. "Did I do that properly?" he murmured.

"It sufficed," Anji replied, and patted his unburdened arm. "Now, that's almost all of us—where's Terj?" she asked me.

My face froze, and I tried not to let my expression shift. "He, uh…he left a few weeks ago. Said he was ready to move on."

Mia frowned. "Really? He couldn't stick around for your wedding?"

"This is best for him," I insisted.

"Maybe, but I'd hoped to meet up with him again…has Falova seen him?"

"I haven't asked—"

"*Susan*," interrupted a familiar voice from behind me, and easily segued into English. "Come here, dear, let's have a look at you."

I spun around, the questions about Terj momentarily silenced, to find Ardith Quince standing a few feet away, a curious smile on her lips. Five centuries old and still mostly brown-haired, my former neighbor arrayed herself like a proper maladeta in a simple, soft blue floor-skimming dress and gray cloak, but in my mind's eye, she would always be the nice middle-aged woman who favored thin twinsets, fed me cookies, and chided me for tramping through flowerbeds. Having done her time as Uncle Malachi's babysitter—superintending a Watcher was regarded as a hardship post, as there was so little Aen that flowed into Cole's Crossing—she'd come home to rejoin the Taln'een as the First Daughter, the clan's second in command. And though she called herself Ardielta among her own people…well, some habits die hard.

"Hey, Ms. Quince," I said, and quickly closed the

distance to hug her.

She held on a bit longer than one would for a casual greeting, my childhood guardian once again, then stepped back and gave me a once-over. "You look beautiful, honey. How are you doing?"

I flashed a weak smile, though part of me felt like falling apart as I thought of home and Dad and Uncle Malachi, who'd never dance with me on my wedding day. "Eh?"

"Figured." Glancing over her shoulder, she called, "This way!"

Spotting a dark-haired woman in a similar cloak passing through the crowd, I pulled myself together and curtsied as Ganeel, the clan leader, approached. "Great Mother," I said, rising. "I'm so pleased you could make it."

"Believe me, child," she said, "I've traveled much farther for far less pleasant reasons than a wedding. This is a welcome change of pace."

"Doesn't Susan look nice?" Ms. Quince prompted.

Ganeel nodded. "Yes, quite…though the sight of you in such finery does take a bit of adjustment. Ah, girls!" she said as Anji and Mia drew near. "And that son of Nokan'ti. How are you?"

Ms. Quince met my stare and shook her head, then gently pulled me away from the group toward a darker corner of the room. "So," she said, wrapping her arm around mine, "I understand that yours is an arranged marriage."

"Politically, it made sense. Did Tonnera give you the details?"

"Naturally. Why would we send one of our daughters here if we could learn nothing?" she asked with a teasing smirk. "Erianthe gets rapid message transit to the other heads of state, and we learn the gossip. A fair trade, I should think."

"You're incorrigible, Ms. Quince."

"*Practical*, dear." She said nothing further until she was

sure we were alone, then drew me close to her and quietly said, "Hear me. I know you think you're doing the right thing, but if you're wrong, or if you need help, you need only ask."

I took a deep breath, then forced a smile. "Thank you, but I'll be fine. Makou is...very nice."

She grunted, unconvinced. "That may be, but should you change your mind—"

"Susan, *there* you are," my mother interrupted, sweeping toward us on a cloud of pale pink lace. "Don't stand in the corner all night, girl—you have guests to entertain."

"I only stole her for a moment, Your Majesty," Ms. Quince smoothly replied, then hugged me again before nudging me toward the room. "Go on, darling. I'll see you later."

With that, Mother rushed me back into the growing press, and I soon found myself at Makou's side once more, making small talk with strangers and struggling to keep names with faces, much less countries or worlds. Finally, Anji sneaked up behind me with a fresh glass of wine, and I took it with a grateful sigh. "Do you see the guy in the wheelchair over by the buffet?" I asked.

"Yes..."

"That's Jerrcoa, my brother. If you ask, he'll tell you how to get to my room."

She grinned through her beard. "That sounds almost inappropriate, lass."

"I wouldn't dream of besmirching your honor. But why don't you three get directions and meet me there for the afterparty? And have you met my fiancé?" I asked as Makou noticed our conversation. "Makou, this is Anjikora of Blackhorn Mountain, who's a large part of the reason why I still have all my limbs..."

Leaving him in Anji's care, I was sneaking toward the food to steal a bite when a tall, dark-skinned woman in a gold sheath gown and a jewel-bedecked headwrap stepped into my path. "Ah," she said with a smile, "the bride. I would know your face anywhere, Watcher."

As photography wasn't a thing in the four worlds, I took a stab at the woman's identity and prayed for the best. Dropping a curtsy, I said, "Your Majesty. Welcome to Deoni. I trust the journey was uneventful…"

"Fortunately so, and much more pleasant than it's been in recent years, now that the river has lost its stench." She gripped my shoulder and inclined her head. "I understand that you recovered the elemental."

"It was a group effort," I replied, fighting back sudden thoughts of Terj, "but yes, I was involved."

"Well, regardless, my people and I owe you a debt of gratitude, young one. Perhaps in time, our fisheries will recover, but for now, we can finally begin to feed ourselves again."

I'd guessed correctly. The woman in the headwrap was Merenel Palta, queen of Ti'cal, Daril's southerly neighbor. Though she was a few years older than my mother, she bore her age better—her skin was still smooth and plump, her dark eyes lively. Flat-footed, she had a head on me, and her headwrap functioned much like Mother's tiara. Had she been cross, she'd have presented an intimidating figure, but Merenel was all grace that night. Then again, she was among friends—by necessity, landlocked Ti'cal had always been more than cordial with Daril, dependent as they were on the river and access to the northern port.

Merenel had come with a decent-sized party, but she lacked a consort. Her much-loved husband had died five years prior, during one of the worst of the recent fever seasons. The area around the Falova was prone to outbreaks of a hemorrhagic fever during the dry months, when bloodsucking bugs hatched and bred, and the die-off in the river had led to rampant insect overpopulation. Already weakened by food shortages, the Ti'calis suffered and succumbed in greater numbers than did the Darilis. With the river's recovery, people once more had hope for better fever seasons in years to come, but that didn't bring the queen's consort back to life.

"I, uh…" I paused, unsure of the proper response—would she be offended if I neglected to mention a particular deity? "I wish you good fortune in your recovery," I said.

"Thank you," she replied with a nod. "And I to you in your marriage."

As she moved on, I hastened toward the buffet before my mother could catch me. Fruit skewers weren't going to do much for my mood, but they were better than nothing.

My marriage didn't need luck. It needed a miracle.

After the last of the dignitaries had drunk his fill and had a word with Mother and Fetull, I bade Makou goodnight and hurried through the castle to my room—well, relatively speaking, as I couldn't breathe deeply enough in that damn dress to even think of running more than a few feet.

Sore, tired, and ravenously hungry, I threw open the door to my apartment to find a most welcome sight: Mia, Anji, and Fanakel lounging in my sitting area, a low-burning fire in the hearth, and a tray of meats, cheeses, and breads awaiting on the table. "Oh, y'all are the *best*," I said, pointing to the midnight charcuterie. "How'd you know?"

"Hell, I could do with a snack, and I noshed all evening," said Mia, who'd by then changed into her Walmart leggings and an oversized T-shirt. "You barely ate. Come here, let's get you out of that contraption."

Grateful for the help, I leaned against the wall while she unknotted the laces holding my bodice together, and Anji grabbed my robe from the wooden screen across the room. "The food was your brother's contribution, actually," Anji told me, stealing a piece of cheese as she passed it. "He had it delivered a few minutes ago."

"Jerrcoa?"

"Edes." Handing me my robe, she said, "Curious thing.

He approached Father, my sisters, and me during the party and apologized for his behavior during his visit. Said he was embarrassed and asked that we convey his regrets to the women he, uh…"

"Propositioned," Mia offered.

"Yes, that," she said stiffly. "I suppose the lad's grown up a bit."

I chuckled as my lungs finally began to expand. "I *might* have asked him about that trip, and I *might* have told him he behaved like a dick and should be ashamed of himself. He really does cringe when he thinks about it," I told Anji. "Kind of a desperate move on his part."

"I won't ask you to confirm or deny," said Fanakel, who was averting his eyes while I undressed, "but there was a rumor floated for a time that Daril's crown prince might not willingly produce an heir, if you know what I mean."

"I'd believe it," Mia muttered.

Anji glanced up at her, frowning. "You think?"

"Well, the vibe I'm getting from Makou is certainly stronger, but I wouldn't be surprised about Edes. Okay, there you go," she said as my bodice fell open, and I quickly belted the robe around my shift before kicking the rest of the gown off. "Now, let's talk about Makou."

I groaned and headed for the loveseat, and Fanakel made room. "What's to talk about?"

"I mean, you're clearly the beard in this relationship."

Fanakel's brow furrowed in confusion, but Anji nodded emphatically. "I spent no more than five minutes with him," she said, settling on the padded armrest of Mia's chair, "and I'm telling you that he's not at all interested in women."

"Oh, yeah. I know," I said, assembling a finger sandwich.

"*Suze*," said Mia with reproach, "you *cannot* marry this clown!"

I looked up and shrugged. "Treaty suggests otherwise.

He and I have had a talk, and I think his plan is to find a position for his boyfriend here—"

"His boyfriend?" Anji protested. "*No*. Not if he's married to you! That's shameful!"

"Perhaps not *shameful*—" Fanakel began.

Anji cut him off with a sharp look. "Shameful to anyone who's not an elf and respects her marriage bed."

I bit into my sandwich to give myself a moment to collect my thoughts. "Look, Makou and I have talked it over," I told the others. "Neither of us is thrilled about this wedding, but we're going through with it for the politics. I don't hate the guy, and I don't want him to be miserable for the rest of his life, so as long as he keeps matters on the down-low, it won't hurt me."

"And that's understanding of you," said Mia, "but Suze, you deserve better than a loveless marriage. Why don't you just say no?"

"Or we could buy time," Fanakel suggested. "Give me access to the castle's herbal stores, and I can put together a draught that will leave you in bed for a few days. Vomiting profusely," he admitted, "but unfit for a wedding."

I finished my sandwich and started making a second one. "That's sweet of you, but I'm out of good options. This was Erianthe's idea to make sure our Ga'beshi colonies stay protected—I'm getting married for a navy."

"Ah, true love," Anji muttered.

"It gets better," I said, piling the cheese high. "Fetull really just wanted her necklace. She proposed this damn marriage instead."

Mia's eyes widened. "That bitch is sticking you in a sham marriage because she doesn't want to part with her *jewelry*?"

"To be fair, she likes her jewelry," I replied, "which is more than I can say for her feelings about me."

"Still…" She glanced out the window, which I'd left cracked that afternoon. "You could always run off. Give yourself time to *really* think this through."

I smirked. "What do you think Anji's father would do if she brought home a second sparring buddy?"

"He'd haul me to the priests for a stern talk," said Anji. "He's not overjoyed that Mia's in my company, and for there to be a suspicion that we were a threesome...*no*."

"But you two..." I said, pointing between them with my sandwich.

They shared a look, and Mia nodded. "Is it obvious?"

"I know you well enough, and I've never seen you look at anyone like you do Anji, so yeah."

The apples of Anji's cheeks flushed over her beard, and she cleared her throat. "This is...*not* something we speak of openly," she murmured. "Father tolerates it because we keep matters quiet, though we all know the gods frown upon such. If you could respect that—"

"Of course. You're two very good friends, and I know nothing otherwise," I said, and Mia snorted. "But between us, I'm happy for you both."

"Small question," said Fanakel, making his own sandwich now that it was obvious I wasn't planning to inhale the entire platter. "Does he know she's..."

He left that unfinished, but there was no need to go further. Among all the heads of state who'd been invited to my wedding, none were tekorish. While elves and maladetas were immune to their power, humans and dwarves were not, and I'd yet to hear of tekoraet spoken of in Deoni as anything better than pests. Still, I could see why it might not be ideal to have a group with mind control abilities roaming the castle, feeding on other guests' lust.

That Mia was half tekori was a matter kept secret by those who knew. The maladetas of Taln'een were certainly aware—Ms. Quince had watched Mia grow up, and after a matter of weeks within the Aen and having accidentally fed, my pretty, rail-thin friend had turned into a voluptuous bombshell in her sleep. Her transformation was proof enough to anyone who'd known her before that there was something not entirely human about her. But given the mistrust, if not outright hatred, for tekoraet among the other races, we tried to pass her off as a beauty with the appetite of a linebacker.

"Father suspects," Anji told Fanakel. "He hasn't demanded an answer of me outright, but he's remarked upon Mia's looks."

"And the amount of food I can shovel away," Mia added.

One of Fanakel's eyebrows rose. "So...we're not feeding on unsuspecting dwarves?"

"I'm not *feeding*, period," she retorted. "As long as I keep stuffing my face, I don't need it."

"But Father has suggested that he's not entirely opposed to her presence," said Anji with a little smile at her girlfriend. "After all, should some man accost me..."

"You'd gut him," Mia replied.

"Assuming I were incapacitated, then."

Tekorish abilities only worked on the opposite sex. While Mia had accidentally turned Fanakel into her puppet once—unfortunately for him, he'd taken after his human mother in the "tekori defense" department—she had no effect on women. Thus, Anji was perfectly safe around her, though the same couldn't be said for half the dwarven population.

"What about you?" I asked Fanakel, eager to shift the topic away from my impending nuptials. "I heard things are better back in Caritulo."

He brightened. "They are. It's not perfect—I'll never measure up to my father's other children—but he can't deny that I was part of something bigger than anything my siblings have ever done."

That Fanakel was satisfied with even those scraps was testament to the curse under which he'd been born. The unintentional result of his father's affair with a human servant, he'd gone all his life knowing that he was less than an elf—and in a society that viewed pure-blooded elves as their gods' greatest creations, he hadn't stood much of a chance at advancement. But Fanakel had not only gone Outside and returned alive, a feat unmatched by any of the so-called True Children, but he'd also helped destroy the monster whose spawn had plagued the four worlds—and Earth, thanks to that damn magic sword—for centuries. Though he still wasn't True, he'd come home an unquestioned hero, and that was *something*.

"I may be mistaken," said Anji, "but watching you tonight, I could almost imagine that you'd discovered a bit of self-esteem in the last months."

Fanakel eyed her as if waiting for the shoe to drop. "Oh?"

"Yeah. Starting here," she replied, running the backs of her fingers along her hair-covered jawline.

He reached up and brushed his hand against his faint reddish stubble, irrefutable proof of his mixed parentage. The Fanakel I'd first known would have despaired at the thought of being caught with anything less than a clean shave, but that night, he merely smiled. "Long trip, thought I might be getting sunburned. Razors aren't kind to inflamed skin."

"Not at all." She chuckled softly to herself as she took him in. "Suits you."

"Likewise."

She gave one of her beard's braids a tug. "Still shorter than I'd like, but it's growing back in. And since this one doesn't complain," she added, glancing at Mia, "perhaps I'll have a respectable face before long."

"This one wouldn't *dare* to complain," said Mia, then leaned closer and pecked Anji on the cheek. "Now, if she tries to get *me* to grow one…"

The two of them laughed, an odd couple but obviously happy together. Their situation wasn't perfect, but then neither was Fanakel's, and he'd yet to mention any suggestion of a girlfriend.

As I got up to open the bottle of wine that Edes had

considerately brought for me, Mia asked, "Have we given any thought to the Crossing?"

"What about it?" I asked.

"Like…everything we left behind. Your house, the cabin, our cars…"

I found the corkscrew and pried the bottle open. "Well, I've got my bills on autopay, your car's paid off—"

"Yeah, but it hasn't been moved in months."

"Dead batteries are fixable."

Mia grunted. "But more than that, what about taxes? And your store?"

"Annie Plunkett can run the store in her sleep," I said. "As for taxes…well…"

"Property's late, isn't it? Didn't you have to pay that before the end of the year?"

I nodded and poured. "And then there's income tax. Do we even know when it is back home?"

"Assuming the days here are about the same, I'm calculating mid-March."

"*Great.* So my property taxes are a few months behind, I'll miss tax season…do you think someone will seize my houses?" I asked.

Fanakel frowned. "If they do, what's the loss? You weren't planning to make that town a Darili colony, were you?"

"No, of course not," I said, "but…you know, my stuff's still there."

Stuff—the detritus of my old life, but also the last traces of my dad and uncle. The thought of strangers rummaging through my property, bagging up those little bits of my family as so much trash, made me sick.

"Maybe, once the wedding's over, I could steal a few weeks and go visit," I said, swishing my wine. "Get my finances in order, pack, officially give Annie the store…"

"Sell your houses?" Fanakel suggested.

I winced. "That would make sense, but, uh…"

"But currently, we've got a place to run off to, just in

case," Mia finished.

Anji scowled. "*Run off to?*"

"You know, in case you get tired of having me hang around," she said—far too calmly, I thought, as if she'd spent time contemplating the possibility.

"Mia, if you run off anywhere, I'll be right behind you. Understand, lass?" Anji took her hand and held her stare. "I can't imagine tiring of you."

She smiled, though she looked a little queasy. "Believe me, it's possible..."

Before Mia could elaborate, Anji pulled her face closer, then kissed her deeply. "Hear me," she said, resting her forehead against Mia's. "I know you've been hurt, but I swear to you by any gods you like that I am *not* Raquel."

I couldn't say how much Mia had told Anji about her cheating former girlfriend, but judging by their expressions, Anji knew plenty where Raquel the Whore was concerned.

"The promises I've made to you...perhaps they can't be repeated in the Great Temple, but the High Queen knows my soul," she continued. "I love you, Mia Randolph, and if Heartfast is no home for us, then I will follow you beyond Blackhorn Mountain, beyond Ildon...beyond the four worlds, if that's what it takes. So know this: should you run back to the Crossing, you will not run alone."

"If you came home with me," said Mia, "you'd have to face my mom."

"I've killed Outsiders. I don't fear Janine."

"That's because you haven't *met* Janine," I told her, but smiled to see the grin on Mia's face.

Anji waggled her eyebrows. "No, but more importantly, Janine hasn't met *me*."

My friends sat around until the wee hours, polishing off the wine and the charcuterie and one-upping each other on stories from the months since our parting. By the time they wandered to bed, the fire had burned down to embers, and I stacked the evidence of our impromptu party on the table for the maid to remove in the morning.

In my bedroom, I changed out of my shift and threw on a T-shirt, then pulled back the covers. Before I retired, I opened the window by my bed a crack, just in case Terj came by. The notion was ridiculous, I knew, but the part of me that cast my eyes to the night sky and waited for shooting stars hoped he'd find his way.

From beyond the castle wall, I heard my father's voice: *You are troubled, soul of my soul.*

It's been a long day. Don't worry about me.

You are not merely tired.

I'll be fine, I told him, and slid into bed.

I would have to be.

CHAPTER 6

Shortly after the first bell, with the sky still inching toward proper dawn, one of the maids awoke me. "Another big day," she said with too much enthusiasm for the hour, lighting lamps around my apartment as I rubbed the gunk from my eyes. "Will you bathe or eat first, Your Highness?"

The tepid bathwater did more to wake me than Erianthe's preferred tisane ever did, and I warmed up by the fire with the small breakfast the kitchen sent up—tea, toast, and fruit, hardly filling but enough to keep me both vertical and laced into a gown. I'd have preferred something more substantial, or at least a bit of protein, considering the event ahead, but I didn't want to get the maid in trouble by sending her back down for more.

Nibbling my toast, I glanced at the hook on the wall where the maid had hung that day's dress, an opulent number in rich blue. The bodice was both decorated and laced with silver, and when it was cinched tightly, the extra material at the hips gave me an admittedly impressive set of curves. The design was great for standing and milling about, but not nearly as much fun for sitting, which comprised a large part of the day's agenda.

My wedding was the following afternoon, and after rehearsing our steps and lines that night, we had a wedding-eve dinner to look forward to. In the interim, however, was a final meet-and-greet: Makou and I would be seated at the foot of the dais in the throne room, and the well-heeled of Daril, both wedding guests and those who didn't rate an invitation to the main event, would be able to see us and pay their respects. I understood the purpose of the reception—Makou was an unknown, I'd been around for less than a year, and this was our first big event—but still, the idea of sitting for hours under Mother's watchful eye, making small talk with strangers and pretending to be madly in love with my fiancé, didn't exactly motivate me to get up and dress.

But the wedding schedule waited for no one, including the bride, and so I'd barely finished my first cup of tea before the maid returned with her minions to prep me for the day. Hair and makeup were first on the agenda, while I sat still in my robe, followed by the bodice lacing. As I leaned against the wall and tried to think skinny thoughts, I recalled Merenel's sheath gown from the night before and resolved that should I survive the wedding, I'd henceforth be importing my clothes from Ti'cal *and* Cirivant.

Sunlight glinted on the castle rooftops as I made my way down to the throne room. As I paused outside the rear doors to check my jewelry, Makou arrived, formally attired but surely far more comfortable than I was. Someone had apparently coordinated our wardrobes, as his bright green tunic beside my blue dress made a not-so-subtle nod to the Darili flag. Dark brown trousers, matching boots, and a fawn-colored cape completed his look. Handsome and polished, he seemed every inch a prince from my imagination, but the polite smile he gave me didn't exactly leave me weak in the knees.

"Ready?" he asked.

I sighed. "We may as well get this over with. Any idea how long it's going to go?"

Makou made a face. "Did you not see the line?"

"What line?"

"Of our well-wishers. It stretches out the main gate and down the road."

I shouldn't have been a brat. The people of Daril had every right to want to see me, and the fact that some of them had probably camped for hours just for a moment's conversation with Makou and me was touching and humbling. At the same time, if Makou was right about the size of the line, we'd be making chitchat for *hours*.

"If we don't stop for lunch and I pass out, just prop me up in my chair, all right?" I told him, and with a snicker, he pushed open the door for me.

Erianthe had orchestrated new decorations for the throne room that day. Her throne and Narod's were pushed to the left side of the dais, with two smaller but ornate chairs placed to the right for Fetull and Cofali. The colors of each realm hung on their respective ends, the blue and green waves of Daril and the red ship's wheel of Cirivant. Neither, in my estimation looked great with the lilac carpet down the central aisle, but I'd had no say in *that*. Positioned just in front of the dais were wooden chairs for Makou and me, each equipped with a thin white cushion that would surely do nothing to help after an hour so or. Arrangements of dried flowers had been set up on the dais behind us and slightly to the side, a sort of floral barrier between us and our parents—who, I noted with a pang of jealousy as Makou helped me to my seat, warranted much more padding in their chairs. Given my mother's bony backside, I was sure she needed it.

We'd been waiting about ten minutes when the platform party arrived. Fetull and Cofali beamed at us as they took their seats, every inch the proud parents. Narod also smiled down at us, while Erianthe, resplendent in a red gown and her usual tiara, mustered up an expression that seemed almost pleasant. On her signal, the rear doors were thrown open, and the head of the line began to snake its way down the aisle.

And *oh*, the people came. Lesser nobles from far-flung corners of the kingdom who might not get a moment with me after the wedding. Wealthy merchants from Daril who dressed as well as any aristocrat but would never be asked to join them socially. High-ranking military officers. Top bureaucrats. Middling priests who wouldn't be part of the wedding ceremony. Senior scholars from Daril's university, who wore elaborate robes decorated with sashes representing their disciplines. Interspersed among them were a few people who I suspected had slipped into the line without an invitation, as they gawked at the throne room and seemed unsure of how to comport themselves once they reached the front, either going tongue-tied or babbling. Our parents said little, leaving Makou and me to manage the line and its tempo: smile, listen, nod, thank, repeat.

We'd been at it for about two hours when I felt a familiar presence at the edge of my mind.

Distracted, I looked up from our latest guest, one of Deoni's finest science masters, and quickly scanned the rafters for any slight distortion in the air. *Terj?* I asked, heart racing.

To my surprise and joy, I heard him answer me: *I'm coming, Susan.*

Where are you?

On my way. Patience.

Excited as I was, I could barely focus on the people walking down the aisle as I kept sneaking peeks in the corners of the room, waiting to spot Terj. He was drawing nearer—I could feel him like the swelling sound of a nearing band, like a building wave racing toward the shore, but I couldn't find him anywhere.

I'm in the throne room, I said. *If you can't find me, I'm down at the front.*

He chuckled in my mind. *Oh, believe me, this line would be clue enough if I didn't know. I'm coming.*

Terj sounded like himself, but I thought I could pick up on a tinge of anxiety in his voice. *Are you okay? You're not hurt, are you?*

I'm fine. Eager to see you.

Likewise. Where the heck are you?

Almost there…

He fell silent, and I tried to be polite to our well-wishers while I waited. Perhaps sensing that my attention was elsewhere, Makou picked up the slack, but I did make an effort not to be rude. Still, the feeling of Terj's nearness was strengthening by the second, and the fact that I couldn't locate him was driving me crazy...

Until the minor nobles at the head of the line stepped away and the man behind them came to the fore.

At first glance, I thought he was a maladeta—the long gray cloak he wore looked like something of their make. Then he pushed back his hood, and I took him in. A soft blue shirt over gray trousers and dusty boots in the maladetan style, yes, but above the V of his neckline hung a sizeable Aen crystal set in silver—a *very* expensive piece of jewelry. His black hair was wavy, lightly tousled, and short by local standards, falling around his ears...which were rounded, so despite his lack of facial scruff, he definitely wasn't an elf. Handsome but unremarkable, in my estimation, unless you considered his eyes, which were the palest gray I'd ever seen, the color of mist at dawn.

I'd never seen him before, but...

No. It couldn't be...

Terj? I asked.

The corners of his mouth twitched in a little smile. *Hello, Susan.*

My jaw dropped, and I was on my feet and rushing toward him before I knew I was out of my chair. *What the hell have you done?* I asked as I gripped his arms. They felt real, muscular and solid and warm through his sleeves, though my brain struggled to accept the notion that *this* could ever be Terj.

I went to see Ganeel, he replied. *Told her the Taln'een owed me.*

But...but how...

Necklace. It's real enough—it's not an illusion—but it's not perfect. I... His brow furrowed, and he gently pulled out of my grasp just long enough to clasp my hands.

I looked down at his fingers—real fingers, flesh and bone and nails—then up into his eyes. He was, I vaguely realized, about a head taller than me. *Why would you do this to yourself?*

Because...because I... He fumbled briefly but recovered. *Susan, there's something I need to ask you.*

"Who is *he*?" Erianthe demanded from the dais. "What's going on down there?"

Terj glanced over my shoulder at her, then focused on me again. *If you love him*, he said, *and he makes you happy, then I'll wish you two well and never say another word about this. But if you don't...*

His breathing had quickened, and his hands held mine like vises.

If you don't love him, he continued, *and if there's any way that you...*

That I what?

I have nothing to offer you, and I realize that, but...maybe not today, maybe not this year, but someday, if you might consider me—

I freed my hands and wrapped them behind his neck, then pulled his face toward mine. When my lips touched his, I felt his sharp, surprised inhalation, and then his mind's shading shifted in an instant from trepidation to...

Yes, that was *definitely* desire.

His kiss was clumsy, but that could be excused. His hands had migrated to the small of my back and were drawing me closer, and when I broke away for a moment, breathless, he looked dazed. *Are you*— I began.

Why does that feel so good? he asked, but he didn't wait for an explanation before darting toward my lips again.

Distantly, through the haze of my jumbled senses, I was conscious of shouting behind us and the rumble of the crowd ahead. Fair enough: I was supposed to be married the following day, and yet I was standing in front of the kingdom, the gods, and my own fiancé, kissing another man.

What was I *doing?*

I looked at Terj, then at the bunting and flowers all around the room, decorations for the sham marriage I didn't want…and in that moment, the fog seemed to lift.

Releasing him, I stepped out of his embrace and turned to the dais to see what awaited me: the Cirivantis' shock, Narod's confusion, Erianthe's red-faced rage…and then there was Makou, who caught my eye and arched a brow as he grinned.

I liked that guy.

As my mother bellowed at me, I raised a hand to cut her off, then looked at Makou's parents. "Your Majesties, I'm very sorry about this," I said, "but I can't marry your son. Makou is a wonderful man, and he'll make the right person very happy someday. I'm not that person, and let's be honest—he doesn't want to marry me, either."

The king looked down at Makou, who nodded.

"I'm sorry for the fuss," I told them. "You traveled all this way, and I'd almost convinced myself to go through with it…but I love *him*," I said, reaching back to take Terj's hand. "And if I'm not mistaken, he loves me, too."

The joy radiating off of Terj was all the answer I needed.

"You *cannot* do this," Erianthe snapped. "You signed a treaty—"

"Under patently false pretenses," I retorted, and she flinched as if I'd struck her. "I'll deal with you later, *Mother*. Your Majesty," I continued, turning back to Fetull, "I agreed to the betrothal only in order to secure naval protection for our interests in Ga'besh. Makou tells me that this wasn't your original idea. You asked for Mother's necklace, and she offered me up instead. Is that correct?"

"Uh…yes, that's accurate," he replied, still shocked. "Not to say that you would not make a fine daughter-in-law, but—"

"I'm really not offended. Would you wait here for just a moment? I've got something that might make this trip of yours worthwhile."

Without waiting for leave, I marched out of the throne room, dragging Terj with me. He stumbled once but quickly righted himself, and I felt his flash of embarrassment. *Sorry, my balance isn't the best—*

I'm going to need full details, but let's wait until I'm out of this damn dress.

He hesitated, then said, *It looks uncomfortable.*

I glanced up at him and grinned. *You're not going to try to tell me that it's beautiful and I need to suck it up and suffer for fashion?*

You know I'm not good at discerning physical beauty.

So you'll kiss me again once I'm in loungewear?

I'll kiss you in anything you like. That was…

I laughed as I pulled him through the corridor and toward a staircase. *Your first time?*

Why does it feel like that? Making contact with my lips has never led to a…cascade like the one I experienced.

Could it be that I turn you on?

He thought about it until we reached the second landing, then seemed to relax as the question resolved itself. *Oh. So that's what that means.*

Pleasant?

Well, since I'm fighting the urge to push you against the wall right now and try again…

"Patience," I murmured in a singsong.

Frustration bubbled up in his mind, but he didn't try to slow me. *I still can't do that*, he said as we stepped off on the level that connected to my apartment.

Do what?

Vocalize. It's far more complicated than I'd thought. I mean, I can make noise, he amended. *The cords work. But words are another matter.*

I don't care if you never speak a syllable, okay? I replied, squeezing his hand. *I love you, and I should have told you months ago.*

Likewise, I just thought you wouldn't want me…and then that fucking betrothal came along, and I was about to lose any chance with you, and I had to do something...

Reaching my door, I turned and kissed him again, then let myself in and hurried to my trunk.

Loungewear? he asked hopefully.

Not yet. Digging around in the bottom, I pushed aside my lingerie to reveal a cloth-wrapped bundle, and I untied it and showed Terj my prize. *Let's hope this does the trick,* I said, then stuffed the bundle into my bodice and hastened back to the throne room.

By the time we returned, the confused crowd had been ushered outside, but my furious mother remained with the Cirivantis and Narod, who seemed torn between his wife and brother. "I'm sorry for the wait," I said, breezing back to the dais, then pulled the bundle out and produced an Aen crystal the circumference of a half dollar. "Not to be crass, but how much protection would this buy us?"

Erianthe gasped—to be fair, the crystal was larger than the one in her necklace—and Fetull's eyes widened as he took it from me and held it to the sunlight. "Merciful gods, Susan, where..."

"That one was set in the pommel of Shadowbane. The rest of the sword disintegrated."

"That's not yours!" Erianthe screeched. "The crystals that went into that sword—"

"Are mine and Terj's," I said, glowering at her. "I came to you *begging* for help to be rid of that damn sword, and you were going to execute me instead. So since I'm the last Watcher, and since poor Terj got stuck in the damn thing, we've got the best claim. Now why don't you shut up and let me clean up your mess, hmm?"

Cofali looked at my mother in horror. "You were going to execute your own daughter?"

Erianthe's flush deepened. "I didn't know she—"

"*Bullshit* you didn't know," I snapped, and looked at Fetull. "Well, Your Majesty? How much protection will that buy us?"

"For this?" He whistled softly. "Five hundred years. I'll

sign a treaty before we leave."

I turned to Terj, who nodded, then stuck out my hand to the king. "You've got yourself a deal."

He smiled and gripped my forearm. "An excellent one. Though I'd have liked to have another daughter as well…"

"Father," Makou muttered, and rolled his eyes.

"*But* I understand," Fetull finished, and looked at Terj as he released me. "Now, who might this fellow be who outranks a prince in your estimation?"

"This," I said, still marveling at the feel of his hand in mine, "is Terj."

Narod frowned in bemusement. "But…that…*how…*"

You'll have to ask the maladetas, Terj replied, and the Cirivantis stiffened at the mental communication. *But if you don't believe Susan…*

Suddenly, my hand closed on air, and I opened my fist and spun to Terj, only to find him back in his insubstantial form, the same as ever…well, almost. A hint of the necklace remained, a small green glow within his chest. Terj waited for a beat while the Terols picked their jaws off the floor, then resolidified in the blink of an eye. *Took them a few days to figure that out. I have no idea how it works, but it* does, *so that's me.*

You're not stuck, I marveled, keeping the conversation between us.

What do you mean?

I was afraid you were trapped in a body…

His thoughts warmed as he recognized my concern. *If that were the only way, I'd have taken it, and gladly*, he told me, *but no. Ganeel really did outdo herself.*

She didn't say a damn word about this last night.

I think she's been trying not to jinx this. We weren't even sure if I'd be able to walk a few weeks ago.

The sound of voices on the dais drew my attention back to the room. "—tell the priests," Fetull was saying. "A pity to cancel tomorrow's wedding…unless you two…"

Terj and I shared a look and reached the same conclusion. "Not just yet," I told the king. "We need some time, and really, after this rushed betrothal, I'm done with weddings for a while."

"But we have plans for a feast tomorrow," said Narod, "and seeing my brother again is as good a reason as I need to bring out the banquet. How about it?" he asked Fetull. "Will you stay? Be our guests a while longer?"

Though Erianthe was purpling by then, Fetull grinned at his little brother. "Of course. This will be a wedding feast for the histories," he said, and nodded to me. "The bride who bought her way out. I fear your legend grows, my dear."

"Just lucky like that," I replied, and took Terj's hand again. "Now, if you'll all excuse me, I'm going to get out of this miserable gown. Makou...no hard feelings?"

My former fiancé chuckled. "None. Best wishes to you both."

"And to you," I told him, holding his gaze, then let Terj escort me from the room.

I had questions. *So* many questions. But while I'd hoped for a few hours alone with Terj to figure out what had happened and what this meant for us, that was not to be.

Back in my apartment, I'd just worked out the knot holding my bodice together when the door burst open, and in ran my siblings—Zadi unencumbered, Edes with Jerrcoa slung over his shoulder like a grain sack. "*What* is going on?" Edes demanded, puffing for breath as he deposited Jerrcoa in a chair. "Mother is raging, the servants are whispering, and Makou says the wedding is off?"

"Sounds about right," I replied. "Zadi, hon, could you please help me with this?"

She set to work, though she looked distressed. "Why aren't you marrying Makou? What about the treaty? And your beautiful gown..."

"And who is *this*?" Jerrcoa asked.

I glanced over my shoulder to find him pointing at Terj, who'd taken the other chair and was watching quietly as my siblings fretted. "Terj came back today," I told my brother. "Somehow piloting a meat suit. And since Makou has a boyfriend back home, and your uncle really wanted an Aen crystal instead of a marriage, the only person who's upset is Mother."

Jerrcoa goggled at Terj. "Wait…that's—"

"Meat suit"?

I shrugged as Zadi's deft fingers ripped through the laces. "Is there a better term?"

Amusement filtered from his thoughts. *Honestly? That works. It does still feel like I'm piloting something foreign half the time, and I keep discovering new buttons to push.*

"I repeat: *what* is going on?" said Edes, looking back and forth between Terj and me.

"Personally, I'm more concerned with the *how*," Jerrcoa murmured, pushing on the armrests to adjust the awkward position in which he'd landed. "And, uh…welcome back, Terj," he added dryly.

By then, Zadi had opened the bodice enough for me to wriggle free, and I stepped behind my screen while I peeled off the dress and threw on my robe. "Let's just take a minute and breathe, all right? Then we can work through this like reasonable—"

Someone frantically pounded on my door, and before I could say, a word, Mia pushed inside, with Anji and Fanakel on her heels. "*Deets!*" she cried. "I need them all. Where are you, Suze?"

She's dressing.

I couldn't see Terj from my crack in the screen, but I caught Mia's face as she gaped. "Oh, my God, *Terj?* What the fuck, man?"

"Seconded," said Edes.

"All right, y'all…find a seat," I said, emerging as I knotted my belt. "Fanakel, would you close that door, please?"

He stiffened, and I mentally kicked myself for slipping up and using his name in front of my siblings, but he let it pass and did as I asked.

We crowded around the sitting area, and as Terj looked to me for a cue, I suggested, "Maybe we could take this from the top?"

He nodded and leaned back in his chair. *Once you resolved to go through with the betrothal, I knew I'd have to do something drastic if I wanted any prayer of changing your mind. So I returned to Taln'een, like I told you.*

"And guilted Ganeel into…this?"

More or less. I explained Erianthe's plan, confessed that I loved you, and told her I needed a true physical form.

"Terj," I said quietly, "I loved you without one."

To my surprise, his face began to pinken. *I thought perhaps there would be less of a scandal if you chose someone with consistent visibility. And…you know, that you might prefer this.*

"But what about you? You had your freedom, you were ready to go…"

And I'm using that freedom to stay by your side.

Edes's face screwed up in thought. "Don't you want to be out there, elsewhere? I thought that was the nature of air elementals."

It is. But I'm…warped, you might say. Broken. Better now, but I'll never be who I was before the sword was forged. He paused, then slowly shrugged, and I realized he'd had to think about the gesture. Terj could read body language well enough, but deploying it was another matter. *All those years spent around humans, never seeing another of my kind…it shaped me. So no, this isn't normal. None of this is normal,* he said, patting his flushed face. *But it's what I want, and Ganeel agreed to help me.*

"What did she do, exactly?" Mia asked, staring at Terj like one might a dog who'd suddenly started singing opera.

A sound escaped him that I vaguely recognized as harsh laughter. *You would need to interrogate her. All I know is that she brought me into her quarters, she and Ardielta started muttering, and a few moments later…boom.*

"Boom?" I echoed.

Terj nodded. *It felt like an explosion, anyway. Waves of pain. Nothing I haven't endured before,* he hastily added as I began to protest, *but unexpected. Ardielta stayed with me until the worst passed. It was a processing quirk,* he explained. *Or so she thought. Basically, I had all of these internal functions going simultaneously, plus the sudden influx of physical sensation, and I didn't know how to interpret what I was feeling. Pain was the default. And then I couldn't quite figure out how to move in anything resembling a coordinated fashion, so…it's been a process.*

That Terj had gone to Taln'een for help when that clan was the one that had imprisoned him to begin with told me how desperate he had been. That he'd asked them to do something so drastic to him was almost more than I could believe, and the thought of him lying there, helpless and in agony…

Sensing my distress, he reached toward the loveseat where I'd perched and took my hand. *I'm fine, Susan. This is fine. So much better now. As far as I can tell, things don't hurt unless they're supposed to.*

"So…you're breathing," said Anji, tugging on her beard as she studied him. "Is that necessary or for effect?"

Not necessary but encouraged, if you will. The meat suit likes respiration and rest. It breathes unless I consciously choose not to, and it gets sore if I push too long without giving it time to repair itself.

"Sleep, you mean?"

No, I still don't sleep, but I can…drift, I guess, he said. *Conscious but not paying attention to anything. I've been doing that when my body tires, and it seems to work.*

"What about food?" asked Fanakel. "Drink? Do you hunger?"

I haven't yet. Ganeel believes that as long as I'm within the Aen, I'll need nothing more. But I can eat, he added. *I've tried a little. It's…bizarre, frankly.*

"And then you're left dealing with the end result," Edes

muttered.

At that, Terj shook his head. *Fortunately, no. I seem to absorb everything I consume. The, uh...the equipment is installed but nonfunctional, if you understand me.*

Edes's gaze flicked lower. "So, um, you—"

"Not in front of Zadi," Jerrcoa snapped.

Our sister folded her arms and pouted. "I'm not a *child*. Go on, ask him."

"Maybe later," Edes mumbled, chastised. "But to be clear—you're stuck like this now? For *Susan?*"

You sound surprised.

"No offense," he said, cutting his eyes my way, "but it's a *massive* change."

It's not bad, Terj protested. *Anyway, no, I'm not "stuck."*

With that, he released me and flickered again, once again only a suggestion of a body and the slight glow of the crystal around his neck.

"All right, that's cool," declared Mia. "What happens if you take the necklace off?"

I can't. It doesn't truly exist in that form any longer—it's part of me. The way it manifests is an illusion, more or less. In a blink, he was back in the chair, not a tousled hair out of place. *So that's me, then. No fantastic new powers, just an optional meat suit.*

I grinned. "You're going to keep calling it that, aren't you?"

Absolutely. But enough about me, he said, looking at our friends. *It's been months! How are you?*

Before anyone could answer him, a heavy knock sounded at the door, and all eyes turned to me.

"Come in," I called.

The door opened to reveal two of the castle guards, my mother's personal defense corps. "Your Highness," said one with a deep nod. "The queen commands your presence."

I gestured toward my robe. "This minute?"

"She was most adamant, Your Highness."

Rolling my eyes, I rose from my seat and headed for

my trunk. "Let me dress. I'll come quietly."

Is that wise? Terj asked. *Going alone?*

"She is *not* happy," said Edes. "Again, I mean no insult, but would you like, uh…backup?"

Anji grunted. "That's not a bad idea, lass."

Pulling a pair of legging out of my pile of clothes, I glanced at the guards, then back at my would-be posse. "Let me handle this. Maybe she'll talk to me like an adult if I can get her alone. *Is* she alone?" I asked the guards.

"Not quite," said their apparent leader. "The prince consort is with her."

"Close enough," I replied, and stepped behind the screen to make myself decent.

The guards escorted me to the queen's private office, where I found her poised as ever but seething, with Narod by her side. "Leave us," she ordered, and the door latched behind me as the guards saw themselves out.

The fact that she didn't immediately criticize my ensemble was proof of how furious my mother was. "What do you have to say for yourself?" she demanded, gripping the wooden arms of her chair as I stood on the rug like a misbehaving student dragged before the principal. "You spoiled, *stupid* child, what possible explanation can you offer for your conduct?"

Maybe that tone would have worked when I was ten— Dad had certainly employed the "disappointed parent" voice to great effect—but I snorted my laughter and folded my arms. "Well, let's see. You lied to me—maybe you both did, I can't say," I added, glancing at Narod, who stood silently. "But we can start with that."

"I never lied!" she protested.

"The *only* way to get Cirivant's navy was for me to marry Makou? You don't consider that a lie?"

Her rouged lips pressed together.

"Makou's a nice guy. At least he had the decency to tell

me the truth," I said. "And you know, even though you lied to me, even though you were about to marry me off to a man who will *never* willingly touch a woman, you almost had me convinced to go through with it. All that talk of duty and sacrifice—"

"Makou is a fine young man—" Narod began.

"Who doesn't want to marry me, either! And that's not a *sacrifice* either of us should have to make," I continued, focusing on Erianthe. "You could have fixed your own problem with a fucking necklace. I fixed it for you, and I did it my way, and now you've got generations of protection for your damn colonies. *You're welcome.* All it cost you was the money you sank into this wedding that should never have been arranged in the first place."

"You defy me," my mother replied through gritted teeth. "You humiliate me. You show no gratitude—"

"Gratitude for what? That you haven't sent an assassin to kill me in my sleep yet?"

She sucked in a sharp breath. "Your presence here is no longer tenable, so here is what I will do. I will negotiate your marriage to an appropriate man. You and he will either reside with his family or in a location of my choosing until such time as I desire to see your miserable face again. That...*creature* with whom you were cavorting is hereby banished from this realm on pain of death..."

Erianthe fell silent as I cackled, which admittedly wasn't the usual response to a royal decree. As I wiped my eyes, I stared back at her and smirked. "I'd like to see you try, Mother. You can't force me to marry, and good luck keeping Terj away."

"I can lock you in a tower cell for the rest of my life. Brick up the window."

"Dear, let's not be hasty," Narod tried, but neither woman in the room paid him any mind.

"You wouldn't dare," I retorted.

"Simple enough. You've contracted a terrible illness and need to recuperate in peace," she said. "It would be too bad if you died of your condition."

"*Erianthe*," said Narod, appalled, "that's enough."

"Bread and water for a decade," she continued, ignoring him. "No visitors. Let's see how your attitude changes then."

I didn't flinch. "You'd have to get me up there first."

"All I need do is call the guards."

"You can try," I replied, cocking my head. "But before you do, you should remember something."

"Oh? And what's that?"

"The human body is about sixty percent water."

My mother didn't blink, but I caught the flicker of uncertainty in her eyes. "Meaning?" she asked with feigned nonchalance.

"If I can lift an acidic lake out of its bed and throw it around," I murmured, "imagine what I can do with the blood in your veins. Or maybe the acid in your stomach. That stuff's strong enough to dissolve metal, so think about the damage it could do if it burned its way through you."

To her credit, she kept up her front. "Every word from your cursed mouth is treason, or are you too stupid to realize the penalty for threatening me?"

"If we're playing this game, I believe you started it." Shaking my head, I said, "You don't like me, and I understand that—"

"I *hate* you," she said, making a point to enunciate each syllable.

Admittedly, that stung, though it wasn't surprising. "I'm sorry. I know you didn't want me—I'm the walking consequence of your actions. But you could have ended your pregnancy," I said, stepping toward her. "I've been here long enough to learn about the ways. *Someone* could have fixed the problem for you if you'd paid. Maybe there would have been whispers, but hearing my friends talk, there were whispers about you and a secret baby before I came back, so *great* plan. Whatever. You carried me, and you gave birth. You could have smothered me easily enough if you didn't care to find someone to look after me. But you didn't even do *that*. You left me in the woods to die of exposure or be eaten or…or God knows what else. You left me to *suffer*," I said, fighting the pricking in my eyes.

She said nothing.

"Look, I know you hate me—you've made that clear since the night I was born. You have no *reason* to hate me. I sure as hell didn't get you pregnant, and I wouldn't fault you if you'd ended your pregnancy. But is there no sliver of humanity in you that looks at me now and sees a daughter?" When she maintained her silence, I pressed, "Was there never a time when you held Edes or Jerrcoa or Zadi and thought of me? Did you never wish things could have been different?"

"My children mean everything to me," she finally said. "You're not even human."

Narod gripped her shoulder. "Erianthe, please…"

"And you barely know the first thing about Daril," she continued, shrugging him off. "My son has prepared his entire life to rule this land and protect it, and then you walk in like I owe you *anything*. Tell me, where do you find the audacity?"

"Yeah, I'm not as prepared as Edes is, and who the hell's fault is that?" I countered. "Sorry that I'm not Darili enough for you—maybe if you'd actually raised me in Daril, I'd fit the part. And I'm *terribly* sorry that you don't find me sufficiently human to warrant basic compassion," I said with all due sarcasm. "Nothing I can do about that. If you've got a problem with my parentage, take the matter up with my parents. Oh, wait…"

"Susan, you're not helping," Narod tried again.

"You're a disgraceful monstrosity," Erianthe spat. "The greatest mistake of my life was not ending yours when I had the chance." Sneering back at me, she said, "You know my people will never accept you, yes? Daril has been a *human* kingdom since its founding. Even if they were willing to overlook your shortcomings, they'd never recognize *him*. Your little plaything."

There, at least, she had a point. I'd been raised human—maybe I couldn't pass for a native Darili, but I certainly had the gist of the species. Terj, on the other hand, was clearly something other. Even if Daril accepted me as their queen, would they balk at a selectively corporeal prince consort?

And did I really want to find out?

I'd been chafing in the castle for months, butting up against the rules and expectations for a princess. The dresses, the tutoring, the awkward moments—not to mention the years of Erianthe's disdain that I had to look forward to…was it worth the effort?

What good was my birthright if it made me miserable?

I still had my life in Cole's Crossing, didn't I? My family home, Uncle Malachi's cabin, a few vehicles of questionable functionality, the store—I had another option. Maybe it wasn't glamorous, and sure, I'd have to leave before everyone realized I wasn't aging…and I'd have to convince Terj to give it a try…but the Crossing was home, comfortable, familiar, and markedly less complicated than Deoni.

I could be Susan Fulquir, miserable princess with a mother who begrudged her every breath, or Susan Cole, small-town business owner and average local girl.

Susan Fulquir would have to fight for anything she wanted.

Susan Cole could metaphorically hang up the sword and make a life with the man she loved.

"What do you want of me?" I asked my mother.

Her answer was immediate: "Renounce your claim to the throne in favor of Edes and leave."

I glanced at Narod, who seemed to realize that nothing he said would help this situation, then back at Erianthe. "And why would I do that?"

"Because it's best for Daril and for the *rightful* heir to my throne. Because you're too selfish to marry well."

"You could visit," Narod suggested, pressing on when his wife shot daggers at him. "On occasion. I'm sure your siblings would like to see you."

"Renounce and depart," said Erianthe, "and you and I will never have to bother each other again."

I paused, considering my options, then sighed quietly and shrugged. "You can announce it tomorrow night. I'm going to enjoy my own damn wedding banquet before I go."

My mother's eyes widened, and her face brightened as my words registered. "You'll do it? Truly?"

"Yeah," I said, and turned to leave.

"Wait, we need to—"

"Tomorrow," I insisted, and glanced back at them— Narod, troubled and conflicted, and Erianthe, practically shining with excitement. "I could have been a really good daughter, you know?" I murmured. "If you'd given me a chance, I'd have made you proud."

"Doubtful," Erianthe replied. "I told you that you were my great shame. What could you possibly do to change that?"

"Guess slaying a bunch of monsters wasn't enough, huh?" I said, and walked out before she could concur.

CHAPTER 7

Edes took the news harder than anyone. "Why would you do that?" he demanded, pacing my living room. His ponytail had come untied during the afternoon, and he tugged at his loose hair in his agitation.

"To be fair," I said, lounging on the loveseat beside Terj, "I *did* just give you a throne. Most people would be all right with that."

He glared at me on his next pass. "Yeah, well, *most people* also wouldn't mind marrying Curin of Eraneg, yet here we are."

"She's very pretty," Zadi offered, and shrank back when Edes turned his glare on her.

"The odds of you getting stuck with Curin again are slim," said Jerrcoa, who hadn't moved from the chair where Edes had deposited him. "Considering that your prior engagement was...what would we call that?"

"A shitshow?" Mia suggested.

"Mm. Crass. I like it. Yes, a *shitshow*," he said to our brother. "I can't imagine that her parents would be eager to risk a repeat."

"If Susan's gone, what's the risk?" Edes muttered. "Unless Mother's hidden other siblings we should know about..."

"None that I'm aware of," I said. "Look, she actually gives a damn about you, so just tell her you'll marry when you're ready. She's been burned on weddings twice in the last year—maybe she'll back down."

"Which I would try if not for the fact that I'm once

again the crown prince, and I've got to marry."

Anji shrugged. "Not necessarily, lad. The throne could pass to a nephew or niece, could it not?"

Edes pointed to Jerrcoa, then to Zadi. "He can't have children, and she's still a child. I'm of age, so guess who's duty-bound to take a wife?" Groaning as he did an about-face at the window, he said, "*Stay*, Susan. Tell Mother you've changed your mind. She has her moods, but she'll get past this."

"Did you miss the part where she and I casually threatened to kill each other?" I replied.

He paused, scowling. "Perhaps it will take longer than usual for her to move on—"

"It's not worth it. I'm not going to live my life in fear of poisoning or a dagger in the back, and I'm sure as hell not going to stay if she's threatening Terj."

She talks, but what could she do to me?

I took his hand, still marveling at how real everything felt, and squeezed. "I don't know, but I'm not willing to find out." *You know what happened to Falova*, I added privately. *I won't risk that happening to you.*

When he answered me, he spoke publicly, keeping my confidence. *You don't have to walk away on my account. I can be sneaky...*

"You shouldn't have to be sneaky," I said, holding his gaze. "So if you want to come with me, let's go find a life out there."

"But where will you go?" asked Zadi, worrying the cuff of her sleeve. "Ti'cal?"

Terj's eyebrows rose in query. *That might not be a terrible plan. You could still see your father.*

"Yeah," I said, "but...I had an idea."

What's that?

"You know how we talked about driving out to the Grand Canyon? Like Uncle Malachi always wanted?"

His mouth began to curl. *As I recall, you thought we could go all the way to California.*

"Could do. Are you still interested?"

"And where is, uh...*California*?" Edes interjected, saying the unfamiliar word slowly.

"Back on the other side of the Crossing. So how about it?" I asked Terj. "We drive out west, see the big hole, maybe go to LA or San Francisco or Portland. Hell, maybe all three. Go take pictures at the Hollywood sign and drive the Pacific Coast Highway and...and tour Alcatraz, maybe, I don't know. We could find the giant sequoias and see the Rockies and Death Valley—I've got the funds. We'll do it for Uncle Malachi. And once we've seen enough, we could figure things out from there. I realize that living outside the Aen wouldn't be ideal, but—"

If you'll have me, I'll follow you anywhere, he said, tightening his grip on my hand.

"I don't want to hurt you."

And I won't let it get to that point. But while we're making plans, why not do so on the road? We know we travel decently well together, he joked.

"Ah, yes. A noble quest to figure shit out," I deadpanned.

"Are you keeping this a twosome trip?" Mia asked. "If not, I offer my DJ skills."

Terj and I shared a quick thought, and I grinned at her. "Sure! We can make room. How about it?" I said, looking at Anji and Fanakel. "Want to get the band back together?"

Anji frowned. "Band?"

"Just an expression," Mia told her. "What do you think? You've been nice enough to show me around your country—I could return the favor, assuming your father would allow it."

The dwarf mulled that over briefly. "I would need to shave, would I not?"

Mia sucked her teeth. "Unless we want to pass you off as a guy—"

"*No*," she said, and snorted with disdain. "Well, that's

not ideal, but it's merely hair, so…"

Fanakel eyed her incredulously. "You're not vexed by the idea of another shave?"

"Survived the last one, didn't I?" Anji retorted. "And what about you? Pressing matters in Caritulo, or would you be interested in seeing whether we get along when we're not faced with imminent death?"

The elf smiled. "I do prefer situations without imminent death, to be honest."

"So you'll come?"

"Since I can't imagine that my father would miss me too terribly…room for one more?" he asked me.

"Sure," I said, "we'll squeeze. Put a hat on you, hide those ears, buy some clothes that don't scream 'Renaissance faire…'"

"Sorry, what?"

"Don't worry, it's nothing a little denim can't fix," said Mia. "And, uh…if y'all wanted a side quest…"

I motioned her on. "Please. Find Bigfoot? Smoke some *really* good weed?"

"Actually," she mumbled, "I was wondering if you might want to help me find my dad. If you don't, it's okay," she hastily added, "I get it. If you'd rather not go hunting for a tekori, I understand."

Edes stopped pacing and gaped at her. "You're *tekorish?*"

"Half," I said, "and if you know what's good for you, you'll forget that."

He held up his hands in surrender and shut his mouth.

"And yes, absolutely," I said, freeing myself from Terj and rising from the loveseat to grasp her shoulders. "I owe you *big* time, Mia. If you want to find him, I'll be there."

"As will I," said Anji. "Your father owes you at least his name."

"Maybe this is a mistake," Mia told me, "but I've been thinking about it for a while, and…I just want to know where I came from. If I approach him like that, keep it cool, then surely he'll give me medical information or something, right?"

"If he doesn't," her girlfriend grumbled, "I'll break his damn knees."

Mia looked down at her with a smile. "You're sweet, lass."

"I'm serious."

"I know, and I love you for it," she said, bending to kiss Anji's forehead. "But let's hope it doesn't come to violence. Maybe he'll be slightly happier to see me than Erianthe was to see you," she added, glancing my way.

That bar's so low, it's underground, said Terj. *So it's decided, then? We return to the Crossing, head west, and see if we can find Mia's father's hiding place?*

"That works," said Fanakel, and the rest of us nodded. "How do we propose to get to the tunnel?"

Terj grunted. *I wasn't planning to walk, if that's what you're asking.*

"I didn't want to presume…"

Trust me, I can get us there. Even you, he teased.

"Then that's settled," I said. "Let's pack tonight, stick around for tomorrow's banquet—I mean, after the last few weeks, I deserve it—and then we'll be off."

"Take me with you."

We turned to Jerrcoa, who had leaned forward in his chair. "Please," he said, "let me come, too. I won't be a problem. I've got a modified saddle, and I do know how to ride—"

"There are no chiquiws where we're going, lad," said Anji.

"*Please,*" he insisted, looking up at me. "I've not left Deoni in ten years. Let me see something of the wider world before it's too late."

"Jerr—" Edes began, but our brother put up a hand to silence him.

"You've been abroad," he snapped. "So has Zadi. I'm left to rot in this damn castle. Please, Susan, I beg you…"

I looked at my friends for their thoughts. "He's got a wheelchair, but it's not portable."

"There's a medical supply store near Walmart," said Mia. "Think we could pick one up? Something foldable, I mean, not a power chair."

"Yeah, that could work." Turning back to Jerrcoa, I asked, "Are you opposed to pushing yourself?"

"Not at all. And I can bathe myself and...uh...manage other matters," he added, blushing. "Anything but stairs."

It wouldn't be overly taxing to carry one more, said Terj.

"Well, then, I guess we'll find a spot for you," I said to Jerrcoa, who beamed.

"Strapped to a luggage rack?" Mia quipped. "If we're taking your Accord..."

"Nah. Dad's old Explorer has a third row. It's been in the garage for a while, but if we jump the battery..."

"Ooh, *yes*. I like legroom."

"Are you sure this is safe?" asked Zadi. "Going so far from home..."

I took her hands and smiled. "We'll be safe, I promise. And I'll bring Jerrcoa back in one piece, all right?'

My sister didn't seem sold on the idea, and Edes grumbled, but eventually, he went down to the kitchen to have food sent up for us. No one wanted to face Erianthe that night, and my apartment was decently out of the way.

Long after sunset, when the last of the food had been eaten and the coast seemed clear, our little party broke up. Anji and Mia returned to break the news of their side trip to Rokund, Fanakel slipped off to pack, and Edes once again tossed Jerrcoa over his shoulder as they and Zadi took their leave. Finally, as the door clicked shut behind them, I was alone with Terj.

He perched on the arm of the vacated loveseat and watched as I double-checked the locks—I was in no mood to be awakened by a maid in the morning. *You should rest, Susan*, he told me. *Today has been trying, I'm sure.*

I'm okay, I replied, slipping back into our effortless

conversation as easily as I pulled on Edes's oversized tunics. *Are you?*

Just fine. He hesitated, rubbing one elbow, then asked, *Might I stay with you tonight?*

I headed for my bedroom. *Of course.*

Terj followed me, then averted his gaze as I shimmied out of my leggings, not turning back until the bed creaked. *Comfortable?*

I sighed as I pulled the covers to my chin. *Close enough.*

Good. He carefully blew out the candles, leaving only the chamber pot lantern aglow, and I saw him dematerialize in its faint light. *Sleep well.*

What about you?

What about me? he replied.

Where are you resting?

Oh, uh…here, I suppose. A slight gust opened my window a little wider. *This ledge is convenient.*

Do you, um… I started to ask.

Yes?

Do you want to sleep with me?

The color of his thoughts changed in an instant, first to surprise, then to trepidation. *I…don't know if that's a good idea.*

You don't have to, I quickly assured him. *Just an offer. There's plenty of room in the bed.*

I don't truly sleep, though, so what if I grow too restless and wake you?

We can cross that bridge if we come to it. I paused, considering his reaction, and then the gears clicked. *Oh, no, I wasn't suggesting that we, uh…get intimate. This is purely about sleep.*

Ah. Terj sounded relieved. *In that case…if you're certain…*

I slid over and patted the mattress. *Come on, join me.*

He appeared once again, silhouetted against the window, then unclasped his cloak and let it puddle on the floor. Carefully, he eased onto the bed and worked his feet out of his shoes, and then, still more or less dressed, he slipped beneath the covers and lay on his back, staring up at the ceiling. *How's this?* he asked.

Could be better. Roll over this way.

Terj obliged, and I spooned against him, then pulled his arm around me. *Is this okay?*

Judging by the emotional cast on his mind, it was better than okay—his body was weary, the bed was decent, and something within him reacted to our proximity.

Why does this feel so good? he asked as my breathing slowed.

If you were human, I'd say it's because we're hardwired for touch, and because I'm probably giving off an interesting bunch of pheromones right now.

Mm. I wonder if the maladetas built in similar reactions for me. Does this feel good to you as well?

Uh-huh, I replied, holding his arm a little more tightly. I snuggled into him, and he carefully kissed a spot behind my ear.

Goodnight, Susan.

Goodnight, I echoed as my mind began drifting toward unconsciousness. *Don't let me go.*

I've got you, he said, and I released myself to the encroaching darkness.

When I awoke at the sound of the first bell, Terj remained beside me, pressed against my back. He was warm—such a strange deviation from the coolness I'd previously associated with his touch—and his chest moved slowly, his breathing soft and calm.

You don't have to wake yet.

You're still here, I thought, rolling over to face him. I couldn't see much, but I felt his presence as if he were alight.

Where else would I be? he replied, bemused.

You didn't have to stay here all night! I'm sorry, that had to be boring—

Somehow, his lips found mine, and my protestations died as he kissed me.

It's actually rather pleasant, said Terj once we'd slightly parted and my forehead was resting against his on the pillows. *And the meat suit feels better, so…*

Oh, I've done a <u>bad</u> thing.

He chuckled. *Not at all.*

We lay together silently for a moment, listening to the distant sounds of Deoni waking beyond the open window.

Second thoughts? I asked.

About our road trip?

About this.

His response was immediate and firm. *No. I would stay like this for the rest of my life if it meant having you beside me.*

I love you with or without the meat suit. You don't have to—

Truly, I don't mind. It's…interesting, he said. *After observing for so long, I'm finally trying it out.*

Minus some of the less pleasant bits, I reminded him.

And I'm not complaining.

A question I'd been wondering about popped into my mind, but I quickly suppressed it. Terj, however, was perceptive. *Is something bothering you?*

Nothing to worry about.

No, tell me. What's up?

I paused, putting my thoughts in order, then said, *This is going to seem…indelicate.*

I'm a big boy.

Right. So, uh…I know your digestive system isn't fully functional, but what about…you know?

To my relief, he didn't sound offended. *I'm not entirely sure. Ganeel believed it should work as usual, but it seems to have a mind of its own. Stiffens at strange moments. I've yet to fully work out how to control it.*

I don't think most guys can.

Really? Well, that's annoying.

Maybe you should chat with Fanakel.

Terj sighed. *Somehow, I don't think he'd appreciate the*

conversation.

Maybe, but since I'm no expert, Jerrcoa's a special case, and the rest of our party are lesbians, perhaps Fanakel can suck it up and help a bro.

When he hesitated, I could sense his unease. *If it doesn't function properly…*

If it doesn't, or if you're not comfortable being intimate with me, I won't love you any less.

I <u>want</u> to be what you need, he insisted, cupping my cheek in the predawn gloom. *I just don't know how.*

That's fine. There's no rush. I like this, too, I said, kissing him again. *We can take this slowly and figure out what's best for us.*

Relief mingled with his doubt. *You're not upset?*

Remember how I was supposed to marry Makou today.? I <u>really</u> don't mind if we do this by baby steps.

As Terj pulled me closer beneath the blankets, I said, *I need to talk to Falova. Tell him what's going on.*

He'll be disappointed that you're leaving.

Can't be helped. If Erianthe and I don't get some space from each other, we'll come to blows at <u>best</u>.

True, but my money's on you. And you don't have to do this, he insisted. *Let her try to lock you away and banish me—she's one human, so what's she going to do?*

I don't want to risk finding out, I replied. *You're worth more than that.*

More than a kingdom? he asked incredulously.

When you put it like that…yeah. To me.

I don't deserve you—

Another kiss cut short his train of thought. *I'm glad you chose me. Okay? No matter why you did it, no matter how much it sucked at the time, I'm glad I was the Watcher, because now we're both free to choose each other.* I laughed to myself, then asked, *Is that horribly sappy or what?*

That's perhaps the nicest thing anyone's ever said to me.

And I meant it, sap and all. But, I said, easing out of his embrace, *this isn't getting it done, so it's probably time to face the day*. Sitting up in bed, I tugged my shirt straight and kicked off the blankets, baring my legs to the cool morning. *Excuse me.*

He stretched while I availed myself of the chamber pot behind the screen—*that*, at least, would be a feature of Darili life I wouldn't miss—and once I emerged, I ran my hands through my tangles. *A bath would be a good idea. You, too.*

Thank you, but that's unnecessary.

What do you mean?

He flickered in and out of corporeality. *Whenever I do that, it basically resets me. The clothes, now*—he sniffed his underarm—*those will need to be washed eventually, but I should be otherwise presentable. Hope you don't hate this haircut—if you do, it'll take the maladetas to change it. Otherwise, this seems rather convenient, yes?*

"Men," I muttered, then pulled on my robe and headed into the corridor to find a maid for bathwater.

The sun was fully up by the time I'd bathed, willed the water out of my hair, thrown on a tunic and leggings again, and eaten the modest breakfast the maid brought. I offered to share with Terj, but he declined; content to carry on as usual in the presence of so much Aen, he felt no need to subject himself to the weirdness of tasting, chewing, and swallowing. Decent and satiated, I headed up to my usual battlement overlooking the river, which sparkled below in the morning light, a thick, glassy ribbon dotted with small fishing boats and a larger vessel heading north toward the sea. At the bottom of the section of wall on which I stood was the bricked-up place through which the river had once flowed into the castle. I wasn't surprised that Erianthe hadn't seen fit to reopen the wall once the stench of the dead water faded.

Want a lift? Terj asked.

Sure. I braced myself as he dematerialized and a strong

gust lifted me off my feet.

Don't look down, he teased. *You and heights...*

I glanced back at him, a translucent figure with a small green glow at its core. *When the meat suit's not optional, you grow to appreciate the power of gravity.*

Well, no need to worry about it right now.

The cushion of air on which I sat gently descended to the grassy bank, and I slipped over the edge and found my footing as Terj landed beside me. *There, all better*, he said as I smoothed my wind-ruffled hair. *A little warmup for the big trip...*

He fell quiet as the water before us stirred and rose into a humanoid form slightly taller than I was. *Morning, Father*, I said, approaching the river's edge.

Soul of my soul. His pleasure rippled through the thought. *This is your wedding day, is it not? You need not have wasted precious time here.*

The wedding's off, I replied, and glanced at Terj, who remained insubstantial. *Erianthe lied to me, my intended prefers the company of men, and I love Terj, so I cancelled the wedding.*

He paused, taking that in, then turned his attention to Terj. *I see you finally told her, brother.*

I did.

And you could not have done so months before now?

Terj seemed to sigh in my mind. *It was a process.*

Oh?

Show him, I pressed.

He obliged, effortlessly flickering into view.

My father retreated a few inches from the bank in his shock, then swiftly drew close again. *How...what have you...*

Maladetas with a debt to repay, Terj replied, *and that's all I know of their art.*

He looked back and forth between Terj and me, and after a moment, I felt his comingled surprise and contentment. *I understand, though I cannot imagine how you, of all people, endure such...*

It's different, yes, but not painful. And...I think, in a way, it suits me.

Falova reached for me, and I took his hand. *Truly, daughter, I believe he would be a better match for you than would anything out of Cirivant. Be happy.* Releasing me with a little squeeze, he asked Terj, *I should expect to see you around here on a more permanent basis, then?*

Well…that's what we came to tell you, I interrupted. *Erianthe and I have reached an impasse, and frankly, I don't feel safe here any longer. She's threatened both of us,* I said, nodding to Terj, *and so I decided it would be wiser to do what she wants and renounce my claim to the throne.*

My father did nothing to hide his shock, which was quickly followed by anger. *She threatened you?*

And I threatened her in turn. Our relationship has hit a new low, if that's possible. But she does make a good point: Edes has been trained to be king, and I'm the interloper.

Whose birthright just so happens to be the throne… Terj added.

I shrugged. *And since I made it pretty plain yesterday that the only man I'm at interested in is this guy,* I continued, nodding to Terj, *Erianthe's furious. Imagine a Fulquir ruler who's only, say, a quarter human. It's possible that if I were to try to take the throne with Terj as my consort, Daril would revolt. So to avoid that, and because this place isn't nearly big enough for Erianthe and me to share, I'm moving out.*

Where will you go? Falova asked.

I winced at his stab of fear. *For starters, I've got some unfinished business back beyond the Crossing—*

There? That is not safe!

I'm not going alone, I soothed. *And we're not doing anything dangerous—mostly tourist activities. This is in honor of my uncle.*

And to give us time to work out our next move, said Terj.

Right. I'll be back, I assured my worried father. *If for no other reason than that Jerrcoa is coming with us, and I'll have to bring him home eventually. But this isn't goodbye forever, I promise you.*

He opened his arms, and I stepped to the edge of the

river, where he hugged me fiercely. *If you must do this, then go and be safe*, he told me. *Know that I await your return. And as for you*, he said, turning his attention to Terj, *protect her.*

My life for hers, Terj said simply. *Always.*

Falova retreated from me slightly but held on to my shoulders. *Would it help if I confronted Erianthe?*

I shook my head. *This is fine, Father. She'll mellow toward me or she won't, but in either case, she won't live forever, and Edes likes me. I'll be back.*

He hugged me once more before releasing me—and as always, despite the fact that his form was composed entirely of water, my clothing remained dry. *Should you have need of me, soul of my soul, just ask. Anything that I can do for you, I will.*

I know, I replied, and smiled at him. *And I'll miss you. But hey, we'll take plenty of pictures and show you the good ones when we get back, huh?*

His head cocked. *Take pictures?*

Uh...with a camera. You'll see, I insisted too brightly. *And we'll be very careful.*

Terj dematerialized and scooped me into the air, and my father began to shrink toward the river's surface. *I will be waiting*, he said, and slipped beneath the light chop as Terj carried me away.

I hid for most of the morning, packing what little I'd brought with me to Deoni and adding a few items I didn't want to leave behind—a necklace from Narod, a little embroidered bird Zadi had made me, and a couple of Edes's tunics, since they were surprisingly comfy. By the lunch hour, however, I resolved to emerge for a meal, at least, and headed down to the midsized dining room set aside for the wedding guests. The kitchen had put out a buffet, which was rather picked over when I arrived.

I was pleasantly surprised to find Mia and Anji sitting at a long table across from Ms. Quince, and I hurried to join them. "She emerges!" said Mia as I pulled out a chair. "Where's Terj?"

"Resting up. Also, seeing as Erianthe has banished him, we didn't want to risk a scene. He's not hungry, anyway," I said, tearing a roll in half. "Are we still on for the trip?"

"Very much so," she replied, and Anji nodded. "Rokund thought it would be a good idea for us to get out of the house for a bit, and this seemed pretty tame."

"Fanakel also confirmed at breakfast," said Anji. "And we saw to Jerrcoa midmorning."

"He's still in?"

"Absolutely. I just wanted to check the limits of his forging before we go beyond the Aen." Seeing my confusion, she explained, "All forged items are powered by the Aen, yes? When we create them, we build in a reservoir, if you will, so that the objects won't stop working if they were somehow temporarily cut off."

"A battery," Mia offered.

"Some have larger reservoirs than others," Anji continued, pulling the crystal pendant from beneath her shirt. I recognized it as one of the pair of two-way translators she'd forged the previous summer in Taln'een, and a glance at the chain around Mia's neck suggested that she was still wearing the pendant's twin. "I built this with a reservoir for about two months. Fanakel's ring has a similar capacity."

"Firebrand had a much more limited reservoir," Ms. Quince added. "The forging was so complex that it drained quickly, which is why Terj was too taxed to speak almost as soon as the sword was brought beyond the Crossing."

"Lovely," I muttered.

"We should be set for a trip of modest duration," said Anji, "at least as far as translators are concerned. If something should happen to them, I suppose you could assist in an emergency. But I was concerned about Jerrcoa's equipment—I didn't know whether he had accounted for the lack of Aen."

I frowned. "Is his ring not designed like Fanakel's?"

"Oh, his translator is solid work," she replied with a wave of her hand. "*Old*, yes, but certainly adequate. The crystal is of good quality. The piece is Ga'beshi in provenance, I assume."

The tone of her voice did nothing to disguise her disdain. Dwarven forging was overseen by their guilds, and unauthorized forging was illegal...well, in dwarven countries, at least. Anji was an incredibly talented forger, one of the few who could work solo, and Ganeel had given her books, time to practice, and a firm nudge during our stay with them. (If Rokund wondered where his daughter had acquired the translator she wore, he obviously hadn't punished her for making it.) Dwarves were willing to forge a few items for human clients, but nothing involving Aen crystals—humans had no limits on their use of whatever power they could scrabble together, and so the various dwarven leaders had wisely decided not to sell them items that would enhance their abilities. The great exception to the rule were the freelance forgers on Ga'besh, who sold on the black market, rejected guild regulations, and charged enormous sums for their work.

"It was his other gear I wanted to inspect while I can still forge," she continued.

"What other gear?"

Anji grimaced. "The illness that crippled your brother can affect us in much the same way. Partial paralysis is rare—it's more common in humans—but one of my cousins suffered his fate. The swellings appeared in her back, and then she lost control of herself below the waist. We grew up together, and I knew how she cared for herself. Obviously, Jerrcoa doesn't have the braces she used to walk—"

"He can't walk," I interjected. "No feeling at all in his legs."

"Yes, just like my cousin, but there are ways to forge

around such issues…and before you ask, we don't sell those braces to humans. I would procure them for him if I could," she said apologetically, "but the guildmasters agree that it's too risky. Aen crystals power them, and they could be abused."

"By *Jerrcoa*?"

She shook her head. "I'd be more worried about Erianthe. But there is one piece of my cousin's equipment that Jerrcoa uses, and I'd suspected he did—we don't mind exporting that. It's a matter of dignity."

"Which is…"

"It's a forged garment that—"

"Magic underwear," Mia interrupted with a slightly giddy smile.

Anji rolled her eyes. "Self-containing, self-cleaning, and only requires washing about once a week. It's a practical solution for the aged and infirm. *Anyway*," she continued, shooting Mia a warning look, "as I'd expected, his were of export quality. The ones we produce for our own use, like everything else, are designed with generous reservoirs. Jerrcoa's reservoir capacity was only a few days, so I tweaked his supplies to give them a longer useful period outside the Aen."

"That's, uh…that's really nice of you," I said. "And something I hadn't considered…"

She reached across the table and patted my hand. "Neither had Jerrcoa. That's one unpleasant surprise avoided. Now, Mia thinks you can procure a mobile chair for him."

"She's right," said Ms. Quince between sips of tea. "The medical supply store is decent—I made a few trips for sick shut-ins over the years. They carry foldable wheelchairs, and just about anything in there would weigh less than that contraption the poor boy is using now."

She had a point. While Jerrcoa's chair gave him limited freedom within the castle, its heavy wood and iron construction made moving it between floors a nightmarish task.

"It'll set you back a few hundred dollars," she told me, "but if you're reasonably gentle with the chair, it'll do him for years to come."

I took a bite of stewed meat. "I don't mind the price, just as long as it'll fit in the Explorer."

"It should. Now," said Ms. Quince, looking at Mia, "what's this you were saying about finding your father?"

"We're going to look for him while we're back over there," she said. "I'm not sure *how*, but since Mom met him in Vegas, that might not be a bad place to start."

"Can you help?" I asked Ms. Quince. "Didn't you tell me you might be able to do something for Mia?"

My best friend perked, and even Anji leaned closer.

Ms. Quince glanced around the room, found most of it empty, then lowered her voice. "I can, but I'll need something to work with. When you first came to Taln'een, you were wearing a translator—a moonstone pendant, yes?"

Mia nodded. "Yeah, one of Anji's projects."

"Do you still have it?"

"It's in my luggage…"

"Why would you bring that with you?" Anji asked, bemused.

"Well…" Mia began to flush. "It's a backup translator, and…you gave it to me."

"But it's a poor thing," Anji protested. "It's only a one-way piece—"

"It's the first thing you gave me."

The princess stared at her for a moment until she comprehended what Mia was saying, and then her hand went to her breast as she murmured, "*Oh*."

"Of course I keep it with me, silly," said Mia, leaning down to kiss Anji's forehead. "And even if it didn't work, it's pretty."

"May I borrow it?" asked Ms. Quince. "I won't destroy the forging," she hastily added before Mia or Anji could protest. "What I can do is add a layer to the spells worked on it, essentially."

Though Mia seemed suspicious, she retrieved her necklace and hurried back to the table. Ms. Quince waited until a pair of servants had finished refreshing the chafing dishes, then took the necklace and produced a small knife from within her dress. "I'll need a drop of blood," she explained, holding out her hand.

Mia's reservation only mounted at this pronouncement. "That *can't* be sterile."

"This is *magic*, dear," Ms. Quince replied, fixing her with a look I knew all too well from childhood, but with a huffed sigh, she rose and pulled a bottle of clear liquor from the beverage table. Returning to us, she held the blade over a plate and slowly poured alcohol on both sides, then muttered under her breath.

I almost fell off my chair when the booze ignited in purple flame, but Ms. Quince held the knife steady until the last of the alcohol had burned off. Satisfied, she flicked the blade back and forth to cool it, then beckoned at Mia. "Sufficiently clean. Let's see your hand."

Mia braced herself, but to our relief, Ms. Quince didn't go for a dramatic palm slash. Instead, she used the tip of the blade to prick Mia's finger, then held it over the necklace and muttered as a drop of blood coalesced and fell. The impact site on the moonstone flashed pink, and Ms. Quince continued to mumble and gesture until the blood vanished and the stone returned to its usual appearance.

"There," she said, passing the necklace back to Mia, who'd wrapped her finger in a napkin. "The stone will glow more brightly as you near one of your parents. I can't limit it to just your father," she said apologetically, "so when you get back to the Crossing, don't get your hopes up—it'll pick up on Janine. But if your father is still alive and you get within, say, about twenty miles of him, you'll know."

She grinned as she fastened the necklace in place, layering it with the better translator. "Thanks, Ms. Quince."

"It's a start, at least. And, uh..." She paused, her eyes cutting between Mia and me. "You know, girls, you can call me Ardielta."

"Yeah, but that would be weird," I replied, and surprised her with a quick hug before I turned to the business of lunch.

CHAPTER 8

I attended the banquet alone that night. Terj offered to escort me—in all honesty, I think he was worried that my mother might be waiting with a hit squad—but I assured him I'd be okay and asked him to sit it out. As much as I'd have liked to roll up on his arm, I decided to do the mature thing and keep him out of view, or at least not flaunt him in front of my would-be in-laws.

Hell, I even let Mia lace me into a dress for the occasion, which I thought was pretty generous of me, all things considered.

Erianthe's lips pressed into a thin line when I arrived with my friends, but she said nothing as I took the open seat between Edes and Zadi. Jerrcoa smiled at me from the end of the table, where his bulky wheelchair was best able to fit. He'd assured me that afternoon that he was packed and ready to go, but whether he'd yet bothered to tell our mother remained an unanswered question.

To my surprise, Narod spoke first that night while the soups were being passed out. He apologized to the guests who'd made the trip but were deprived of a wedding, but he closed on an upbeat note: "Having not seen my brother in years, and having not hosted his family in a far longer time, this is still a celebration, and we're pleased that you could join us. So while there is no marriage to toast tonight," he said, lifting his glass, "we hope you will enjoy the feasting and drinking, the music and dancing, and that you will leave Deoni with fond memories of this place."

I clapped for him, and he winked at me as he took his

seat.

A few minutes later, Fetull took his turn. "Though the gods have blessed me with many daughters—possibly too many," he joked, and the crowd tittered—"I admit that I'm sorry to leave without adding another to their ranks. But I understand," he said, leaning past Erianthe and Narod to meet my stare. "As my brother probably remembers, our parents had selected a perfectly nice wife for me, but I ran off to the temple by night with the woman I loved." He pointedly glanced back at Cofali, who smiled and waved him on. "Did Narod tell you of this, Susan?"

"He did not, Your Majesty," I replied, "but I congratulate you on your fine choice."

"I did choose well, didn't I? A better woman than I merited, that's certain."

"Oh, *you*," the queen muttered, but the twinkle in her eye outshone her protestations.

He grinned at her, then turned to me again. "I bring this up to say that while parents make betrothals with the best of intentions, sometimes their children simply know better. We wish you happiness, our almost-daughter."

The room laughed again, warming to his good humor.

"And we are happy to announce that our nations' strong relationship continues," said Fetull. "While our previous treaty was unfortunately broken, your generous gift has more than satisfied Daril's part of the bargain between us. We pledge tonight that for the next five hundred years, should anyone attack Daril's Ga'beshi holdings, Cirivant will treat this as an act of war against ourselves."

Applause followed this declaration, particularly from the Darili aristocrats, and I nodded my acknowledgement. Erianthe seemed less thrilled—she stared straight ahead, her face a mask—but then I hadn't expected her to fawn over me for cleaning up her mess, especially not in public.

"I'm pleased that Cirivant is satisfied," I told the king,

"and we thank you for your understanding. As is said beyond the Crossing, the heart wants what it wants."

He considered that briefly. "Mm. Curious turn of phrase, but I believe I see your meaning."

"To Makou, I echo Your Majesty's good wishes," I continued, glancing past him at his son, who flashed me a conspirator's smile. "May your heart find the person it wants. I know I wasn't that person, but I have to believe that a better option awaits you."

The prince lifted his glass in salute.

"Makou, you've been gracious throughout these proceedings," I said. "It's been a pleasure to meet you, and I hope our paths cross in the future…though perhaps not in a temple, just to be safe."

The other guests laughed again, and Makou's smile widened before he drank. His brother patted him on the back as he set his glass aside, the two of them chuckling together while their mother spared them an indulgent glance.

The dinner continued uneventfully from that point, with new dishes being brought every fifteen minutes or so. The court musicians played, a troupe of dancers cavorted in the aisles, and I made quiet conversation with my siblings while my filling stomach pressed up against my bodice. But the peace couldn't last, and as the first desserts appeared, Erianthe stood and waited for the room to fall quiet.

"I have an announcement," she said—unnecessary, really, as the eyes of the room were already on her. "After the chaos and *unpleasantness* of the last days, the princess has decided that she does not possess the temperament necessary to rule well. She realizes now the sacrifices that one must make as queen," she continued, staring down at me, "and she does not feel that she can give what is expected of her. Therefore, she has decided that in the best interest of Daril, she is renouncing her claim to the throne in favor of my son Edes."

The rumblings echoed around the high-ceilinged hall immediately, and I cut my eyes to Edes, who looked grimly at his plate.

"So you see, dear brother," said Erianthe, turning to Fetull, "Daril *will* uphold its treaty with Cirivant."

"This is...unexpected," Fetull replied, looking past Erianthe at me. "And while I certainly support a future in which my nephew rules in Daril, I have to wonder if this is truly in the realm's best interest."

Erianthe laughed softly, though her cheeks began to redden. "*Your nephew* has been preparing since birth to guide Daril with a steady hand. Educated by the finest tutors in the kingdom, fluent in multiple languages, instructed at arms and diplomacy alike. He will make a fine king in time. *She*, however, is only now beginning to pick up the rudiments of our people's tongue. She knows little of our history, our culture, our gods. Besides," she said, directing her attention toward the assembled Darili nobles, "this is a human kingdom, and the princess, regardless of what virtues she may possess, will forever be wanting on that count."

I sat down the table from her and took it, clenching my fists in my lap and trying to school my expression...but I was surprised to hear the rumblings continue, and from their tone, it seemed that not every mind in the room was aligned with my mother's.

"If the princess is unschooled in various respects," said Fetull, "it would be unfair to place the blame on her head. After all, having grown up outside of Daril, she cannot be expected to possess a full knowledge of its ways."

"And do correct me if I'm mistaken," Cofali interjected, "but the fault for Susan's foreign upbringing lies with *you*, does it not?"

I glanced down the table and caught the eye of her daughter Velia, who nodded sharply back at me.

"The past is behind us," said Erianthe. "What matters now is the future of Daril, and that has once again been settled. A child of Terol blood will sit the throne when I am no longer able to fulfill my duties to the realm." Smiling at her brother-in-law, she added, "It seems that the new treaty for Cirivant's naval resources is now unnecessary, as the original bargain is being kept."

Fetull looked at his wife, then back at Erianthe. "This is true."

"Then perhaps Cirivant would consider returning the item with which its support was purchased."

He reached into a pocket and produced the Aen crystal. "This, you mean?"

"Indeed. As Daril has kept faith—"

"*Daril* has not kept faith. *Susan* has." Pushing himself to his feet, he looked down at my mother, who simmered with quiet fury. "When I learned that Daril could not keep its bargain, I asked for your necklace in compensation for the continued protection of our colonies. You offered your daughter's hand instead. It was *she* who offered this crystal to Cirivant, not you—and if our new treaty is unnecessary," he continued, looking at me, "then I will return the crystal to its rightful owner."

"You are mistaken, brother," Erianthe replied through a forced smile. "That is a *Darili* treasure—"

"No, it's not."

Erianthe wheeled around and glared at Edes, who shrugged in the face of her anger. "That came from Shadowbane," he continued. "It's Susan's, or maybe Terj's, but it's not ours."

She laughed weakly. "Perhaps my son's education is not yet complete. He should recall that Daril provided the crystals used in the forging of that sword—"

"That matters not," said a woman's voice from out in the hall. "The sword belonged to the Watcher."

Shocked, I watched Enarl, Fanakel's beautiful aunt, rise from her seat at one of the nearer tables. "Daril freely gave the crystals necessary to forge Bright Blade," she said, her voice carrying impressively. "As all of us who participated in the sword's creation gave freely of our resources and our people. The sword belonged to the Watcher for life, and as the princess was the final Watcher, the sword is hers. That would include its components."

The scraping of a wooden chair on stone drew my attention to the other side of the main aisle, and I feared the worst as I saw Rokund stand. "The elf's correct," he said, folding his arms as he looked back at Erianthe. "Daril relinquished its claim to those crystals when Heart's Blood was forged. You've got the girl's birthright, Erianthe—are you going to beggar her as well?"

That little speech sent the hall's chatter to a new pitch, and I watched as Rokund turned to Enarl and curtly nodded. She reciprocated and started to speak again, but Ganeel beat her to it.

"Taln'een agrees with Blackhorn Mountain and Nokan'ti," she said, stepping into the aisle to better stare down my mother. "And need I also remind you, Erianthe, that you took no action to free *your own daughter* from Firebrand?"

The fact that the peoples who'd made the damn sword still refused to agree upon its name wasn't lost on me, but at least the non-Darili representatives looked equally peeved.

"We sheltered Susan and her companions when you threatened to execute her," Ganeel continued. "You have no claim to anything of the Watcher's."

"Perhaps I misheard you, Great Mother," said one of the nobles from a table near her, "but did you just accuse our queen of trying to *execute* the princess?"

"It was a misunderstanding," Erianthe hastily interjected.

"No, it wasn't," said Anji, who stepped onto her chair to be seen in the sea of taller diners. "I was there, or have you forgotten?"

"As was I," said Fanakel, rising with her. "We stopped in our travels to aid a village that had been attacked by

Outsiders. We *saved* most of those people. And when they showed their appreciation by shackling us and carting us to you, you threatened to kill the princess for dereliction of duty." He folded his arms and glared at my mother, who'd gone scarlet. "The dwarf's correct," he said, cocking his head toward Anji. "I mean, you don't forget your first time breaking out of this castle. *That* was a night."

"A *misunderstanding*," Erianthe insisted.

"Really?" I asked. "What part of it was a misunderstanding when you came to my cell and told me about this Darili princess who'd gotten pregnant by a water elemental and abandoned her baby in my backyard? The choice you gave me—"

"That's enough, Susan," she snapped.

"*The choice*," I repeated, "was either returning to the Crossing to work off my mother's sins or face execution in the morning. You didn't even have the decency to tell me who you were," I said as I stood. "So here's how this is going to work, Mother. I renounce my claim to the throne, just like you want. Your Majesty," I continued, looking at Fetull, "if Cirivant is satisfied with the original treaty and unopposed to returning that crystal I gave you *for Daril's sake*, then I would appreciate its return. Then my friends and I will depart," I said, looking back at Erianthe. "Not permanently, but for a time."

Narod cleared his throat. "How long?"

"I'm not sure yet. We're going to make a journey in honor of my uncle," I explained. "He was the previous Watcher. Spent almost forty years trapped by the Crossing, living alone in a little cabin, and he never got to go anywhere. Worse than that, he knew he couldn't have a family or live closer to town because the Outsiders would come, those monsters he was condemned to fight, so he lived and died alone. Some kid found his body in the woods. He spent most of his life cursed so that you people could sleep safely at night," I said, turning to face the room. "You should have statues erected in his honor. You should tell stories about him. But you don't even know his name. Or that of his granduncle, who was Watcher before him. Or any of the other Watchers. Those men had no choice but to live by that hole in the ground you made and spend their nights killing creatures that most of you can't even imagine, and you'd all but forgotten about the people you'd damned until I came here."

Silence greeted my spiel, and I maintained it for a long, awkward moment.

"Malachi Cole, if you're curious," I said. "That was my uncle's name. So we're taking a trip to see some of the places he always wanted to go but could never reach because of you. It should be at least a few weeks until I return. Oh, and my brother is accompanying me."

Erianthe's eyes opened wide as she reached for Edes. "What are you—"

"*Me*, Mother," Jerrcoa interrupted from the end of the table, and waved for her attention. "Susan's taking me."

"*You*? Absurd. No."

"Actually," said Narod, "I think that's a fine idea." Erianthe spun toward him, mouth opening, but he calmly said, "Jerrcoa is nearly a man, and Edes had certainly traveled at his age. This will be good for him."

"Yeah," I added, "this is *sightseeing*. It's not like, you know, we're going off to fight monsters or anything."

My mother started to protest again, but Narod had fixed her with an unusually stern expression, and she found no help among the Cirivantis. With a brusque huff, she raised her chin and turned back to her guests, most of whom had yet to touch their desserts. "Thank you for coming," she said stiffly. "I wish you safe travels home."

And with that, she marched from the room in a swirl of skirts.

Narod shared a look with his brother, then rose and nodded to the other diners. "The queen is indisposed, and I should attend to her. Please enjoy yourselves in our absence," he said, and hurried after his wife.

Once the door closed behind them, Fetull rose and walked down the table toward me, "My dear, this belongs to you," he said, putting the Aen crystal in my hand. "And should your travels bring you to Ga'besh, you and your companions would be honored guests in our court."

I thanked him and forced myself to eat—the spiced fruit tarts were too good to waste—and the rest of the room eventually dug in. But after the last of the three dessert courses had been brought forth, the dancers had ended their routines, and the guests were beginning to disperse, I headed to Jerrcoa's spot and sought my friends in the crowd, and they quickly joined me. "I think we should leave tonight," I murmured. "Just in case someone gets interesting ideas by morning."

"We're packed," said Anji, and Mia nodded.

"As am I," said Fanakel. "Shall we wait for moonrise?"

"Shouldn't be more than an hour or two," I replied. "That's a plan. Meet in Jerrcoa's apartment."

"I'll show you the way," he offered, pushing his chair back from the table, and the other three followed him out of the dining hall.

Before I could make my excuses and leave to fill Terj in on the change in plans, Enarl approached. "Princess," she said, regarding me with an inscrutable expression.

I curtseyed. "Your Serene Majesty. That was, um...unexpected."

Her mouth twitched. "Considering our previous meeting, you mean?"

"Well, I wasn't going to bring it up. I've already angered one queen tonight."

"Most effectively." She glanced down at her dress and smoothed an invisible wrinkle. "I...may have been hasty. In my prior treatment of you."

I frowned, waiting for elucidation.

Though Enarl struggled, she soon managed to corral her thoughts. "Though I am a queen, I am also a mother," she said softly. "My youngest daughter is but thirty-seven.

I admit that I was furious when you abandoned your duty and allowed Outsiders into our worlds—"

That wasn't my duty, I started to say, but bit my tongue.

"—and yes, I blamed you for our dead. Much as your own mother did, it seems," she added with a brief, wry smile. "But then I saw the recording. A maladetan copy of the one my nephew brought home with him. And…"

When she fell silent, I asked, "Yes?"

"I saw that massive *thing*. The one you slew. You looked so tiny beside it, and…and all I could think of was what if that were my daughter in your place, and no one would help her? And she had to kill something like that creature?"

"But then I'm not True, so it doesn't really matter what I had to fight, does it?"

"No," she agreed, "you are not True, but…" Her face softened. "You down below, with only my nephew, a dwarf, another human, and whatever that other person was, perhaps the Divine know—"

"She's Unaran and the queen of Banilgh. Younger than I am."

Enarl shuddered. "Though you are not True, there is a standard of decency that the Divine direct us to uphold to lesser beings. You were mistreated."

That was, I reasoned, the closest I was going to get to an apology from an elf, and I treated it as such. "Your support tonight was much appreciated."

"It was fairly given. Be safe in your travels, Watcher," she said, and glided off to rejoin her brother without another word.

Terj concurred with my misgivings about overnighting in Deoni, and we were soon on our way through the corridors to Jerrcoa's apartment. Having changed into leggings, a sweater, and a cloak against the night chill, I moved quietly through the castle, clutching my nylon backpack straps and listening for footsteps in corridors. My Banilghish sword rested in Shadowbane's old leather scabbard at my side, a comforting object lying against my leg. Terj moved beside me, nearly invisible, and darted ahead as necessary to look for unfriendly faces. After dodging a pair of guards on patrol, we made it to my brother's rooms and let ourselves in, where we found Jerrcoa waiting with Fanakel. The elf carried a pack made of waterproofed cloth, while Jerrcoa sat with a daypack-sized satchel at his feet.

We would really need to make shopping a priority once we got home, I mused.

Home.

A pang in my chest made me reflect upon the absurdity of the situation. Deoni *should* have been home. That castle should have been the place where I'd grown up, now as familiar to me as my own name. Instead, I was fleeing it by night for the little community in the middle of nowhere that I'd griped about for so many years, a town that barely warranted mention on maps and to which my only tie was one of accident. For all its shortcomings, however, Cole's Crossing was home to me in a way that Deoni would never be, the place that came to mind unbidden, fuzzed with the haze of nostalgia. My people were there—not my blood, perhaps, but the folks who remembered me as the mayor's daughter and shopped at my family's store and waved when they passed. They would never know about the things I'd done beyond the Crossing—that I was anyone other than Susan Cole—and that was for the best.

Whatever else I'd done, home still awaited.

I'd barely had time to drop my gear when Mia and Anji arrived, locking the door behind them. "This is us, then," I said, turning to Terj. "Are you sure you're okay to do this tonight?"

Absolutely. Out the window?

Fanakel unlatched it without hesitation, and Terj slipped through the opening and into the night sky. *Step out*, he told us. *I've got you.*

Anji went first, tapping the air with her toe until she realized it was thick enough to support her and sat down on the cushion Terj had created. She scooted back to give Mia room to board, and then Fanakel and I awkwardly carried Jerrcoa to the ledge and slid him over. Mia helped him move into place and tuck his useless legs out of the way as Fanakel stepped out. I was last, taking care to close the window, and I reached for Terj as I settled in. *Are you sure? If we're too heavy, we'll make other plans.*

He didn't even sound strained when he replied. *I'm much stronger than I was the last time we did this*, he assured me. *Ready?*

As ready as anyone would be before a long-haul flight. We had a considerable trip ahead of us, and though Terj had the advantages of speed and being able to avoid the terrible roads, it would still be at least half a day to the tunnel back to the Crossing.

Just don't forget to put the windshield up.

Ooh. Right.

I winced at the thought of what could have been as I felt the walls of air rise around us like the doors of a car. Terj estimated that he could cruise along at about sixty miles an hour on a calm day, and for the rest of us, getting blown off his homemade conveyance midflight would be a quick and messy end.

He flew slowly at first, as if testing our weight and maneuverability, then headed over the castle wall and down toward the river. As we neared, I saw my father rise from the surface to meet us, and I stuck my arm through the dense air beneath me to touch his hand as we passed. *I'll be back*, I promised him.

Be careful, soul of my soul, he replied, and sank again as Terj steered us away.

Once we'd cleared Deoni and were speeding over the moonlit countryside, I stretched and settled in. *All right?* I asked Terj.

Just fine. I could do this all night.

He sounded confident, so I allowed myself to relax. "Well," I said to our crew, "if no one minds, I think I'll sleep while I can."

Go ahead, Terj urged.

Anji and Mia had already made beds for themselves with their packs and cloaks, and Fanakel stretched out beside them. Jerrcoa, however, huffed his disbelief as we bedded down. "How are you *sleeping*?" he asked indignantly. "We're high above the ground, going faster than anything, and you're taking a nap?"

"Not our first flight," said Mia. "And if you think this is fast, you should see Suze's driving."

"Assuming the cars will start," I pointed out.

"One problem at a time." Spooning behind Anji, she said, "Stay up if you want, Jerrcoa, but you're not going to see much until daylight."

I'll keep an eye on him, Terj told me, and with that reassurance, I wrapped myself in my cloak and soon knew no more.

Morning dawned over the wasteland, and I woke to the sound of Fanakel munching on crackers. He offered me the bag, but after the banquet, my stomach wasn't in the mood for more. Terj put us down by some lonely dunes for a pit stop, then insisted he was fit to keep going. As Anji combed her hair and Mia did a number on Fanakel's cracker stash, Jerrcoa stared at the unfamiliar world with wide eyes, taking it all in while Terj steered us toward the southwest.

A few hours later, after I'd drunk most of the water I'd packed the day before and was beginning to come around to the idea of breakfast, the tunnel entrance appeared, a dark hole set into a hillside at the end of a rough path through the scrubland. Unlike my last trip through, Erianthe had recalled her soldiers, and the way was unguarded—appropriate, as the tunnel opened in the no-man's-land between Daril and the Meali Republic. Terj guided us to the edge of the tunnel and landed, and most of us stood for a moment to get our bearings before proceeding. Jerrcoa couldn't go far without assistance, but he studied the horizon like he was trying to burn the unforgiving land into his memory.

Soon, we regathered for the final push. *Here's the plan,* said Terj, not bothering to materialize. *I can fly us through there, but I'll need to stay low, and I'll go slowly. It's too dark to risk travel at speed.*

"Why has no one bothered to rig real lights in there, anyway?" I asked. "The light streaks in the walls are pretty, but they don't do enough to give you visibility."

"And what happens when you meet someone coming from the opposite direction?" Mia chimed in. "Dwarven carriages take up most of the tunnel width—what do you do if two meet?"

"It's customary," said Anji, "that if one is in a vehicle like that, one sends word ahead. The hub at the Crossing is large enough to permit multiple vehicles to pass—"

"But how do you send word?" Mia interrupted. "You're not traveling with maladetas."

"No," she replied, chuckling. "All of our carriages are built with a relay system. There's an indicator set among the controls. When you traverse any narrow passage, such as the tunnels, you turn your beacon on, and anyone who comes close will see your position and trajectory on their instruments. That's how we avoid crashes."

Obviously, I don't have anything like that, said Terj, *but if we encounter an oncoming carriage, I'll take us to the ceiling. Ready?*

Without further ado, he gathered us up again, and we proceeded, using Anji's forged lighter as a tiny torch through the darkness.

The tunnels weren't particularly large, maybe twenty feet wide and fifteen feet tall, and though I had no firm idea as to their length, I estimated that it was about ten to fifteen miles from each entrance to the midpoint anchored on Earth. Colorful lightning zipped through the stone walls as we passed, always heading in the opposite direction, toward the Aen. While there *was* Aen within the tunnels, it decreased in concentration as we progressed, and the air began to take on the curiously prickly quality I'd only noticed after having been on the four worlds. Standing at the tunnel mouths, I could feel the sheer potential in the atmosphere, the raw power available for the taking. Back in Cole's Crossing, where only a trickle of Aen flowed out, I found myself missing that sensation, but I had it easy. My elemental abilities were unaffected by the presence of Aen, whereas Fanakel's skill with magic and Anji's forging talents were useless once past the Crossing. I didn't know how Mia would fare once we were home. While she'd scored her share of free drinks in college, she'd never attempted anything approaching her full-blown tekorish mind control in our hometown, and I had no idea how effective it would be beyond the Aen.

After about an hour of slow flight, we emerged from the tunnel into the hub of the Crossing, an artificial cavern bigger than our high school gymnasium through which crosswinds constantly blew from the connected worlds. The squared-off openings were arranged like an X, with the opening to the Honslia tunnel straight ahead of us on the far side, Ga'besh somewhere to our left, and Ildon to our right. Terj aimed us toward a smaller opening between the Ildon and Honslia tunnels, which instead went to the surface, and set us down at the foot of the staircase. *You'll need to walk from here to the top*, he said. *It would be difficult to maneuver so many people up a winding path like that.*

As we shouldered our packs, Jerrcoa slipped his on, then said, "I'll be slowest in climbing. If you want to go ahead and perhaps wait for me—"

His sentence ended in a yelp as he floated off the floor. *I can take one*, Terj told him. *We're not leaving you to crawl if possible.*

"Thank you," he mumbled.

Rest easy, kid. You'll be pushing yourself soon enough.

With Terj bringing up the rear and Anji leading, torch in hand, we ascended and emerged into afternoon sunlight, and I did a double-take before recalling that the Kopaati exit's time zone was a few hours behind home. The Earth exit had been camouflaged as an abandoned asbestos mine, an unassuming pit surrounded by a ten-foot barbed wire fence. The hole that Outsiders had ripped through the fence would have easily admitted spelunkers, but the threat of mesothelioma kept the curious away. I still wasn't sure who in Cole's Crossing had fenced off the area in the seventies and why the town had seemingly accepted the explanation that the place was a dangerous mine without question, but between the influence my family had long exercised over the place and Ms. Quince's stories of the occasional maladetan son being guided to Earth in search of a better life, I had theories.

Staring up at the budding trees in the woods around us, I caught my breath and acclimated. Mia thought it was mid-March, and the weather seemed to support her conclusion: high fifties and breezy with a few passing clouds, that transition period between the threat of snow and the onset of true spring.

Mia cracked her back and grinned. "Home sweet home, yeah?"

"Yup. Want to see if the cabin's still standing?"

"Cabin?" echoed Anji. "I thought you said we would use your other house…"

"Oh, absolutely," I reassured her, "assuming it hasn't been seized for tax delinquency. But we'll want to drive there from the cabin, and until we get everyone properly disguised, we should avoid the locals."

"*Ah.* Do you recall if there was an extra razor in the bathroom?"

"We'll get you fresh ones if there aren't," said Mia, slinging her arm around Anji's shoulders. "All right, y'all, last push. Let's do it."

With Terj continuing to float my brother along, we made the twenty-minute hike through the woods. My guts unclenched as the cabin came into view, whole and apparently as sound as it had ever been—the windows and door were intact, and nothing had punched a hole in the ribbed steel roof over the winter. I lifted the flowerpot on the porch and found the key, then let us inside.

The place was covered in dust, and I spotted a few dead roaches lying belly-up along the baseboards, but when I flipped the switch by the door, the bulbs in Uncle Malachi's beloved deer antler chandelier illuminated. "Thank God," I muttered, and started assessing the damage while the others dropped their bags. A quick inspection of the place showed that it was much as we'd left it the previous July, albeit with the addition of grime, cobwebs, and insect corpses, and the water ran clear after a few minutes. Fortunately, the toilet still flushed, though the bowl was stained. The ancient avocado-colored fridge hummed and opened to a blast of cold air, though there was nothing edible within—even the few condiments Ms. Quince had left behind were expired. The microwave clock blinked, unsurprising evidence of a power failure, but the fact that the microwave itself seemed to be operational was welcome news.

Terj blew the dust off Uncle Malachi's ratty brown leather recliner and deposited Jerrcoa in the chair, then switched into his physical form once more. *Pull the handle to your right*, he instructed, and smiled as the footrest popped out. *There, that should be comfortable for the moment. Give me your bag.*

Jerrcoa handed it over and bit his lip as Mia opened the closet and began producing cleaning implements. "I can help…"

"You're fine, lad," said Anji, pressing a broom into Fanakel's hands. "The rest of us can make short work of this—*ah*, not you," she snapped as Terj tried to commandeer the vacuum cleaner. "You've been working all night. Sit."

I'm not tired—

"Then keep Jerrcoa company, eh? Please?"

Fanakel nodded, and Terj, with a soft sigh, gave in.

I rummaged through the bedroom drawer in which I'd hidden my purse, then plugged in my phone to charge and checked my driver's license. Satisfied that at least one piece of identification in my possession was still valid, I grabbed my keys and Uncle Malachi's, then headed for the door. "Wish me luck," I called over my shoulder, and silently prayed.

My Accord was a sturdy, decent sedan, but months of sitting in the woods had left its battery with barely a flicker of life. The car sputtered, and the dashboard indicators illuminated, but there wasn't enough juice to make the engine start purring. But my inheritance from Uncle Malachi had also included his beater Chevy pickup truck, which was at least sixteen years old, equal parts red paint and rust, and dented in the bed from its encounters with Outsiders. That thing must have been magical, as it rumbled to life as soon as I turned the key. I had half a tank of gas, plus sufficient washer fluid to get the winter's dirt off the windshield, and when I cautiously backed up and turned the vehicle around, nothing fell off.

"We've got wheels," I announced on my return to the cabin. "The truck started."

"What about my Corolla?" Mia asked, looking up from her dusting.

"Where are your keys?"

She fished them out of her purse, which she'd squirreled away in the storage closet, and went out to check. I heard the engine turn over and gave her a thumbs-up as she came inside. "Filthy but functional," she declared. "Which is good, since now we can divide and conquer."

I frowned. "What do you mean?"

"Well, you need to check on the house, right?"

"And see about my taxes, and get Dad's license plate renewed—"

"Yeah, the *fun* stuff. Meanwhile, yours truly can zip on down to Walmart and the medical supply store. We need a wheelchair, clothes, food, toiletries, all that good stuff."

"I need to take my debit card with me—"

"No sweat, I can handle this."

"And your plate's expired, too," I pointed out.

"Only since February. If I get pulled over…well…" She batted her long lashes and flashed a gorgeous pout. "I'm *so* sorry, Officer," she said in a voice that suggested silk sheets and mirrored ceilings. "Can't you let me off with a warning?"

I smirked at her theatrics. "*If* that works here."

"Guess we'll find out. So, is there a tape measure handy?"

While I took over on the dusting, Mia attacked the rest of our crew with the tape we'd found with Uncle Malachi's tools, making notes. Her list was long by the time I finished, and she headed out the door, dead cell phone in hand. "I'll charge this in the car," she told me. "Back as soon as I can. Good luck with your, uh…taxes," she said, grimacing.

By then, my phone had powered up enough to start, and I finally had confirmation of the date—Mia was right. It was a Friday afternoon, which wasn't great for renewing tags and such, so I decided to bypass the county office and ask for help. Ignoring my overflowing inbox and the massive notification numbers on my socials, I traded my cloak for one of Uncle Malachi's black windbreakers, kissed Terj goodbye, and headed into town.

CHAPTER 9

Cole's Crossing was never a bustling community, not even in its eighteenth-century heyday. Dad and Uncle Malachi's ancestor, Samuel Cole, came west from Virginia with his family and settled along the forested shore of a wide lake in 1736. He'd probably have moved on had he not stumbled upon the last Native American Watcher, who was sick and dying alone. Since Samuel was the only human for miles, Terj chose him, and the maladeta who had been living near the previous Watcher explained the gig. Unfortunately but unsurprisingly, Samuel didn't bother recording the name of his predecessor, but *his* name soon became attached to the area after he began supporting his family with a ferry business. Most people thought "Cole's Crossing" was a reference to that long-defunct operation, never imagining what lay hidden underground.

The Cole's Crossing I knew was a typical small town of minimal importance to anyone who hadn't been raised there: an honest-to-God Main Street with a few shops and eateries, a tiny bank, a lawyer and a doctor to handle the locals' emergencies, two large-animal vets to handle the more important problems on the farms outside of town, and a police force of three who mostly saw drunks home safely and gave them stern talking-tos. A committee of local biddies kept the flowerboxes and hanging baskets blooming in our commercial strip. The only option on Sunday morning was Grace Methodist, but since most of the town had been baptized and married there, attendance remained steady. My family's general store offered pantry essentials, Antoinette's would fry up anything that stayed still long enough and serve it with vegetables cooked in bacon grease, Donna King cut hair and shared gossip in a one-woman beauty parlor, Dirk's Hunt Camp kept outdoorsmen ready through the seasons, and old Mrs. Fielding ran a dress shop that might have last offered fashionable attire during the Reagan administration. People who hadn't set foot within Harris County High for decades still came out for Friday-night football games to pull for the Jaguars. It was, in sum, a place that you might be *from*, but one to which few people ever moved.

And God, I'd missed it.

I'd missed the root-cracked sidewalks. The one lady who painted her mailbox pink and stenciled flowers all over it. The house with the icicle lights dripping off the eaves, which I knew damn well would still be there in July. The guy on the corner who flew an American flag in front of his house only slightly smaller than the massive one flapping over the car dealership twenty miles away. The winter-brown lawns and neighborhood watch signs and Jason Crewe, who'd built himself a jacked-up monstrosity of an F-250 in senior year and kept driving it as if hoping he'd stumble onto a pro-am monster truck rally. The Baker dogs, a pack of mutts that never left their yard but barked at anything that came within fifty feet of the property line. The lone stoplight at the corner of Main and Church, which really should never have been upgraded from a four-way sign. For once, seeing everything I'd wanted to run from left me strangely contented, like I'd come in from the cold and shoved my feet into a pair of fuzzy slippers. For all its flaws, I belonged here.

Or I had, once.

I pulled up in front of City Hall, a two-story brick building that also housed the library, the police station, an underused community center, and the town archives—a place I knew like my own house. The thought of walking through the double doors made my stomach knot. I'd grown up in City Hall, playing with my dolls and blocks beside Dad's desk, sneaking off to the library when he was in meetings to read yellow-paged bodice rippers, conning candy from the administrative staff who did much of the job of keeping our town running. Since Dad's death, I hadn't darkened the door—I didn't *want* to see City Hall without him working in there. But I needed an adultier adult, and that afternoon, I'd pinned my hopes on Joel Rogers.

Joel had been Dad's right-hand man for most of my life, a short, slightly chubby fellow with graying brown hair and blue eyes that squinted in any light more powerful than a forty-watt bulb. He was a genuinely nice man, the kind who'd happily manned school bake sales, shepherded Boy Scouts into the woods, and drafted hopeful but unlikely plans to increase local tourism. He wasn't a great leader, but he was a known quantity, and since he'd stepped up after Dad's death, he'd won a term in his own right. Joel wouldn't have been my pick of a person to turn to during a true emergency, but I figured he'd been around long enough to know a thing or two about paperwork.

Steeling myself to face a City Hall turned foreign and strange, I pushed my way inside and headed to the back of the building, where the mayor and town council kept their offices. The secretary wasn't on duty when I entered the suite—unsurprising, as little business was ever accomplished on Friday after lunch—so I let myself into the back and knocked on the door that should have borne my dad's nameplate.

"Come in!" called a familiar voice.

I cracked it open. "Joel? Hey, I'm sorry to bother—"

"*Susan!*" he cried, leaping to his feet. "Oh, my goodness, honey, come in! Where've you been? What…" He paused briefly as I stepped closer, and his jaw dropped. "Sweetie, what happened to your *face*?"

My hand rose to my cheek, too little, too late. "Oh, um…"

"Shit, I'm sorry, that was…*wow*, that was rude of me," said Joel, flushing. "Wow. Okay, uh…removing foot from mouth—"

"No, no, it's fine," I reassured him, "uh…car accident a few months ago. It's still healing."

"Jesus. Did you go through the windshield?"

"Something like that." I closed the door and stood awkwardly on the well-worn rug Dad had left behind, the one with the fringe I'd braided as a little girl. "I'm sorry to just show up like this, but I need help."

"Of course, honey. Sit down," he urged, pointing to the guest chairs. When I sank into one, he resumed his seat and steepled his fingers on the desk. "What's going on?"

"So…I left town for a while, yeah?" I said, beginning the story I'd mentally rehearsed on the way over. "First Dad, then Uncle Malachi…"

Joel shook his head. "Say no more. I get it."

"Thanks. And I'm still not sure what I'm doing in the long term. But I'm back for a few days, and I realized that I never bothered, like, stopping my mail or paying my taxes…"

He chuckled softly. "It's been taken care of."

"Huh?"

"Well, Annie Plunkett said you left her in charge of the store, and she has access to all the accounts. She's been keeping the books for years, so she handled that. And since you didn't draw a salary last year, I got together with Annie and Paul Croaker, and we figured that what the IRS didn't know wouldn't hurt them."

The mention of Cole's Crossing's only lawyer didn't soothe my anxiety. "What do you mean?"

"We filed a return for you. You actually got a reimbursement, and since I paid your property taxes, Annie gave that to me. I hope that's okay. Oh, and Annie's got your mail, too."

The knot in my gut unraveled just as my throat started to tighten. "You…paid for me?"

Joel's face softened, and he rose from his desk and grabbed a box of tissues, which he brought over as he took the chair beside me. "You listen to me, honey," he murmured. "Your dad pulled my butt, and this town's collective butt, out of the fire more times than I want to remember. He paid town debt personally on more than one occasion. I'm not going to see his little girl turned out of her house, got it?"

"I didn't know about—"

"Barnaby never made a fuss. Just said it was his duty." He waited while I blew my nose, then said, "I'd heard you were staying out in Malachi's cabin for a bit, but the place was locked up when I came by. Please tell me you're not actually thinking of moving out there. It's not safe."

"I was cleaning it up," I fibbed.

"Mm." Joel hesitated, cutting his eyes away from me as he thought. "Susan, what happened to your face...that wasn't really a car, was it?"

Saying nothing seemed like the best strategy at that point, but Joel found all the confirmation he needed in my silence. "I know about the monsters in the woods," he whispered. "Your dad told me all about them. He said that's why Malachi moved out there."

"He *told* you?" I whispered back.

Joel nodded. "I think Barnaby needed someone to confide in, and he knew he could trust me." When my brow furrowed, he shot me a sly smile. "My dad's dad was a weird guy. Just showed up on the edge of town one day. Had an accent, but he'd never say anything about where he came from—it's like he fell from the sky. He was a carpenter, and whenever he'd bash his thumb or whatever, he'd cuss a blue streak—or that's what we thought, since he never swore in English."

One of my eyebrows rose.

"I remember when your dad and Malachi and I were in our twenties and Ardith Quince moved to town," he continued. "I didn't think too much of her until I drove my granddad to your family store to pick up a few things, and she was there. He almost stumbled with his cane and cussed, and she overheard, and the next thing I knew, they were talking like old friends—and I couldn't understand a damn word of it."

I started to nod.

"Ardith left about the same time you did," said Joel. "I always kind of wondered if you came from the place where she and my granddad belonged. Like, maybe she came to look after you."

"She came for Uncle Malachi," I replied. "I was a surprise."

He nodded. "Barnaby said Ardith wasn't human."

"Yeah."

"So…my granddad…"

"They move here from time to time," I explained. "Their men, I mean. Their women are long-lived and have incredible…*talents*"—I wasn't sure that I wanted to go into magic with the mayor—"but their men are pretty normal. Some of them come here for a better life."

"Huh," he grunted. "And by 'long-lived', you mean…"

"Ms. Quince is at least five hundred years old."

"*Shit.*"

"They sent her to look out for Uncle Malachi—"

"Because he got the Cole Family Curse," he finished. "Barnaby told me about that. Said it always fell on a male Cole, so he was glad you'd be safe. But since it seems that you've met the monsters in the woods…"

I wadded up the tissue in my fist and forced myself to smile at Joel. "The monsters are gone. Trust me."

"You think?"

"I *know*. I broke the curse. So go ahead and build that campsite by the lake that you've been talking about forever—it's safe now."

Joel studied my face as if trying to spot a glimmer of deception, then leaned closer and took my free hand. "Did you find your people, honey?"

I nodded.

"And?"

"And I'm proud to be a Cole."

He gave me a squeeze and released me. "Glad you're back. Your house should be okay...is everything accounted for?"

"Honestly, I haven't been by yet," I replied, and groaned. "Need to get our car tags updated."

"Mm. Wait right there," he told me, then returned to his desk and picked up the phone. "Hey, Amy, this is Joel Rogers...yeah, hi," he said, brightening. "Listen, I know it's Friday, but I've got a favor to ask. I've got a young lady here who needs to get her plates legal. She's been away, and she doesn't want to drive around on expired tags. Would you mind waiting for her this afternoon?...Aw, that's great. Thanks so much."

Hanging up, he smiled at me and gestured toward the door. "Daylight's burning, kiddo, but she'll wait for a bit."

"Thanks, Joel," I said, going to my feet. "For everything. If my reimbursement didn't pay you back enough—"

"Nothing to worry about, sweetie," he replied, and shooed me on my way. "I'll see you around, now."

We headed to my home under cover of darkness that night, with Mia and me driving our sedans. I'd gone by the house on my way to the cabin to pick up jumper cables, and I had my car up and running before nightfall. By then, Mia had returned from her shopping excursion with a trunk full of plastic bags—clothing, certainly, but also pantry staples, snacks, and toiletries—plus a foldable wheelchair for Jerrcoa and a pair of fingerless gloves.

My brother had regarded the chair with suspicion at first, given the unfamiliar construction, but once Terj had deposited him in the seat and he'd dragged his feet onto the metal rests, he'd begun to grin as he pushed himself around the cabin. "It's lighter," he'd marveled. "Easier to turn."

Mia had then given him the gloves and explained their use, and soon, Jerrcoa had been lifted out of the cabin and off the porch, where he could wheel around to his heart's content.

I drove over with Terj beside me and Jerrcoa buckled in the back, while Mia took Anji and Fanakel. "This is going to be a little bumpy at first," I told Jerrcoa as I eased up the trail away from the cabin. "Once we hit the paved road, things will be easier, and I'll be able to pick up speed. We're not going incredibly fast around here, so don't worry about that."

He gripped the door handle as I maneuvered around trees and rocks. "How fast is fast, anyway?"

Faster than I can fly, said Terj.

"And this is safe?"

"Relatively," I replied, and said nothing more until we cleared the woods.

Jerrcoa didn't seem to be entirely on board with our mode of transportation by the time we pulled into the garage, but he didn't complain as I unpacked his chair and helped him scoot out of the car. "The door should be wide enough," I said, eyeballing the entrance, "but there's a little step up, so Terj, if you could help me get him over the hump…"

Working together, we had Jerrcoa in the house in short order, and I returned to the garage to await Mia. "She was right behind me, wasn't she?" I muttered.

At first. I think she took a detour.

"Going *where*?"

He shrugged and grunted, and so we carried our share of the luggage and purchases inside. I came back out again to update the tag on Dad's Explorer—by some miracle, the engine started without a jump—and I was checking the fluid levels when Mia finally drove up.

Fanakel jumped out of the back, pumped his fists into

the air, and shouted, "*Wooo!*"

"Shh!" I hissed, and motioned him into the garage. "Where've you been?"

He staggered toward me as Mia and Anji disembarked, the former smiling in the security light, the latter unnerved. "Took us out on the highway for a few minutes, just to get her up to speed," Mia explained, popping the trunk. "There wasn't much traffic."

"How fast did you go?"

"Oh, about eighty."

"That was amazing," said Fanakel, clapping me on the shoulder. "Exhilarating. I need a drink. Please tell me you have alcohol here."

Dad had left me with a decently stocked bar, and in short order, Fanakel and Anji were decompressing over bourbon while Mia sped off again to pick up pizzas. While she was gone, I put away the groceries and opened a beer for myself, then divvied up the clothes and passed around bags for trying. "You can use the master bedroom," I told Fanakel. "I still have all my stuff in my room, and Mia never moved out. I'm assuming you two will be bunking, yeah?" I asked Anji.

"If it won't cause offense."

"Of course not. Terj, you're with me?"

Is there space?

"For you, I'll squish. That leaves Jerrcoa," I continued, turning to him, "and I'm afraid the best I can do tonight is make up a bed for you on the couch. There are no bedrooms downstairs, but the couch is *comfy*. I've fallen asleep down here oodles of times—"

"That's fine," he said. "I wasn't expecting luxury."

I smirked down at him. "After months in Deoni, running water, flush toilets, and electricity feel luxurious to me."

He pointed to the fluorescent light over the kitchen sink. "And that's not forged?"

"That is one hundred percent human made. Electric

power, not Aen. Can't you feel the difference in the atmosphere?"

He made a face. "A little. I suppose you're more sensitive to it."

Believe me, there's a vast difference between here and Kopaat, Terj told him, then peeked in his bag of goodies. *Should I try these on?*

"I'll assist," I offered, and led him toward the staircase. "Back shortly."

Even with the two of us working together, it took a few minutes to get through Mia's haul, especially as Terj required explanations for each piece of his new wardrobe. I found a rolling weekender bag for him and packed everything away except his pajamas, a striped cotton set that seemed oddly formal but pleased him. I loaned him my spare bathrobe—the house was chilly, having been empty and barely heated all winter—and we returned to the kitchen just as Mia walked in with hot pies and garlic bread.

As we spread out between the table and the kitchen island with our plates, Jerrcoa looked up at Fanakel between bites and said, "Question."

Noticing the direction of his stare, Fanakel put his slice down. "Yes?"

"What do I call you?"

The elf paused to consider that, and I wondered how far he was willing to go. He'd given the rest of us permission to use his name, but Jerrcoa was a different matter. Elves only addressed their equals or inferiors by name, and while my little brother was also a born-and-bred prince, there was the *slight* matter of the elven superiority complex to consider. Sure, Fanakel was half human, but that didn't leave him ready to buddy up to every human in sight.

It was Anji, however, who came through with an answer. "Seeing as you'll need to choose a false name while we're here," she told Fanakel, "perhaps the boy could employ that without causing offense."

Fanakel frowned. "You think false names are necessary?"

"I do," said Mia. "If we're trying to sneak y'all around without being noticed, we need to come up with cover stories. I think we can pass you off as our college buddies, but that still means fake identities."

"Very well. What's your name?" he asked Anji.

She grinned. "Angie," she said, stressing the short *a* instead of the long *ah* of her usual nickname.

"That's hardly a change," Fanakel protested.

"Yeah, but she's lucky," I said. "Angie is short for Angela. It's not the most popular of names, but it's not weird."

Anji pulled off a fresh piece of garlic bread. "And once I shave, Mia thinks I can pass, especially if I keep my mouth shut."

"You're still too short," he pointed out.

"Dwarfism is rare but known among us," Mia explained. "And it comes in a few physical varieties. No one's going to ask Anji too many questions because that would be rude."

"What about me?" asked Jerrcoa.

I blotted grease off my pepperoni slice. "Once we get you dressed, you'll be fine—just don't say anything if you can avoid it. That translator won't cover your accent."

He nodded. "Is my name passable?"

"No…Jerry?" I suggested.

"Jerry," he repeated, trying it out, then smiled. "Sure, that works."

Mia and I looked at Fanakel, who wiped his hands clean before rooting through his clothing bag for the brown ski cap she'd bought him—not exactly ideal for mid-March, but it'd do in a pinch. He pulled it down almost to his eyebrows, keeping his ears tucked inside, and spread his hands. "And?"

"Hm. Still pretty," Mia declared, "but passably so. Just

don't talk to strangers."

He pointed to his jawline, which had begun to sprout reddish stubble. "Would it help if I let this happen?"

"It wouldn't hurt," I said. "Might work with the hat aesthetic. But if you're going to be miserable—"

"If she can shave hers off, I can grow mine out," he insisted, pointing to Anji. "And what am I to call myself?"

I chewed while I contemplated the question. His name didn't lend itself to easy transposition. "What about Phil? Would that work?"

"Seems inoffensive," Fanakel replied, and picked up his pizza. "Which leaves the one guy here whose accent won't be a problem."

Very funny, Terj replied, leaning against the counter as he watched us eat. He'd accepted a glass of water but declined all food. *Far simpler for me to feign mutism than to attempt verbal speech. Or just dematerialize—that's no trouble.*

"And what are we to call you?" he asked.

Terj cut his eyes to me. *Suggestions? The current moniker won't do.*

"Nothing leaps to mind," I replied. "Does anything appeal to you?"

He thought briefly, then said, *Sean. I could live with that.*

I laughed to myself. "Wish you'd said something months ago. If that's a name you preferred—"

No, he insisted, hurrying around the island to grip my shoulder. *No. You gave me my name. I want no other.*

I pulled him closer and kissed him, but he made an odd face as he straightened and licked his lip. *Is that what pepperoni tastes like?*

"Maybe? Or pizza sauce."

Interesting. I don't hate it…

"And I'll brush my teeth before bed," I said before finishing my slice in two bites.

After we ate, I fixed up the couch for Jerrcoa, who could

barely squeeze into the downstairs half-bath but made it work. Promising him a trip up a flight for a bath in the morning, I made sure he was comfortable and within easy reach of his new chair before going upstairs to join the others. While the evening was still fairly young, our body clocks were confused, we were exhausted, and Anji and Fanakel were embracing the massage showerheads Dad had installed.

I was too tired to bother with cleanliness that night, and despite his protestations that flying us for hours hadn't worn him out, Terj didn't argue when I suggested retiring. By then, the house had warmed to a comfortable sleeping temperature, and it took only a few minutes' work for me to put clean sheets on the bed and shake the worst of the dust from the comforter. With that accomplished, I stripped and threw on a T-shirt, then turned to catch Terj watching me. He immediately averted his eyes, but I chuckled and crossed the room, then guided his face back toward mine. *See something you like?* I asked.

Very much so.

I thought you didn't have real opinions on physical beauty.

I don't, he confirmed. *That hasn't changed. But I enjoy being in your presence, and I…I like it when you touch me.*

I ran my hands over his sleeve-covered arms. *Like this?*

Not quite.

He unbuttoned his shirt and tossed it aside, which only improved my view, and I let my fingertips trail over the muscles of his shoulders and chest. *How about this?*

Much better. He kissed me, first tentatively, and then with greater urgency as I reciprocated. *Does this please you?*

It's a start, I said, and slipped off my shirt. His eyebrows rose, and with great hesitation, he reached for me, exploring my unfamiliar curves. When he quickly abandoned his examination to resume kissing me, however, I almost laughed. *Not a boob man, huh?*

Sorry.

That's okay. They've never done much for me, either.

Terj followed me into bed, and as he made himself comfortable, he noticed me watching him and smiled. *Yes?*

Just curious—who designed the meat suit? I asked, brushing my fingers along his jaw.

Ganeel and Ardielta, I assume.

You didn't, say, pick your hair color?

They never offered me the option. Why, is something wrong with it? If there's a problem, they can make adjustments—

It's great, I assured him. *I just didn't know if this was a look you liked, if you were trying to cater to my taste, or if it was random chance.*

The shading on his thoughts brightened. *You like it?*

I think you're handsome, I replied, and rolled over to cut off the bedside lamp. *The maladetas do good work.*

I wasn't sure whether you would be disappointed, Terj told me as I settled into the old dip in the mattress. *Considering your preferences.*

What do you mean?

His laughter came out as a soft huff. *I've seen the way you look at Fanakel.*

Because he's objectively pretty. Even Mia appreciates that bit of scenery. But Fanakel is sleeping alone tonight, and you're in here with me, so what does that tell you?

That the maladetas know you decently well?

That I love you, silly boy.

He pulled me closer as I kissed him. *You could have had a prince.*

I don't want a damn prince. Terj's Aen pendant slid toward the mattress, and I reached for it in the darkness. *You're sure this doesn't hurt?*

It's painless.

Because if it does, I'll understand. Look, if my parents were able to figure it out, then surely you and I could do likewise.

Amusement flashed in his mind. *I thought the rule was that we didn't talk about your conception.*

We absolutely do not, but I'm trying to make a point.

And I appreciate that, he replied, finding my lips, *but you needn't worry. This is…growing on me.*

Yeah? Would you be up for a little experiment?

I sensed his sudden trepidation. *What sort?*

Just tell me how this feels, I said, and carefully reached past the elastic waist of his pajama pants.

After a few seconds of gentle manipulation, Terj's thoughts shifted from fear to a mixture of confusion, desire, and pleasure. *What…*

Well, nice to see that is operational, I teased.

He groaned as his body reacted. *Oh, that…okay, I get it. That's why they…*

Are you sure you get it? Because we could keep going. For science.

Another little groan told me *exactly* how Terj felt about that idea, and I released him for a moment to roll over to the nightstand. Opening the drawer, I felt around until my fingers found the small box Dad had given me when I was in high school, shortly after I started birth control for my acne. Though he'd been awkward about the whole situation, he'd wanted me to be safe.

I suspected that the condoms were long past their best-by date, but they'd do for the night.

What's that? Terj asked as I ripped a pack open.

Trust me, I said, returning to our experiment with protection at the ready. *If this goes how I think it will, you'll thank me shortly.*

I would say that I was the first awake the next morning but for the tiny fact that Terj didn't sleep. He perked up when I disentangled myself from his embrace and shifted behind me in bed. *Going somewhere?*

Bathroom, I replied, *and then I need to check in with Annie at the store. If I get there midmorning on a Saturday, she'll wring my neck. That, or I'll have to stock shelves.*

Do you need help?

Nah. I bent and kissed his forehead. *Rest up. I'll be back as soon as I can.*

I took full advantage of the shower, melting beneath the pounding jets, then brushed my teeth and contemplated booking a visit with the dentist while I was home. Daril didn't seem to have discovered the benefits of semiannual cleaning, and I didn't want to explore the wonders of premodern cavity treatment. Finally, I was clean enough to face polite society, and I braided my hair back and willed the water from my braid into the sink. Terj had vacated the bedroom by the time I emerged, but I found him in the kitchen with the coffeepot full and waiting for me, and I gratefully grabbed a travel tumbler to go.

The shop wasn't bustling when I arrived shortly after eight—for most locals, Cole's Crossing General Store was the convenient option when you forgot something at the big supermarket outside of town—but I found Annie and her son Dewey hard at work ringing up and bagging the purchases of one of the biddies who feared any drive of more than five miles. As soon as she left, Annie abandoned the register to give me a hug and fuss over me—where had I been, was I eating, what on earth happened to my face? I gave her my cover story about trying to get my head on straight and going through a windshield, then thanked her profusely for keeping the place running in my absence and handling my finances. She tutted, but I insisted that she give herself and Dewey five percent raises, then explained my plans. Some of my college friends had come back to town with me so I could check in on things, and then we were going west for a bit to see some of the places Uncle Malachi always wanted to go. Annie gave me a sympathetic smile at that, then started running through a travel checklist with me. Since I'd been decidedly under-mothered as a child, Annie had made it a point to pitch in, and though I was technically her employer now, some things never changed.

Once Annie was satisfied that I wasn't about to drive into the desert and drop acid, I thanked her and Dewey again, then headed home to get the house properly in order. When I arrived, I found Fanakel at the stove, tending a skillet of scrambled eggs, while Mia handled a pack of bacon and a bag of hashbrowns. Anji, who'd shaved off her beard that morning and looked a little naked without it, gamely chopped fruit. My brother and Terj were upstairs, they explained; Terj was the only one who could carry Jerrcoa around without breaking a sweat, and he was hanging out by the bathroom in case of emergency while Jerrcoa cleaned himself up. They appeared in short order, and after I willed Jerrcoa's hair dry for him, we tucked in.

The plan was to hit the road soon after breakfast, we decided. I'd covered my bases in Cole's Crossing, and Mia was doing her best to avoid detection by her mother. The necklace that Ms. Quince had enchanted for her had glowed pink the whole time we'd been in town, warning her that Janine was nearby. Having not spoken to her mother since our final semester of college, Mia had no desire to run into her on the street, especially now that she looked like she'd had massive amounts of high-end plastic surgery.

I couldn't blame her for her reluctance to have a chat with her mom, considering the things Janine had said to her during their last conversation. I'd sat beside her on our crappy dorm couch and held her hand for support while she came out to Janine, and so I'd heard nearly everything that had followed from Janine's end of the line: denial, anger, and virtual disownment, all topped with a heaping helping of threats of Hell. Unlike most of our neighbors, Janine attended the tiny fire-and-brimstone nondenominational church outside of town, widely regarded among my peers as a place where fun went to die. Though Grace Methodist wasn't officially on board with non-hetero relationships, the minister didn't condemn Mia to her face. Janine's pastor would surely have had no such reservations, assuming Janine had ever let her newest shame slip.

I didn't understand why Janine had turned out the way she had. She'd gone through her rebellious phase—after all, Mia was the result of a one-night stand with an exotic dancer in Vegas, a scandal for the daughter of such a conservative family—but while Janine had little to do with her parents, she'd continued to attend their church even after their deaths, where, per Mia, the *nice* people regarded her as the Whore of Babylon and the pastor used her as an example every time the sermon veered toward fallen women. True, Janine would have received whispers and similar side-eyed glances at Grace—small towns can be shitty like that—but at least folks would have been subtle about it. I imagined that Janine's standing among the church ladies wouldn't improve if anyone learned of her daughter's deviancy, but the fact that Janine had chosen *that* over Mia made me sick.

Mia offered to handle the breakfast cleanup while the rest of us packed, and since Terj had little luggage to speak of, he assisted her. Meanwhile, I went into Dad's study and dug in the closet until I found the fire safe, the place where he'd always stored our important documents. As I'd been away for months, paranoia made me open it and riffle through the contents—the deeds to the house and cabin and vehicles, an old bundle concerning the general store, my adoption paperwork, birth certificates, unused passports, all accounted for. I'd discovered after his death that Dad went a step further than many with his safe, as he also kept photo albums and some VHS tapes of home movies tucked in there as well—my first steps, protected against disaster.

My dad might not have created me, but he'd loved me. I knew that with my whole heart, which only made these reminders of his absence the more painful to bear.

Mia looked up from the soapy sink when I returned to the kitchen and began taking photos off the refrigerator. "What's up?"

"I don't want these to fade," I said, though it hurt to dismantle the display as Dad had last had it—I hadn't disturbed his fridge gallery since his death. Pictures of him and Malachi, of his parents, who'd died years before I came along, of his friends from City Hall, of me—all went into my stack for preservation. I hesitated before removing the last photo that Dad and I ever took, a throwaway image of the two of us on New Year's Eve ten days before his heart attack, but I pulled it from the door like ripping off a band-aid.

I carried the pictures back to the study and tucked them into the safe, then ran up to my room and returned with my pouch of Aen crystals. They wouldn't be of any use to me in Arizona, I thought, and at least they'd be safe while I was away. When I eventually returned to Kopaat, I'd need to support myself, and those blue-green rocks could sustain me for a good while.

By ten, the dishes were put away, the Explorer was packed—even my Banilghish sword, which recent experience made me loath to leave—and I'd locked up and lowered the heat again. We helped Jerrcoa into the seat behind me, Mia took shotgun, Terj claimed the other chair in the middle row, and Fanakel and Anji shared the back bench, where Anji, at least, fit comfortably.

"So," said Mia, having plotted our route on my phone, "if we don't stop, it's about twenty-eight hours to the Grand Canyon."

"Is anyone in a great rush to see the big hole, or can we make this an easy drive?" I asked my passengers.

"We're not being chased," called Fanakel from the rear, "and I'm in no hurry."

"Agreed," said Anji. "Let's take the easy route."

I turned to Mia. "Thoughts?"

"We could make Paducah by midafternoon," she replied. "Let's have a short day to be sure that no one gets carsick, and we'll push on tomorrow."

"Works for me."

The garage door closed behind us, and I glanced in my rearview mirror as the town I called home gave way to fields and trees.

CHAPTER 10

Our first day on the road wasn't particularly eventful for Mia and me, but the rest of our crew had a ball.

Having never been outside of Cole's Crossing until our previous trip, Terj sat with his face inches from the window, watching the towns and farms go by. The scenery wasn't great that early in the spring, but judging by the way he stared, he wasn't disappointed, especially once I hit I-64 and picked up speed. As for the others, that Saturday was a day of firsts: eighteen-wheelers, cows, and a roadside vulture feast, and that was just in the first half hour. They marveled at the radio—not only that such a thing existed without magic, but that the broadcast was partly recorded and partly live. Jerrcoa shouted at the sight of a jet flying overhead toward Lexington, and Anji and Fanakel craned their necks to see a vehicle that high above them. I wasn't sure how I was going to break the news to them about satellites, but I decided that this was a topic for another day.

We bought burgers for lunch and junked up at a gas station, at which time Jerrcoa earnestly declared a Snickers bar to be the best thing he'd ever put in his mouth. Fortunately, no one seemed to suffer from motion sickness, even the two in the back, and they didn't complain over the fact that the Interstate wasn't the most scenic of routes.

That afternoon, having switched time zones, we pulled off at a hotel outside Paducah, and I parked at the far end of the lot. "How do we want to do rooms?" I asked, turning to face the rear. "Most of the rooms should sleep four…"

"I'll pay for Anji and me to have our own," Mia volunteered.

"And it might be nice for the two of you to have some privacy," said Fanakel, pointing to Terj and me. "If you can afford a third room, the boy and I can share."

Jerrcoa perked at the offer. "You don't mind?"

The elf smirked back at him. "I've shared quarters with your sister. You can't be any worse."

"*Hey*," I protested.

Fanakel winked at me, then feigned injury when Anji punched him in the arm.

Mia and I took care of getting the rooms and keys, and the others joined us inside once we had a place to land. Dinner that night was easy—more pizza, courtesy of a joint across the road, which we ate in Mia and Anji's room—and I slept well and deeply, full of carbs, tired from the drive, and comfortable in Terj's arms.

We'd planned to meet in the lobby for breakfast at seven, Fanakel and I having arranged that I'd come knock once I awoke. Instead, Fanakel's polite but insistent knocking pulled me from sleep around five Sunday morning, and Terj got up to investigate.

What's wrong? he asked, opening the door.

"It's Jerrcoa," Fanakel murmured, stepping into the room with his hat pulled low over his tangled red hair. "He's been in discomfort for hours, and I can't do anything to help him—not this far from the Aen."

I slid out of bed and grabbed my leggings from the chair beside me, grateful for the wall blocking Fanakel's view. "Did he hurt himself?"

"No, but you should see this."

Concerned, I followed him down the hall to his room with Terj on my heels. When I walked in, I found Jerrcoa dressed in his pajamas and sitting in his wheelchair, rubbing his sticklike thighs. "What's going on?" I asked as

Fanakel locked the door behind us.

Jerrcoa looked up at me, his face tight. "Do you know the feeling when you lie on your arm for too long and it begins to tingle?"

"Sure. We call it pins and needles."

"Well, I woke to that sensation radiating through my legs," he said, continuing his agitated massage. "It's only worsened, and it's traveling toward my feet."

I grimaced and sat on the edge of his bed so that I wasn't staring down at him. "I'm sorry, that sounds like a mess. Does this happen often?"

"*Never*," he said slowly. "Not since before the fever. I've felt nothing in my limbs since I was three."

"Shit," I muttered, then glanced up at Fanakel, who shrugged.

"We're unaffected by that disease," he explained. "Most diseases, actually. I mean, *I* might be susceptible, but elves in general don't fall ill. I don't know anything about the course of his condition."

"But Anji does," I replied, rising. "Jerr, I'm going back to my room for some painkillers. I don't know if they'll help, but they shouldn't hurt you. Terj, could you please get Anji in here?"

By the time I returned with a bottle of aspirin, Anji had swept into the room in her new blue bathrobe and kicked the guys out. We waited awkwardly in the hall with Mia for a few minutes until the door opened again, and Anji motioned us inside. While I filled a glass of water for my brother and gave him a couple pills, Anji folded her arms and considered Jerrcoa as if studying a particularly tricky riddle.

"I'll remind you that I'm no expert," she began as he swallowed the medicine. "What I know of this comes from my cousin. So, uh…the humans have their own names for the illness that crippled Jerrcoa, but we call it Growing Fever. It's often mild and passes easily, but when it doesn't and paralysis sets in, you find growths in the patient's back.

Sometimes small, sometimes large. They're normally near the mid-back to the base of the spine."

"Like…tumors?" I asked. "They press on the spinal cord?"

She frowned, considering my terminology. "Perhaps?"

"Can you remove them?"

"You *can*, but they always return. Our doctors have tried. Sometimes, there's relief, but it never lasts, and the growths are often larger when they reappear. Best not to touch them," she said, then pointed to Jerrcoa. "He has the growths, just like my cousin did. But he felt them a moment ago, and—"

"They're smaller," Jerrcoa interjected. "I *know* what they feel like, I've had them most of my life, and I swear to you that they've shrunk."

I turned to Mia. "If he's got tumors back there that have been pressing on his spine, and the pressure is letting up…"

"That could explain the tingling," she finished. "Though who's to say what kind of damage has been done to the nerves?"

"And why would the growths spontaneously shrink *now*? What would trigger that?"

Unless pizza has medicinal properties, the only variable I can think of is the lack of Aen.

"We're barely affected by it," Jerrcoa countered. "Adepts can use it with study, but the loss of Aen shouldn't change anything about *me*."

It's not you that's changed. It's the growths.

"Assume the fever causes the growths," I said. "Whatever bacterium or virus is behind the illness…maybe it never leaves you after you're infected."

"Herpes," Mia muttered.

"Right. Say it lingers. It can be weak, but if conditions are right and it gets a toehold, it starts producing the growths."

She nodded. "Plausible…"

"Okay. But think of this," I continued, speeding up as an idea crystalized. "In the four worlds, you've got species that arise with Aen sensitivity and abilities. Dwarves, elves, maladetas—"

Forget them, said Terj. *We're born from it.*

"Of course. But while humans might be somewhat sensitive to the Aen, their abilities aren't as strong or inherent, right?"

"Yeah…" said Jerrcoa, frowning.

"Why?"

Anji spread her hands. "Because the gods didn't give them those gifts?"

"Well…maybe," I allowed, not wanting to get into a theology debate before breakfast, "but there's a more basic reason. *Humans aren't native to the Aen.*"

Mia's eyes widened. "Oh, *duh.*"

Jerrcoa looked at us like we'd lost our minds. "What are you talking about? We've always lived in Kopaat."

"No, you haven't," I said. "Ms. Quince explained it. Earth's like the barren island in the middle of the four worlds, and tunnels have opened here on occasion, but most of *you* don't like it here because of the lack of Aen," I explained, pointing to Fanakel and Anji.

"Didn't she mention a penal colony or something?" said Mia.

"I think so. But she told us that humans have gone exploring in the four worlds for ages. Daril or its predecessor civilizations may be old," I told Jerrcoa, "but sometime in the distant past, your ancestors came from Earth."

He appeared troubled by the notion.

"But think about it," I said to Mia. "We know that certain species that arose within the Aen can use it. Who's to say that's limited to *intelligent* species?"

Mia's thoughts were heading in the same direction as mine. "Maybe whatever causes that fever needs the Aen to survive."

Anji's eyes widened. "The longer he remains here…"

The rest of us looked at Jerrcoa, whose jaw had begun to sag. Closing his mouth with a snap, he stuttered for a moment, then managed, "Are you suggesting that the growths might *disappear*?"

"Maybe?" I replied. "I have no idea. But if the lack of Aen makes them shrink, and you're getting feeling in your legs—"

"I might yet walk?" he asked, his breathing quickening.

As much as I hated to rain on his parade, I didn't want to raise his hopes for nothing. "Let's not jump to conclusions. Mia's right—there's no telling what sort of nerve damage you might have without the growths. And even if you were to wake up with full feeling tomorrow, you don't have any muscle tone. I'm not trying to be cruel," I said as his face fell. "All I'm saying is that if the paralysis fades, you'll still have a long way to go before you're walking."

"But I *might* walk," he insisted as his eyes narrowed. "And that's more hope than I've had in nearly seventeen years."

"We'll take it a day at a time," I replied, squeezing his shoulder. "For now, give the drugs a chance to work—I don't want you miserable in the car."

While Anji returned to her room to shower and shave, Mia, Terj, and I dressed just enough to go to the lobby and grab breakfast without causing a scandal, and we brought plates back to the others. We checked out around eight, sufficiently fed and caffeinated for the trip, and when the coast was clear, Terj lifted Jerrcoa into his seat in the Explorer with a controlled gust. By then, the aspirin seemed to be doing the trick—the tingling sensation had dulled, my brother reported, though it stretched down to his toes, present but not painful.

"What's our destination today?" I asked Mia as she pulled up the map.

She poked around on the screen for a moment, her

mouth scrunched in thought. "Tulsa?"

"How far?"

"Seven or eight hours nonstop. No time changes."

"Works for me," I replied, and headed for the Interstate.

The day's trip was a long drive across southern Missouri along I-44, mostly small towns and stretches of trees waking to spring. With his painkillers having kicked in, Jerrcoa grew comfortable enough to doze, and he made up for his interrupted night's sleep with a nap against the window. Mia did her best to keep the radio on a pop or rock station, explain the music to Anji and Fanakel, and offer whatever tidbits she could about the area through which we were passing, but as neither of us had spent time in Missouri, she couldn't do much as a tour guide.

I caught glimpses of Terj's mood while I drove—often pensive or contemplative, sometimes concerned when Jerrcoa shifted in his sleep, but with a growing streak of unease. Around two that afternoon, as we neared Joplin, he finally revealed the cause. *Susan, I don't mean to cause trouble,* he began from behind Mia, *but I think there's something wrong with me.*

The others turned toward him, and though I kept my eyes on the road, I sneaked a look over my shoulder in the mirror. "What's up?"

There's an unfamiliar sensation in my torso. It's not pain, exactly—

Before he could clarify, his stomach growled loudly enough for the rest of us to hear.

Mia laughed. "You're *hungry*, Terj."

Oh. He sounded bemused. *Is this what hunger feels like?*

"Probably," I said. "Let's stop for gas, and we'll get you something to eat. Do you feel okay otherwise?"

He paused, taking stock of himself. *Perhaps a bit lethargic. The inside of my mouth feels odd...*

"Sounds like thirst," said Anji, extending her water bottle. "Go on, see if this helps."

Terj took a swig, waited briefly, then chased it with a longer one. *I think you're right.*

"Finish that, lad. I've got another back here."

"You've been corporeal for weeks, yes?" asked Fanakel as Terj chugged. "How are you just now realizing what hunger is?"

The maladetas said that Aen alone is sufficient to sustain the meat suit. Since we're so far from the Crossing now, I suppose it requires fuel of a different sort.

"Well," said Mia, "if the alternative to Aen is greasy fast food, you're in luck. Suze, find an exit."

We've already stopped for lunch—

"My dude. You all know I'm constantly hungry, and *he's* twenty, so he's a bottomless pit," she said, pointing to Jerrcoa. "I could eat again. Jerr?"

My brother nodded. "Could do."

"And fries for everyone else. There."

With my marching orders thus given, I found a McDonald's and stocked up at the drive-thru, then pulled into a parking space while Mia handled distribution. Once the food was passed around, we watched as Terj unwrapped a Big Mac and gave it a cautious sniff. "It's not gourmet fare, but it's decent," I told him. "Think you can try it?"

My saliva production appears to have increased.

"Your mouth is watering. Go for it."

He stared at the burger, hesitating for a few seconds, then took a bite. *Oh, this is so weird*, he reported as he chewed. *The grinding, the spit mixing in—*

"How's the flavor?"

Not horrible. He swallowed and bit off a larger chunk. *How much of this do I need to eat for the discomfort to end?*

"Only you can figure that out," Mia replied, "but you can probably polish the whole meal off. Try your fries."

"They're quite good," Fanakel offered from the back

bench.

Terj rooted in the paper bag for a fry and popped it in his mouth. His eyes widened as the salt and grease hit, and I laughed to myself as his hand shot back into the bag for more. "There should be some ketchup in there—"

Don't need it, he said, cramming a wad of fries down.

"Don't choke! The food's dead—it's not going anywhere," I reminded him, and passed over his drink. "Here, this is just water. Wash it down."

Within a few minutes, Terj had drained his cup, demolished the burger, and licked the last of the salt off his fingers. "Feeling better?" Mia asked between chicken nuggets.

He nodded. *Actually, yes. Not quite satiated, I don't think, but I should be fine for...wait, Susan...*

Terj protested until I made it to the speaker, and then he surrendered and thanked me when I thrust another meal his way. Within half an hour, he was full and comfortable enough to close his eyes and drift, and the back of the Explorer settled in for a group siesta while Mia kept me company.

Our hotel that night outside of Tulsa was nothing special, but it was adjacent to the parking lot of a slightly seedy strip mall featuring a Chinese buffet. After we'd claimed our rooms, Mia and I led the expedition, and the others grabbed plates and followed us as we made our way down the line of questionable dishes. Mia helped Anji, who wasn't quite tall enough, while I took care of Jerrcoa, and we crowded around a table to tuck in. Mia ordered pots of tea and glasses of water, and since the friendly staff barely spoke English, our posse could chat without spurring too many questions.

A couple hours and many cups of green tea later, we wandered back to the hotel, stuffed and groaning. Terj fell into bed beside me, miserable, and I turned on the TV to decompress. *Overdid it, huh?* I asked.

His eyes screwed shut. *How do you know when to stop eating?*

Don't inhale your food, and listen to your stomach. It'll send signals when you've had enough.

Now you tell me.

In retrospect, I mused, perhaps I should have checked in when he left the food line with his third heaping plate of fried rice. *This will pass. And hey, maybe you won't get heartburn.*

He inhaled deeply, then belched and clapped his hands over his mouth in shock. As I cackled next to him, he insisted, *I didn't know that would happen! What—*

It's just a burp. You swallowed air. Better out that end than the other, know what I mean?

Unfortunately, yes. Recall those frozen bean burritos that Malachi so adored.

Oh, God.

We lay there in silence for a moment while a local car dealership made its TV pitch.

I'm sorry, said Terj, *I shouldn't have—*

Don't apologize. Rolling over to face him, I smiled. *He did love those nasty things. Dad would have stopped ordering them years ago if not for Uncle Malachi.*

I shouldn't complain about him.

You were stuck as much as he was, I replied. *It's okay. I'd rather talk about him than forget him.*

If you say so.

I do. And now, I continued, handing Terj the remote, *I'm going to try to sleep and digest this food baby. You're not the only one who made a pig of yourself tonight.*

Do you mind if I change the channel?

Watch whatever you like. I'll see you in a few hours.

When I closed my eyes, I felt him scrunch closer in bed and kiss my forehead. *Susan?*

"Mm?" I grunted.

What's it like to dream?

Kind of trippy most of the time. Or nightmares. You're not missing much.

I snuggled against his chest, and he softly sighed as the commercials gave way to a laugh track.

Terj didn't need to shower, as a quick flicker out of physical form and back again was sufficient to reset him clean. But he'd been curious, and I awoke to a light beneath the bathroom door and the sound of pounding water. When he emerged, pinkened and dripping with a towel around his waist, he grinned sheepishly and said, *Sorry. It feels nice, and I lost track of time.*

Been there, done that, I replied, and slid out of bed to kiss him. *Get dry, you. I'll lather up.*

We beat the others down to breakfast, staking out a table as the business travelers grabbed coffee and runny eggs, and were settling in with our plates when Jerrcoa came rolling up, deftly maneuvering around the tables and chairs, with Fanakel right behind him. "Hey, y'all," I said, waving them over. "Pull up. Jerr, want me to grab you something to eat?"

"That can wait," he whispered, and pointed to his feet—which, oddly enough, he'd left bare. I was about to mention sanitation and the preference for shoes when he said, "Watch this."

After a moment's concentration, his right big toe twitched up and down.

"Holy *shit*," I said, leaning closer. "Do it again."

Jerrcoa repeated his trick, beaming like he'd just won a medal, and Fanakel looked on with a proud little smile. "He's been practicing since the small hours," he said quietly, conscious of the groggy guests around us. "Isn't that marvelous?"

"And the growths are still shrinking," said my brother. "Susan, they're *shrinking*. At this rate…"

If he kept going like he had been over the last two days, he'd be tap dancing by the end of the year. While I suspected that was unlikely, I couldn't bring myself to be a realistic downer. "That's wonderful," I said. "Who knows what you'll be doing in a week's time?"

Jerrcoa was still nearly floating when we packed up and hit I-40 for the trip out of the lower Midwest and into the desert Southwest. Now that everyone had spent a couple days on the road, Mia suggested a longer haul, and she aimed us toward Albuquerque. Our drive that day took us all the way across Oklahoma, through Amarillo and the northern chunk of Texas, and halfway across New Mexico. Never had I been so grateful to see the warm lights of our hotel, though I still felt like I was moving as I stood in front of the reception desk.

Having gained an hour, we'd arrived around six, and Mia declared that room vegetating wouldn't do. "I mean, we don't have to go hiking in the dark," she said, "but couldn't we do something together?"

Despite the long drive, the group eventually decided that a movie might be fun, and I found a quiet six-screen theater playing an inoffensive buddy comedy. We settled in with popcorn and candy for dinner, and Mia and I glanced at the others as the lights went down and the previews began. I'd expected Jerrcoa, Anji, and Fanakel to be pleasantly surprised, but Terj's nearly palpable excitement puzzled me until I realized its cause. Despite all the years he'd lived in Cole's Crossing, he'd never been to a theater—our closest option was twenty miles away, well outside the sword's radius. He smiled like a kid, contentedly munching on popcorn, and I couldn't help but be happy for him. Sure, Terj had a few centuries on the rest of us—he made even Fanakel look like a stripling— but so many of his experiences in the last few days were new, and in some respects, he seemed almost childlike as he explored the world beyond the Crossing in a body he didn't fully understand. Truth be told, my heart melted a little whenever I caught a glimpse of his pure delight.

We could keep doing this, I thought, as the movie

began. There were plenty of corners of the country that were new to me, and even without passports, we could stay out for weeks, maybe months. As long as the funds lasted, we could drive and camp and eat new foods. Once we'd seen the Grand Canyon, maybe they'd want to push on to Yosemite or Death Valley or Yellowstone. We could drive through the Rockies or to California, where I might be able to get Anji into a pair of board shorts if I pressed my luck. North or south, west or east, we had sprawling options and nothing but time.

Looking to my left, I saw Jerrcoa staring raptly at the screen, and Fanakel, his hand in his popcorn bag, was similarly enthralled. To my right, Mia and Anji seemed less interested in the film than in each other, as they were taking advantage of the darkness and noise to make out. Though I didn't want to distract Terj, I leaned closer and rested my head against his shoulder, and he raised the armrest between us and pulled me toward his side. When he laughed, I felt the vibration in his chest as much as I sensed the amusement in his thoughts, and I couldn't believe that five short days ago, I'd been on the precipice of marrying freaking *Makou*.

Part of me hoped the credits would never roll.

Tuesday morning, I came down to breakfast to find Jerrcoa already waiting, eager to show off his latest developments. His left big toe had begun to twitch, while the heel of his right foot could rise ever so slightly from its rest. The pins-and-needles sensation had abated somewhat, but he told me that he'd put up with it forever if it meant regaining mobility.

The others soon joined us, and Mia made herself two waffles, plus a heaping plate of eggs and bacon. As she settled in with her breakfast, Jerrcoa said, "I don't mean to be rude, but how can you eat so much?"

"You've got a healthy appetite," she said, pointing to

his full plate with her fork.

"Yeah, but not *that* healthy."

She sighed and leaned closer to keep her voice down. "You know how Terj is having to eat now because there's no Aen around? I'm in a similar situation."

His mouth moved in a silent *oh*, and he cut his eyes to a group of guys at another table—backpackers, I assumed, given the snippets I'd heard of their discussion.

"Exactly," said Mia. "If I don't…you know, *feed*…then I make up for it like this."

"She's always been hungry," I added. "Couldn't put weight on for ages."

"I still can't," she griped. "The girls"—she glanced meaningfully at her full chest—"filled out of their own accord, remember?"

I picked up my coffee and took a bracing sip. "*Oh*, yeah. Overnight."

Jerrcoa's face screwed up in confusion. "I, uh…I didn't think it worked like that…"

"Not under normal circumstances," said Mia between bites of syrup-soaked waffle. "But I didn't feed for the first time until last year, and…well, have you ever seen pictures of a desert blooming after a rainstorm? Kind of like that, we think."

"So…you *have* fed…"

Fanakel cleared his throat. "She didn't know what she was doing. And no one was hurt in the long run."

Mia looked down the table at him and lowered her fork. "That's…really decent of you. Thanks."

My brother's eyes widened. "Wait, did—"

"Everyone here is off the menu, so can we drop this, please?" she interrupted.

He ate in silence for a while, then turned to Fanakel when Mia got up for more juice and whispered, "What was it like?"

The elf rolled his eyes. "I don't recall much about it, but what I do remember was the feeling that my mind had sunk into a warm bath. Like I was intoxicated but didn't want to look away from her. I seem to recall a certainty that she was the most beautiful, captivating creature I'd ever seen."

"She *is* pretty," Jerrcoa allowed.

"That's not how she looked at the time," said Anji. "And we were travel-worn, too. But this isn't a conversation for breakfast, lad," she added with a hard stare, and Jerrcoa, though curious, bit his tongue.

The day's itinerary was the final push to the Grand Canyon, which still left us with options. Mia, who'd taken over the role of travel planner, had determined that we'd go to the South Rim—not only was it the more touristy side of the canyon, but the higher North Rim was still closed to vehicle traffic for the season. She suggested a less expensive hotel near the park instead of paying a premium for rustic lodging on site, which no one minded, and with that, we loaded up for another day on I-40, a drive across the other half of New Mexico and then partway across Arizona.

The land rolled on along either side of the road as we headed west, brownish-red dirt and scrub vegetation with the occasional rocky prominence rising in the distance. When the afternoon arrived and we pushed on for Flagstaff, the temperature dropped as we gained elevation, and pine trees appeared once more. The land soon veered back toward arid wilderness when we lost a bit of altitude, but before we could turn north off the Interstate, Mia called a halt in Williams, where the lodging was far cheaper.

"It's about another sixty miles to the canyon," she reported once we'd huddled up in her and Anji's room for planning. "Maybe an hour and a half, depending on traffic—we won't be able to drive as quickly," she explained. "But if we're out of here by eight tomorrow, we'll have plenty of time…unless someone was planning on riding a mule to the bottom."

"A what?" asked Fanakel.

"Imagine a less intimidating chiquiw. There are mule rides you can book, but...ew," she said, scrunching her nose.

"Why are you making that face?"

"Imagine mule trains going up and down the same narrow trails, day after day, in fairly arid conditions...the smell's got to be rough."

We concurred that the view from the top would probably suffice, and with that, we set aside the rest of the next day's itinerary. It was only about three in the afternoon, and Mia had plans. "We're putting serious miles on this SUV," she told me, "and *when* was its last oil change? I know you didn't get it checked out before we started."

Dad would have killed me for my carelessness, but we'd avoided disaster thus far, and Mia wanted to keep it that way. Taking the keys from me, she insisted that she was going to get the oil changed, the tires rotated, and the fluids topped up, then suggested a few hours playing around in town. Williams wasn't large, but a stretch of Route 66 ran through it, and there was at least a small museum to visit. "Plus brewpubs," she said, waving her phone. "We could have a little fun tonight."

"Except for the fact that we're the only two with valid IDs," I pointed out. "No one else has identification, and Jerrcoa's underage."

"I can stay here," he offered.

"Absolutely not, lad," said Anji, and Fanakel nodded. "What's the problem, Mia?"

She sighed. "You've got to be twenty-one to drink alcohol here, and if restaurants don't check your identification card, they can lose their liquor license."

"Well, that's annoying," Anji muttered, folding her arms, "but I'm sure we could last an evening without ale. Right?" she asked, looking around the room.

"We could go to dinner, and then I could buy booze on

the way back to the hotel," Mia offered. "I mean, room drinking is still drinking, right?"

Anji, Fanakel, and Jerrcoa deemed this a promising proposition, but I begged off. "I've been driving for a few days, and I could use some vegetation time," I said. "Take the Explorer and enjoy—I'll grab a bite around here."

Though I encouraged Terj to go with them, he refused to leave me behind by myself. With that, we split up for the afternoon. Having noticed a stack of board games in the lobby, Fanakel brought one up to play with Jerrcoa and Anji while Mia handled the oil change. Terj and I retreated to our room, where I kicked off my shoes, sank onto the comforter, and was asleep in minutes.

When I awoke, the sky beyond our sealed window had shifted toward the golden light of sunset, and Terj smiled as he sat on the mattress beside me. *Feeling better?*

Closer to human, I think, I replied, yawning. *Are you hungry yet?*

Not quite. Is there room for one more on here?

I slid over and patted the empty spot, and he faced me on his side. *Do you want to go out tonight?* he asked. *Take a walk? If you need time alone, I'll find the others—*

This is nice, I insisted, and moved closer to kiss him. Sensing his interest, I kissed him again, lingering that time, then raised myself up a little to look down at him while he considered that. A moment later, he sat up and kissed me...and I had to admit that he was getting better at it. Even if the technique left something to be desired, the enthusiasm was there.

I gathered up handfuls of his shirt and tugged it over his head, baring his chest and the Aen pendant. Terj seemed perplexed as to the next step until I pulled off my own shirt, then my leggings. *Susan...*

Down to my mismatched underwear and feeling rather vulnerable with my extra padding on full display, I bit my lip and kept my distance. *Too much? We don't have to—*

No. He reached out and ran his fingers over one of my

bra cups. *No, I want to, but…*

You're nervous?

He hesitated, then laughed weakly. *You would think that I would have a decent grasp of the mechanics by now, but I'm afraid I'll disappoint you.*

It's okay, I said, inching closer to him. *What if I lead?*

You don't mind?

I'm not going to be upset if you don't pin me to the wall and ravage me.

Mm. The people in the next room might complain.

Forget them—they're probably out to dinner. Let's take this slowly and see what happens, yeah?

I won't say that what followed was the most passionate hour of lovemaking in history. It didn't crack the top ten, or probably even the top ten million. But Terj wanted to please me and was willing to take instruction, and by the time I opened a condom—a girl can never be too prepared—and straddled him, he was putty in my hands. I came first, arching my back and shuddering as a guttural cry escaped me, and that was all it took to push him over the edge. I returned to myself in time to see his pale gray eyes staring up at me, wide with shock, and kissed him as his breathing slowed.

We lay together for a long moment, limp, sweaty, and coming down, letting the silence between us say everything.

Come with me, I told him after a time, though I wanted nothing more than to burrow beneath the sheets and pass out. *Let's get cleaned up.*

His thoughts seemed unusually fuzzy. *I don't need to bathe…*

Your new accessory needs to go, remember?

What…oh. That. Uh…

Let me. I pulled him after me into the bathroom to assist, then considered the shower. *Actually, I might rinse off. Want to join me?*

He didn't protest, especially once I had the hot water

going full-blast, and watched while I shampooed and soaped myself clean. *See something you like?* I teased, having switched places with him to let the conditioner work while he slumped beneath the pounding massage jets.

Very much so.

I stepped closer and ran my hands up and down his arms. *Are you okay? Was that too much?*

No, that... He hesitated, and I could feel his jumbled thoughts. *That was amazing. I get it now. Before, when you did that thing with your hand, that was great, but...wow.*

You know, shower sex is a thing.

And I'm aware of that, but honestly, I don't think I have it in me to go another round quite yet. He slid past me as I moved beneath the showerhead to rinse the conditioner out, then tentatively asked, *Did I do okay?*

You were absolutely fine.

Please be honest with me. If that wasn't right—

Terj, I interrupted, wiping the water from my eyes, *did you hear me yell?*

Yes...

Then take that as a compliment.

His thoughts brightened instantly, and I returned to rinsing my hair, content to let him bask in the post-coital glow of a job well done.

CHAPTER 11

We hit the road right on schedule the next morning, with Mia navigating between bites of her third bagel, Jerrcoa recounting the wonders of the Route 66 museum, and Terj and me playing off our evening of television. I wasn't convinced that Mia believed me—she'd known me *far* too long—but other than flashing me a private cheeky grin, she didn't press me for details.

Our drive to the Grand Canyon was smooth, the day clear and cloudless, the Wednesday-morning traffic minimal. Soon enough, I pulled onto the narrow park entrance road, and then I stopped at the visitor center. "So," I said, turning off the engine, "informational exhibits first, or would we rather go straight to the big hole?"

The unanimous vote was to come back to the visitor center later, and so Mia led the way up the trail to the lookout points, with Jerrcoa wheeling along behind her almost on her ankles. I chuckled to myself at his excitement, but then Mia, who'd reached the fence, stopped and said, "*Whoa.*"

We hurried to join her, and I had to agree with her sentiment.

The canyon stretched before us, reddish-orange rocks rising and falling beyond the edge of the cliff on which we stood. Somewhere far below was the Colorado River—I could feel it—but much more pressing in my mind was the sheer scale of the scar in the land that the water had carved over millennia. The austere beauty was unlike anything I knew back in Cole's Crossing, and so taken was I with the scenery that I almost jumped when Terj put his arm around my shoulders.

"Incredible, isn't it?" I murmured.

He nodded. *Malachi would have loved this. We actually made it*, he said, almost in disbelief. *He always wanted to see this place in person...*

Movement out of the corner of my eye drew me to Mia, who was rummaging through the backpack hanging from Jerrcoa's chair. "What are you looking for?" I asked. "Are we doing pictures?"

"In a minute." She paused, saw that the coast was relatively clear, then pulled a small bottle of bourbon from the bag and cracked it open. "Got this last night. Huddle up, y'all." We hastily circled her, and Mia raised the bottle in a toast. "Here's to Malachi," she said, "gone but never forgotten. Wish you were here."

With that, she took a quick swig, then poured at least a healthy double into the dirt before recapping the bottle and hiding it away. Putting on a smile, she said, "Well, now, are we doing group photos or what?"

We stayed at the park until around four, having eaten an overpriced lunch and taken dozens of pictures of each other and the landscape. I think Jerrcoa enjoyed the experience more than anyone—he happily wheeled around the accessible areas, rode the shuttle bus, and read every exhibit he came across, and he conked out like an overly tired kid once we hit the road for the trip back to Williams.

Mia, who'd compiled a list of brewpubs the day before, took us to one the group hadn't tried on Tuesday night, and we sat out in the cool spring evening, eating burgers and looking through Mia's and my camera rolls. She and I laughed as the others took sips of our soft drinks—only Anji liked my Coke—and we promised to buy more beer on the way back to the hotel.

As dinner wound down, Mia cleared her throat. "So,

uh…any chance that y'all are still up for a trip to Vegas? I mean, my father's *probably* not there anymore—it's been decades—but as long as we're out here…"

"I'm with you," I said, and the others nodded their assent. "How long is the drive? Have you found a route yet?"

"It's not too far." She pulled out her phone and opened her mapping program. "From here, maybe a little over three hours, plus we gain an hour once we cross into Nevada. We could be there by lunchtime, maybe drive around the city and see if my necklace lights up?" She pulled it from beneath her shirt, but the moonstone had lost the pink glow it had shown in Cole's Crossing. "And assuming this is a bust, we could pick up I-15 in Vegas, and it's only another four hours to LA."

"LA?" Anji echoed.

"Los Angeles. Big city right on the coast, and there's always a chance of seeing movie stars."

The dwarf's eyebrows rose. "Like…the movie we saw…"

"Exactly! We could go to Hollywood, do the tourist thing—they have busses that'll drive you around to the mansions and stuff. It's tacky as hell, but it might be fun."

"And there's shopping," I said. "Rodeo Drive…"

"Oh, right," Mia scoffed, "like we've got the budget for Beverly Hills."

Anji reached into her backpack, then pulled out a small felt bag and unknotted the drawstring. "If this would help…"

Mia glanced inside and quickly pushed the bag away. "Holy shit, woman, you can't just flash that!" she whispered. "I told you not to bring all that gold."

"In case of emergency," Anji protested. "Since you and Susan have been paying our way to this point, it's only right."

"Your father has put me up for *months*. I can buy you a burger."

"I brought a bit of silver, if that would be easier," Fanakel offered. "We can contribute."

Mia and I traded glances, then looked back at the members of our party who'd come loaded with precious metals and shook our heads. "More trouble than it'd be worth to sell it and explain its provenance," I said. "But that's sweet of y'all. Thank you."

"This is our treat for helping keep us alive," said Mia.

"It was no trouble—" Anji began.

"What part of 'fight a giant monster Outside' was no trouble?"

She chuckled at that. "Point. But I think I've been amply rewarded for that, lass."

"Oh?"

Anji reached across the table and took Mia's hand with a knowing smile. "Yes."

Mia looked back at her, faintly blushing. "You're pretty cute yourself."

At that, Fanakel stood and pointed to the weathered cornhole set at the edge of the patio. "Come on, kid," he said, grabbing the handles of Jerrcoa's chair. "Let's test your aim."

When we parted in the lobby that night, everyone seemed to be in good spirits but Terj, who'd been unusually quiet all day. I waited until we were alone, then asked, *What's on your mind?*

He sat on the edge of the bed we hadn't used and sighed. *Malachi.*

I figured. Sitting beside him, I rubbed his back and rested my head on his shoulder. *Do you want to talk about it? I'm here.*

Terj said nothing for a minute, and when I raised my head to look at him, I saw tears running down his face. *Oh, babe,* I said, reaching over to dry them, *it's okay—*

It's not, he replied, blinking hard. *It will never be okay. I'm sorry, Susan, I don't mean to be depressing—*

You're allowed to feel what you feel. I'm here, I said again. *Talk to me if that'll help.*

When he held his silence again, I assumed he might just want time alone with his thoughts, but then he said, *Malachi should be here. He desperately wanted to see the world beyond the Crossing, and I stole that from him.*

You didn't want to.

But I did it anyway. I stole his life from him. From Pericles, Zachary, Richard, Joseph…all the ones before… He shook his head, still staring at the wall. *You were the sixteenth. That's fifteen lives I destroyed.*

I cupped my hand against his damp cheek and turned his face toward mine. *You were a victim, too, Terj. You didn't want to curse them, right?*

Of course not, but that means little. I did it.

But the sword hurt you if you resisted, I pointed out. *You told me the pain worsened if you didn't choose a Watcher.*

And what should my pain matter to them? he countered. *Why should it matter to you? Had you been anyone else, you'd have been just as damned as the previous fifteen Watchers.*

As Terj turned back to the wall and stewed, I tried to think of a rebuttal…and then an idea occurred to me. *Show me what it felt like.*

He whipped toward me again with a look of horror on his face. *Absolutely not.*

Help me understand. You told me once that it was like hot chains running through you. I can already see your thoughts—can you show me a memory?

Susan—

Can you? I pressed.

After a moment's deliberation, he nodded miserably. *I think so, but I don't want to hurt you.*

I know you don't. I'm asking you to do this. Show me what it was like. Scooting back on the bed, I gripped the edge of the mattress and flashed a tense smile. *I'm ready. Hit me.*

Susan…

Please.

Terj held my stare, perhaps looking for a way to dissuade me, then reached for my hands. *I think this might be easier if I touch you.*

I linked my fingers through his. *Now what?*

Brace yourself, he replied, and closed his eyes.

Before I had time to reconsider the wisdom of my request, I felt like I'd been impaled six ways on burning spears. The scream I tried to release on instinct refused to leave my mouth, and as I writhed in my private agony, searching for relief, I only succeeded in intensifying the sensation that I was being seared alive. Despite my struggles, I could barely move; my limbs refused to cooperate, my lungs stilled, and the only thing of which I was cognizant was the pain, the *constant* pain, the fire that burned without consuming, that pinned me in place like a beetle in a shadowbox. So focused was I on my newfound hell that I forgot where I was and what was happening, and even my own name escaped me.

And then, as quickly as it had begun, the pain ceased. In its place, I felt a new sensation: someone patting my cheeks and shouting into my mind, repeating syllables with no meaning...

Soo. San.

Suddenly, my mental fog cleared, and I recognized Terj's voice as he frantically called for me. *Susan, honey, come back. Please, Susan, you need to wake. Wake, Susan, I'm so sorry—*

"Terj?" I mumbled as my fingers twitched. The scratchy surface beneath them didn't feel like the hotel comforter, and I surmised that I'd fallen to the carpet. "What..."

Relief flooded through my mind. *Susan...*

Gasping, I sat up—yes, I'd landed on the floor—and found him kneeling beside me. With a sob, I threw myself into his arms, and Terj held me as I cried. After a moment, he picked me up and carried me to our bed, but I clung to him as my chest hitched and my nose ran.

I'm sorry, he said, rocking me as I wept at the memory of fear and pain. *I shouldn't have done that, I'm sorry...*

When I finally pulled myself together enough to raise my head, I asked, *That was what it felt like when you didn't choose a Watcher?*

No. That's what it felt like the rest of the time. When I didn't choose a Watcher, it worsened—

Terj! I sat up and stared at him through watery eyes. *You were fucking tortured!*

I... He paused, his face tight. *It doesn't change what I did.*

In response, I pulled him back against me, wrapping my arms around him as my tears ran their course. *I forgive you*, I insisted. *If I haven't made it clear yet, I forgive you.*

You shouldn't, he replied, tightening his hold on me.

You told me you were kept in pain. You didn't say anything about that.

I condemned you—

That's how you lived in the Crossing? Five fucking centuries of that? And then I dragged you into Unara...oh, God...

You saved me.

Not before I made it worse! No wonder you couldn't speak to me there! And I was taking my sweet time with those damn trains—

Susan, no, he said, running his hands over my back. *We had to go Outside. Why would you blame yourself for—*

And you went back to the maladetas? They did that to you, and you went back to them? Because of me?

You're worth it, he said simply.

I pulled away just enough to stare him in the eye. *Say the word, and I'll wash that village off the map. If you want, I'll sweep everything out to sea.*

His brow furrowed, and I felt his bemusement. *You're serious.*

I love you. They locked you in that damn sword, and even when they knew you were still alive, they wouldn't free you. If it'll make you feel better, I'll turn Taln'een into a salt marsh.

He held my gaze, then kissed me.

There was desperation in that kiss. Longing. Sorrow. Guilt. I tasted hints of his tears on his lips and felt the self-loathing circling his thoughts like an oil slick.

You are not to blame for what they made you do, I told him as my mouth lingered on his.

If I were stronger—

Terj, no. No.

We sat together on that rumpled bed, holding each other until our eyes dried and Terj's darkest thoughts retreated, and then, without bothering to put on the television or shuck off more than our shoes, we turned back the blankets and held each other until I fell asleep.

At breakfast the next morning, Jerrcoa proudly showed off his ability to lift his right leg and move his knee. The left lagged behind, but Fanakel was confident that we'd see similar improvement there in another day or two. "The growths are rapidly dwindling," he said as we ate. "I've seen him with his shirt off for several days, and there's a visible difference. Who knows?" he said, turning to Jerrcoa as he spread jelly on his toast. "A few months here, and you could be on your feet."

Why wait that long? Terj, who'd awakened with a grumbling stomach, had helped himself to ten sausage patties from the chafing dish and was popping them into his mouth like Oreos. *You've regained a range of motion, however limited,* he said to Jerrcoa. *Your body may not be strong enough yet to support you, but if we assisted now, you might recall how walking is supposed to feel.*

My brother grimaced over his eggs. "Considering that I've not walked since I was three…"

It's not simple, but it can be learned. Trust me.

An eyebrow rose. "You have experience here?"

What do you think I was doing in Taln'een for weeks, sunbathing? I didn't wait until the day before Susan's wedding to come back because I wanted to be dramatic—it took practice to learn more grace than a drunk toddler.

"Oh," he mumbled. "Sorry, I…I guess I thought you could walk already."

Never had a need to learn until now. So let's put my recent fumbling to good use once you've got a bit more motion in your left leg. Yeah?

Jerrcoa grinned. "If you're willing."

Certainly. "Phil," are you in?

Fanakel gave him a pointed look, then glanced at Jerrcoa, who waited with expectant eyes. "Of course. And, uh…among ourselves, at least, I suppose we can drop 'Phil.'" My brother's smile widened, and Fanakel reached over to muss his dark hair. "You're all right, son of Daril."

That constituted high praise from an elf, even one rocking a five-day beard and a ski cap, and Jerrcoa faintly flushed as we finished our meal.

As I headed west on I-40, cutting across eastern Arizona, Mia turned to the back of the SUV with her phone and played tour guide.

"The fun part of Las Vegas is basically this neon playground in the middle of nowhere," she explained. "Southern Nevada is pretty populous when you look at the state as a whole, but that's not saying much. Lot of desert. Las Vegas is known for the Strip, which is actually right outside the city proper. That's where most of the casinos are."

"Casinos?" asked Jerrcoa, repeating the untranslated word.

"Places to gamble. Card games, dice games, slot machines—if you want to risk your money on the slim chance of a jackpot, Vegas has you covered. But all the casinos are competing for business, right, so things get a little ridiculous. Fancy resorts, restaurants, high-end shopping, shows, amusement parks—"

"They've even got choreographed water fountains," I

added.

"Right. Basically, if you've got money to burn, someone in Vegas will be happy to set it on fire for you."

"It's popular for wedding parties," I said as I pulled around a slow-moving tanker. "Fly out, do a little gambling, see a show or two, and hit the nightclubs."

"Yeah, and if you're *really* lucky, you end up with a souvenir like me," Mia joked. "They've got wedding chapels there, too, in case you want a kitschy ceremony."

I glanced over my shoulder and caught Terj's eye. *Don't get any ideas, bub.*

Amusement colored his thoughts. *You mean you don't want to get married by Elvis?*

I was hoping for something slightly more formal, if it's all the same to you.

But this means you will marry me?

I chuckled to myself. *Have I not made that clear?*

I didn't want to presume…

At that, I laughed in earnest, and though Mia glanced my way, I ignored her querying look. *Terj, at some point when we've made plans for more than a week in the future and aren't actively running from danger, will you marry me?*

I'd like nothing more, he replied, and I felt his love radiating toward me from across the vehicle.

The traffic gods were with us, and we pulled into Las Vegas around ten-thirty that morning. Though Mia was itching to at least coast around and look for changes in her necklace, she agreed that the first step was to secure a hotel for the night. We pulled over on the outskirts of town and made a quick search for prices, then settled on a surprisingly decent place in Paradise with a ridiculously low rate. True, it was off the Strip—we had I-15 between us and the action—but my bank account approved, and no one complained as we checked out our rooms. There was a casino on the premises, I had a king-sized bed, and the view faced the mountains instead of the neon lights, which suited me nicely.

I was unpacking my toiletry kit and trying to gauge how much clean underwear I had left when my phone beeped with an incoming message from Mia. *Come here*, it said, plus her room number, and so Terj and I obliged.

We found Mia alone when we knocked, and I was surprised to see that she'd pulled the curtains, leaving the suite in twilight. "What's up?" I asked. "Where's Anji?"

"Gone to get the guys. Look at this," said Mia, and pulled me into the dark bathroom.

Though it was faint, I could make out the pink glow of the moonstone around her neck.

"Holy shit," I murmured. "He's still in town."

"Looks like it. Terj, tell me I'm not crazy."

He leaned over my shoulder and grunted. *It's been activated. I don't suppose that necklace offers directional assistance, does it?*

"Nope. I get to play 'Hot and Cold,' I guess."

Sensing his confusion, I explained, "You send one player away and hide an object. When he gets close, you say he's hot, and farther away is cold. We used to play it in gym class when the teacher was feeling lazy."

Just then, Anji returned with the guys. "You've got to see our room!" Jerrcoa announced as he wheeled in. "It's *huge*, and there are handrails everywhere, and the bathroom is completely flat!"

Our previous accommodations not having offered the greatest of handicapped rooms, I was happy for him. "Come check this out," I said, and stepped aside.

Fanakel whistled when he saw Mia's necklace. "How close is he, then?"

"Don't know. It was brighter than this when we were at the cabin, so he's farther away than the distance from there to my mom's house. What do we want to do?"

"Get your purse," I said, heading for the door. "We're loading up again."

Mia rode shotgun as usual, albeit sneaking frequent peeks down her shirt at the necklace hidden within. I made my way to the Strip, then got into the slow lane and cruised north. But when we started reaching the wedding chapels at the far end, Mia had no news to report. "It's still faint," she said, looking for all the world like she was hunting for something lost in her bra. "Want to try the other direction?"

That proved similarly fruitless, so we turned north again and headed into Las Vegas proper, rolling through small business districts and more residential neighborhoods. We looked up casinos off the Strip and sought them out, just in case he was working there, but by one, having driven past both the Air Force base and the hospitals with no luck, we stopped for lunch to strategize.

"He might work nights," I said over pizza, while Mia, though frustrated, demolished a four-meat calzone. "Especially if he's still an adult entertainer. Maybe he lives outside of town."

"We could widen our search radius, could we not?" suggested Anji.

"Maybe," said Mia, "but do we want to roll up on him at home? What if he's got a family here? You think they'd appreciate it if I knocked?" She sighed and sawed off another bite. "I think it's safer if we try to catch him at work. Scope him out in public. If I can approach, great, but if not, at least we'll have a starting point."

Anji squeezed her arm. "Don't despair, lass. We're on his trail."

"And what if he doesn't want anything to do with me?" she mumbled.

"My offer to break his knees still stands." She leaned closer and stabbed a runaway piece of sausage with her fork, then grinned as she stole it.

"Perhaps we should wait a few hours before driving out again," said Fanakel. "Is there something we could do in the interim that wouldn't result in us losing all our funds?"

With two-thirds of our group either underage or lacking ID, we couldn't have gotten into any reputable casino had we tried, but Madame Tussauds proved distraction enough, followed by a museum of movie cars. The fact that most of the faces and films were unknown to the majority of our group wasn't nearly as much of a problem as I'd feared, as they were good sports, and Mia kept her phone handy to look up pictures and video clips. She was practically sparking with nervous energy, but if museums kept her occupied, I didn't mind paying the entrance fee.

Mia's necklace had yet to change by the time we emerged, and so I suggested an early dinner and a nap. "We may have a long slog around town tonight," I reminded her, and though Mia wasn't tired, she never turned down food. A few overpriced burgers later, we returned to our hotel to crash until nightfall.

When we rendezvoused in the lobby a couple hours later, Mia cupped her hands around her necklace and called me closer, her eyes bright. "It's stronger," she said— and I had to agree. There was no writing off the glow as a trick of the light now, and Mia practically ran out of the lobby toward our ride.

As before, she settled in beside me, and I directed us back toward the Strip. This time, the stone's glow intensified as we traveled east, and I paused at the intersection with the main drag. "Left or right?"

"Let's try right," she replied, and so I turned and started down the road. A few blocks later, however, Mia said, "It's dimming. Other way."

I pulled a U-turn as soon as possible and started north again, and soon, I noticed the intensifying pink light out of the corner of my eye. "Keep watch on your necklace," I told Mia. "Let me know when it starts to fade again. We'll set up a search area."

The necklace reacted before we reached the end of the Strip, and I headed south until the full glow returned. Detours down side streets to the east and west confirmed what I'd suspected: Mia's father was somewhere on the Strip, perhaps hidden on a packed casino floor or hanging out in a hotel room. "Okay," I said, "we're going to have to take this on foot. Let's find a place to park."

Two blocks and an expensive parking fee later, we set off through the sea of light and color and excited crowds behind Mia, who kept consulting her necklace like a compass. After a ten-minute hike, she paused and doubled back, then turned again, eventually settling outside a smaller theater building with thumping bass and dark windows. *Club Xotic*, announced the neon sign, and the posters in the windows revealed the draw: enough gorgeous, half-dressed men to make a bachelorette reconsider her nuptials. One wore a tight variant on a cop's uniform, while a pair were dressed as shirtless firefighters with suspenders and smoldering gazes. Another straddled a backward chair in leather pants, pinning the passersby with a come-hither gaze.

"Goddamn it," Mia muttered. "Couldn't he be a valet or something?"

"Maybe he's a bartender," I offered. "Or maybe he's just…seeing the show?"

She fixed me with a look of deep incredulity, then considered her necklace, which was glowing brighter than ever. "I'm going in. If y'all would rather not—"

"I'm with you, lass," said Anji with grim disapproval.

For a moment, I thought her declaration might have been premature, but Club Xotic wasn't the sort of institution with a strong "no minors" policy. The only person at whom the bouncer balked was Jerrcoa, but as Mia leaned close to the impediment, her voice slipped into a husky register I recognized as her tekorish charm coming out to play. "He's legal," she purred, trailing her fingertips over the bouncer's tight black T-shirt. "You wouldn't want to make me cry, would you?"

While the bouncer looked like he could bench-press a Cadillac, he was male and all too human, and so he quickly fell under Mia's sway. She gave him a peck on the cheek as thanks when he unlatched the velvet rope, and we hustled Jerrcoa inside before anyone less susceptible to her influence could think twice.

Our tickets put us on the floor, a few tables back from the edge of the stage, and we settled in. "How did you do that?" Jerrcoa asked Mia once a waiter—attractive but fully clothed—had taken our drink order.

She shrugged. "That's my party trick. His brain gets a little fuzzy for a minute, I get a snack, and we get inside."

"Speaking of snacks, do you want wings?" I asked, pointing to the laminated menu.

"May as well. That was barely a bite." She slumped down in her chair as Anji rubbed her back. "Look, I know it's gross," she said to Jerrcoa, "but on occasion, it comes in handy. Might be more fun if I were into guys…"

"Not for me," murmured Anji.

Mia turned to her with a little grin. "You're a good sport."

"I love you," she said simply. "And if that means standing by while you take the occasional nibble…well, every relationship has its challenges, does it not?" She glanced around the theater—more tables like ours, a big stage with a center walkway that extended into the room, an array of lights and disco balls hanging from the rafters. "So, what should we expect from this performance?"

Mia and I traded glances. "Uh…scantily clad dudes," I said.

"Yes, I gathered that from the pictures outside, but doing *what*?"

"Dancing and losing their clothing. That's the attraction."

As I was apparently the only member of our party for whom a stage full of oiled-up men with six-packs was at all titillating, the others made up for it with stiff drinks—having gotten past the bouncer, we weren't carded inside, and even Jerrcoa ordered a beer. The wings were mediocre, obviously having come from the freezer, but if they gave Mia something to do with her hands while we waited for the show to begin, they were worth every penny.

Finally, the last of the tables in the back filled, the lights went down, and a few tables of women (and one bachelor party) started screaming. The music pounded, the fog machine hissed, and the stage lights came up on a trio of dancers in baggy black pants that were quickly ripped off and tossed to the side. I glanced at Mia, who was concentrating on her necklace, then cut my eyes to Fanakel, who smirked behind his scotch.

See something you like?

I reached under the table and took Terj's hand. *They're pretty, I'll grant you that.* Catching the burst of uncertainty that he quickly tried to suppress, I squeezed his hand and added, *This is all flash, no substance. I'm not going home with anyone here tonight but you, mister. Besides, we're being supportive—that's it.*

I just don't see the appeal, he remarked as one of the dancers thrust his pelvis toward the nearest cheering bridesmaids.

Fantasy, libido, alcohol…it's a powerful cocktail.

But what's so great about…that? he asked as the thruster jumped off the stage and started gyrating by the women's table.

Just take it from me that this is an appealing display to quite a few people, and if the dancers were female, Jerrcoa would probably be drooling.

Only Jerrcoa?

He's young. Fanakel would have a bit more class, Mia's preoccupied, and Anji seems properly scandalized.

Methinks the High Queen is not amused, he replied, and I caught the twinkle in his eye when I glanced away from the show.

The show continued in much the same vein: buff, model-esque men in a variety of costumes and stages of undress. Police in booty shorts, firefighters who quickly stripped down to bright red underwear, a few who looked like they'd just come from one of the leather clubs elsewhere in town—it was certainly an eye-opening display, though maybe a touch repetitive when one wasn't as drunk as the bachelorettes.

But after about forty minutes of thrusting and posing, the house went dark, and over the constant bass, the announcer said, "You know him, you love him…"

To my surprise, the tables in the *back* of the room began to cheer, and I suspected I'd found the regulars' section.

The announcer waited a beat before finishing his spiel. "Let's give it up for the one, the only…*Richard Maximus*!"

As the volume rose, I snorted and rolled my eyes. *"Big Dick." That's creative.*

He said the man was named Rich…oh, Terj replied. *Well, that's probably appropriate…*

His thoughts on our next performer ended abruptly as Mia pulled her necklace from beneath her shirt. The moonstone glowed like a pink beacon in the darkness.

For the briefest of seconds, I wondered whether we should hustle Mia out before he took the stage, but then the lights flashed, the regulars clapped along, and a man strode forward from behind the black curtain.

Richard Maximus had a body designed to grace calendars. About six feet tall, tanned, and built like he dabbled in strongman competitions, with shaggy blond hair, blue eyes, and a dazzling smile, he looked like a naughty version of Captain America, the kind of man who'd turn heads if he were wearing a burlap sack. Instead, he'd opted for black leather chaps over a gold G-string that evening, which, while perhaps not the sartorial choice I'd have made, lent support to the appropriateness of his name.

For years, I'd wondered where Mia got her looks, even before her overnight glow-up. Now I knew without a doubt.

As Richard started strutting and the audience's excitement grew, I glanced at Mia, who held her necklace and watched with slack-jawed disbelief. Her eyes widened as he ripped off the chaps, and there he was, nearly naked and reveling in the crowd's enthusiasm.

Then I felt it—just the faintest hint of something strange pressing against my mind, a power that was not my own.

Richard, who'd progressed to some admittedly impressive dance moves around a fireman's pole, was spinning with his head thrown back and a sultry smile on his face. I scanned the crowd visible in the stage lights and saw the women goggling at him, leaning forward in their seats, some with their mouths hanging open. They clapped mechanically. One woman at the table beside ours actually began to drool.

When I turned to Mia to ask if she was feeling something strange, I found her leaning in front of Anji, snapping her fingers and trying to shake her girlfriend from her sudden stupor. "*Anji,*" she insisted over the club mix and the screeches from the enraptured women around us. "Come on, wake up! Look at me!"

"I've got this," said Fanakel, then lifted Anji from her chair, slung her over his shoulder like a bag of cement, and unceremoniously carried her toward the lobby.

Mia started to follow but paused, frowning at the stage. Sensing her dilemma, I spoke to her without trying to shout: *Go. I'll watch him. Take care of Anji.*

She nodded and hurried out, leaving Terj, Jerrcoa, and me to endure the awkwardness of our introduction to Mia's father. I mean, truth be told, he was a *fabulous* dancer, and he made the splits look effortless, but I could only imagine what had to be going through my best friend's mind.

Richard was the climax of the show—probably in more ways than one, considering the dazed expressions on some of the patrons' faces as they staggered out—and we soon met up with the others in a corner of the lobby while the rest of the revelers wandered into the night.

Mia had bought a Coke for Anji, who sat on a folding table and absently rubbed her forehead as she drank it. "I lost time," she said between sips. "He came out, he started dancing, he, uh…removed his trousers…and then I was here." Looking up at Fanakel, she asked, "Is that what it felt like for you?"

She sounded shaken, and I couldn't blame her. Apparently, I'd inherited the elemental immunity to tekorish influence, but Anji had no such protection, and she'd been a zombie in there.

"I recall bits," he told her, "but everything feels dreamlike. You remember nothing once he mounted the pole?"

"I…no," she admitted, scowling. "I remember the noise and the lights, and the cheering, and this…*wonderful* feeling of…um…"

"Lust?"

Her cheeks were, by then, well on their way to scarlet.

"It's nothing to be embarrassed about," said Fanakel as Anji held the cold paper cup to her face. "That's what they do. You couldn't fight it."

Mia stood close to her as if to shield her from the crowd. "I'm so sorry, I didn't even *think* of what could happen—"

"Lass." Anji patted Mia's shoulder with her free hand and looked her in the eye. "I'm here to help you. And if that means making a fool of myself while your father dances in his underwear…"

"Oh, *God*," she muttered, flushing in turn.

Anji offered her the drink cup. "It could always be worse, right? Could be Susan's mother."

He's quite talented, Terj offered, which earned him matching incredulous glares from Mia and Anji.

I was about to offer to buy another Coke so the two of them wouldn't have to share when Richard, now sporting baggy gray sweatpants and a black T-shirt with the club's logo splashed across the front, approached us. "Uh…hi," he said with a brief, awkward wave.

Of course he had the sort of baritone voice that gave me sudden unchaste thoughts.

"Sorry to bother you," he continued, pushing his hair from his sweaty face. "I, um…I saw you get sick, there, and I just wanted to make sure you were okay."

He was, I noticed, speaking English, and though he sounded generically American, I couldn't pin him to a region.

"Oh…thank you," Anji replied, smiling politely as she continued to chill her cheeks. "A little faint, that's all."

He started to speak, then locked eyes with Mia, whose necklace was glowing hot pink against her shirt. Frowning bemusedly, he asked, "Have we met?"

She took a deep breath but didn't look away. "By any chance, do you know a woman named Janine Randolph?"

Richard's blue eyes—and God, those were Mia's eyes—widened in shock. "Janine! *Wow*, that's a name from the past. Yeah, sure, I remember her. How is she? *Where* is she? She just up and disappeared one day…"

Something clicked with him, and his voice faltered.

"Back in Cole's Crossing," Mia murmured. "Where she raised me."

He stared at her necklace, then looked back at her face and slowly pointed to himself.

Mia nodded and tapped her necklace. "A maladeta enchanted this to lead me to you."

His mouth opened and closed soundlessly, but he soon recovered and gently gripped her upper arms. "I want to know everything," he said in a soft rush, "but I have two more shows to do tonight. It's my last night here, I—"

"It's okay—"

"No, it absolutely is *not* okay. I...I don't even know...what..."

"Mia," she murmured.

"Mia. I'm Cary," he said, and though his face twisted, he swallowed hard and smiled. "It's nice to meet you. I had no idea..."

"I know." She glanced away for a second, composing her thoughts. "Look, I...I'm not here to ruin your life. I don't want anything from you. But I have some questions, and—"

"I'm sure you do." Releasing her, he pulled a phone from his pocket and unlocked it. "Would you be willing to meet me at my place later? All of you," he hastily added, "I wouldn't ask you to go to a stranger's house alone. Let me get through tonight's shows, and I'll answer anything you want to know."

Mia fished her phone from her purse and gave him her number, and he texted her an address. "I live in Henderson, south of town," he explained. "Meet you there around one?"

Her head bobbed twice, and her eyes began to fill.

"I'll be there as soon as I can," Richard—well, Cary—promised, and then, with obvious reluctance, he ducked through an employee door.

When it slammed behind him, I turned to Mia, who clung to her phone and stared at the place where he had been. "Y'all?" she mumbled.

Terj grunted. *Let's get back to the hotel. Susan, can you find alcohol along the way?*

"In Vegas?" I said. "Absolutely."

Great. I think Mia's going to need it.

CHAPTER 12

To keep Mia from climbing the walls, I bought her a bottle of prosecco, something that would go down easily and maybe dull a bit of her nervous energy. By the time we left the hotel for Cary's house, she'd drunk most of it and seemed slightly more relaxed, relatively speaking. I couldn't blame her for being on edge—I'd certainly been a mess when I went in search of Falova—but as we wound our way toward the southeast, she fidgeted in the seat beside me, fingering her necklace. I was relieved to see it brighten, proof that Cary hadn't given us a false address.

Cary's neighborhood was a subdivision nestled in the southern reaches of Vegas's sprawl, right up against a nature preserve, or so my phone told me. Driving through an unfamiliar city at one in the morning, I had little to orient me and saw virtually nothing familiar, but at least the suburbs had streetlights. The neighborhood seemed to be a planned build, given the closeness and similar construction of the homes—single-story houses of brownish stucco with tiled roofs, a suggestion of adobe if something rather different. Unlike my childhood neighborhood with its verdant lawns, this one had been landscaped with drought-tolerant plants, gravel, and mulch. Sure, it was a practical choice, given the climate, but I couldn't imagine planting cacti in my front yard.

I slowed as I turned onto Cary's street and began checking the house numbers. Really, there was no need, as his was the only one with the porch light still on at that hour. The garage door was closed, but I pulled up the driveway and turned off the engine. "Ready?" I asked Mia.

"I think so."

"We need not stay," Anji reassured her from the back row. "The moment you want to leave, say the word."

"I know," she said, her voice tense with anxiety, and I squeezed her hand before I opened my door.

Terj and Fanakel were helping Jerrcoa into his wheelchair when the garage door opened and warm yellow light spilled onto the driveway. "Hi, there," said Cary, standing between a black Toyota Corolla and a makeshift home gym. "Come in this way—there's a step if you use the front door."

We followed him through the garage and into the kitchen, where a pair of large pizza boxes and some paper plates awaited on the simple pine table. "Go ahead, help yourselves," he offered, leaning against the counter. "I'm stuffed."

To my relief, he'd opted for the T-shirt and sweatpants again instead of his stage ensemble.

Mia glanced at the steaming pies. "You didn't need to do—"

"You're starving. I can see it in your eyes, honey. When's the last time you fed properly?"

"I had to get Jerr here into the club today, but other than your bouncer…"

Cary considered my brother, who was also gazing hungrily at the pizza. "How old are you, kid?"

"Twenty."

He snorted. "Boys your age can't eat enough. Dig in, don't be shy."

That was all the encouragement Jerrcoa needed, and Mia was right behind him. As the rest of us took a slice or two apiece, Cary asked, "Want to go to the den? It might be more comfortable."

We settled on his couch, and he brought kitchen chairs in to make enough seating. Finally, when Cary could delay with hosting duties no longer, he sighed and turned to Mia.

"First of all, I'm *so* sorry for not bringing you here straightaway tonight. Like I said, this was my last night on the job, and I promised the owner I'd do the shows."

"It's fine," she replied around a mouthful of cheese and vegetables. "Gave me a chance to drink."

He chuckled weakly. "Well, I've got about a million questions, and I'm sure you do, too, but would you mind if I started?"

Mia motioned him on.

"Okay. So, if your mom raised you, then where the hell did you find a maladeta to do *that?*" he asked, pointedly glancing at her pink moonstone.

She and I traded glances as she chewed.

"Do you know where Cole's Crossing is?" I asked him.

Cary frowned. "I know it's back east somewhere. Janine said that was her hometown, but…"

"It's in Kentucky. It's also the town founded right next to the opening to the Crossing. You must have passed through it at some point," I continued as his eyebrows rose, "but yeah, that's where Mia and I come from."

"And where the Watcher was stuck," she added. "Know about that?"

He grimaced but nodded. "Unfortunately. My people had nothing to do with that, but yes, I've heard of the Watcher. And sure, I passed through that place, but only long enough to hitch a ride out. One of my cousins explained the practice…" He paused, thinking, then asked, "You have maladetas there?"

"Just one," said Mia. "Sent to babysit the Watcher. We didn't know what she was until Suze here got the gig last year."

To his credit, Cary's expression shifted toward horror. "Merciful gods, you're a *kid!*"

"Almost twenty-four," I replied with a shrug. "It wasn't ideal."

He whistled low. "And the maladeta got you out of that mess?"

We laughed aloud, and as Cary's forehead wrinkled, Mia came to the rescue. "Not exactly. She told us about the Crossing, and Suze and I went through to find someone to help her. Do you want the long version or the condensed one?"

"For the moment, let's start with condensed."

"Sure. Long story short, last summer, Suze, Anji, this son of Nokan'ti, and I went Outside, met the local queen, and killed this massive spider monster *thing* that was actually creating all the Outsiders. The people in the area had been worshipping it as a god, so that was a little tricky."

"Susan did most of the killing," said Fanakel.

"Oh, absolutely," Mia concurred. "Anyway, once the monster was dead, the Watcher's sword fell apart, and voila, Terj," she continued, thumbing one hand at him.

"Here," I said, digging in my purse for a Unaran recording device. I'd kept both mine and Terj's, and I'd brought them along on the trip, just in case. "We've got it on tape."

Mia started the playback for him, and Cary watched, gobsmacked. As the recording ended, he stared at Mia, his eyes wide and watery. "Janine let you *do* that?"

"She had no idea. We haven't spoken in a while," Mia muttered, and handed me the device.

He softly swore—in Common, I assumed, as the nonsense my translator seemed to provide struck me as idiomatic instead of gibberish. "And not to be rude, but you've got a strange group. This is…" he began, gesturing to Fanakel.

"A son of Nokan'ti," said Mia as Fanakel removed his ski cap, revealing his pointed ears and a bad case of hat hair.

Cary rubbed his blond stubble. "Not fully elven, though, no?" he asked—definitely in Common that time.

Fanakel, whose week-old beard was coming along nicely, shook his head. "What gave it away?" he asked dryly.

"I mean, the fact that you're sitting in my den with a dwarf suggests you've got more people skills than the average elf." Turning to Anji, he said, "I'm assuming that you're not just short."

Anji, whose stubble was also in need of a shave, smirked back at him. "Anjikora of Blackhorn Mountain."

Cary goggled for a second. "You're one of Rokund's kids?"

"I am."

"Rokund *Elf-Bane*?"

Her smirk deepened. "You've heard of him?"

"I'm from Ragatanu, not Nevada. So," he said, puzzling us out, "we've got a half-elven prince, a dwarven princess—"

"She's also my girlfriend," Mia blurted. "Hope that's not a problem."

"Really?" Cary seemed surprised, not scandalized. "Good for you two. Nice to meet you," he told Anji, "and, uh…sorry we had to meet *quite* like we did. I'm sure your father would be appalled."

Anji brushed it off. "He's already trying to cope with the reality of his wayward daughter and her dear, live-in *friend*, so I don't think he'd faint with shock if he knew where I'd been tonight."

"Does Rokund know that Mia is—"

"Father saw her before her second puberty, so he's likely aware. He also knows that Mia can be trusted not to feed on anyone," she said, a note of challenge in her voice.

But Cary didn't rise to the bait. "What do you mean, *second* puberty?" he asked, looking between Mia and Anji.

Mia cleared her throat. "So, uh…the three of us were in Nokan'ti, trying to break out of jail…well, the three of us girls and Terj, I mean, but we didn't know he was there yet—"

An easy mistake.

Cary twitched at the mental speech. "Jail?"

"Um…Suze managed to piss off the Twins, and they locked us up."

Her father turned to Fanakel, who lifted his hands. "I had nothing to do with it."

"No, he just got stuck on guard duty that night," said Mia, "and I was trying my best 'score free drinks' routine, hoping he'd come close enough that we could get the key or something, but I accidentally, uh…psychically roofied him," she finished in a mumble. "Anyway, I woke up looking like this the next morning, and he and Anji figured out that I'm part tekori. Guess it was the first time I'd fed."

"The first…" His jaw started to sag, but he snapped his mouth closed. "*When* was this?"

"Last May…maybe June? We were on the run, so the dates are kind of fuzzy—"

"You never fed until *last year*?" Cary covered his mouth as he stared at Mia, who took the opportunity to finish one of her pizza slices. After a moment, he asked, "Did Janine never tell you that you might need to feed?"

Mia frowned at him. "How would she know?"

"I told her all about tekoraet when we were dating. Surely she knew you were my daughter—"

"Dating?" Mia echoed. "Mom said I was the result of a one-night stand."

Cary's face fell, and he took a moment to process that. "No," he finally said, and I knew I wasn't imagining the slight tremor in his voice. "No, Mia, you weren't some random accident between strangers. Your mom and I dated for several months."

Though there was still pizza to be had, she put her plate aside and studied him as if trying to spot the lie. "She told me that she flew out here with friends for a spring break trip, went to see some, uh…exotic dancers"—Cary didn't flinch—"and she hooked up with one of them in a dressing room after the show. She was too drunk to bother to get his name, and by the time she realized she was pregnant, she was too embarrassed about the whole thing to call the club and make enquiries." When Cary didn't jump in, she pressed on. "My family's pretty religious—my grandparents went to this hardline church, and there's where Mom brought me up—so while Mom's parents didn't want anyone to know she was pregnant and unmarried, they also wouldn't have considered an abortion. She had me, but then she *kept* me, and my grandparents didn't have much to do with us after that. I mean, we went to church together for years, and they hardly ever looked at us."

Cary reached for her, and Mia took his hands. "I don't know what happened once Janine went home," he murmured, "but that bit about a drunken romp on spring break is a *complete* fabrication. I loved your mother very much. And I can prove I'm not full of shit," he added, releasing her as he stood. "One moment, I'll be right back."

As he hurried deeper into the house, Mia scarfed down the last of her pizza, then headed toward the kitchen for more. "You're still *hungry* at a time like this?" Fanakel asked.

"This is stress pizza," she called back. "Jerr, you want seconds?"

By the time Cary returned, Mia had found a pair of trivets to keep the box grease off the coffee table and brought the pizzas into the den. "Oh, no, go ahead," he said as a flash of guilt crossed her face. "Please. I know you must be famished."

He took his seat and opened a shoebox, then pulled out a stack of photos. "Look familiar?" he asked, holding one toward Mia.

She put down her slice as she stared at the image. "Shit, that's *Mom*."

I scooted closer for a better look, and I had to concur. Long brown hair, blue eyes, barely upturned nose—I knew Janine's face well from my childhood, though the girl in the picture was fuller in the cheeks and, weirdest of all, *grinning*. The Janine I knew was a dour woman, quick to snap if we made noise or a mess, which was one reason why Mia and I had spent so many Saturdays at my house.

The man with his arm around her, sporting dark dress slacks and a button-down shirt with the top three buttons open, was unquestionably Cary. Sure, the fashions in the picture screamed "nineties," but he'd barely changed in the two and a half decades since. Then again, tekoraet could live for five hundred years, so what was a mere twenty-five?

"I've got plenty more," said Cary, putting the photo away. "She bought a Polaroid camera and loved to play with it…"

Craning my neck, I caught a glimpse of the rest of the shoebox's contents: pictures, folded pieces of paper, a pink velour scrunchie.

"I believe you," Mia said quietly. "Tell me the truth."

He looked into the shoebox for a moment, then closed the lid and put it behind him. "Guess I'll start at the beginning. So…I'm from Ragatanu." When Mia looked at him blankly, he added, "It's in Ga'besh—"

"Borders Cirivant," Jerrcoa offered.

Cary nodded. "You're Cirivanti, kid?"

"My father is. I'm of Daril."

"He's second in line to the throne," I explained, grabbing more pizza.

Jerrcoa scowled at me. "Only because *someone* renounced her place."

"I'm sorry, *what?*" asked Cary, and pointed to me. "I thought you were from Mia's hometown…"

I shrugged. "Technically, yeah. I'm a rogue elemental, he and I share a mother," I explained, nodding to Jerrcoa, "and she dumped me beyond the Crossing before anyone back in Daril was the wiser. Anyway, she hates my guts, the feeling is close to mutual, and so I gave up my spot about a week ago. Didn't want to deal with her stupidity or give her a chance to come after Terj," I said, taking his hand.

Cary's forehead wrinkles deepened. "And...*he* is an elemental?"

Piloting a meat suit, as it were.

"O...*kay*. Huh."

As Cary tried to absorb the weirdness, Mia hinted, "You were telling me about Ragatanu..."

"Right. Sorry. Uh...so, we have this tradition in which you leave for about twenty-five years and make your own way. It's to prove that you're not lazy or inept—that you're an adult who can look after himself without someone else's funding to fall back on. Earth is a popular destination because it's big, it's fascinating, and feeding opportunities abound."

Mia's mouth twitched. "I wouldn't call this 'fascinating.'"

"You say that, but do you have any idea how interesting computers are to someone who grew up without guaranteed plumbing? And we're better off than most," he added, crossing his legs. "Dwarven forging can do wonders, but for true tech, there's nothing like human ingenuity. Those of us who've come here in the last few centuries have made a point of taking careful notes and bringing tools back for our engineers to play with. When I left, we'd finally established a small electrical grid—only for a few buildings—but I hope it's grown by now. I know cell service is too much to ask for, but if we could get landlines established, I'd be a happy camper."

"You have literal *magic* to play with," said Mia.

"Doesn't do us much good. Guild forgers won't work for us, and the free agents in Ga'besh charge a *stiff* premium. We have one unusual talent, and it doesn't require Aen, so it's not like we're living in a magical wonderland," Cary replied. "But that's a discussion for later. Anyway, I came over in early '94—I was a bit shy of sixty, a little young for exile, but my parents thought I could manage."

Quickly, I did the math. Cary was only a few years younger than Fanakel, and the elf was nearly a hundred. For a nonagenarian, Mia's father looked pretty damn good.

"My most recent cousin to return from his exile suggested Las Vegas. He'd worked as a dancer and said the money was easy. I took his advice and hitchhiked out here, and I had a job and a little apartment of my own within days. It's not the most glamorous work, but I've made a comfortable living...though I'm sorry that was your first impression of me tonight, Mia," he added, making a face. "Not the father you would have wanted, eh?"

"Mom didn't lie about the dancing part..."

"Yeah, but seeing the routine in person was probably unnecessary."

She didn't disagree.

"You feed off the crowds," Anji interjected.

Cary nodded. "Easy meal for me, and it doesn't hurt them."

The dwarf arched a brow. "Doesn't it?"

"Nah. Humans are *very* resilient." Seeing the skeptical expressions around the den, Cary sighed. "Let me guess: tekoraet are to be avoided at all costs because we'll seduce you before you know what hit you, then fuck you to death. Right? And we keep stables of helpless sex slaves for that very purpose?"

"So I've been told," said Fanakel, and Anji and Jerrcoa nodded.

He groaned. "*Massive* exaggeration. We don't roam the four worlds, constantly looking to feed. It's necessary that we feed on occasion, now, but if you leave corpses in your wake, you're doing it wrong. I've certainly never killed anyone by feeding. Don't know anyone who has."

"But can't you just, like...*not* feed?" Mia mumbled. "I mean, tonight was the first time I've done it in a while, and it feels gross, and...and if I've actually got to screw a dude, you may as well put me out of my misery now."

"Whoa, *whoa*," said Cary, and took her hands again. "You don't have to have sex with anyone, honey."

She cut her eyes to Anji and Fanakel, then back to her father. "I don't?"

"Not unless you want to. I've got an uncle who's repulsed by the notion of bedding another person, and he's perfectly healthy. When we feed properly, we trigger that sort of lust state in others, and we siphon off some of their energy. They can be *really* suggestible during that period—"

Fanakel pointedly cleared his throat.

"—but you don't need to make them do anything. And unless you do something crazy while feeding, they'll be unharmed. Most of our donors say it's a relaxing experience, and they have a nice nap once we're finished."

"So you *do* keep slaves," the elf interrupted.

"*Donors*," Cary insisted, releasing Mia. "Fed, clothed, housed, and well paid by the Crown. Free to go at any time without repercussions. Most opt to stay with us because it's an easier life than they'd find elsewhere, and we respect them for the service they provide. Some of them end up marrying us. I admit that it must be a strange system in your eyes, but it's a mutually beneficial arrangement."

"Oh, sure," he scoffed, "live well for a few years until you're drained and die young, right?"

Cary stared at him, then slowly exhaled. "Wow, you people must really think we're monsters."

"Am I wrong?"

"Completely. Tell me, son of Nokan'ti, have you ever pricked your finger? Maybe nicked your jaw while shaving?"

Fanakel began to redden but held his temper. "Of course."

"You've lost blood, then, and suffered no ill effect greater than a little sting at the wound site. Here, humans actually donate blood—they let medics take whole bags from their veins. Some make a bit of money from it. Sure, they can't do it every day since that lost blood takes time to be replenished, but it does come back, and they're unharmed by the experience." Turning to Mia, he said, "It's much the same when we feed. We're not taking blood, but rather energy. It's why substantial feeding will leave the donor sleepy. Now, we can feed on other tekoraet—it's what we did in the long-ago—but we're slower to recover from donation. Our scholars have experimented over the years, and we've found that most humans can donate every two or three days without hurting themselves. They're incredibly resilient in that way."

"But what about all those people at the show tonight?" Mia asked. "You were feeding on them…"

"Barely sipping from each. Morally, maybe it's a gray area, but the way I see it, people come to shows like that to be titillated—they want to feel that lust and excitement and lose themselves. I get up there, turn it on for a few minutes, get a little sip from the ladies in the room, and they go home remembering only that they had a *great* time." Cutting his eyes back to Anji, he said, "That's why your table stuck out to me tonight. Mia had that glow-in-the-dark necklace, but you got carried out of the room, and neither Mia nor Susan reacted to me."

"So you knew we weren't regular patrons, huh?" I said.

"Well, I knew you weren't regular female humans. It's amazing what you can learn when you work a room like that."

I frowned. "What do you mean?"

"Our power works on people of the opposite gender. I've seen many an audience member who passes for male or female but isn't truly so. Sometimes, they're trying to blend; sometimes, they're lying to themselves. I've actually met a couple over the years before and after they transitioned, and I'm happy they figured themselves out. That's why I wasn't sure what to make of you—I thought perhaps you were truly male."

"But what if someone's nonbinary?" I pressed.

Cary chuckled. "It happens. I'd have a lesser effect on them, but then Mia would also have an effect, so it would balance out."

"What about a nonbinary tekori?"

"Same principle. They're able to feed on males and females, but to a lesser degree."

Mia coughed and gave me a meaningful stare. "So, about my mom…"

Sorry, I mouthed.

"Sidetracked. Right," said Cary. "Okay…I got to Vegas in early '94 and set myself up. There was a bar near the club where I worked, and I used to hang out there in the afternoons—not to drink, but because they had cable and these really good club sandwiches. The owner and I were friendly. So I stop in one day in December, and there's this new girl behind the bar. Young, brunette, *pretty* blue eyes…"

"Mom?" Mia asked.

He nodded. "And she was about to have a come-apart. The place was quiet—it was me and a couple of old guys who came in every afternoon for beers and the sports shows—but she couldn't get the orders right. Couldn't even pour the beers correctly. Well, she looked like she was about to cry, so I called her over to my end of the bar and asked what was wrong, and she confessed that she had no clue what she was doing. She'd just run away from home, she had a fake ID, and she'd bluffed her way into a bartending job. Said she grew up in a family of teetotalers."

"Oh, yeah," Mia muttered.

Cary laughed to himself. "I wasn't working that day, and I didn't want to see her lose her job, so I offered to give her some pointers. By then, I'd learned a bit from the guys who tended bar in the club, so I could at least walk her through the basics of beer and liquor. She didn't know the first thing about cocktails, and neither did I, really, so I ran to work and copied the cheat sheets our bartenders used, and Janine and I practiced that evening." He smiled at the memory. "When she got off, she thanked me and asked if she could buy dinner. I wasn't about to take money from her, but I did take her out that night. Just Chinese—nothing inappropriate. We ate, and then I walked her home, and that was that."

"You didn't feed on her?" Mia asked, suspicion laced through her words.

His answer was immediate and vehement. "*Absolutely* not. I never had so much as a taste from Janine." When Mia remained skeptical, Cary explained, "The people who came to watch me were one thing, and the donors back home were willing and compensated. But Janine had no idea what I was, and I had no right to do that to her."

"You dated her, and you never told her?" Mia countered.

"Not at first. I kept stopping by for sandwiches, and she and I would chat. We didn't have a date, as such, until nearly the end of the year. I took her out to get her mind off the holidays. First Christmas away from home. She told me about her parents," he said, absently rubbing his knees. "How they were overbearing. She'd wanted to leave town for school, but they'd convinced her to go to the community college instead, and she was still living with them. She waited until her twentieth birthday, told them she was meeting a few friends for dinner, then headed west and was long gone before they realized she skipped town."

That sounded nothing like the Janine I knew, who'd perhaps become her parents as she grew up.

"She'd called them once, just to let them know she was alive, and they'd laid into her. She didn't tell them where she was. I said she'd done a brave thing and to keep her conversations with them minimal—she needed a chance to find herself before letting them try to wheedle her back home. She agreed, but that didn't make the holidays any easier for her."

For the first time in my life, I felt a twinge of sympathy

for Mia's mother.

"After that, we started seeing each other more outside of work, and we were exclusive by February," Cary continued. "I don't know about Janine, in retrospect, but I fell *hard*. Your mother is the first and only woman I've ever loved," he told Mia. "And because I loved her, I had to be honest with her. If we were going to be together, she had a right to know the truth. So...in early March, I set her down and told her what I was. Told her about the four worlds."

"How'd she take it?" Mia asked.

"Well, she thought I was joking at first, then she thought I might be crazy, so I took her to a bar that night and demonstrated. We got *thoroughly* drunk, and we didn't pay a dime. Once we sobered up at my place, I made her breakfast and swore I'd never do that to her...and I thought she was fine," he murmured. "She called me 'Spaceman' from time to time, but only when she was flirting." He paused for a moment, his face twitching, then said, "I went by the bar one afternoon in late May. Brought her flowers—you know, just because. The manager said she'd called in sick the previous day, so I went by her apartment, but no one answered the door. I tried calling her. She never picked up. Went back to the bar and said I thought something was really wrong with Janine—I thought she might have had a heart attack or something. So the owner and I went to her apartment, and we found the property manager and asked him to let us in. He was confused. Said she'd broken her lease and left town the day before. He opened the door to show us. The furniture was still there, but all of Janine's clothes and things were gone."

Holding Mia's gaze, he said, "She didn't leave a forwarding address or phone number, and she never called me again. I had no idea she was pregnant. Our fertility rate is pretty low, and she said she was on the pill—"

"You didn't use protection?"

"I offered, but once I explained that we don't contract or transmit STDs, she didn't see the need. Truly, we don't," he said as Mia's eyebrows rose. "I don't know what it is about our physiology that makes us immune, but it works. And it's not like I was having sex with anyone other than Janine, anyway. But...Mia, please hear me," he said softly. "If I'd known for a second that you existed, I'd have tracked you down and demanded to be part of your life. I'd have supported you, raised you...hell, I'd have cut my exile short and brought you home so at least you could be educated. To think that you grew up like that...and Janine let you *starve*..."

Cary's voice had thickened, but his distress seemed genuine to me, and a quick consultation with Terj strengthened that conclusion.

"You were not an accident from a random fling," he said. "Maybe a *little* accidental, sure, but I loved your mother to pieces. And I am so sorry that I'm just now meeting you..."

"You didn't know," Mia replied as he began to tear up. "I...look, if she never told you, I can't blame you for not being there."

"But I should have been. My kid suffered, and I could have prevented that." He shook his head. "Mia, honey, I'm sorry."

Her eyes filled, and though she sniffled, she nodded.

"Let me start to make this up to you. Come home with me," he offered. "Your grandparents will be delighted—I'm an only child unless something has changed in my absence, and I know they'd love to meet you."

She forced a strained smile. "A half-*human* grandchild?"

"It's honestly not a big deal for us. Most tekori–human crosses lean tekori, anyway, and from the sound of it, you're no exception. They'll be thrilled. It looks like you've got another necklace on—is that a translator? Do you speak any Common?"

"Just a few words," she admitted. "Anji's language

tutor was trying to work with her, and I sat in a time or two…"

"No worries, it's not important," he assured her. "You've got plenty of time to pick it up, and a translator will be great until you do."

Mia hesitated, then mumbled, "I don't want to hurt anyone."

"What are you…*oh*. Feeding?" She stiffened, and Cary's face softened. "It's okay, sweetheart. You've never had anyone teach you to do it properly, have you?"

She shook her head.

"My lease here is good for another week. Let me take you out tomorrow. I can show you how to feed safely."

"Can't I just…not?" she asked. "I'm fine eating extra food…"

"No, you're not. Not indefinitely. Be honest with me: you can feel the difference, can't you?"

"Yeah," she whispered.

Cary paused, choosing his words. "I know this is uncomfortable for you. It's different when you grow up tekorish—you still have your occasional moral qualms, but feeding is natural. Ever have a cat?"

"No…"

"Cats are interesting. They're obligate carnivores—they *have* to eat meat. You hear stories of well-meaning vegans trying to raise cats on that sort of diet, and the poor animals end up malnourished or worse. We have it a little easier," he said. "I mean, you can get by for a *long* time on cheeseburgers alone. But to be truly healthy, we need to feed, and the longer you starve yourself, the greater the deficit you'll need to make up. Let me teach you, Mia. I'll make sure you don't hurt anyone."

Her lip began to tremble, and she turned to Anji, torn.

"I love you, lass," Anji murmured. "If you need this…"

Mia looked back at Cary. "You promise I won't hurt anybody?"

"I swear it. I'll help you learn to control it, okay? You

don't have to be afraid of yourself." Glancing at the pizza boxes, he said, "Might want to eat up before it all goes cold, kid. Unless you like it that way—"

"Nope," she said, and shoved half a piece in her mouth.

As Fanakel got up to pass one of the boxes to Jerrcoa, his gaze landed on Cary's hand, and he frowned. "Your ring."

Cary raised his hand slightly, and the light flashed off a gold signet I hadn't noticed earlier. "I don't wear this at work."

"I would imagine not," he said quietly. "I am Fanakel. And you?"

Even with the brief time I'd been around the four worlds, I understood what he'd done. An elf willingly gave his name only to a superior or an equal, which eliminated the possibility of almost any non-elf being on a first-name basis with one of the True. For Fanakel to have offered his in such a fashion was a sign of respect, and anything less than reciprocity would be a grave insult.

Evidently, the meaning wasn't lost on our host. "Cerian Venel," he replied.

Given his true name's unfortunate homonym, I could easily imagine why he'd opted for "Cary."

One corner of Fanakel's mouth twitched. "I suspected." Turning to Mia, who stared back at him bemusedly, he said, "Do you recall some months ago when you bemoaned the fact that of our company, only you and Terj were untitled?"

Her confusion grew with the non sequitur. "Uh…yeah?"

"Well, it's down to Terj now, because unless I'm gravely mistaken, *that* man is the heir to the Amethyst Throne."

Mia's head slowly swiveled toward her father, who sighed and rubbed his eyebrows. "I was thinking we could do this one shock at a time…" he muttered.

"Are you *shitting* me?" she cried.

He looked at her wearily. "Crown prince of Ragatanu. The elf's perceptive, I'll give him that."

"Only because I've heard of the Ragantanese exile," said Fanakel, settling back into his chair. "And I was led to believe that it's limited to those close to the throne."

"You're not wrong." Focusing on stunned Mia, he said, "I never got around to telling Janine that part. I would have, but she left town."

"Holy shit," she mumbled.

I patted her on the back. "So, uh…welcome to the awkward princess club. We should make T-shirts."

"Ooh," said Anji, perking, "can I get in on this as well? Could we consider something in leather?"

"I…" Mia tried. "Y'all…"

This has been…informative, said Terj, tugging her to her feet, *but since Mia's mind is somewhat blown, and the alcohol and the hour probably aren't helping, we should get her to bed.*

"Oh, absolutely," Anji chirped. "Come on, lass, back to the vehicle…"

"But…but I…"

She'll text you once she's awake, Terj told Cary, who seemed poised to protest. *Jerrcoa, you can bring that in the car*, he added, and my brother, sheepishly smiling, clung to his pizza box as Fanakel pushed him out of the house.

CHAPTER 13

An insistent knocking at my hotel door woke me far too early the next morning. Rolling over, I found Terj's side of the bed empty, then forced myself upright and headed to the door, muttering undeserved curses about efficient housekeeping staff.

Instead, I found Mia in the hallway, puffy-faced and still in her pajamas. Her beautiful platinum waves had snarled into unruly tangles, and the smudges around her eyes told me she'd been too shaken or exhausted to remove her makeup before crashing—from the looks of her, probably both.

I stepped aside to let her in, then bolted the door behind her. "We're alone," I said. "Terj has probably gone out." I paused, considering Mia's expression. "You okay?"

She shook her head, and then her face crumbled.

I hugged her as she cried on my shoulder in ugly, hitching sobs that left her shaking. I'd seen Mia upset on plenty of occasions—hell, what were friends for?—but she seldom fell apart. Even when she'd called me from New York to tell me that she'd caught her girlfriend in bed with another woman, she'd held it together, understandably weepy and furious but not snotty crying. Raquel the Whore did not *deserve* her tears.

No, I hadn't seen Mia like this since the night her mother called her every name under the sun and disowned her, when I'd held her on our couch as she broke and bawled.

As much as Erianthe loathed me, at least I hadn't

grown up with her hatred in my life. Dad and Uncle Malachi had never left me feeling less than loved, and even when I'd thrown a childhood tantrum or tested my boundaries as a teenager, I'd known that I was wanted. Sure, my birth parents had tossed me out, but the Cole brothers had chosen me to be part of their family, and I'd gone through the world secure in the knowledge that whatever happened, they would have my back.

Mia hadn't been nearly as lucky. While we'd both been children of single-parent households, I'd always had the sense that Janine hadn't really wanted her daughter—an impression that had only solidified when Janine told Mia that she was the byproduct of a random, ill-advised fling. Mia's mother had been strict with her—perhaps the effect of her conservative church, or perhaps an overcorrecting attempt to keep her daughter from making the same mistakes—and the only reason Mia was allowed the freedom of my house was because Janine knew that Dad or Ms. Quince was always keeping an eye on us.

When we reached adolescence, Janine had tried to tighten her grip on the leash, nudging Mia away from the county high school events and toward her church's small youth group, where surely nothing more scandalous than handholding would be tolerated. That had been the start of Mia's rebellion, and when she'd caught the youth pastor fondling one of the sophomore girls behind the church, she'd put her foot down. The Randolph women's relationship had devolved into shouting matches, toothless threats, and Mia storming off to spend the night with me. Tempers had cooled somewhat by the time Mia and I left for college, but Janine had nagged Mia toward a purity-centered student organization and hinted that it was time for her to find a "nice" boy before temptation led her astray. Mia had demurred as to both suggestions, her announcement that she was accepting an internship in New York had led to more shouty phone calls, and her coming out had blown up what was left of the fragile peace.

I mean, it's one thing to be familiar with homophobic slurs, but hearing them from the person who's supposed to love you unconditionally, along with screamed denouncements that you're bound for Hell…that's a new level of hurt.

If Cary had told the truth—and neither Terj nor I had sensed that he was lying—then Janine had known how to find him but had unilaterally decided that Mia wouldn't have a father. Janine had been told about the tekorish peculiarities but hadn't seen fit to mention them to her daughter. Shit, Janine had known about the existence of worlds beyond Earth but hadn't said a peep. And while Janine had rejected Mia, Cary hadn't batted an eye when she'd introduced her dwarven girlfriend. Cary *wanted* to be her father.

Mia could have had that all along, if not for Janine.

So I guided her to the bed and held her as she cried, and when Terj returned and found the door locked, I quickly explained, and he gave us space. I knew why Mia had come to me instead of Anji: we were the closest thing either of us had had to a sister for a long time, and Mia didn't have to explain to me the years of greater and lesser hurts behind her tears. Maybe she'd already told Anji part of it—maybe all of it—but I'd been there as it happened.

When her sobs began to quiet, I rubbed her back and murmured, "You're worthy of love, Mia. You always have been. And there's nothing wrong with you."

She raised her head and wiped her runny nose on the back of her hand. "What if Cary spends more time with me and realizes—"

"Realizes what? That your mom's a raging psychopath? That he's missed out on *so* much? That you're an awesome friend?"

She smiled weakly. "That I'm absolutely not princess material."

I snorted. "*Please.* At least you've got the looks for it."

She waved that aside.

"Honestly! You want to know how many times Erianthe found a way to call me fat or complain about my scar? But more importantly," I said, leaning closer, "if the heir to the throne of this Ragatanu place has spent your entire lifetime dancing in his skivvies, then what do you possibly have to worry about?"

"Maybe he won't like me once he actually gets to know me…"

"Mia." I hugged her again, holding on until her breathing slowed. "After last night, I really don't think that's going to be a problem. Clean yourself up and call him. Let him give you some pointers. If *you* want to get to know *him* better after that, then so be it. Whatever else you may be," I said as she sat up again, "you're one of the best people I've ever had the privilege of knowing, okay? And you deserve to be happy. Whether that means going home with Anji or giving Ragatanu a try or…I don't know, heading back to New York and working three jobs until you figure out what you want to do with your life, that's up to you. But whatever you do, you are so worthy of love."

She wiped her face on her T-shirt, further smearing her old makeup, then composed herself sufficiently to give me a little smile. "You really think I should go out with Cary?"

"Without question. If nothing else, let him help you learn to feed."

Her mouth tightened. "Yeah. *That.*"

"You are what you are," I said, "and I know it's weird for you, but look at it this way: you've been feeding without guidance to this point, and you haven't hurt anyone yet."

She arched a brow. "Fanakel might disagree."

"He's perfectly fine. One bad night on the beach and a little introspection. And if that's the worst you've done…"

Mia huffed a sigh. "Maybe."

"Go on, text Cary. He's probably waiting by the phone."

She raised up enough to pull her phone from the thigh pocket of her leggings and turned it over in her hands. "My father," she murmured.

"The exotic dancer—who has damn good moves, you know?"

A snort answered that. "Yeah, and also the crown prince of fucking Ragatanu…which is where, exactly?"

"Borders Cirivant, apparently, but that's the best I can do."

Mia stared at the phone for another moment. "And I'm a goddamned princess, huh?"

"It's fun!" I said with forced cheer.

She smirked at me, then unlocked the phone and opened her messages.

While Mia showered, I sat in the lobby with Terj, eating a muffin and looking over tourist brochures. I'd narrowed the options to shopping and an aquarium—things we could do without needing fake IDs or expensive tickets—when Fanakel came running off the elevator and made a beeline for us. "There you are," he said, absently tugging his ski cap lower over his ears. "Come with me, both of you."

I jumped to my feet. "Is Jerrcoa—"

"Come see."

We rode back upstairs and jogged after Fanakel, who let us in and swept one arm toward my brother. "All right, show them," he ordered.

Jerrcoa, who'd moved his wheelchair in front of the window, turned to us and beamed. After a few seconds' concentration, he managed to lift his right leg off the chair seat and move his knee back and forth.

"Oh, my God!" I cried, and ran across the room to hug him. "Jerr, that's amazing! Can you move the other?"

"It's a bit harder," he admitted, but managed to elevate the left leg. "I don't know what the problem is on this side.

The growths feel like they're gone, but my left half still lags."

"It may always be weaker," I said, sitting on the edge of his bed. "If that whole area has been compressed for so long, you might have damage that takes years to heal, if ever. But you've made miraculous progress in *days*, and if this keeps up…"

He sighed and manually moved his left leg back into position. "Maybe I'll walk again someday."

I don't have plans.

We turned to Terj, who'd observed with his arms folded. *Susan, if you want to go out, don't let me stop you, but unless Jerrcoa is dying to see some fish—*

He frowned bemusedly. "What fish?"

"There are aquariums in town, but never mind," I said. "You think he's ready, Terj?"

I'm willing to try if he is.

Jerrcoa's eyes brightened. "Really?"

Sure. Don't panic.

"Why would I—"

His thought ended in a yelp as he floated from his chair.

Get your legs under you, Terj told him. *Straighten them, if you can.*

His breathing had quickened, and he flailed as his body rotated upright. "I'm—"

You're not falling. I've got you, and I will not drop you. Terj stepped closer and held out his hands, and Jerrcoa grabbed them. *You're just learning what this feels like*, he soothed. *If your knees buckle or you can't balance, I'm here.*

Jerrcoa clung to him like a life preserver as his feet touched the ground. "I don't know…how do I…"

Balance? Amusement colored Terj's thought. *It's not easy, and that's with fully functional legs. But let's experiment. Want to work on it?*

He started to answer, but his brow knit with worry. "You don't mind?"

I wouldn't offer if I did.

"And seeing as I'm similarly at a loss for plans," said Fanakel, "why don't I grab food and...assist? Superintend?"

Perfect. Terj glanced at Fanakel and smirked. *Would we consider this male bonding?*

"Only once Susan leaves."

"Y'all," I began, "I—"

"*Out*," said Fanakel. "You've been driving for days. Take Anji and try to relax, won't you?"

You know she'll be a wreck while Mia's gone, Terj added.

I looked from him to my brother and Fanakel, then rolled my eyes and threw up my hands. "Fine. Sheesh. *Men*," I muttered, and saw myself out.

As anticipated, Anji was nervous all afternoon, hopeful for Mia but afraid of what might happen if things went poorly. "I just don't want Cary to hurt her feelings," she said as we strolled past a saltwater tank. "She tries to hide it, but she's sensitive, you know?"

"Absolutely." I paused to watch a small shark glide by, and Anji stopped beside me, arms folded. "How *are* things back home for you?" I asked quietly.

"Fine." When I turned and looked questioningly down at her, she grunted. "As good as can be expected. Father likes Mia. My siblings like her. And we all proceed on the understood falsehood that she's my friend. Well, that's not entirely false," she amended, "but it's not true, either."

"Have y'all talked about anything more long-term?"

Anji sighed, and her crossed arms tightened. "She's the one for me. I know it. I think she feels the same..." she began, though her voice drifted off before she could finish.

"But?" I prompted.

"But I know damn well that we can never be acknowledged spouses. The priests wouldn't allow it."

Knowing Anji's religious sensibilities, I tried to be

political in my questioning. "Is that a priest-made rule, or is it something the, uh...High Queen came up with?"

She grinned at my awkward attempt. "The gods have never spoken on the subject. They direct that marriage is for life and thereafter, and that one should not remarry after the death of a spouse, but nothing in Their pronouncements concerns the specifics of what a married couple must be. The priests are quite sure that They meant a couple to be female and male, which does make sense from a procreative standpoint," she allowed, "but to answer your question, there's no firm divine instruction."

"And they...speak to your people often?"

"Rarely. There's only one oracle at any time, and she cannot force the gods to speak through her. We find that They are more likely to make Themselves known during major festivals, but that's never guaranteed. You know, when Father and Mother were married, my grandparents arranged for the oracle to accept a question from each of them, but they went unanswered. The gods speak as They choose."

"Well, that's inconvenient."

"What," she retorted, "yours are any more forthcoming?"

"Not lately."

Anji watched as the shark circled and passed by us again. "I love Mia," she murmured. "I know you do as well, and since she has no close family to consult, I...hope you approve."

I saw the anxiety in Anji's eyes and tried to reassure her. "I do. As long as Mia is happy, I'm happy, and I've never seen her quite so...*easy* with anyone as she is with you."

"Do you suppose this would be enough for her? Devotion without the trappings of marriage? The understood fiction?"

"I mean, I can't read her mind," I replied, "but I'm pretty damn sure she loves you."

"But is that enough?" she pressed.

"I think you'd know by now if it weren't."

The shark drifted by, lazily swimming toward the far side of the tank.

"Worst comes to worst, you could stay here," I said. "I wouldn't know how to go about getting fake documentation for you, but you two could get married. Figure out a life together."

Anji smiled sadly. "My father is lenient, but only to a point. Permanent relocation might push him too far. Still," she mused, staring at the faux reef in front of us, "if it meant either angering Father or losing Mia…"

"Not something you have to decide today," I said, and steered her on. "Want to hit the gift shop?"

As we headed toward the exit, my phone chirped, and I found a message from Mia. "They're at a bar," she said, and showed Anji the grinning selfie that Mia and Cary had taken. "She wants to know if we all want to grab dinner tonight. He's got a recommendation."

Anji studied the photo for a moment, then nodded, satisfied. "That would be nice, I think."

Cary's recommendation turned out to be a quiet steakhouse far from the Strip, the sort of place where seven people could eat in relative peace and for less than a grand. He was in high spirits and insisted on paying, and Mia seemed almost giddy as she chatted with Anji at the table. The afternoon had been a rousing success all around: Mia had fed without harming anyone, scoring several free drinks in the process, Jerrcoa had managed to "walk" across the room with Terj supporting him, and…well, Anji and I had passed several high-end boutiques and shown what I felt was admirable restraint.

After our steaks arrived, Cary turned to Mia and cleared his throat. "So, I've got a proposal for you, kid."

She put down her fork and smiled expectantly.

"Come home with me. I'll be making the trip in a few days' time, and I want to introduce you to your family. We won't have far to go once we're through the tunnel—it opens in the border area between Ragatanu and Cirivant, and I'll be able to send word for transportation once we're there." Before Mia could object, her father hastily added, "I know you've got your own thing going on here, but this is long overdue. Anji, you come, too. Hell, all of you are welcome," he said, looking around the table. "If my parents have seen that recording, then they'll be pleased to host you."

Anji softly coughed. "In...Ragatanu?"

"You'll be perfectly safe. We never have more than a handful of dwarven visitors at any time, so no one will mistake you for a donor, especially not in the palace complex. Let me prove that we're not all a bunch of voracious monsters, eh?"

When I caught Mia's eye, I saw the unspoken request there.

"Could be fun," I said. "I'm certainly in no rush to get back to Daril...what about the rest of you?"

Terj was unopposed, and though somewhat unconvinced, Fanakel and Anji agreed, but Jerrcoa picked at his dinner and said nothing. Noticing him, Cary said, "You're welcome, too, Jerrcoa—we can make accommodations for you."

"Thank you," he mumbled, "but I don't want to go anywhere."

I mentally kicked myself. "The growths. *Shit.*"

Cary frowned. "Growths?"

"He contracted the Growing Fever young," Anji explained. "I don't know what you call it, but the afflicted have—"

"Growths in the lower back," Cary finished, nodding. "Yeah, I know what you're talking about. It's almost always mild with us..." His voice trailed off as he considered my brother in his wheelchair. "Are you worried about contracting it again in Ga'besh?"

"No," said Jerrcoa. "We think the growths need Aen to survive—ever since I've been here, they've been shrinking. I think they're gone now, or at least too small to feel, but if I leave…"

I could only imagine his desperation. He'd come closer to walking that day than he had since he was a toddler.

Fortunately, Cary got it. "An experiment," he suggested. "You say the growths may have disappeared. Come to Ragatanu with me, and let's see what happens. If your condition deteriorates, we'll have confirmation of the cause, and I will *personally* see you back to Earth. And have you told your parents of this development? You can contact them—we always have a maladeta or two stationed in Enead. If you linger on Earth without a word for weeks or months, I'm sure they'll worry."

He smirked. "You haven't met my parents, have you?"

"I've yet to have the pleasure," Cary replied with measured politeness, and I wondered what Mia had told him about our experiences with Erianthe. "But what do you say? Come be my guests for a time, see what our land offers, and perhaps you'll find something redeeming about our people. *Especially* you," he said, squeezing Mia's shoulder. "This is your heritage, little one—let's make up for lost time."

"I'm in."

The table turned as one to Anji, who smiled and lifted her Coke. "If you're not comfortable—" Mia began.

"I want what's best for you, and you need this, lass. I'm with you."

"A daughter of Blackhorn Mountain would be an honored guest," said Cary, "and my daughter's girlfriend even more so."

Fanakel grinned at Anji in challenge. "If you think I'll allow you to show me up—"

"It's not a contest," she replied primly.

"*Right.* I'll come," he said to Cary.

"Splendid! Now, I apologize," Cary said as Fanakel started to take a sip of water, "but I didn't catch this earlier—whose are you, Enoul's or Enarl's?"

Fanakel coughed in his shock, and Jerrcoa gave him a hard thump between the shoulder blades. After a moment's wheezing, he managed, "My father is the king."

"Thanks—I didn't want to botch introductions. Are you all right?"

"Fine," he said, and coughed again.

I kept eating but heard Terj's voice in my mind: *It's not just dwarves who regard elves as stuck-up assholes, is it?*

It is not, I said, and winked at him. *Are you okay with this?*

Sure. What's a tekori going to do to me, anyway?

Yeah, but I know we talked about California…

He stopped playing with his fillet for a moment and smiled at me. *We can see California another time. You need to go to Ga'besh to support Mia, and I just want to be with you.*

Have I mentioned lately that I love you? I replied.

Maybe, but I like to be reminded. He glanced at his steak. *Do you think you could ask for some mustard?*

Not in a steakhouse, babe.

Terj rolled his eyes. *I was afraid of that*, he said, and soldiered on.

We decided to stay in Las Vegas for a few more days while Cary packed what little he wanted to take home with him. I'd have a chance to rest up for the drive, Jerrcoa could continue to practice his long-lost walking skills, and Mia and her father would have a little longer to get acquainted before he introduced Ragatanu to its newest princess.

But our plans fell apart shortly after two the next morning, when I awoke to my phone ringing on the table beside the bed. Rolling over, I saw an unfamiliar number with a 606 area code—eastern Kentucky, but no one I knew. Assuming it was a wrong number, I answered and croaked, "Hello?"

"Susan? Is this Susan Cole?"

The anxious voice on the other end made me sit up, and Terj, who'd been drifting beside me, looked over to see what was going on.

I cleared my throat. "Ms. Randolph?"

"Oh, thank God. I was afraid you'd have gotten a new phone by now—"

Nothing good could come of an early morning call from Janine. "Is something wrong?" I asked. "I'm sorry, I'm out of town—"

"Is Mia with you?"

"Uh…"

"*Please*," she begged, "is Mia there? I don't have her number anymore, and something's happened, and I need to know that she's okay…"

I frowned in the darkness. A frantic call at that hour suggested nothing less than a death in the family, but Mia's grandparents were dead, and she had no other close kin. "She's with me," I said cautiously, "but it's very early here, and—"

"*Jesus.* Thank you, Jesus…"

Terj turned on the lights while I swung my legs out of bed, unsure how to proceed with Mia's mother sobbing on the other end of the line. "Uh…do you want me to pass a message along?" I asked once I could get a word in. I wasn't about to give up Mia's number—she'd changed it after Janine disowned her—but I figured it wouldn't hurt to put the ball in Mia's court. Janine just kept crying, however, and after a moment, I snapped, "Ms. Randolph, it's two in the morning, so what the hell is wrong?"

That seemed be the long-distance shake she needed, and she released a shuddery breath to steady herself. "It…it's gone…everything is g-gone—"

"*What* is gone?"

"Our home!" she wailed.

Terj looked at me and cocked his head. *Janine,* I told him. *Hang on, she's a mess.*

He grimaced, then pointed to the coffeemaker, and I nodded my gratitude.

"Ms. Randolph," I tried again over her crying, "you need to calm down and tell me what's going on, okay? Did someone break in your house? Was there a fire?"

The next words she said turned the pit of my stomach to ice: "Not just my house. The whole town. It's gone."

"I don't understand," I said, distantly aware of the sounds of Terj filling the water reservoir. "What's happened? An earthquake or something? Need me to call Joel Rogers?"

My questions were answered with more tears, until finally, I reached my limit. "Janine, for fuck's sake, pull yourself together and *talk to me*!" I yelled into the phone.

She gasped—one did not use *that* word around Janine Randolph if one were wise—but the shock distracted her from her latest crying jag. "I...I don't know exactly what happened," she blubbered. "I was out of town last night, staying with a friend who just had...had eye surgery, and I got the call two hours ago and hurried home, and there's police and fire trucks and ambulances and some reporters—"

"Did something blow up?"

"I...I don't—"

"Janine," I said, fighting for calm, "I need you to take a deep breath and focus."

Shaken as she was, she proved willing to follow instructions. "There wasn't an explosion," she said once she was able. "Not like a gas line or anything. I mean, I think there *were* some explosions, but small ones—"

"Why? What's damaged?"

"I don't know the full extent, but as far as I can tell...everything. The fire at my house wasn't that bad— they got the shed, but it rained yesterday, and it didn't spread to the garage. But no one's being allowed downtown, and I didn't even try to get into your neighborhood with all the trucks there, and...and I didn't know if Mia…"

"She's safe," I heard myself say, though my mind reeled. "What…what started the fires?"

"Maniacs," she said. "In costumes or something. They got away, but my doorbell camera saw them run past."

"Can you send me a link?"

"I think so…"

My phone dinged a long few seconds later with the incoming message, and I said, "Let me take a look at this, and I'll call you back."

"Susan—"

"I'll call you, Ms. Randolph," I repeated, and hung up.

Terj carried over a doctored cup of coffee for me as I queued up the video. *What happened?*

"Someone attacked Cole's Crossing," I muttered, taking the mug from him, then hit play.

Janine's door camera wasn't top-of-the-line, nor was it designed for nighttime filming, but she'd installed a security light in the front yard when Mia and I were kids, which offered a decent enough view of the sidewalk to show me the crowd moving past. Perhaps a dozen figures all told, they wore helmets and what looked like light leather armor, they seemed to glide over the asphalt on hovering skateboards, and they carried long tubes like rifles. Before I could try to puzzle out what the tubes might be, a man aimed one toward Janine's shed, and a brilliant green fireball exploded from the business end and flew offscreen.

"The fuck is *that*?" I asked Terj, coffee forgotten.

Firethrowers. They're Aen-based weapons, forged pieces, he replied. *I saw some in the armory in Deoni and skulked around there long enough until I had a chance to watch them employed at target practice.*

As dread clawed at my gut, I paused the video, then zoomed in as far as the picture would allow. The men on the sidewalk were horribly grainy, but one had angled himself just enough in the security light's glow to give me a fuzzy frontal view.

Even in the darkness, the wavy blue and green bars of the Darili flag were clear as day.

Ten minutes later, after a phone call to Mia and a rude door pounding to wake Fanakel and Jerrcoa, the six of us huddled in my room to watch the recording again.

"That's the royal guard," my brother said when I froze the picture. "They're the only ones with access to the firethrowers and the floaters."

"The boards?" Anji asked.

He nodded. "Dwarven construction. They're expensive, but they can move as quickly as a chiquiw, or so I hear."

Who controls those men?

Jerrcoa glanced from Anji to Terj. "They answer only to Mother."

I said nothing, trying not to cry.

Erianthe had sent her men to firebomb my hometown. Putting aside the obvious implication that she *really* didn't want me to return from my visit, I had no idea how many homes and businesses her hit squad had destroyed—how many people might have lost their houses, their livelihoods...their lives...because of me.

Mia's hand landed on my shoulder. "Suze..."

"I have to get home," I said, and passed Anji my phone. Pacing to the window, I ran my hands through my hair and tried to spot the clear path forward, but my mind whirled with a storm of fear, guilt, and anger.

I'd leaned my forehead against the cold glass when I heard Mia's voice across the room: "Mom? It's me. Where are you?"

I turned and saw that Mia had taken the phone from Anji, and she put a finger to her lips as she triggered the speaker.

"—you're okay. Thank *God*, I was so worried about—"

"Where are you?" Mia repeated with impressive calm.

"I...they let me back in the house..."

"Are the men gone? The ones from your video?"

"I don't know. I haven't seen any, and the cops aren't talking."

"Okay. Listen to me, all right? Do you have any guns in the house?"

Janine stuttered briefly, then said, "Just a .38. I haven't fired it in years."

"Load it. Keep it loaded," Mia replied. "Stay inside, lock your doors, and keep the hell out of the woods. I'm on my way."

"Mia—" her mother began, but she'd already hung up and tossed the phone onto my bed.

"You don't have to do this," I told Mia. "Go back to Ragatanu with Cary, and I'll deal with Janine."

But she shook her head. "Those bastards hit the Crossing. We've got business first."

A night owl by virtue of his trade, Cary was still awake and packing when Mia called with the news. "He's not happy," Mia reported, "and if there are really Darili soldiers lurking around there, he doesn't want me anywhere close, but he also knows it's not his decision."

Fanakel raised a brow at that. "No?"

"Nope," she said, folding her arms. "He's been cool thus far, but he hasn't unlocked that level of dad status yet."

Still, Cary had offered to compress his packing schedule and come with us, and since I had no idea what we were heading into, I didn't mind bringing a more adept adult along for the ride.

We checked out of the hotel and were at Cary's place by four, where I found a pair of suitcases and a duffel bag waiting by the garage door. "This is it," he said, lugging a black garbage bag out to the bin. "Let's hit the road."

I glanced around at the kitchen, which still seemed put together but for the empty pantry and refrigerator. "What about the rest of your stuff?"

"The house came furnished," he explained, "and I told my landlord to do what she likes with the rest. She knows I've got a family emergency," he said, and popped the trunk of his Corolla.

Mia, who'd joined me by the garage, watched uncertainly as he packed. "We came west largely on I-40. I think it's about the same from here if we take I-40 or I-70 east…"

He lifted his suitcases into place with a grunt. "It's late in the season for snow in Denver, but since we're in a hurry—"

"I-40 it is. About thirty hours if the traffic gods are gracious."

Cary slammed the lid and considered us. "Who's driving?" When I raised a finger, he asked, "Are you okay for that? Did you get any sleep?"

"Caffeine is a wonderful drug," I replied. "And *you* haven't slept—"

"Which is why I'm claiming the first shift," Mia interrupted, holding out her hand. "Keys, please."

He paused, taken aback. "I can—"

"*Keys*, Cary. You're not driving into a ditch on my account." To me, she said, "I'll take point with the map, and you follow, okay?"

"Can do."

"Great. Anji!" she called into the house. "Want to ride with Cary and me?"

In short order—and probably against his better judgment—Cary found himself sitting shotgun in his own car. Mia pulled up to the mailbox so he could leave the housekeys and garage door opener, and then she peeled off through the chilly predawn, speeding southeast toward Arizona.

In the Explorer, Terj had migrated to the front, giving

Jerrcoa and Fanakel each one of the middle-row chairs. As we picked up I-11 out of town, Terj asked, *What's the plan for today?*

"Drive as far as we can push it," I replied, and looked in the mirror at my other passengers. "Strap in, guys. It's going to be a long ride."

Though Mia and I were keyed up and anxious to get home, we were also under-slept, and the rational heads prevailed an hour east of Albuquerque. Covering only nine hours of driving was disappointing—even with stops for lunch and gas and a time zone change, it wasn't yet dinnertime—but I'd had to jerk the wheel on too many occasions to keep fighting when Terj insisted it was time for a break. We found a halfway decent motel and grabbed four rooms, and while Cary drove off in search of pizza, the rest of us gathered in my room so I could check in with Janine.

She picked up on the second ring. "Susan! Where are you?"

"About two days away," I said, stifling a yawn. "Coming as fast as we can. What's the latest?"

Janine hesitated, and I heard so much in that brief silence.

"I'm sorry, hon," she finally said. "Your house is gone."

My chest clenched, and though I fought it, my eyes started tearing up. "All of it?" I asked stupidly.

"Looks like a total loss. Most of the ones on your street were hit hard," Janine reported. "There's a neighborhood group that's started compiling whatever people can salvage from their security and doorbell cameras, but I haven't seen any footage yet from your block. The county deputies are keeping order."

I wasn't surprised that the county was involved. Chief Brundage was a nice man, as police officers went, but as he comprised a third of the town's force, backup was necessary. "What about downtown?"

Janine hissed. "Looks like a warzone. City Hall is gone, and so is everything for two blocks around it." Again, she hesitated. "Susan, I'm so sorry, but your family's store was hit hard. I haven't been close enough to see it, but I wouldn't hold out much hope."

I squeezed my eyes closed to stop the tears from falling. "Are the Plunketts okay? I haven't heard from Annie yet, but if you see her before I talk to her, could you please tell her that I'll help them? Once the insurance comes through, I can give her and Dewey at least a few months' pay to get them on their feet."

Her silence that time was deafening, and I squeezed the phone so hard that my fingers ached. "Ms. Randolph? Are you there?"

"The Plunketts' house caught fire," she said softly. "There were no survivors."

I dropped the phone as if it were cursed, and it bounced off the thin floral comforter. Mia caught it and held it close to her face. "Who else?"

"Too many," her mother replied, and started to cry again.

CHAPTER 14

As Mia refused to give her mother her phone number, the news from home came to me over the next day's drive.

Charity Ludlow, the sweet old lady who ran the town's lone sandwich shop, and her housebound husband, Warner, hadn't survived their injuries.

Chief Brundage had lived, but his wife, Emmaline, had been helping their daughter with her newborn that night, and that entire branch of the family had been snuffed out.

Duffy Shoemaker, who'd carried a torch for Mia despite logic and against all odds, had succumbed to smoke inhalation.

Antoinette O'Leary, Mia's former employer, had survived, though her restaurant was a burned-out shell. Her home was one of the few close to the center of town that had made it through the night largely unscathed, and she'd turned it into a combination shelter and walk-in clinic. The only true medical professional left in Cole's Crossing was Tanya Crooks, an EMT, who'd received permission from her boss to run triage out of Antoinette's kitchen. The town's lone doctor, Elizabeth Nichols, had died when the top floor of her house collapsed on her and her trapped children.

Reverend Houghton and his wife had died—both Grace Methodist and their adjacent home had been hit hard—so the clergy and congregations of the nearby Methodist, Baptist, and Episcopal churches had pulled together to assist with work crews and pastors. With no large buildings left intact downtown, the Baptists had erected their revival tent in the park, and everyone was making the most of it, passing out blankets and warm meals to the shellshocked and suddenly homeless populace. The reporters parked their vans nearby, partly for easy access to interviewees, and the church ladies kept slipping them sandwiches as they worked.

But what hit me as hard as the news of the Plunketts was the report that Joel Rogers had died of his burns. He'd gone out a hero: upon seeing flames down the street, where Opal Vaughan, the elderly head librarian, lived, he'd run from his house to see if she needed help. The place had been burning hot when he arrived—no one could as yet explain why the fires had seemed so *green*—but Joel had pushed past the onlookers and run in to find Opal. While he'd managed to carry her to safety, he'd been badly injured in the process, and he'd succumbed in the ambulance.

Seemingly every time the phone rang, it was Janine with more bad tidings—bodies found, children left orphaned, parents bereft of their kids, my former classmates' names added to the register downtown. Paul Croaker, our lone attorney, had stepped in to help where he could, running an information booth under the Baptists' tent with phone numbers for shelters, updated lists of the injured and dead, and advice for people who had no idea how to arrange burials, deal with life insurance policies, or settle estates. He'd called in favors and enlisted his friends, and by lunchtime on the second day after the attack, a pack of old lawyers and a cadre of paralegals had descended to help manage the chaos.

At my request, Janine had driven out to the woods and reported that Uncle Malachi's cabin was untouched. "It's locked up tight," she said, her feet crunching over the decaying leaves as she circled the building. "But considering how far away this place is, I'm not surprised that those maniacs missed it."

Knowing where they'd come from, I was rather more

surprised, but I kept my thoughts to myself. Then again, the cabin was dark and small—maybe the Darilis had assumed it was uninhabited, or at least not worth burning.

We drove hard that day, stopping only for gas and drive-thru meals, and coasted into the outskirts of St. Louis by the grace of strong coffee around eleven-thirty that night. As Mia dealt with the desk clerk, I brought Jerrcoa's wheelchair around, and Terj and Fanakel lifted him down. He'd passed the time by working out behind me, lifting his thin legs over and over until he was red in the face, but he'd said little since we'd left New Mexico.

"Tired?" I asked as he settled into his chair.

He looked up at me, his expression blank. "Numb."

I closed the door and rolled my stiff shoulders. "Sorry, man. I know this drive isn't fun—"

"I don't mind the drive," he interrupted. "It's everything else."

"I shouldn't have gotten you into this mess," I said, leaning against the Explorer.

"I'm glad you did." When I frowned, Jerrcoa shrugged. "In the last days, I've had confirmation of something I'd heretofore only suspected. I'm expendable to Mother."

"She loves—"

"She sent the royal guard to burn down the town where she believed you to be, knowing that I was with you. That's the very definition of expendable. I mean, she has two other children who are reasonably healthy, so I'm no great loss. I'm not politically useful."

"She likes you a hell of a lot more than she does me," I protested.

"Perhaps. But she hates you more than she loves me," Jerrcoa countered, "and...well." He sighed. "It's not always fun to be proven correct."

"I'm sorry."

He reached for my hand, and I squeezed his. "Don't be. You've given me something to hope for, and...I know I'm not the easiest traveling companion—"

You're not a burden, said Terj, coming around the vehicle to join us. *In case no one has told you that.*

Jerrcoa smirked up at him. "Says the person who spent a day holding me upright."

Exactly. And if I don't find you burdensome after that, then no one else should. But give yourself time—you'll be walking soon enough.

"Assuming the growths don't return after I'm back within the Aen," he muttered.

Terj crouched in front of his chair and said, *Look at me.* When Jerrcoa did, Terj told him, *Sometimes, things must worsen to improve. The most agonizing experience of my life—and I've known my share of pain, mind you—was the time I spent Outside, but going there was the only way to be free of that damn sword. Soon enough, whether you're bound for Ragatanu or elsewhere, you'll pass through the Crossing again. Perhaps the growths will come back. Perhaps they won't. In either case, you'll learn more about your condition and how you may eventually cure it. Or help someone else be cured*, he added, holding Jerrcoa's stare. *You're a pioneer here. That can't be easy, but if what you find now can save another from a youth like yours…*

"I shouldn't complain," Jerrcoa mumbled.

You have many reasons to complain, Terj replied, standing, *but for whatever it's worth, I'm proud of you.*

My little brother really did look like a kid when he smiled, I mused, and let Terj escort me to bed.

Given our late arrival that night, we didn't leave Monday morning until close to eight, better rested but anxious to be on our way. We picked up I-64 for the last push, and by three-thirty that afternoon, we were speeding past the familiar pastures and stands of trees toward Cole's Crossing.

I'd taken the lead for the final stretch, but as I neared the town limit sign, I saw a pair of cop cars and some wooden barricades stretched across the road. Slowing, I approached the roadblock and pulled to a stop, then rolled down my window as a sheriff's deputy walked up.

"Ma'am," he said, giving the inside of my vehicle a cursory inspection. "I'm afraid this road is closed to through traffic. You need to turn around, go back about half a mile, and pick up—"

"Oh, hell—Susan? Susan Cole?" Another officer appeared behind the first, and I recognized one of Cole's Crossing's two police deputies. "Shit, kid, you picked a great time to be out of town," he said, and nudged his partner aside. "You heard, right?"

I nodded. "Bits and pieces. I came home as quickly as I could…"

He reached into the SUV and patted my arm. "Nothing you can do, hon. Come to see what's left?"

"And Mia Randolph," I said, thumbing my hand toward the black Corolla behind me. "She lives here, too."

"Sure, sure." He tapped the top of my window and retreated a few paces. "You're good to go. Stay out of the way of the search and recovery crews, there's food downtown if you need it, and try not to make more work for anyone, okay?"

"Yes, sir."

"Y'all be careful, now," he cautioned, and moved one of the barriers to the side.

As much as I wanted to see what remained of my home and business, the first priority was the living, and that meant a trip to the Randolph home. Avoiding the blocked-off avenues leading to Main Street, I cruised through the residential roads, horrified at the devastation. For every home with busted windows or a little smoke damage, two or three were nothing but charred debris. I'd seen photos of towns destroyed by tornadoes—flattened blocks, splintered boards everywhere, dazed people digging through piles of rubble in search of baby pictures—but never had I imagined my hometown approaching that level of destruction.

And I knew, as I skirted a haphazardly parked pickup truck, that we would never recover.

At least tornado victims tended to have warning—radios, TV meteorologists, sirens, or hell, a funky-looking sky portending trouble. My friends and neighbors had been asleep in their beds when Erianthe's men came flying through. Maybe some had awakened to the crash of breaking glass. Maybe some had heard fire alarms. Judging by the growing number of dead and wounded, plenty had awakened to find their houses in flames around them and the exits blocked off.

Cole's Crossing was only a town of about six hundred people. At least a hundred of them were dead, hundreds more had been hospitalized, and most of the place had been rendered uninhabitable overnight. If the downtown blocks were as ruined as Janine had suggested, then what would people have here besides memories? Lake tourism was nice, but it wasn't enough to justify the rebuilding of an entire community. Our larger neighbors would absorb whatever part of the population remained, and in time, Cole's Crossing would become a curiosity of overgrown lots, perhaps reabsorbed by the woods from which it had been carved.

Driving through was like viewing a corpse.

When we reached Mia's street, I saw a few houses in decent condition, and her mother's was one of the best of the bunch. Suddenly weary and fighting the urge to cry, I parked on the street and slid out while Mia pulled Cary's car into the driveway.

Before I could unpack my brother's chair, the front door opened, and Janine ran out—same gray-streaked brown hair, same pinched face, same light-washed denim jacket as she'd worn for twenty years tossed over dirty pink corduroy pants. Seeing me, she cried, "Susan! Where's…"

Her question ended in a strangled gasp as Cary stepped out of the passenger seat, tugged down his shirt, and scowled at her. "Hello, Janine," he said, folding his well-toned arms.

Janine's eyes widened to saucers. "C-*Cary*?" she stuttered. "How...but..." She looked away from him at the sound of the driver's door slamming, and her mouth hung open as Mia walked around the car to join him.

"Are you hurt?" Mia demanded.

It took Janine a few seconds, but she recovered enough to remember how words worked. "Mia Elizabeth Randolph, what have you *done* to yourself?" she shouted.

Janine hadn't seen her daughter since Mia had developed her pinup figure and ridiculous good looks, so the question was fair. Mia, however, was in no mood for critique.

"Are you hurt?" she asked again. "Is the house in decent shape?"

Her mother struggled, overwhelmed by the dual shocks of her daughter and her ex, and finally managed, "It's fine. Just the shed..."

"Glad to hear it." With that, Mia took the spot by Cary and mimicked his pose. "I think you owe us an explanation, don't you?"

As Janine floundered and Anji slipped out the back of the car, I considered the three of them, then returned to the Explorer. "Change of plans," I said to the guys. "We're going to the cabin while they hash this out."

Fanakel moved aside to let Anji climb into the third row, then whistled low. "Yeah, I don't think they need our help."

"Absolutely not," Anji concurred. "Better drive before Janine starts running this way," she added, and I threw the SUV into gear.

Just as Janine had said, the cabin was undisturbed—the one home left to me, I thought, as we unpacked, and might have laughed had my heart not been so heavy. Watcher or no, I was stuck here again, if only for the night.

"Make yourselves comfortable," I told the others. "I don't think there's anything in the pantry, but I'll shop in a bit. Going for a walk."

Anji followed after me. "Stretching your legs?"

"Looking for evidence." I closed the cabin door and lowered my voice. "Erianthe had this town destroyed and innocent people murdered. I'll be damned if I let her get away with it."

"And how to you propose to bring the queen of Daril to justice, lass?" she asked, trooping after me down the stairs. "You and what army?"

"Don't know yet," I muttered. "One step at a time."

We walked in silence through the woods toward the faux asbestos mine, scouring the ground for abandoned weapons or hints that the royal guard had passed that way. Not until we reached the hole in the fence did we have any luck—a scrap of cloth bearing the Darili colors was caught on the sharp wire—but at that moment, I was so shocked that I almost overlooked it.

The opening to the tunnel down to the Crossing had caved in.

I stepped through the fence and walked closer, irrationally concerned about sinkholes, but once I got up to the rockpile where the cave entrance had been, I knew this was no natural occurrence.

"High Queen have mercy," Anji mumbled beside me. "What happened here?"

"You're the one who carries portable explosives," I replied. "What do you think—could something forged do this?"

She nodded. "Janine never mentioned an explosion, did she?"

"With all the fires in town, I doubt anyone noticed." Staring at the well-sealed hole, I muttered, "*Shit.* Anything in your luggage that could, I don't know, pulverize that?"

Anji grimaced. "To my shame, I didn't come prepared for such, nor would I recommend more explosives."

"No?"

"We have no idea how stable the cavern is beyond that point. Maybe the rock plug is superficial, but maybe the whole staircase has collapsed. Additional explosives would only exacerbate the problem…and we'll need equipment to dislodge even that," she continued with a grunt.

"Right. But where the hell am I going to get heavy machinery here, *now*, to work on a fucking asbestos mine that I don't even own?" I closed my eyes and rubbed my forehead. "Erianthe really took no chances, did she? If the fires didn't kill me, maybe this would keep me away."

"And Jerrcoa," Anji replied. "*And* Fanakel and me. You know what this means, yes?"

I looked down and found her grimly smiling. "We're all fucked together?"

"This is now an international incident. An attack on the crowns of Nokan'ti and Blackhorn Mountain…albeit indirectly, but an attack all the same. The Twins might let it pass, but my father will be *furious*."

Perhaps I seemed skeptical—after all, what I'd seen of Rokund to that point had been a generous host and a competent politician—because Anji's smile developed teeth. "People tend to underestimate dwarves. They only do so once." Giving the rockfall another moment's study, she asked, "Do you suppose Terj could get through that? Scout it for us, tell us what we're up against?"

It was worth a shot. We hurried to the cabin and informed the guys of our predicament, and Terj dropped everything to ferry the two of us back, turning the twenty-minute walk into a frighteningly fast weaving skim over the forest floor. He didn't bother materializing as he studied the blocked cave. *I can feel Aen leaking through*, he said after a moment, *so it's not solidly plugged, but…*

"Yikes?" I offered.

Yeah. Back soon.

Even his airy form disappeared then, leaving only the slight green glow of the Aen crystal around his neck, which seemed to zip toward the rocks and vanish. Anji and I waited on the surface for about five minutes before I heard Terj's voice from the other side: *The staircase is largely intact. The cave seems sound once you get down, oh...say twenty feet, and the Crossing itself is unharmed.*

How thick is the rockfall? I asked.

About twenty feet. Looks like they took down the roof of the cave on their way out. On my way.

By the time he appeared, I'd filled Anji in, and she scowled as she pondered the solution. "Are the rocks wedged fairly compactly?" she asked Terj. "Or is it packed at the top but loose below?"

It loosens the deeper in you go, but just finding gaps at the start took some work. We've got a mess on our hands. Now, assuming no one in town will be in a hurry to loan us an earthmover, he continued, turning to me, *what are we thinking?*

"Anji doesn't have her explosives," I replied, "and I don't think there's enough Aen here for Fanakel to be of much use."

Agreed. It's a trickle at this point.

"I don't suppose you could blow the rocks out of the way, could you?" Anji asked him hopefully.

But Terj shook his head. *Pebbles, perhaps, but some of those stones are enormous.*

"You've been able to carry all of us," she pointed out.

That's different. It's not hard to pick you up and move the air in a given direction, but this... A strong gust blew past us, sending a spray of grit away from the cave but barely nudging the boulders. *I can't get purchase.*

Which left one option. My awakened senses were all too aware of the lake nearby, but since it was still daylight, I couldn't call that water to me just yet—the last thing we needed was snoops following a stream heading the wrong way into the trees. "I have an idea," I told the others, "but it'll have to wait until nightfall."

Which is? Terj frowned at me, and then his face smoothed as I showed him the basic contours of my plan.

Ah. That might work, assuming you can generate the necessary pressure…

"What might work?" asked Anji, looking back and forth between us.

"Maybe I can use water like a drill," I explained. "There's plenty I can snag from the lake, and if I narrow the flow to a point and keep the pressure high, I might be able to break through."

She looked up at the afternoon sky. "Which means returning here tonight?"

"Unless we want to stay crammed in the cabin indefinitely. In the meantime, we're going to need food," I said, and pointed toward the path back. "Who wants to go shopping?"

No one was really feeling up to a trip to the supermarket in the next town, but Terj rode with me, and our other local cop waved us through the barricades.

We'd only just unloaded our groceries when Cary's Corolla pulled up beside Uncle Malachi's beater truck. Mia jumped out and slammed the door, and the car turned around and headed for the road. I had the front door unlatched before she'd made it to the porch. "What happened?"

"Ugh," she groaned, and flapped one hand toward town. "Is there anything to drink here?"

Fanakel tossed her a barely chilled beer as she pulled a kitchen chair into the sitting area. "Where's Cary?"

"He went off to try to find a motel with availability. I told him about the cabin, and then he took one look at this place and said no. It was bad enough when we were trying to sleep four adults in here, but _seven_?"

I could lose the meat suit to make room, Terj offered.

"And we'd still have one bed and the recliner. Let's see if we can do better." She sat down and cracked open the can. "So. _That_ was a fun talk."

I dragged another chair over to join her. "Dare I ask?"

"Shock. Tears. Shock and tears." She sipped her beer and closed her eyes as it went down. "She fessed up. Confirmed everything he told me."

"Why did she run off?" Anji asked, climbing into the recliner.

Mia sighed and stared at the can in her hands. "My grandparents' church, the one I grew up in…you've got to understand, if it's not a full-blown cult, it flirts with the notion. They sucked her back in."

"How?"

"Well…you don't grow up being browbeaten by your pastor and warned that you're eternally damned for every little failure and make it out unscathed. Mom was raised in that toxic stew, and then she made a break for it, met Dad, started dating…"

Dad, I noticed, not *Cary*. However miserable the drive had been over the last three days, maybe something good had come of it for Mia.

"But it's damn hard to cut off the only family you've ever known," she continued, "and she called home. Felt guilty. Her parents cried and yelled and told her to come back, that she'd be forgiven, but she held out until that May, when they and the pastor showed up at her apartment. They'd hired a private investigator to find her."

"Shit," I muttered.

"Yeah. She let them come in, which was her next mistake, and they started laying on the guilt in person. She was literally living in Sin City, she was going to Hell…and then the pastor noticed a sweatshirt Dad had left draped over a chair. Mom said she'd never forget the look on her parents' faces when they realized there'd been a man in the house. They interrogated her until she cracked and admitted that she was dating him, and then the pastor pressed until she confessed that they'd been intimate, and *then* all hell broke loose. By the time Mom was supposed to go to work, she was a mess, and they'd convinced her she had to leave. So she called in sick, packed, broke her lease, and was heading east by morning. Her parents and the pastor had flown out there, so they rode back with her. She said her dad drove her car."

Fanakel, who'd helped himself to a beer as well, leaned against the wall. "And when she realized she was with child?"

"Oh, that happened almost immediately. Her mother dragged her to the doctor once she was home to get her checked out, and to Mom's surprise…" Smiling bitterly, she said, "Mom hadn't been on birth control when she left home—her parents would never have allowed it, even though she was a goddamned adult—so she didn't know how to get it once she reached Vegas. She bought *something* from a woman who came to her bar. Probably a sugar pill. She said she took one a month…so much for sex ed. Anyway, Mom's parents marched her back in to see the pastor, because now she wasn't just a disobedient whore but a *pregnant*, disobedient whore, and that asshole lit into her. How could she do this, how could she let herself be tempted to sin, et cetera."

She shot me a knowing look, and I nodded.

"So Mom was young and getting screamed at on all sides, and she cracked. Told them that the guy who seduced her wasn't human—he was an exotic dancer who fed on lust. Well, *that* went over well, as I'm sure you can imagine, but at least some of the heat was off Mom. The pastor said she'd been raped by an incubus."

"A *what*?" asked Jerrcoa.

"It's a kind of sex demon," I replied. "Tell you later."

"Anyway," said Mia, "that led the pastor to the oh-so-logical conclusion that I was literal demon spawn, and he actually suggested an abortion."

My eyebrows shot up. I'd caught a soundbite of the current pastor of that church a few years ago in which he suggested that pregnancy following rape was a gift from God. "*Seriously*?"

"I know, right? Guess there's an exception in their abortion ban for demon babies. But Mom refused—she said she was confused about Dad and all after getting preached at like that, but she wanted to keep me. Well, they weren't crazy about *that* plan, but the pastor and her parents told her that the only way to save me from damnation was to bring me up in the church. She agreed, and then the pastor did some sort of ritual to bless the pregnancy and destroy Dad's unholy influence over me, or whatever. Her parents went through all her belongings, looking for anything that might be his, and they found a scrap of paper with his phone number. They burned it and scattered the ashes."

"And she just couldn't remember how to call him?" I asked, crossing my arms.

Mia shrugged. "Religious abuse is real, and they'd wormed their way into Mom's psyche. She said she really believed for a while that he might have been a demon, and she was doing the right thing by protecting me from him. Didn't make either her or me popular with her parents—I mean, you know how little they had to do with their whore daughter and her bastard, right?" she said to me. "But she kept dragging me to that hellish place and tolerating all of the jabs about her sins because she was convinced that this was what God wanted. She deserved the abuse, and if we kept going there, I'd be okay."

She paused for a long swig of beer. "And then I came out."

"All for nothing," I murmured.

"Bingo. She'd done everything for me, and I was still damning myself. Guess that explains why she was so pissed when she disowned me…"

As Mia drank again, I said, "She sounded pretty worried about you this week for someone who didn't care."

"Because apparently, she's been doing some *heavy* soul searching in the last year," Mia replied. "She kept going to that fucking place for a while, but she said her failure gnawed at her—if she'd done everything right, if she'd followed the pastor's directions, then why had God let me turn out the way I am? Eventually, she broke down and sneaked off to a therapist two towns over—not a church counselor, but a real psychologist. Lucked into finding one who'd grown up in a similar church and spoke the lingo, who recognized the signs of abuse and opened her eyes. And once the therapist started to make inroads there, she worked with Mom on her issues with me—you know, if that church was fallible, then maybe they were wrong that I was on the expressway to Hell for liking girls. So Mom gradually started coming around, which meant she had to deal with the shit she'd told me."

I nodded, recalling the venom in Janine's voice that night.

"She said she wanted to reach out to me and make amends," said Mia, "but by then, you and I were somewhere beyond the Crossing, and Mom had no idea where to find me. She said she managed to learn that I'd been working at Antoinette's, but Antoinette is good people, she knows what Mom was like, and so she told her to fuck right off—she wasn't giving out my contact information without my say-so. Mom said she called you," she told me, "but of course, you weren't anywhere near your phone, so that was that. She didn't know if I was living nearby and avoiding her or if I'd run back to New York forever, so when everything burned, she started praying for a miracle, and you picked up."

"So…you've reconciled?" Fanakel asked.

Mia snorted. "I wouldn't go that far. Dad let her have it—she should have known he's not a fucking demon, she knew I was half tekori but let me starve, she stole my entire childhood from him, and so on. He told her at one point that if she kept me around only to make me suffer for her sins, then she should have given me to a parent who would have actually loved me. Cue the waterworks."

She rolled her eyes and drained her beer. "The sad thing is, I think Mom does love me, in her way. However warped she was, she wanted the best for me—she just had a very different idea than I did as to what that might be. And she did apologize *profusely* for what she said the last time we talked, so that's something. Minimal progress is still progress. But I wouldn't say we're buddies by a long shot. I mean, I'm glad Mom's been working on herself, and I can see where she may have been somewhat of a victim in this, too, but that doesn't undo everything, you know?"

Did Cary confront her about leaving like she did?

Mia looked at Terj, who'd staked out a spot against the wall near Fanakel. "Not really. He seemed mostly upset about me. Then again, I guess she gave him an explanation—I'm not sure what more there is to say when your ex-girlfriend tells you she ran off without a word and never called again because she was convinced you're a demon." Sighing, she considered her empty can, then rose to get a fresh beer. "Well, I did my duty, Mom knows I'm alive, and there's not a damn thing I can do to fix this fucking town, so are we still on for that Ragatanu excursion?"

"That depends," said Jerrcoa. "Would you bring me one of those, please?"

She pulled two cans from the old fridge and passed him one. "Depends on what?"

"On whether Susan can blast through the pile of rocks that's currently blocking the way back to the Crossing."

Mia turned to me, her eyes wide. "I'm sorry, *what?*"

"My dear mother's goons left us a parting gift," I explained. "I'll go out there once it gets dark and try to make headway."

Softly swearing, she sank onto her chair and opened her beer. "Do you think you can get past it?"

"Guess we'll find out." I ran my hands through my hair and groaned. "Erianthe's got to pay for this. I don't know how, but she's got to fucking *pay.*"

Jerrcoa watched as I pushed myself from my chair and stalked to the kitchen. "What are you thinking?"

"Don't know yet," I muttered. "Gonna stress-eat a bag of Cheetos first."

"And that will help?"

"It won't *hurt*," Mia told him, and my brother wisely shut his mouth.

Cary returned to the cabin around seven to inform us that our accommodations had been arranged. "You're not staying in this…*hovel*," he said, taking in the ratty recliner and ancient appliances.

"Susan was stuck here," Mia reminded him.

And her uncle spent decades in this place, said Terj. *It's cramped, yes, but for one night—*

"It's nowhere near large enough for everyone, and on the off chance that any of Daril's men are still lurking, it's not safe. As for the rest…" He looked at me, his expression grim. "It's fucking appalling what was done to you and the other Watchers. Ragatanu had no part in that scheme, but at least let me put you up in a decent place tonight. I've got money to burn."

While most of our group accepted the offer, Terj and I declined. I explained what I was going to attempt in the woods, and while Cary didn't like that plan in the slightest, Terj insisted that he would stay with me. *Malachi kept a small arsenal here*, he said, opening the storage closet where the gun safe was wedged. *I'll go armed and keep watch.*

You've never fired a gun in your life, I said to Terj privately.

It can't be that difficult. And Erianthe's men are long gone. What's the worst that will find us out there, an ill-tempered raccoon?

But before I ventured into the woods that night, I had a stop to make. Once the others had headed for the hotel—Cary insisted that he'd have a room reserved for us, just in case—Terj and I climbed into the Explorer for a trip I'd been dreading.

The sheriff had yet to impose a curfew on Cole's Crossing, but there seemed to be no need—the streets were dead as I crawled toward my house, and even those few homes left mostly standing were dark and empty. Thus it was that no one was around to stop me when I pulled up to the trampled, charred lawn on which I'd played as a little girl and jumped out to see what was left of my home.

I stood on the cracked sidewalk and stared at the blackened pile of rubble, its contours still visible in the waning twilight but in no way approximating the shape of the house I remembered. The front porch, the dormer windows, the garage, Dad's bushes...nothing remained but ash and debris.

The weight of an arm wrapping around me pulled me from my stupor, and I leaned my head against Terj's shoulder, too overwhelmed by the sudden wave of fresh grief to do more. He tightened his hold and didn't bother asking what I was thinking, and when I pressed my face against his chest and started to silently cry, he hugged me and let me fall apart for a moment.

As my sobs began to calm, I heard an unfamiliar voice near my ear—a male voice, not as deep and sultry as Cary's but still pleasantly low. "Love," he murmured.

I stepped away from Terj and saw the anxiety in his pale eyes. "Did you just..."

"Love?" he tried again uncertainly.

"*Oh,*" I sighed, and pulled him close again.

I didn't want to leave Terj's embrace. I didn't want to confront the ruins of my house and the long night ahead. But I couldn't stay on the sidewalk forever, and so I kissed him and turned on my flashlight as I broke away. *Let's get this over with*, I said, heading up the lawn.

Terj followed, his light bobbing along beside mine. *What do you hope to find in there? They burned this place to the ground.*

Maybe not all of it. I swept my light over the wreckage, trying to map the floorplan I knew onto the piles of half-burned boards and roofing shingles, then headed around the side and aimed for the back, where I thought Dad's study had been. *Could you do me a favor?* I asked.

What do you have in mind?

Any chance that you could move some of the junk out of the way? I need to get under the remains of the second floor.

A strong wind blew past me, and debris began to lift from the pile and fly toward the street. I watched for a minute as Terj individually moved some of the larger pieces, and then I patted his arm to stop him. *That'll do for now. Let me see if I can get in.*

He followed me closer to the house. *When was your last tetanus shot?*

Do you think I can still get tetanus?

Do we really want to test this now? he countered.

Just give me your arm. Steadying myself against him, I waded through the mess until I bumped into something unyielding. *Here we are*, I said as my light glinted off metal in front of me. *Let's hope this isn't part of the fridge…*

Terj stood by, ready to jump in, as I manually tossed aside a few handfuls of unrecognizable scrap. After a moment's digging, Dad's fire safe appeared, and I hoisted it from the wreckage. *This thing weighs a ton—*

Let me. The safe floated out of my arms on a cushion of air, and Terj helped me pick my way back to the grass. We returned to the SUV, and once I had the dome light on, I opened the safe and held my breath.

The papers inside—deeds, handwritten notes, precious photographs—were unharmed.

Relief loosened my muscles as I started to pull items out, the only scraps remaining of my home and possessions. But then my fingers grazed something small, hard, and round, and I held my Aen crystals to the light.

Do you think they tracked these? I asked Terj. *My street looks like ground zero…do you think they came with something that sniffed out Aen?*

I don't know, but it's possible. Anji might have a better idea.

My guts clenched. *I led those bastards here. If I'd taken the crystals with me—*

They still would have burned the town. Susan, he said, reaching across the center console to turn my face toward his, *no. Don't do this to yourself.*

I said nothing as I repacked the safe and stowed it behind me—all but the damned crystals, which I shoved into my pocket. If Erianthe's hit squad was still around somewhere, let them come to me.

Terj didn't ask where we were going when I aimed us for Main Street. We couldn't drive downtown—the roads remained blocked off, and I didn't see any good coming of me blowing through police barricades—so I parked as close as I could and started walking. Terj took my hand as we skirted a wooden blockade and made our way past a half-collapsed structure that had once been a florist's shop with an apartment upstairs, and then I let my light slowly rove over the destruction of the downtown district until I saw the pile of brick and burned wood that had once been Cole's Crossing General Store.

My inheritance, my family's legacy, was nothing but ashes.

I pulled a piece of broken brick from the pile and pocketed it, then stepped back and stared at the rubble as sorrow and rage warred within me. *She's got to pay.*

She should.

I turned back to Terj and squinted in his flashlight's glow until he lowered the beam. *I don't understand—I gave her everything she wanted. She won! Why would she do this?*

Because she didn't win, he said gently. *Because you will always be the Watcher—the one who went Outside and slew a monster Daril could never imagine. Because you've exposed Erianthe's secrets, and she can never hide them again. You may have relinquished your claim to the throne,* he continued, drawing closer to me, *but everyone with the slightest understanding of the situation sees that it was unjust. You publicly humiliated Erianthe at Edes's engagement, and you did so again when you bought your way out of your marriage—or so Jerrcoa tells me. And even if Edes takes the throne someday, as long as you're around, people will whisper that you are the true queen. Erianthe knows this.* He shrugged. *Does she truly love her other children? I don't know—she's certainly willing to sacrifice Jerrcoa. But if Edes is crowned without another contender to challenge his claim, then Erianthe can tell herself she kept her bargain with Cirivant…and the only way to guarantee his succession is to eliminate the threat.*

I wasn't planning to challenge Edes, I protested. *My word is good.*

But hers isn't, and why would she assume anything better of you? Terj gripped my shoulder with his free hand and looked me in the eye. *What happens next is up to you, Susan. We can disappear here, we can go to Ragatanu and start over…or we can embark on the uphill path to bring Erianthe to justice. This is your decision.*

What do you think?

He paused, considering my face, then said, *I don't think you'll find rest until you face your mother again. That's not my call. But know this: whatever you choose, I'll be with you.*

I can't ask that of you, Terj—

You're not. All I'm telling you is that whatever you choose, wherever you go, however many monsters you face…I'll be at your side.

I let that hang between us for a long moment, then nodded and kissed him deeply. *Want to go play in the woods?*

CHAPTER 15

Forests are *dark* places at night. If you've grown up in town, you don't know true night darkness—there are always streetlights, the glow of windows, cars passing, maybe a dog walker with a flashlight for poop retrieval. You don't really think about how black the night can be in a place in which the only illumination is starlight and whatever little equipment you carry with you.

The moon was waxing but not yet to the first quarter, minimally helpful with the leafing trees, and we lost it by two in the morning. I didn't pay it much mind as I sat on a fallen log beyond the fence surrounding the opening to the Crossing and focused my will on the water I was siphoning from the nearby lake. Bright as noon to my awakened inner senses, the lake was an easy source from which I could draw—far simpler to access than had been the moisture I'd needed to make a downpour in the Kopaati desert—and it flowed through the air at my command, winding past the trunks as if suspended in an invisible pipeline.

I took that flow and narrowed it to a small, strong stream, like pressing a thumb over the opening of a garden hose to concentrate the emerging jet, albeit on a grander scale. The result was thin as a pencil and strong enough to snap a limb off a tree—I'd tried it to be sure—but when I directed it at the rocks, it seemed harmless as a squirt gun. For hours, I forced water at various places in the blockage, looking for a weak spot, a crack I could use, but as I stopped for a quick break around three, I had to admit to myself that my power was insufficient. Sure, erosion would triumph over years, but it wasn't enough in the short term.

I was shivering with cold and exhaustion, and Terj held me to warm me up while I took a sip from the water bottle I'd brought along. He'd been nothing but encouraging all night, but I knew he saw the futility in my efforts just as well as I did.

As I sat there, tired, shaking, and wondering what I was going to tell the others, the shadows in front of me seemed to take on definition.

A light.

Panic clawed at my guts. I'd kept my lake stream suspended, hovering at the ready, and if someone from town wandered out here and saw the impossible thing happening around me…

I jumped to my feet and wheeled around, trying to come up with a plausible lie, but what I found behind me wasn't an insomniac out for a stroll.

There was a light, yes, but far fainter than the beams of our flashlights…and it was emanating from a pale, glowing form I'd have known anywhere.

I dropped my water bottle in my shock and whispered, "Uncle Malachi?"

He stopped a few feet away from me and smiled. "Long night, Susie?"

Part of me insisted that I should be terrified, but a louder part cried out in comingled joy and sorrow as my vision blurred. "Is it…it's really you?" I asked—stupid, yes, but I was down to my physical dregs, and my emotions weren't faring much better.

He nodded. "It's okay, honey, don't be scared. No one's here to hurt you."

"No one…"

The words that would have followed died away as more glowing shapes appeared from the trees behind Uncle Malachi—men in various styles of dress, two of whom I recognized from old photographs but the others strange to me. There were fifteen in all, and a quick glance at their faces and garb suggested that about half of them were Native American.

Uncle Malachi glanced over his shoulder, then looked back at me with a quirked mouth. "The boys and I thought you could use a hand."

The Watchers, I realized. These were the Watchers who had come before, the men who'd been chained to this patch of land and told to fight whatever emerged from the ground. They'd died with that curse on them...

My face fell as a horrifying thought occurred to me. "You're still trapped here?"

"Oh—no, baby, *no*," Uncle Malachi reassured me, and the men closest to him fervently shook their heads. "No, this is a...special reunion, you might say."

"Those assholes destroyed our town," said the man in overalls to his right—Pericles, I thought, Uncle Malachi's granduncle. "You want to go after them, girl?"

I stepped away from Terj toward the crowd of spirits. "My mother sent them. I want to go after *her*. Take out the queen, not the pawns."

He rubbed his chin as he considered that. "Think you can do it?"

"I don't know, but I've got to damn well try."

A third man, a bearded fellow who wore oversized trousers held up with dark red suspenders, gave me a careful study. "You've got one hell of a gift, there."

I followed his gaze to the suspended lake water. "It's not enough. I can move it around, but I can't sufficiently concentrate the flow to break through the rockfall." Pointing to the blocked opening, I said, "All I've managed tonight is getting it wet."

He chuckled—Zachary, I guessed, Ganeel's Watcher, the man who'd died when an Outsider bit his arm off. In death, at least, he'd regained his detached limb. "Which is why Malachi suggested this meeting. Looks like you could use a little help."

I swiped at my leaking eyes. "Why would you help me? I'm the reason Erianthe burned down the town…"

One of the Native American men spoke, and though his words were foreign, it seemed that my internal translator worked just as well for the dead as for the living. "You are one of us."

An unfamiliar Cole nodded. "And for a goodly number of us, you're kin."

"Adopted," I mumbled.

"Since when has that ever made a difference?" Uncle Malachi interjected. "Whoever else, *whatever* else you may be, Susan, you will always be a Cole. Hell," he added with a grunt, "adoption wasn't enough to save you from the family curse, was it?"

Several of the Cole men grimaced.

"Now, let's get you on your way," he said, and pointed to my pocket. "Pull out the big one from the pommel."

Frowning, I dug around and quickly extracted the largest of the Aen crystals. "This?"

"Yep. You're going to use it as a focusing tool."

My fingers clenched around the stone. "I…I've never done anything like that. No one's taught me to use Aen crystals. That's not the way my talent works…"

Uncle Malachi shook his head to stop my babbling. "Honey, you're still learning to use your talent, but I'm going to let you in on a little secret: you've only been using *part* of it."

"What do you mean?"

"Don't get me wrong, that's pretty damn impressive," he said, gesturing toward the waiting water, "but you're not using your full potential." Stepping closer to me, he said, "All of us who spent a couple decades or more with the sword got a bit of power from it. A little magic. Not enough to shoot fireballs or anything useful like that, but enough to, say, change the channel without the remote. Know why?"

"Because you were constantly around Aen crystals," I

murmured.

"Uh-huh. Humans...well, we're magical duds. No great inherent skill here. But if we're around Aen long enough, it changes us. We respond to it. Maybe we'll never be maladetas, but we're *primed*, so to speak. And that's where those crystals come into play. We may not have much power on our own, but we can use the crystals to amplify what we have. "Now—" He tried to plant his hand on my shoulder, then muttered in disgust when it went right through. "*Shit*. Sorry, honey. What I'm trying to tell you is that you've got that elemental ability, sure, but the other half of you is human, and you're holding one big-ass Aen crystal."

"Give it a go," Pericles urged.

Unsure of what I was doing, I turned to face the rocks. My hand tightened until it felt like the facets of the crystal were cutting into my skin, but I couldn't sense anything different—no burst of energy, no tingle telling me it was working.

"You've got this, Susie," said Uncle Malachi. "Your power is like water. Flow *through* it."

I took a deep breath to clear my mind, then opened my consciousness until I was fully aware of every drop of moisture around me—in the lake, in the air, running in my veins. I felt Terj's rushing blood, pumping by a racing heart, but pushed that aside. In that moment, all I needed was the water waiting for me. I aimed my clenched fist toward the hovering stream, then swept it toward the Crossing.

The water hit like a jackhammer, slamming into the rocks with the resounding crack of rifle fire. I kept up the pressure, drawing upon my dwindling reserves to force more and more water into the flow, to widen the hole trying to split the stone in two...and as I began to flag, I felt a tingle against the skin of my back, growing and moving through me toward the crystal. Glancing behind me, I found Uncle Malachi with his insubstantial hand pressed against my shirt and the other Watchers coming closer to join him. Some touched me, while others gripped the shoulders and arms of the men in front of them, a surreal laying-on of hands. The shadows stretched all around us, sharp in the brightness of their combined glow, and I felt my power surge on the swelling current, a voice rising to join the song.

The rock *shattered*.

"Clear it!" Uncle Malachi bellowed, but not at me. From the corner of my eye, I saw Terj vanish. A strong wind swept away the chunks of stone, giving me an unobstructed shot at the rock beneath, which was already beginning to break under my assault. "Good!" my uncle shouted. "Keep it up! Don't make her waste power on the broken bits!"

The next rock fractured a moment later, and the parts were blown aside before they could fall.

I maintained the pressure on the rocks, though I don't know how. By that time, after having toiled for hours, I was cruising on empty—so much of what came through me was surely borrowed from the strange fraternity at my back. But within about ten minutes, my jet broke through a rock and hit empty space behind it, where it splashed down to the stone staircase beneath.

"Holy shit," I mumbled.

"Come on, honey, stick with us," said Uncle Malachi. "This ain't over yet."

He was right—while I'd bored a hole through the rockfall, the pile was structurally unsound, and a slight shift would undo my work.

"Aim higher," my uncle instructed. "Break the ones above to widen the gap."

And so we went, me riding the wave and Terj cleaning up the debris. Unable to see him, I hoped he could stay out of my way, but I was too focused to give that worry much consideration. The Aen crystal felt like an extension of myself, an external manifestation of my mind and soul, perfectly channeling my will and narrowing it to a beam of power. Water slammed with devastating force, rocks cracked and broke and fell away, and for a seemingly endless moment, Susan ceased to exist, replaced by an implacable force with a singular goal.

But then, as I penetrated the rockfall yet again, I heard Terj: *Susan, hold your fire!*

Snapping back to myself, I stopped the flow, keeping the water hovering at the ready. *What's wrong?* I called to him.

Nothing. Let me see if this works...

For a moment, nothing happened, and I was about to ask Terj if he needed help when I felt more than heard him cry out as he strained. From deep within the cave came the moan of a rushing wind, and then, like a bomb going off, the plug over the opening exploded. Large rocks slammed into the fence, denting it and bouncing off, while smaller ones flew through the holes or over the top. I quickly called the lake water to me and formed it into a shield—an imperfect barrier, sure, but one thick enough to slow the missiles. When the sounds of banging and crashing ceased, I turned on my flashlight and saw the cave open once more, perhaps a little deformed from the damage rendered by the royal guards but passable.

Terj? I asked. *You okay?*

Fine. Clearing the staircase. Just a moment...

With a long sigh, I sent the water back to its source, then felt the loaned power ebbing from me. Turning, I saw the waiting Watchers and sagged to my knees. "Thank you," I said, bracing myself against the dirt and leaf litter as I sought strength. "I...I don't know how..."

"Put that rock away before you lose it in the dark, Susie," said Uncle Malachi, and I slid the Aen crystal back into my pocket. "Are you all right?" he asked, crouching beside me. "Can you stand?"

"Just...give me a minute."

"Is she okay?" asked Pericles, drawing closer.

"She's fine, give her room. That's my girl," Uncle Malachi coaxed as I got a foot beneath me. "Easy does it, honey, don't fall…"

I staggered upright, wobbling briefly before I recovered my balance, then nodded to my anxious companions. "I'm fine. Exhausted, but I'll…uh…"

"Live?" Uncle Malachi finished, and grinned as I flushed.

"Oh, my God, I'm sorry," I mumbled, but his laughter stopped my apology.

"You'll have to try a lot harder than that to hurt my feelings, kid," he said. "Besides, I'm finally free of this place—I don't think any of us would rather go back to the way things were, right, guys?"

The other Watchers shook their heads and muttered firm denials.

"See?" he said to me. "No harm done."

I sniffled as my eyes started pricking. "You're okay? You *promise* me you're okay?"

"I'm better than okay," he said gently. "Better than I ever was."

"I miss you."

"I know, baby girl, but I'm never far."

My tears began to fall I fought against the tightness in my throat. "We saw the Grand Canyon last week."

"You did. And Mia poured one out for me," he replied with a chuckle. "Waste of good liquor, but she's a sweet kid. Thank her for me, eh?"

"You…you saw us?"

"Oh, honey," he said, and rested his glowing hand on my shoulder—well, on and slightly in, but it was close. "I've loved you since the day you were born, and I'll love you until the end of time. You really didn't think I'd keep tabs on you?"

I tried and failed to choke back a sob, and my uncle leaned closer. "Don't you mourn me, Susie. Don't you dare. Miss me all you want, but be happy for me. I've seen wonders beyond human understanding."

Nodding, I wiped my eyes and breathed deeply until I didn't feel quite so choked.

"Now," said Uncle Malachi, "you've got work ahead of you, and you need sleep before you leave. Go back to the cabin and get some shuteye—it's good for one more night. And as for your shadow…"

I glanced behind me and saw that Terj had returned. Once more corporeal, he stayed back a few paces and stared at the Watchers, and I'd barely reached for his mind before I felt his guilt and fear.

I'm sorry, he said. *All of you, I…I'm so very sorry*—

But Uncle Malachi's expression shifted to a sad smile. "Hello, friend."

I didn't want to do it. I'm sorry, I should have fought harder, I'm sorry, I'm sorry—

"What the hell did I tell you about leaving Susan alone? My last damn words, man!"

I shouldn't have—

He held up both hands to stop him. "I'm glad you did. For both of you and for all the Watchers that might have been, I'm so fucking glad you did."

Terj's babbled apology petered out, and he regarded Uncle Malachi with confusion. *But…but I…*

"Ain't your fault," said one of the Coles. "You did your time, too, old son."

The others rumbled their agreement.

"But if you want to make it up to us," said Uncle Malachi, "there *is* something you can do."

Terj nodded. *Anything. What would you ask of me?*

My uncle pointed to me. "Protect her. For the rest of your life, however long that may be, you protect our Susie. You want to make amends for screwing up our lives, you look after her."

As I caught Uncle Malachi's eye, he dropped me a quick wink.

He *knew*.

You have my word, said Terj, moving closer to take my hand. *My life for Susan's.*

Uncle Malachi nodded. "Then I think our business here is concluded. Boys, give me a minute, won't you?"

The other Watchers vanished, leaving only my uncle's glowing form and my flashlight against the darkness.

"Barnaby wanted to be here," he told me. "*So* badly. But this is Watcher business, and he dodged that bullet."

"I understand."

"Yeah, well, your dad's not happy about it, but I promised him I'd pass a message. He loves you so much, and he's damn proud of you, and he's sorry y'all didn't have longer together."

I nodded, not trusting myself to speak.

"Also, he said to tell you that he's not upset about Falova." My eyebrow rose, and Uncle Malachi chuckled. "Honestly. Look, we know Barnaby's always going to be your dad, but since he can't be here to hold your hand and give you advice and embarrass you, he's glad you've got someone you can count on. And if that someone just happens to be your progenitor, Barnaby's not threatened."

I smiled, though my heart ached at the thought of Dad. "Thank him for me, will you? Give him a big hug for me…"

"Don't you cry anymore, Susie," said Uncle Malachi. "Save those tears for someone who needs them. Your dad is just fine. Well," he amended, "I mean, he's worried sick about you, but he's fine otherwise."

And *there* was my dad. "I'll be careful."

"Yeah, right. I'd tell you to stay out of trouble, but I think you'd just ignore me. Like *you* did," he added, cutting his eyes to Terj.

Malachi, I—

"Relax. Let me have my fun." He stepped back and looked at us both. "Not who I'd ever imagined for you, Susie, but sometimes, it's good to be surprised. I love you, little girl."

"Wait!" I said before he could vanish. "Will I ever see you again?"

My uncle smiled. "You just might."

"I love you," I told him. "Thank you for this tonight."

"Of course." He began to fade. "Last of us, best of us, go do what we could not. Oh, and should you see Ardith," he added, "give her my regards, eh?"

I stared at the place where he had been until the afterglow faded, and then I realized Terj was still holding my hand and gave him a squeeze. *Feel better?*

Actually...yes, he replied, though he sounded a little dazed. *Weary.*

I hear you. Bed?

Instead of answering, he scooped me off my feet on a cushion of air and sped us back through the woods to the cabin. I'd left a light on in the main room, and as it grew brighter in my vision, I didn't think I'd ever seen such a welcome sight.

Terj gently deposited me on the porch, and I pushed open the door, which still bore deep gouges in the weathered paint from Outsider attacks. "Come on," I mumbled, heading straight for the bedroom. "I'm about to drop."

I kicked off my shoes, tossed the flashlight on the rug, and collapsed into bed, and Terj followed suit. "Goodnight," I whispered as a sudden gust blew the bedroom door closed.

He pulled me closer beneath the blankets and murmured, "Love."

My phone rang around seven the next morning, and I groaned into the pillow.

Want me to destroy it? Terj offered, only half in jest.

No, I might need that...

A burst of wind picked the phone up off the night table and dropped it beside me, bringing the power cord with it.

Oops…sorry. Forgot it was attached.

I smiled wearily at him and glanced at the screen. Mia. "What's up?" I croaked.

"Plenty. Any luck last night?"

"It's wide open, and I'll give you the details after I've had, like, all the caffeine. Y'all okay?"

"Maybe?"

I rubbed the grit from my eyes. "Going on about three hours of sleep, so you've got to do better than that."

"*Yikes.* Sorry, Suze." Mia paused, and I heard a slurp that was almost certainly coffee. "Mom came looking for us last night. She drove all around town until she spotted Dad's car."

"Shit. Did it get messy?"

"I…honestly, I don't know. I slept through it."

It didn't sound like Janine had launched into a screaming fit outside the hotel, at least. "What happened?"

"Well…from what I've gathered, Dad was sitting up late in the lobby, and she walked in, and the two of them have been hanging out by the breakfast buffet for hours. They're being weirdly civil, from what Fanakel says. I'm trying to avoid them."

By the time that I'd showered, dressed, and driven with Terj to the hotel to meet the others, Anji was outside waiting for us, and she jumped into the SUV for privacy. "They're making up," she said incredulously. "Or that's the best I can deduce. Perhaps the High Queen understands what's happened between them."

"Making *up?*" I echoed.

She nodded. "Insane, is it not? They've been talking all night."

The long and short of it was that Cary hadn't been exaggerating when he'd said that Janine was the only woman he'd ever loved. Despite the years, her disappearance, and the whole messy situation with Mia, he was somehow still pining for her. Now that she'd finally had enough therapy to work past some of the abuse of her youth, Janine remembered how much she'd loved him, too, and after their blowup the day before, they'd taken the night to more calmly reconnect. While Janine had hurt Cary deeply, she was apologetic. They'd talked about the intervening years—Cary's moves around the country with a new alias every few years, Janine's struggles to raise a child by herself while living under the fear that any wrongdoing on her part would send her daughter catapulting straight to Hell.

Cary told Janine that he was going home and taking Mia with him, as she needed to continue to safely explore her abilities and learn about the other half of her heritage. Janine wasn't thrilled about this development—she hadn't spoken to her daughter in about two years, and now Mia was leaving not only town, but the world—but she agreed that this was probably for the best. She'd screwed up, she knew it, and at the end of the day, she wanted the best for her daughter. Cary promised her that he'd keep in touch, and the two exchanged phone numbers. While Cary's phone wouldn't work past the Crossing, at least Janine would recognize the number the next time he returned and called her.

And he *would* be returning.

"I guess I should be happy that my parents are trying to get along," Mia told me over a plate of powdered eggs and greasy sausage, "but this is *weird*."

"Could be worse," I reminded her. "My mother tried to have my father killed, remember?"

"Yeah." She stabbed at a blob of uncooperative egg and scowled. "But Mom was horrible to Dad, she kept me in the dark, then she disowned me...and now they're hanging out, talking all night?"

I shrugged. "Maybe there's still something between them."

"Doesn't undo the last twenty-four years." She chewed for a moment in silence, then said, "Maybe Dad's ready to forgive and forget, but he didn't grow up with Mom breathing down his neck. Don't get me wrong, I'm glad she's in therapy and trying to make amends, but I'm not ready to hug it out."

"That's okay."

"Is it? Because part of me feels like shit for rolling my eyes when my own mother starts sobbing in front of me."

"Hey." I took her free hand, and she dropped her plastic fork. "She's the one who hurt you. Now, she can be as sorry as she likes, but any reconciliation has to be on *your* schedule. She doesn't get to be upset if y'all don't have a perfect relationship because she's the one who torpedoed it in the first place."

Mia smiled sadly. "She wrecked *that* long before I came out. You know, I used to be so jealous of you."

"*Me?*"

She nodded. "My mom was a pain in the ass who always assumed the worst about me. Your dad was your biggest cheerleader...and he didn't mind ordering pizza when I stayed for dinner," she added with the ghost of a grin. "I'm sure he wasn't perfect, but from where I was standing, looking in..." With a sigh, she said, "I guess Mom did her best, messed up as she is."

"That doesn't mean her best has to be good enough. You can do your best and still fail."

She looked at me, considering that. "Yeah. Guess you're right."

"And if it makes it any better, at least Janine has never tried to kill you. When it comes to mothers, I'd take yours in a heartbeat."

Mia smirked and poked at her eggs again. "You only say that because you've never lived with her."

"I'm talking about attempted *filicide*," I groused. "Sure, Janine thought you were going to Hell, but Erianthe tried to speed me on my way! And the rest of us, and this whole fucking town," I muttered. "God," I said, dropping my head into my folded arms on the breakfast table, "what am I going to do?"

She patted my back. "You're going to get up, and you're going to drink a big-ass cup of coffee, and then we're going to blow this popsicle stand and figure out our next move once we get to Ragatanu."

I groaned.

"Suck it up, princess."

"Oh, look who's talking."

Mia chuckled. "If I get you your coffee, will you at least drink it?"

"Fine," I mumbled.

She rose, then quickly returned with a steaming paper cup of cheap brew, heavily doctored with sugar and vanilla creamer. "And might I suggest availing yourself of the facilities once you've finished with that?" she said, sliding the coffee in front of me. "Dad can talk up Ragatanu all he likes, but I'm withholding judgment until I see the plumbing situation for myself."

Around nine, with Fanakel and Cary taking turns helping push Jerrcoa through the woods, the seven of us reached the entrance to the Crossing. My brother stared grimly at the hole in the ground, then lifted each leg and gave his feet a wiggle. "It's been fun, I guess," he said to himself.

Terj gave his shoulder a brief squeeze, and Jerrcoa floated into the air. He hung there awkwardly as I folded his wheelchair, then asked, "Does that have to stay here?"

"This?" I said, lifting the chair. "I thought we could take it with us, if that's okay."

The prospect of mobility improved his mood, and he didn't complain as Terj carefully guided him and the chair underground. The rest of us eased our way down the staircase, avoiding patches of rubble by flashlight, and soon arrived in the massive cavern at the nexus of the tunnels. "So," said Cary, shifting his bag, "if we start walking now, we should be there by early afternoon—"

Walking?

He glanced at Terj, then at Jerrcoa. "*Oh*...sorry, kid, I didn't mean to be insensitive. Here, let's get your chair set up again—"

No, you misunderstand, Terj interrupted as Cary reached for the wheelchair. *Unless you just want a hike, I can speed this along.*

Fanakel grunted. "You're up to carrying all of us? After last night?"

Susan did the heavy lifting, and since I can actually feel the Aen again...yeah, I think I'm all right. Come on.

"What do you—" Cary began, then yelped as he was tossed off his feet.

Easy, now, said Terj as he flickered out of corporeality. *I've got you.* He paused, then asked, *Does anyone have a sense of oncoming traffic?*

We listened for a moment, but the tunnels remained silent beyond the usual moaning of moving air.

Right. Let's—

Windshield, babe, I privately reminded him.

Embarrassment flared through Terj's mind. *Sorry*, he told me, then threw up the protective barrier without alerting the others and sped us on our way.

Someday, he said only to my hearing, *I'm going to remember that without being reminded. Hopefully before I send someone to a messy death.*

Even moving at a cautious pace, with Terj's speed, what might have been a four-hour walk to the end of the tunnel turned into a comfortable hour-long flight through the near darkness. From what I could tell, sensing him as I did on the edge of my thoughts, he felt better than he had in days, and I had to concur—now that I knew what the Aen was like, I missed its energetic potential when I was away.

While we traveled, Cary, who'd acclimated quickly enough, tried to give us the lay of the land on the far side, as only Fanakel had ever visited Ga'besh. "Ours is a watery world," he explained, leaning back on his elbows. "Three continents form a rough doughnut, if you will. I have no idea if this is just the way they drifted or if it's actually one continent with a massive crater in the middle, but it doesn't matter. The important thing is that most big cities are ports built along the Central Sea." He started to trace a circle in the air, then realized that we couldn't make out fine details in the dark and gave up on the visual aid. "Ragatanu is in the southernmost continent, Axit. Ours is a decent stretch of land—a little smaller than Daril, I should think," he said, turning to me, "but respectable."

I laughed sadly. "You know, this is going to sound awful, but I really have no concept of how big Daril is. I've flown over a good chunk of it, and I've spent time in Deoni, but that's really about it."

"For Daril...think France," he replied. "But so much of it is wasteland that it seems smaller. Anything of note lies along the Falova. Ragatanu, now, we're about the size of Austria and Germany if you melded them together. Or so I imagine—this is educated guessing."

"It helps."

"Nothing like being asked to learn the political geography of four worlds, is there?" he replied with a smirk in his voice. "So that's Ragatanu. Enead is both our capital and largest port. It's about half a day's sail from the tunnel exit—"

"That's near the coast on the border of Ragatanu and Cirivant," Jerrcoa interrupted.

"Right," said Cary. "So my plan is to leave the tunnel, go north to the border port, and see if I can hire passage for us to Enead. I'm not carrying much gold," he admitted, "but if I'm recognized, perhaps that will be sufficient to convince one of the ferry captains that he'll be reimbursed."

Or you could just give me directions and save the money.

Cary looked back, though he surely couldn't pick Terj's natural form out of the darkness. "That's a long haul," he protested. "I can't ask that of you."

This isn't nearly as taxing as you must imagine. Show me the way—I can get you home.

"A generous offer—"

And one freely made. Unless you're desperate for a ferry ride…

With no one dying to go for a sail, Cary gave Terj the basic route before we exited the tunnel, and Terj warned us to hold on as we neared the exit, a steadily growing hole through which gray light glowed. *I'll gain altitude and speed once we're out of here*, he explained, *but I've got you well in hand. No need to start screaming.*

Duly reassured, we braced ourselves as we entered Ga'besh, only to immediately realize why the light had seemed so dull. A storm had come in, and our destination required Terj to fly through the wind and pounding rain.

Susan, he said as water blew in my face, *can you—*

Yeah. I concentrated for a few seconds, and a bubble like an invisible umbrella formed around us, repelling the rain. "Sorry, wasn't expecting a car wash," I muttered, and willed us dry one by one. The extra moisture coalesced into a sphere in my hands, which Terj allowed to fall through the floor.

"You've been practicing, lass," Anji said with approval as she straightened her hair.

Cary, the only one among us who hadn't had a chance to acclimate to elementals in close proximity, patted his suddenly dry shirt and stared at me with wide eyes. "How…how did you…"

"Suze is super-useful in storms," said Mia, nudging me in the side. "And at other times, I mean, but it's nice to travel with someone who can pull that off."

"Rogue, remember?" I told her father.

"I see." Cary quickly checked the rest of himself, then asked, "And your power is…*only* over water?"

"Eh, I've had decent luck with most fluids," I replied. "Not magma, and I've never had a chance to play with, say, mercury, but things that are water-adjacent seem to cooperate." I held his gaze as his mental gears turned, then softly said, "Yeah, I'm aware of the implications. Not really shocked that some of y'all are freaked out by rogues."

He swallowed hard. "You do understand why, yes?"

"Oh, sure. But I like to think I'm not a homicidal maniac, so—"

"This is my *bestie*, Dad," Mia cut in, throwing an arm around my shoulders. "Don't give her a hard time."

If Cary had other concerns, the warning tone of his daughter's voice ensured he kept them to himself.

CHAPTER 16

Enead was a sprawling city of winding roads and multistory buildings that hugged the C-shape of a natural harbor. From the air, I couldn't make out many indications of urban planning—there was a curving road where a protective wall had once been, Cary pointed out, as well as the remains of a later wall half a mile further inland, but the town those walls had once enclosed had burst its bonds in a warren of mixed-use districts. A few more solidly residential neighborhoods had taken root on the outskirts, and the coastline was completely given over to docks and slips, but beyond that, I could make out only two aberrations from the riot of rooftops: a manicured park in the northern section of the downtown district, ringed with the marble buildings that comprised the capital's university, and the castle complex, a turreted structure atop a natural hill on the southern side of the city. The castle's towers came to points, gray, conical stone structures pocked with windows for defense, but even through the pounding rain, I noted several courtyards within and the lush green of apparent landscaping.

Where should I land? Terj asked as we circled the castle.

"Main courtyard," Cary suggested, pointing to the largest of the open spaces. "We'll probably be rushed by guards as soon as we're down, so let me handle this."

Terj made a final pass, then slowed and carefully performed an almost vertical landing. We climbed off our invisible cushion, though I kept the rain barrier in place, and I adjusted my sword and shouldered my bag. Just as

Fanakel was opening Jerrcoa's wheelchair, the promised guards arrived—about a dozen of them, men and women in metal armor with apparent rifles at hand.

Well, I noted, at least one of the nations of the four worlds had discovered gunpowder.

As the guns were raised and aimed at us, Cary stepped forward and held up his empty hands. "It's me," he said, turning his head to search the stern faces around us. "Cerian. I—"

The woman in the front, a stunning brunette—par for the course among the tekoraet, I gathered—quickly lowered her weapon. "Your Highness!" she cried, and flashed a dazzling smile. "Merciful gods, boy, couldn't you use the *door?*"

He grinned back at her and stepped closer to meet her hug. "Good to see you, Captain. I'm glad *someone* here still remembers me—"

"*Cerian!*"

I looked up at a balcony two floors above us and found a handsome, brown-haired man in a long skirt clutching the railing. Like the guards, he was getting soaked, but he seemed not to care.

Cary released the captain and waved. "Hello, Dad! I'm home!"

"What…how did you…"

He struggled briefly until a beautiful blonde in a loose-fitting dress joined him and shrieked. "Son!" she called, and clapped her hands as she beamed. "You're back! And you brought friends?"

"Hi, Mom. Maybe we could take this inside," Cary suggested.

The guards hustled us onto a covered patio—two simply lifted Jerrcoa's chair up the short flight of stairs—and Cary had almost reached the arched doorway when his parents burst through. "Oh, my *darling*," said his mother, rushing to greet him, and Cary grunted with the force of her embrace. "When did you arrive? *How* did you get in?"

"Him," he wheezed, and she released him to turn and give us a better look.

As she took us in, recognition dawned, and her mouth fell open. "You're the ones who went Outside!"

"You've heard of us?" I replied.

"Of course! Our maladeta showed us a recording…you're the rogue of Daril, are you not?"

I spread my hands, resisting the urge to rub my distinctive scar. "Guilty."

"Blackhorn Mountain," she continued, pointing to Anji, "and Nokan'ti, and…Earth, yes?" she asked Mia, who was awkwardly hugging herself. "I apologize, I've not been there in years, and the maladetas didn't offer any details about you."

Mia nodded. "That's, uh…that's partly right, um…Your Majesty?"

Cary, who'd stepped away from his parents, intervened. "Mom, Dad…this is Mia. Your granddaughter."

They wheeled on him, shocked, then quickly turned back to Mia, who offered an uncertain little wave.

The queen slapped a hand over her mouth as her blue eyes turned to saucers. "Cerian," she whispered, "are you…"

"I'm absolutely serious. This is my daughter, and—"

"*Why* am I just now hearing of this?" she shouted, then looked past him as Mia shrank back and quickly switched to reassurance. "Oh, no, sweetie, I'm not yelling at you. Your father, however, owes us a *damn* good explanation—"

"Which I'd be happy to give you if we could perhaps go inside," Cary interrupted.

His parents exchanged glances, and his father beckoned the captain closer. "Tell the secretary to clear our appointments for the rest of the day, won't you?" he murmured, then pushed the door open and motioned us through.

As near as I could tell, Ragatanu was about two hours behind Cole's Crossing, and we'd arrived just after lunch. While Cary's parents ordered up a late meal from the kitchen, we sat around a richly appointed parlor as Cary told them everything—Vegas, Janine, his travels, and his unexpected introduction to his daughter five days prior. The rest of us filled in the gaps as necessary, wrapping up with my mother's attack on my hometown and the Crossing itself.

For Parrian and Coshta, the queen and prince consort, emotions ran high: joy at seeing their son again, shock and delight at Mia's existence, dismay that she'd been denied a childhood in Enead, anger at Janine—and to my surprise, simmering *fury* at Erianthe. "She had *no* right," Coshta growled. "Daril can take what liberties it may in Kopaat, but the Crossing is to remain free and open."

Parrian gripped her son's hand, then reached for Mia's. "She could have trapped you there. Had you not found a way down…"

Cary chuckled. "That wasn't *my* doing. They're the ones to be thanked," he said, pointing to Terj and me.

"Yeah," I muttered, "except for the bit about how she wouldn't have touched the Crossing had she not been trying to kill me."

"And the rest of you as well," said Parrian, her eyes narrowing.

Mia shook her head. "We would have been incidental casualties—she's after Suze."

"That god-forsworn whore knew you were traveling together," her grandmother protested. "To attack her own children is unforgivable, but what she did…that's an attack on Nokan'ti, Blackhorn Mountain, and Ragatanu as well."

"At least we're alive," Mia murmured. "That's more than I can say for a lot of our neighbors."

"I'm not trying to start some big international incident," I told the queen. "And I'm not attempting to claim Daril—I stepped out of the succession. But Erianthe killed a bunch of people and destroyed that town in trying to kill me, and I want to bring her to justice. How do I do that?"

Parrian released Mia and Cary, then rose and crossed the parlor to stand in front of my chair. "Dear girl, there is no path forward *but* an international incident. You can't simply walk into Deoni and demand your mother's arrest, can you?"

"No, ma'am…"

"Precisely. You will need assistance. Now," she continued, glancing at her husband, "assuming Erianthe hasn't become completely lawless, and I'm not sure that's accurate, she's bound to the Peace of Meali."

I frowned. "Wasn't that about ending the war between the dwarves and elves?"

"It wasn't just us," said Fanakel as Anji shook her head. "Our allies joined the conflict, including Daril. The Meali Republic remained neutral, but that was an uncommon stance."

"There's a provision in the Peace concerning grievances between nations," said Parrian. "To avoid another war, should a sovereign be accused of wrongdoing, the sovereign of the wronged party may insist that the claim be heard, and the matter may be considered by a neutral jury. I would certainly have standing to bring a claim on behalf of my son and granddaughter."

"But would that be sufficient?" Coshta asked. "Could we not raise the princess's claim as well? And the prince's?" he added, nodding to Jerrcoa.

Parrian winced. "Officially? No. The Peace makes no such provision. However…"

"Oh, I know *that* look," said Cary under his breath.

His mother ignored him. "I have to believe in light of her behavior that Erianthe won't simply turn herself over if I send notice of a grievance. This means I will need to make a show of force to…get her attention, shall we say? And should I be joined by a sufficient number of similarly aggrieved parties with their own armies, then the matter would have to be heard—and one way or another, the full scope of Erianthe's actions could be brought forth for consideration. It's not precisely contemplated by the Peace," she allowed, "but I think it could work."

I looked around the room at the solemn faces, then up at the queen. "Are you truly willing to do that, Your Majesty?"

Her mouth moved into a grim smile. "Erianthe's deeds have threatened *my* house. I would bring a claim for that alone, but when I see what she tried to do to the rest of you…" She grunted and shook her head. "You four—uh, *five*," she amended, glancing at Terj—"faced unknown dangers and defeated a creature that had endangered all of us for centuries. We owe you an incredible debt. So yes, Susan, I'm willing. Who else do you want to call upon?"

"My father," said Anji without hesitation. "You say you have a maladeta here—could I send him a message? In any case, he'll want to know that Mia and I are safe."

"I should probably mention that Anji's my girlfriend," Mia said from the adjoining couch.

The queen's expression brightened. "*Really?* Well, now, that's lovely news. Is Rokund aware?"

She seemed sincere, and Mia and Anji traded confused glances. "He suspects, I'm sure," said Anji, "though such is not acknowledged by my people."

"No, I'd think not. Dwarves have always been rather limited in their relationships—no offense intended," she hastily added. "But he's tolerated the two of you?"

"I mean, there's an elaborate pretense," Anji replied, "but he hasn't banished us yet."

Parrian moved closed to Anji and stooped slightly to grip her shoulder. "You needn't worry about such here, my dear. I'm pleased to host you all for the time being…and should my granddaughter's partner wish to remain with her, I'd have no reason to object."

"You're not going to try to force me to marry a guy?"

Mia asked incredulously. "Have kids, continue the line?"

"That, darling, is what cousins are for. Or perhaps a sibling or niece or nephew—your father's quite young, after all. But no, I have no intention of attempting to foist you onto some prince you don't want. A princess would be perfectly acceptable."

Anji arched a brow. "A *dwarven* princess?"

"One bold enough to go Outside and face monsters? Absolutely. So yes, send a message to your father and see what he says. Given what I know of Rokund, I'll be shocked if he doesn't offer soldiers."

As long as we're talking to maladetas, said Terj, *let me go back to Kopaat and convey the news to Taln'een. Ganeel has standing among the clan mothers—she may be able to draw others to our cause.*

The queen turned to him and folded her arms. "You think you can safely make the journey?"

Erianthe can't hurt what she can't see, he replied, and vanished from view. *I'll stay out of Deoni.*

As much as I disliked the idea of sending Terj alone, I knew I couldn't go with him. Should my mother learn that I'd not only survived but returned from Earth, there was no telling what she might attempt.

"Tell Falova what's happened," I said to Terj. "I know he still has feelings for Erianthe, but he needs to be made aware."

Of course. He flickered back into view and pointed to Jerrcoa. *What about Cirivant? Do you suppose your uncle could be prevailed upon to take our side?*

He shrugged. "I could ask. After Mother's stunt with Susan's wedding, he might be convinced. I could send a message through your maladeta," he said to Parrian, "but this might work better if I could make a personal appeal."

The queen nodded. "You wish to go to Perem?"

"Is that possible?"

"Why wouldn't it be? We've had peaceful relations with Cirivant for years. I know Fetull—he won't turn away my envoy." Considering his chair, she asked, "How do you fare on ships?"

"I don't know, Your Majesty. I've never been aboard."

"Never..." She rolled her eyes. "One would think that a child of Cirivanti extraction would take his first steps on a rolling deck."

My brother smiled weakly. "I fear I won't be walking across *anything* in the near future."

"And I apologize for that comment," she replied. "Unwarranted. If I may ask..."

"Fever."

"Growing Fever," Anji offered. "But the growths shrank outside of the Aen, so perhaps, with time..."

Coshta nodded vigorously. "Yes, that's *precisely* the cure. My sister is a medical scholar," he explained to the rest of us. "She says that's the only illness we can't treat in Ragatanu. Most of our cases are mild and clear up on their own, but whenever a patient begins exhibiting growths, he's taken through the Crossing and removed from the Aen for a few days. The growths shrink and die, and paralysis is avoided."

Jerrcoa grunted. "Wish someone had mentioned that to my parents."

"You heard what he just said, though, right?" I asked. "The growths *die* outside the Aen. You were away for, like, eleven days, so surely they're dead by now."

He patted the arms of his wheelchair. "I'm not exactly walking—"

"Because your muscles are weak, lad," said Anji. "Give yourself time."

"And my sister would be eager to meet with you," the prince consort told him. "A case like yours would be worth studying."

"Perhaps after he speaks with his uncle," said Parrian, drawing the conversation back on track, then turned to Fanakel. "What about you? Do you suppose your...mother? Father?"

"Father," he replied, "and I would also like to make the appeal in person. Nokan'ti is treaty-bound to Daril, so convincing them to bring a grievance might be difficult."

Her head tilted. "On their own son and nephew's behalf?"

He rubbed the red stubble on his chin. "If you know anything of the True, it shouldn't surprise you to learn that I'm not the favorite child. That said," he continued, looking at me, "if you went with me, it might sway them."

"*Me?*"

"My aunt might be convinced. It's worth a try."

You want to send Susan to Nokan'ti? Without backup?

Fanakel turned to Terj, who bristled beside me. "No one's going to lock her away this time, I swear to it. I'll bring her back safely."

I should come—

"You need to talk to Ganeel and Ms. Quince," I said, taking Terj's hand. "We won't do anything stupid."

I promised to protect you.

And you are, I told him privately. *By going to Taln'een. I'm a big girl.*

Though Terj didn't seem convinced, he accompanied me to our guest room and let me doze in peace instead of listing the many ways that hanging out with the Twins was ill-advised. I awoke around sunset to find his arm around me, a dissipating mist beyond the castle walls, and Mia knocking at the door.

Anji had sent word to Rokund, and Blackhorn Mountain would not stand idly by.

The following morning dawned clear and cool, and the four of us set off aboard a ship bearing the royal standard of Ragatanu—not the worst way by far to get around on Ga'besh. We traveled with an envoy, who would accompany Jerrcoa through Cirivanti waters and see him safely to the palace in Perem. I wasn't thrilled with the notion of my brother traveling with only the envoy, but Fanakel had pulled me aside before I could dispute the arrangement. "He's striving for independence, and it's been denied him all his life," he'd murmured. "Don't coddle him."

"I'm not coddling him," I'd protested.

Fanakel had shaken his head to silence my argument. "His brother has traveled the worlds. His *sister* is a slayer of monsters. Show him that you trust he's capable enough to speak with his own uncle without a nursemaid at his side."

The elf had a point, so I backed off and made my own preparations, packing for a few days in Nokan'ti, including my sword belt. Once aboard the ship, Jerrcoa was all smiles, perhaps a little nervous but intrigued by the rigging and the bustling sailors. The captain proved to be an avuncular sort, a silver fox with twinkling dark eyes and a deep tan, and with the judicious use of a few pieces of scrap wood, he wedged Jerrcoa's chair in place so that he wouldn't go sliding across the deck. Once we'd cleared the harbor, he was happy to talk with us about the ship and the Central Sea, though he laughed when I asked about the ocean on the other side of the continent. "Nothing out there for any man without a death wish," he said. "Monstrous waves, storms beyond your imagining, creatures that swallow ships whole…oh, the waters are rich, but the price is far too steep."

I frowned. "If the waves are so big, then how do you settle along that coast?"

He chuckled. "Who says we do? The crown maintains the sea wall, but it's breached at least a few times a year. Salt marsh and fisheries close to the wall, and that's it. Much the same in Cirivant," he added, nodding to Jerrcoa, "and in any other sane place." Turning to the wheel to make a fine adjustment to our heading, he said, "We're native to Ga'besh, and we know her moods. Others have settled her lands, bringing their own ideas of how to tame her, and when those inevitably fail, they look to us for the answers."

By lunchtime, we'd reached the docks near the tunnel, and I hugged Jerrcoa before we disembarked. "Be safe," I told him, and gave him a last squeeze as I released him. "I'll see you in a few days, eh?"

"Try not to end up imprisoned again," he replied with a teasing smirk.

Fanakel roughly ruffled my brother's hair. "I'll keep her out of trouble…assuming she can ride."

"Right," I muttered as one of the sailors led a pair of chiquiws off the ship. The queen had asked her stablemaster to select mounts for Fanakel and me, and they were a splendid pair of geldings: a tall brown mount for Fanakel, who stomped his paws as he readjusted to solid ground, and a smaller gray for me. The gray had soft eyes and short horns, and his floppy ears gave him a sweet, almost endearing look until his lip curled back, revealing far too many pointed teeth. While I appreciated the loan— a long hike through the Greenwood wasn't high on my list—I'd spent very little time around horses, and their nightmarish cousins left me ill at ease.

As Jerrcoa waved goodbye from the deck, Terj gave me a boost into the saddle, then gestured toward the tunnel. *Shall we?*

He dematerialized and drifted beside us as we rode through the darkness at a trot. I didn't want to go any faster—not only because I was uncomfortable in the saddle, but also because of the limited visibility of my flashlight—but given the size of the chiquiws, a trot was still a good clip. We reached the central cavern after about an hour's journey, and Terj solidified briefly as he reached up to take my hand. *If you haven't returned in a week, I'm coming after you.*

Be careful, I told him.

His grip tightened. "Love," he whispered, and released me.

The tunnel to Kopaat was to our right, while the one to

Honslia was to our left. Once Terj had vanished and sped off, Fanakel and I rode in the other direction, staying close to the wall and watching for the opening. "Was that my imagination," he asked after a time, "or did Terj *speak*?"

"He's trying."

He laughed softly to himself, and I glanced his way, scowling. "What? He's had vocal cords for less than two months. Give him a break."

"You misunderstand," said Fanakel, sobering. "I'm not belittling his efforts—I'm just still shocked at the lengths to which he goes to earn your favor."

"I've never asked any of this of him," I protested.

"Oh, I'm well aware. And I know you love him—I'd have to be blind and deaf to miss that. But I suspect that part of him fears you'll wake from whatever grand delusion convinces you to love him," he said sarcastically, "and so he's trying to make himself suitable for you, delusion or not."

I sighed and adjusted my position in the saddle, dreading the ache in my thighs to come. "Maybe he'll relax once we're married."

"Which will be…when?"

"When we're ready. Once I'm not being hunted by my own mother." I shrugged. "Hell, I'm still a princess— maybe this should be a royal wedding. Give the people a show. They were excited enough about Makou…"

"Yes, the relatively handsome *human prince*."

"Terj is handsome," I countered.

"That's hardly the most important criterion."

I stared at him until Fanakel turned to face me. "I got cursed with that fucking sword for Daril's benefit. I got sent out to kill the Great One for Daril's benefit. So if you think I give two shits about what Daril thinks of my love life…" I paused as he started chuckling again. "*What?*"

"Nothing," said Fanakel. "I *have* missed you, Susan."

"Oh, so I amuse you?"

"No. You…surprise me," he replied. "You have a way

of looking at matters that so many of us consider important and casting them aside like they're nothing, and…I don't know, it's refreshing."

I mulled that over for a moment. "Thanks…I think."

"Of course. This way," he said, and turned down the tunnel toward home.

I understood why the tunnel exits had been placed where they were—politics, concessions, and compromise resulted in the final design. That didn't mean I had to *like* it.

While the Ga'beshi exit was about two hours behind Cole's Crossing, the Honslian exit was closer to six hours ahead, which put us out in the Greenwood around ten that night by my estimation. "Think of it this way," said Fanakel as he urged his chiquiw into the lead. "At least there are no Outsiders to worry about this visit, yes?"

"Yeah," I conceded, "but don't y'all still booby-trap the woods?"

He looked back at me, snorted, then gestured at the low-hanging branches ahead until they rose and bent out of our way. "You were saying?"

"Sometimes I forget you have actual talent."

"I just don't feel the need to constantly employ it," he replied, and let the branches fall back into place behind me. "Also, yours and Terj's are more impressive."

"More limited in scope."

"Perhaps, but what you can *do* within that limited scope is slightly terrifying. Especially you. If you two ever worked together, imagine the storm you could create. You could mitigate against drought in Daril," he continued. "Send in rain from the north. Erianthe was a fool to mistreat you. If she truly had her people's best interest at heart—"

"Big *if.*"

"Exactly." He rolled his shoulders as his mount trotted ahead. "If we're lucky, we'll reach an outpost by midnight."

I looked up through the heavy canopy and was barely able to make out a few stars and the distinct glow of a moon. "Got a good sense of the time?"

"Not great, but the second moon doesn't seem to be up yet. Approximation."

I kept close, wary of triggering a trap along the path. "It's too bad we couldn't just use a maladeta to convey a message."

"Well, there isn't one in permanent residence in Caritulo, so honestly, I don't even know if that would be an option now."

That surprised me. "I thought they loitered around all the centers of power."

"In the other three worlds. Not here. Notice how the Aen is weaker?"

I *had* picked up on a slight decrease as we'd traversed the tunnel. "Yeah…"

"Weakest concentration in the four worlds, so maladetas tend to build their settlements elsewhere. More advantageous locations. Oh, there are transient bands who come through—at least two regularly check on the ogrim population—but I think even they are based in Ildon."

"I've never even seen an ogre."

"And you won't. Not unless you get severely lost out here." He gestured a fallen log out of the way. "The ogrim are the original inhabitants of Honslia. We moved in, and humans after us, and the land wars began. Well, they weren't actually about land at all," he amended. "The issue was water. We have no oceans, nothing even approaching the size of the Central Sea, so access to lakes and streams is key. Anyway, ogrim are formidable, but between our inherent talents and what humans can do with forged items, they were driven back to the wilder places. We have an unofficial truce," he explained. "They stay on their lands, and we don't bother them. No one but the occasional maladetas—them, plus the odd elemental. I've heard that some of the ogrim bands have protective elementals, but I can't prove it."

"They're intelligent?" I asked. "Ogrim?"

He nodded. "Larger than we are, far heavier. Often one-eyed, but not always. They have a speech of their own, and while they seem to lumber, there is an intelligence within them."

"And you took their land?"

He hesitated before answering me. "Not just us, and this was ages ago."

"Yeah, but…" I grunted. "What do the Divine have to say on the subject?"

"Little in particular. Anything that isn't True is inferior, so it's fair for the taking."

"Nice," I muttered.

Fanakel sighed. "I'm not defending it, but if you could kindly refrain from insulting my people's religion while we're here asking for an army, that would be much appreciated."

"I'll behave. I don't have to like it, but I can behave."

"*Thank* you." He glanced over his shoulder at me. "Need a break?"

"I know for a fact that there are bathtubs and beds in the outpost, so let's push through."

"A fair plan," he decreed, and led us onward.

There was, I found, a certain satisfaction in returning in the middle of the night to the elven outpost where I'd previously been dragged as a prisoner. Fanakel might have been the least of his father's children, but a low-ranking prince was still a prince, and he milked it for all it was worth. Imperious, brusque, and barely deigning to look at the guards who scrambled to prepare accommodations for us, he kept up the act until our chiquiws were stabled and we were led to a spacious room with two well-made beds and a large tub behind a living screen of vines and branches. Locking the door as the obsequious men exited, Fanakel waited until their footsteps faded, then made a face and muttered, "Sorry you had to see that, but I didn't want to take any chances."

"You play a convincing asshole," I replied, dropping my gear by the nearer bed.

"I've learned from the best," he replied with a wry smile. "Are you bathing first, or shall I?"

"If you'll promise me a bit of privacy…"

"Believe me," he said, retreating from the tub, "I don't wish to cross you. Take all the time you need."

We slept comfortably and were offered a hearty breakfast the next morning. Fanakel dined without speaking to the guards, though I made a point of thanking them for their hospitality. Sure, I knew the lodging hadn't been given for my sake, but I didn't want to be *rude*.

The outpost's commander, at least, remembered me, and he took the chair beside mine as we ate. "You travel on official business, Watcher?" he asked, his hooded blue eyes wary.

Though gray-haired and obviously an elf of considerable years, he was still a handsome man, I thought—though as I'd just come from Ragatanu with its preternaturally pretty citizenry, even the elves' luster dimmed in comparison. "I do, sir," I replied. "This son of Nokan'ti has offered to bring me to the Twins."

He grunted. "No dwarf this time?"

"She was needed elsewhere—"

"That *dwarf*," Fanakel interrupted, turning to glare at the commander, "is a daughter of Blackhorn Mountain and a more capable fighter than any I've known in the palace guards. You will address her with respect."

The commander stiffened, surprised. "But Your Highness, she—"

"She went Outside with us. How many of your men can say the same?"

That shut him up, and the rest of breakfast was a quiet

affair.

We set off under sunny turquoise skies—or as sunny as it ever was in the Greenwood, considering the lush canopy—and though our chiquiws made good time, it was still a long ride to Caritulo. After about eight hours in the saddle, I was grateful for the painkillers I'd slipped in my bag before leaving Cole's Crossing, and I was aching to dismount as we approached the thirty-foot-high living chain-link fence around the capital, a treehouse city I'd have loved to explore without saddle sores and a pressing need to speak to its rulers. Casual sightseeing wasn't in the cards that evening, but the guards at the gate were far more accommodating than they'd been on my previous visit, and they escorted Fanakel and me straight to a stable. With our chiquiws being fed and attended to, Fanakel led me through the maze of narrow streets in the city's lower level to the thick tree trunk that hid the elevator into the Twins' palace. The guards bowed at Fanakel's approach and moved aside, and he softly exhaled as we rose toward the treetops.

"Perhaps I should have shaved this morning," he said, running one hand over the short stubble on his chin. "Honestly, I forgot. Between our trip west and the chaos at the Crossing, I've grown careless of late."

"Anji's right—it suits you."

He rolled his eyes. "She's just partial to beards."

"I don't know, I tend to agree. Gives your face character," I said, and nudged him in the arm. "And between you and me, it's kind of fun watching the True fall all over themselves in front of a guy who's at least a *little* human."

Fanakel grinned at that. "It is, isn't it?"

When the elevator reached the top level, we walked out into the soaring throne room, which we found empty. "This way," said Fanakel, not stopping to take in the view—really, if the elves did nothing else well, their arboreal architecture was a sight to behold—and led me down a corridor toward a pair of arched doorways. Pausing before the nearer one, he knocked twice and waited.

"Enter," came the curt command from within.

Fanakel pushed the door open to reveal an office space—wide widows overlooking the setting sun and the canopy, an ornately carved wooden desk, and four padded chairs situated before it. Behind the desk sat his father, who regarded us with surprise as I closed the door. "*Fanakel?*" he asked, dropping his pen. "I thought you were abroad."

"I was, Father," he replied, and angled himself to usher me forward. "Until Daril attacked without provocation."

The king cut his dark eyes to me in query. "Explain."

I tried to put on my best manners. "Your Serene Majesty," I began, nodding. "Several days after we came through the Crossing, my mother sent her guards to kill me. They burned down much of my hometown and murdered at least a hundred people. Many more were injured. The place is currently uninhabitable—"

"And that is unfortunate, though hardly my problem."

"They killed indiscriminately," I said. "We believe they targeted my Aen crystals, as my home was completely destroyed. Had your son been there that night, as the guards suspected I was, he may well have perished."

That, at least, seemed to pique his interest. "Go on."

"Erianthe knew your son was traveling with me, along with her own son, my partner, a daughter of Blackhorn Mountain...and, as it turns out, a daughter of Ragatanu."

His eyebrows shot up. "I beg your pardon?"

"My friend Mia, the pretty blonde? Her father is Cerian Venel. The queen is *furious*."

"Indeed?" he murmured, his eyes troubled, and glanced at Fanakel. "You traveled with a *tekori?*"

"A loyal friend," he countered. "Who also has a grievance against Daril."

"Looking past the arson, murder, and attempted

murder," I cut in, "Mother had the opening to the Crossing blown up once her guards finished."

"Had Susan and Terj not worked through the night, we might still be stranded," said Fanakel. "My claim against Daril is legitimate, Father. Pursuant to the Peace, you can bring suit on my behalf...ah, Aunt, good evening," he said as the door beside the desk opened and the queen stepped in, nearly identical to her brother but for a slightly different shape to their pale faces. She wore her long brown hair in a simple braid, which fell over her left shoulder.

"Nephew," she replied, bemused, and looked at me. "Watcher. What brings you here?"

"Apparently," said the king, "Erianthe has tried to kill the girl."

"Again," I muttered.

"Through the mercy of the Divine, we were far from Susan's home when it was set afire in the dead of night," Fanakel told her, "though we returned to the ruins of her town to find that Erianthe had caused the opening to the Crossing to collapse. It would have been beyond my power to reopen without days of labor, but one should never discount elementals," he added, cutting his eyes my way.

She grimaced, then folded her arms over her minimal chest. "That is indeed troubling news. The Watcher escorted you home?"

"No. I escorted her here so that we might ask for my claim to be vindicated. Erianthe's actions could have taken my life and damaged the Crossing. I want justice."

He didn't mention the dead and wounded, but then I supposed a bunch of murdered humans wouldn't make much difference to the Twins.

"Erianthe is dangerous," I said. "She's tried to kill me, my brother could have died, my friends and neighbors *did* die, and for what? I renounced—you were there, yes? You heard me."

They nodded.

"She needs to be stopped," I pressed. "I mean, hell, did Fanakel ever mention what she did to my father?"

The Twins seemed momentarily surprised that I'd deployed his name, but they let it slide. "No, he did not," said his aunt.

"She's the reason the Falova ran dead for the last couple of decades. Sent a team to rip my father out and kill him so he couldn't reveal her infidelity to Narod. They took pity and dumped him in a pond in the desert, and he was hours from death when Terj and I found him. That's *cold*," I said, looking each of them in the eye. "Falova never hurt her. My town never hurt her. *He* certainly never did her wrong," I added, cocking a thumb toward Fanakel. "She's ruthless because she knows no one will stand in her way. That's why we need your help."

The siblings turned to each other briefly, and then the king cleared his throat. "I hear your concerns...both of you. If what you say is true, this is a matter for deeper consideration and observation. Should Erianthe prove untrustworthy, that could damage our relationship with Daril."

"Will you raise a claim, then?" I asked.

"No."

Fanakel stared at him, aghast. *"Father—"*

"We have treaties with Daril. Demanding that Erianthe face accusations such as those you level against her could cause us to break faith. We've not been directly provoked."

"She could have killed me," he said slowly. "She knew I was with Susan, and she attacked anyway. Is that not enough for you?"

The king said nothing.

Fanakel chuckled bitterly and fixed his father with a stare. "And if it had been one of your other children? One more True?"

The continued silence contained all the answers he needed.

Shaking his head, Fanakel said, "Incredible. You know,

Rokund is sending his forces. All Anji had to do was pass a message through a maladeta. I'd never have imagined that *Blackhorn Mountain* could have more honor than Nokan'ti…"

"What Rokund does with his resources is no concern of ours," the king began, but Fanakel cut him off.

"He's defending his daughter's claim, and I tell you in truth, if he's anything like she is, then he's joining us to defend Susan as well. *Every* nation of our worlds owes that woman a debt," he said, pointing to me. "She did more than any of us."

"It was a team project," I protested.

"Yeah, which is why *you* were the one down with the monster and the rest of us were shooting from above," he replied. "But Nokan'ti offers nothing, does it?" he said to his father. "No, you were content to sit here in safety and send a *child* to fight for you."

"The True—"

"Are worthless cowards content to suffer injustice," Fanakel snapped, and gestured the door open. "Including you, Enoul."

The king hissed at the blatant disrespect, but before he could respond, Fanakel raised his hands. "We're leaving. Don't bother showing us out. But a word of advice, if I may," he growled. "Think carefully next time about where you put your dick if it's not in your wife. I deserve better than scraps."

We were halfway down the hall when the queen called, "Fanakel, wait!"

He turned, pushing me behind him. "What?"

"Your claim is valid," she said.

"So you'll confront Erianthe?"

Her mouth tightened. "This is not a decision I can make alone. Your father has spoken, but—"

"Goodbye, Enarl," he said, and pushed me toward the elevator before they could come after us.

Though Fanakel was eager to be off, our chiquiws had just settled in for the evening, and we decided it would be cruel to take them for another long ride through the night. Instead, Fanakel chose a small inn on the outskirts of the city, near the gate and the stables, and ordered dinner for us before paying for a room. The proprietor recognized him—I could see it in the expression she was trying to mask—but since she ran the sort of establishment that promised anonymity, she merely bade us goodnight as she handed over the key.

"She totally thinks we're hooking up in here," I said as I flopped onto the bed, which was just barely wide enough for two. While the evening was still young, I was worn out from a day in the saddle, and Fanakel didn't seem to be in the mood to go out.

He groaned as he lay down beside me. "If that means what I think it means…"

"Yep."

"Well, I'm sure she's witnessed worse." He kicked off his shoes and rolled over, not bothering to change into nightclothes. "See you at first light."

I removed my shoes as well, then drew the curtains and plopped my flashlight by the bed, just in case. "Hey, Fanakel?"

"Mm?"

"I'm proud of you."

He said nothing further, but soon, his breathing slowed toward sleep.

CHAPTER 17

We left early, bought breakfast to go, and rode hard that day—or as hard as we could, considering the forest terrain. Though we reached the outpost in the late afternoon, Fanakel didn't suggest stopping, and I didn't press the issue. The shadows stretched by the time we found the tunnel opening, and we paused only long enough to give the chiquiws a rest before we mounted up and pushed on.

My body had no idea what time it was supposed to be when we emerged into the early afternoon light of Ga'besh. Weary and disoriented, we rode down to the nearby docks and stared in silence at the sparkling blue water.

"What now?" Fanakel finally asked. "There's bound to be a coast road…"

But I lifted a finger to silence him, conscious of a presence near the shore. *Hello*, I said. *I mean no harm.*

A humanoid form rose from the shallows to what would have been his waist. *Who are you?*

Susan. And you?

I am myself.

Figured. *Is this your sea?*

His amusement rippled across my mind. *In part. Far too large for any one of my brothers to claim.* Pausing, he considered me, then cocked his head. *Or <u>our</u> brothers, should I say?*

I was born of he of the Falova. In Kopaat, I explained.

Recognition dawned. *Ah. I have heard whispers of you, little sister. Where are you bound?*

I pointed toward the west. *Enead. My friend and I are*

returning to the queen. These are hers, I added, patting my chiquiw's thick neck. Scanning the empty waters, I asked, *Do you know of a ferry that comes this way?*

I know of several, the elemental replied, *but none that will pass today. The cannieg migration has begun, and every boat along this coast is in pursuit.*

"What's a canniee?" I asked Fanakel, and glanced back to see that he and his mount had retreated a few paces from the water.

"A type of fish. Ga'beshi delicacy. They're normally deep dwelling, so they're difficult to catch."

Except now, when they rise to give birth and mate. This is a long-established pattern. Should you require a boat, I fear you will be waiting for some time.

"Shit," I muttered. I'd been hoping for a bed that night, not a campout, especially since neither of us had packed tents. But there was one other option...

Would you be offended if I made passage for us? I asked the elemental.

I could sense his confusion. *Offended?*

With a moment's concentration, I pulled together a flat boat comprised of water, which bobbed lightly by the dock. *This is your sea, not mine, but may I use it to transport us and our mounts back to Enead?*

I understand. No, little sister, I would not be offended.

I paused, trying to parse any hidden meaning. *Would our brothers?*

No, he replied. *But to save you any interrogation, perhaps I could escort you.*

I don't mean to inconvenience you—

You are not. Come.

"Good enough for me," I murmured to Fanakel, then coaxed my chiquiw aboard the boat. He wasn't thrilled— to be fair, anyone would be uneasy standing on unusually solid water that wasn't ice—but Fanakel's chiquiw followed him with a jingle of his harness. "Let's hope I hold this one together," I said.

Fanakel smirked. "Since I can't think of any waterfalls between here and Enead…"

"Don't remind me," I said, and sped us away from the dock.

About three hours later, I had only just convinced my chiquiw to step back onto dry land when, to my delight, I sensed Terj's approach. He manifested, almost faceplanting as he did so in his haste to reach us, but recovered and was laughing by the time he embraced me.

Hey, you, I said to him alone, smiling as our lips parted. *Miss me?*

Always. Glad to see you safely back. Releasing me, he nodded to Fanakel and asked, *Any luck?*

"None," Fanakel muttered. "Nokan'ti is useless. What about the Taln'een?"

Horrified by my account, particularly Ardielta. It's unpleasant to bear the news of death, but that couldn't be helped, and she knew most of that town. Ganeel is angry. To me, he quickly added, *I passed along Malachi's message. Ardielta appreciated it.*

"So they'll support Susan's claim?" said Fanakel.

They can make their own. An attack on the Crossing provides a claim to any nation that wishes to present it.

That, I'm sure, did nothing to raise Fanakel's spirits, but he let it go.

I spoke with Falova as well, said Terj, turning back to me. *Informed him of what Erianthe ordered done.*

"How'd he take it?"

To put it mildly, he's infuriated.

"Really? Considering how much he was willing to forgive—"

That was before you. Perhaps you don't need a father these days, but Falova seemed very upset at the thought of you being burned alive.

"Nice of him to care."

Trust me, he more than cares. Glancing past me at the water, Terj paused, then raised a hand. *Hello, there.*

The water elemental—who, true to his word, had seen us safely back to Enead—mirrored the gesture. *Brother?*

I am.

I had heard whispers of one born to air who had chosen corporeality, he said, *but I confess that I had thought them absurd...*

He chuckled and shrugged. *Absurd enough, I suppose.*

But...why?

Why? He pulled me close, and I felt his pleasure at our touch. *Need I explain further?*

The other elemental's confusion shifted toward amusement. *You are a strange one, but be well. And you, little sister,* he added before slipping beneath the surface.

"Nice guy," I told Terj, and we started up the dock with Fanakel leading both chiquiws. "Any word from Jerrcoa?

Better than word. He returned late last night, hours before I did. Cirivant will raise its claim and support his as well—the Terols care for their own.

"So that's Ragatanu, then, plus Cirivant, Blackhorn Mountain, and whatever Ganeel cooks up..."

"Not a bad beginning," said Fanakel.

"Beginning?" I echoed, looking back at him. "That's a pretty damn good fighting force, isn't it?"

"Sure, if you're conducting a naval battle. Cirivant's strength is on the water, and Ragatanu's armies aren't much better. Blackhorn Mountain, now, can fight on any dry terrain, but do we even know how many soldiers Rokund is sending?"

There's a maladeta traveling with their band, and she says they should arrive on the morrow, Terj replied. *Cirivant won't be far behind. We can count swords then, but for now,* he said, almost holding me up, *you're exhausted.*

"Nokan'ti is quite a few hours ahead of Ragatanu," I said, stifling a yawn. "And I did just take us for a long boat ride..."

Back to the palace with you both, he ordered, *and straight to bed. I'll brief the others.*

We had barely sat down to breakfast the next morning when aides interrupted with murmured messages for the queen. She listened and dismissed them, then looked down the table with a smile. "It seems there's a Cirivanti fleet headed this way, flying peace banners."

"Good news," said Cary.

"You didn't let me finish. They're traveling with a maladeta, who reported a dwarven force massing at the tunnel exit."

Anji perked. "On foot?"

"No. They're coming through in carriages." Glancing at the aide standing by the door, she said, "Ask Junil to relay to her sisters that I've given them permission to approach. Have the dwarves follow the coast road."

She bowed and departed, and Parrian sipped her tea. "I would eat well, were I you," she told the rest of us. "This should be a long afternoon."

The queen wasn't wrong. While dwarven carriages were speedy by local standards—not as fast as Terj, but certainly better than a trotting chiquiw—Blackhorn Mountain had sent ten loaded with troops, and they didn't leave their staging area until all had cleared the tunnel. Finding the coast road wasn't difficult for the newcomers, but the flying vehicles moved slowly in an attempt not to alarm the locals traveling below—considerate, though ultimately futile. Still, the delay gave Parrian time to arrange accommodations, and using her maladeta to coordinate with the dwarves', she had them quartered at a coastal fortress by midmorning. One of the carriages flew to the palace shortly thereafter, and Rokund, first out of the vehicle as it landed in the largest courtyard, quickly hugged his waiting daughter before greeting his hosts.

"Be welcome," said Parrian, who'd made it a point to have Mia by her side when the delegation arrived.

"Cirivant is on the way. Can I offer you refreshments? Are your people's quarters satisfactory?"

"Most satisfactory, and thank you," Rokund replied, gripping Anji's shoulder. "I apologize for the imposition—"

"It's no imposition—far better to plan here than in the wilds of Kopaat," she said. "At least we have water."

The under-king chuckled. "No one has ever accused Ga'besh of being overly dry."

"It's home." Taking Mia's hand, she said, "I understand you've been hosting my granddaughter."

Rokund's dark eyes widened, and he absently tugged one of his beard braids as he turned to his daughter. "Did you forget to mention that your friend was a Venel, Anjikora?"

"She was unaware," Anji replied.

"As was my son, unfortunately," Parrian grumbled. "But there's no denying this one," she added, giving Mia a fond smile. "Thank you for your hospitality. Perhaps you would allow us to return the favor. After all, Mia will need to stay with us for some time to attend to her education."

Rokund was no fool, and he read the subtext as clearly as any of us did: the youngest of his children could be happy with her girlfriend, far from the gossip and disapproving stares of Heartfast. "A generous offer," he replied. "Though I hope you won't take offense if I share my concerns for leaving my daughter here."

"I assure you," said Parrian, "that she's perfectly safe. It seems our...*peculiarities*, shall we say, are poorly understood beyond Ga'besh. No one would be fool enough to mistake the princess for one of our donors."

His thick eyebrows rose. "Donors?"

"Humans, all of them. Well compensated, well kept, and free to go at any time. They perform a valuable service."

"At the cost of their lives?" he pressed.

Parrian cocked her head. "We all die eventually, my

friend. Those humans who work as donors regularly see their ninetieth year, though I regret that the species is so short-lived."

"Only ninety?"

"That's way above average," I offered from the sidelines.

"Susan's absolutely right," said Mia. "Trust me, Your Excellency, if humans were being farmed and killed young, I'd be the first to complain."

He grunted, perhaps not entirely convinced but willing to drop the matter for the time being. "Well...if there are refreshments on offer, I wouldn't say no, though please don't put yourself to any trouble..."

"It's my pleasure," said the queen, beckoning him toward a door. "Come, let us become better acquainted before Cirivant arrives."

"I don't think I'm out of turn in speaking for Blackhorn Mountain when I say that Erianthe's behavior at my son's aborted wedding was concerning to all of us." Fetull Terol looked down Parrian's long conference table at Rokund, who nodded. "Assuming that my nephew is correct, and I have no reason to doubt his account," he continued, cutting his eyes to Jerrcoa, "I fear for the safety of my brother and his children. That Erianthe would act...*rashly*, I suppose, might be the most political term, as a young woman in difficult circumstances is one thing—"

I kept my thoughts about *that* characterization to myself.

"—but this, now...this is greatly concerning. I would be appalled if she had targeted Susan alone, but her apparent disregard for you four, who've done her no wrong, not to mention Jerrcoa..."

"An unprovoked attack on any of my children is an attack on my house," Rokund murmured. "Erianthe has shown herself to be both faithless and ruthless. Now, I understand that Ragatanu has not been witness to her recent behavior—"

"Mia and Anji have been quite thorough," said Parrian. "And your reactions only corroborate their account. I don't require convincing." She sat back in her chair and twirled a pen between two fingers. "How do we play this?"

"With a modicum of diplomacy, I would think," Rokund replied. "I've come with a contingent of about a hundred fifty—enough to make a point without giving Erianthe concern that we're planning an invasion. But if the consensus is that a larger force is required, I can call for more…"

Fetull grunted. "My thoughts were leading in a similar direction. I've come with about two hundred, but of course, our ships will be useless once we leave Ga'besh. We don't have the immediate resources to launch a prolonged land war in Kopaat."

"How do you propose to get there?" Rokund asked him. "On foot? The dry season has commenced."

"We have sufficient chiquiws, though drinking water will be a concern."

The king and the under-king looked at me, and I shrugged. "Can't promise miracles, but I'll do what I can to keep you hydrated until we reach the river."

"I could easily afford another two hundred soldiers," said Parrian. "Five hundred fifty marching on Deoni would certainly send a message—"

"What of Nokan'ti?" Rokund interrupted, turning to Fanakel.

The elf looked like he wanted to sink through his chair into the floor. "They declined."

Rokund considered that briefly, and an expression I couldn't quite read flashed in his eyes. "I'm sorry, lad."

Fanakel nodded curtly.

Ganeel promises assistance from Taln'een, said Terj, taking the spotlight off him. *They'll meet us in Deoni. She's spreading the word through her network.*

"If there's one thing maladetas do well, it's share information," said Fetull. "That said, I'd rather not count on armies that may not join us—if their claim is simply the damage to the Crossing, that may be too tenuous to risk offending Daril. Ti'cal probably can't afford that."

"Eraneg has a grievance," Jerrcoa muttered.

I grinned at him. "They've got just as much as a grievance against me for screwing up Edes's wedding."

"Eraneg would also face a long sea journey," Rokund pointed out. "As would any of the larger dwarven presences in Kopaat. Those dwarves across the northern sea from Daril are primarily miners and merchants. Silverhold could be formidable, but again, there's the matter of travel across the northern regions in the dry season."

And much as I'd like to help, I can't carry an entire army.

"That's more than anyone can ask of you," Parrian told Terj. "But it might be worthwhile for us to delay our departure by a few days and see whether Taln'een can deliver additional claimants. If they spread the word as far as I suspect they can, then surely someone will respond."

As the more seasoned attendees rumbled their agreement, a thought occurred to me. "There's one the maladetas can't reach."

"Several, actually," said Fanakel. "They don't have a great presence in Honslia—"

"Forget Honslia. What about Unara?"

His eyebrows rose. "You're suggesting—"

"Sanniah might be persuaded."

"Who, now?" asked Parrian as the other two monarchs frowned.

"Sanniah oo'Kral sha'Volng," I replied. "Queen of Banilgh. Outside. She's the orange woman in the recording—you know, short, hairless, four purple eyes?"

Parrian's forehead wrinkled. "She's not a signatory to the Peace of Meali…"

"No, but she owes us. And no offense, but since

Banilghish tech puts to shame a lot of what I've seen in the four worlds…"

"Speaking of tech," Cary interjected, "we've got a problem."

His mother's mouth tightened. "Which is?"

"The best evidence that Daril is responsible for the damage is the camera footage from Cole's Crossing. Doorbell cameras, security cameras, whatever, everyone with recordings uploaded them to a cloud drive…never mind, I'll explain later," he said as she regarded him bemusedly. "Janine has access. We need to save those recordings as evidence."

"And figure out how the hell to play them over here," Mia added.

"A laptop, a projector, and a few solar-powered batteries?"

"Could work," she agreed, then sighed. "I left my laptop in Susan's house, so it's toast."

He grinned. "Then it's probably a good thing I brought mine back with me."

"*Ooh.* Yes," said Mia. "But for the other equipment and the videos, I guess I'll be having a chat with Mom—"

"Let me." He reached over and took her hand. "I know she's hurt you. *She* knows that, too, but I'm not going to ask you to make nice for cloud access."

"You propose to go back there?" Parrian protested. "Already? But you just got home!"

"And with any luck, I've still got a car waiting by the cabin," he replied. "It's all right, Mom—leave this to me."

Mia smiled. "Thanks. In that case, I'm with Suze."

Cary's expression shifted in an instant. "Wait…you want to go *Outside*? That's—"

"A great idea," Fanakel interrupted. "If the five of us go, perhaps she'll be more inclined to take this seriously. I'm in," he said, turning to me.

"Naturally," said Anji, and Rokund, who'd just started to open his mouth, snapped it shut. Glancing his way, she said, "Father, could we borrow one of the carriages? Their transportation systems are quite good, but since we don't have any of their currency…"

"Nor do we know how the general populace is feeling right now," Mia reminded us. "It's been months—let's hope Sanniah still has a throne, you know?"

There's no need for a carriage, said Terj. *I'm faster.*

"Granted," I replied, "but we're talking about a three-day trip. Remember, it was a day's ride from Acanna to Joh, then another to Dalienn, and then half a day more to Volng."

By rail, you mean. The return trip was quite a bit faster by air—

"And you know I love you, but you're not *that* fast."

No, he grumped.

Turning to Rokund, I said, "Your Excellency, if we could borrow a carriage, please…"

The under-king looked at his daughter, who flashed a winning smile, and then he sighed. "You'll have whatever I can give you. What else do you need?"

"Well, slight hiccup," said Mia, "but does anyone have a spare maladeta?"

Dwarven carriages were lovely things, long, black flying craft with rows of benches split by an aisle and windows made of thin sheets of quartz. They varied in size from a stretch limo for more personal craft to vehicles three or four times that length. The ones Rokund had used for troop transport were on the larger end of the spectrum—not so great for Anji, who was stuck piloting the cumbersome thing, but a far more comfortable ride for those of us of the non-dwarven persuasion, for whom leg room was a concern.

A second carriage followed us that morning, flown by a soldier and carrying a pair of maladetas: Junil, who was then stationed in Enead, and Taliem, her sister from

Cirivant. I knew little about the women other than their faces. Both were dark-skinned and wore their long hair in intricate twists, and Junil had mentioned that they were of the Murieg, a Ga'beshi clan—she was the fourth daughter, while Taliem, a much younger woman, was the seventh. More worryingly, the two had looked uncertain when we'd run the plan by them. There was, apparently, a good reason why Ganeel was respected by her far-flung maladetan sisters: the woman was *talented*. The two maladetas we had on hand weren't sure that they could manage the trick of breaking through to the Outside, but they agreed to try.

With the carriages, our trip from Enead to the central cavern at the Crossing took only about two and a half hours, and we stepped out to stretch our legs while the maladetas worked in the bright glow of the headlights. Like Ganeel and Ms. Quince, they chose a space between the openings to the Ildon and Kopaat tunnels, where they felt the skin between our worlds and what lay beyond was thinnest, then started chanting and gesticulating. It was, we'd discovered, far easier to pass in the other direction— pressing against the barrier was like pushing against thick pudding, though whether that was due to some property of the Aen or of Unara, I had no idea. But the maladetas had their work cut out for them, and my nervous stomach unclenched a little when the part of the rock wall on which they were concentrating began to glow and melt.

With the matter well in hand, Cary shouldered his pack and hugged Mia goodbye. "Be careful," he told her. "If you want to come with me, now…"

"I'll be fine," she insisted, and shooed him on his way to the surface.

After twenty minutes of hard work, the maladetas had managed to open a hole large enough for our carriage, which revealed the familiar dark orange brick tunnel beyond it and the prickly breeze of the Aen-less air. Anji stepped past the puddle of molten stone and into the

Unaran tunnel, then returned to us, scowling. "It's a bit narrow for my taste, especially with a carriage this size."

"Can we blow a hole through?" Fanakel asked.

"Well, we would have to at some point, anyway," she said, and pulled a circular explosive disc from her bag.

"I thought you weren't carrying explosives," I said.

She smiled. "And I wasn't, but Father wouldn't send me off unprepared."

While the maladetas took cover, Anji affixed the disc to the wall, set the timer, and sprinted. Just as she crouched and yelled, "Blast!" the bricks burst outward, leaving a hole through the tunnel wall—large enough to duck through, but insufficient for the carriage.

"Your Highness," asked the dwarven pilot, approaching with another disc, "shall I set a second charge?"

"I'll do it, thank you," she replied, and repeated the procedure while the rest of us avoided the danger zone. The second explosion destabilized a large chunk of the tunnel wall, and after the dust cloud from the cascade of bricks had dissipated, we found ourselves with an opening big enough for a tractor-trailer.

"So…we apologize to Sanniah for destroying her nice tunnel when we see her?" muttered Mia.

Somehow, I doubt she'll be heartbroken, Terj replied, and headed for the carriage. *Let's go. Did anyone bring snacks?*

"There's food in the back," said Anji, kneeling to check her gear. "You're not hungry yet, are you?"

No, but I know what to expect now, and there's no telling what we'll find along the way.

With the maladetas standing by to close the hole, we loaded up and flew through into Unara. The sun was high in the strange lilac sky—noon, I estimated—and the fields below us were still carpeted with the short yellow growth of spring. I tried to orient myself using the tunnel, which curved away from the weakest point in a wide U shape, the arms of which eventually joined up at the volcano where the overly fertile Great One had been corralled. The tunnel's arms ran southeast to northwest, with the capital of Banilgh, Volng, a considerable journey ahead. While I had no way to accurately measure distances, I would have been shocked if the trip was less than a thousand miles. To the west of our entrance point lay Acanna, and I knew what Anji was doing when she banked in that direction. If she followed the tunnel there, she could pick up the tracks of the local trainlike conveyance, which would lead us straight to the city.

It wasn't long before Anji found Acanna. The fields gave way to a modest village, and then I spotted the tracks and the long stone waystation. The building hadn't been torn down in the eight months since our departure, which I took as a good sign—maybe the people hadn't risen up in all-out revolution after their young queen made a live broadcast of a band of creatures from Beyond killing their resident god. The priests ran the waystations, places for travelers to sleep. During our prior visit, all travel was conducted during daylight hours—unbeknownst to most, a form of protection in case any of the Great One's children escaped the tunnel to the four worlds—and I wondered whether overnight schedules had been added since the danger had been eliminated.

Anji didn't pause to sightsee. As curious townsfolk looked up at us from below, she guided us toward the rail line and used it to orient us, keeping it out the left window. "Good day for flying," she said over her shoulder as she made some subtle adjustments. "Hardly more than a breeze, and the only clouds are to the east. Let's hope they stay there."

But we'd barely flown for an hour when I noticed another craft speeding toward us from the north—a pale blue, slightly bulbous vehicle that seemed to be closing on us at a clip. It looked rather like the one in which Sanniah had ferried us into the mountains, though as it neared, I noticed a pair of protuberances in the front that reminded me of guns.

"What do we do?" Fanakel asked.

"The wise thing," Anji muttered, and slowed to a stop. Hovering above a grain field, she tapped at her console until radio static echoed through the carriage, then began scanning for a signal. I had no idea what sort of communications frequency the Unarans used, but Anji's equipment was fairly comprehensive, and soon, she stumbled upon a curt male voice. Even without a translator, the tenor of the message would have been clear.

"Unidentified craft, provide registration," the speaker said. "Your flight path is unauthorized. Land or…uh…"

Anji flipped on her microphone. "This is the unidentified craft. I'm holding position."

"Repeat," he replied, agitated. "Sorry, something's garbled."

"Repeating, I am holding position." Looking over her shoulder, she called, "Susan, get up here. Your accent might work better."

"This is *literally* the first time anyone has ever suggested that," I said, but climbed up into the cockpit with her. Taking the microphone, I cleared my throat and tried to speak slowly. "This is the unidentified craft. We have come from Beyond. My name is Susan Cole, and we are traveling to Volng."

A brief silence answered that, followed by an incredulous, "The *godslayer*?"

I looked at Anji, who grimaced and shrugged.

"The same," I said, hoping that wouldn't get us shot down. "I was hoping for an audience with the queen—"

"I…I will inform central command immediately," he said in a rapid babble. "Of course. Her Majesty will be notified. Is she expecting you?"

"No, unfortunately," I said, thanking my lucky stars. "And we're sorry to come unannounced, but we've got a bit of a…situation."

"She will be informed," he promised. "Proceed, I'm

logging your expected path. You'll have an escort."

Anji whistled softly in relief as she set us back in motion. As we approached the other vehicle, the pilot said, "You can speed up, if you like. The deceleration zone is much closer to Volng."

"We're flying at top speed," Anji muttered.

"This is as fast as we can go," I relayed. "You have the superior craft, I fear."

"Oh! Um…just a moment."

We were almost upon him when he returned to the channel. "Faster transport has been arranged. Follow me down, and we'll see you to Her Majesty."

As it so happened, the Banilghish military had a depot not terribly far from our location. We landed behind the other vehicle and taxied into a hangar, where a bald orange figure in a gray uniform stood waiting. I couldn't tell the person's gender on sight—Unarans looked remarkably similar to my eyes—but judging by the amount of flair on the jacket, they were someone of importance.

The person turned out to be the depot commander, and she was eager to welcome us to her installation. Her sister had been one of the unwitting "acolytes" selected to feed the Great One, and like many of her countryfolk, she took the news of the deception *personally*. Sanniah still held the throne, she assured us, her superiors in Volng had been alerted to our presence, and we would be ferried to the capital with all due haste. Promising that Anji's carriage would be protected in our absence, she ushered us aboard a faster vehicle and bade us a safe journey.

Our pilot, a young man who'd lost a brother and his mother to the Great One, was polite to a fault and eager to chat. Yes, he explained, there had been a few disturbances from zealots in the weeks and months after the monster's defeat. Some of the Great One's most fervent devotees refused to believe that the god to whom their families had prayed for generations was nothing more than a ravenous beast, and it smarted to have taken pride in being the people blessed with an actual *god*, only to learn that they had been deceived. Still, those protests had been decreasing in recent months and sparked little interest. The queen's broadcast had been replayed hundreds of times, and confidence in the Crown was at an all-time high. Those with a bit of savvy recognized that Sanniah had risked her throne, not to mention her life, by attacking the Great One and coming clean about the long lie, but the gambit had paid off.

Plus, the new high priest was much younger than his predecessor, more of a scholar than a politician, and he had initiated a campaign of transparency, opening the temple libraries and educating the people as to the lies their local priests had been told. A few of the clergy had been injured by a vindictive populace, but trust was slowly being rebuilt. "Besides," our pilot added with a smile, "we had one of our best harvests in decades last year. The gods surely favor us for the destruction of the false one in our midst."

We landed after sunset and overnighted at another depot near Joh. The waystations along the carriage lines were still fully operational, our pilot assured us over dinner, but people tended to worry when military craft parked in public. Once we'd eaten, an aide showed us to an empty room set up for ten, and after Anji claimed a bed, she helped us rearrange the other nine. It wasn't the most comfortable night any of us had passed, but at least no one was trying to kill us, which I counted as a win.

The next morning, we rose early and took to the air, then sped toward the capital. Arriving at a base outside the glittering pink city wall that afternoon, we traded our vehicle for a smaller craft, which flew us into Volng and over the maze of streets to the thin blue-gray towers of the palace. As soon as we'd set down on the pad atop the tallest, I opened the hatch to disembark, but I'd barely fit my body through the door before Sanniah was upon me.

The queen was a little woman, maybe four feet tall and only about seventeen years old, but she had a *fierce* grip, and I had to thump her back a few times before she let me breathe. "Hello!" she said, beaming as she looked up at me—or so I thought, as trying to determine the direction in which a Unaran's purple insect-like eyes were focused was more art than science. "This is wonderful! Did you have an easy trip?"

"Very easy," I replied, "and thank you for the lift."

"I *especially* thank you for that, lass," Anji interrupted, coming in to hug the queen. "It was going to be a long few days at the controls otherwise."

"Going forward, we must think of a better way for you to announce your presence...ah, hello!" she cried, pausing to hug Mia and Fanakel in turn. "Welcome, friends!" Releasing her grip, she stepped back and smiled at them, then noticed Terj and cocked her head. "And who is this?"

It's a long story, Your Majesty.

"*Oh!*" she gasped, then grinned more widely and gave him one of her lung-collapsing hugs as well. "You must tell me everything while we eat. Come, I've had your rooms prepared."

As Sanniah hurried toward the tower elevator, her pale yellow dress fluttering behind her in the breeze, I hung back and looped my elbow around Terj's. *Could be a lot worse.*

She's in good spirits, he replied. *Here's hoping.*

Sanniah had done her best to make us comfortable, ordering that extra beds be brought into our guest rooms to accommodate us. She apologized, having neglected to set up a room for Terj, but he assured her it was no trouble. *This is optional,* he explained, and dematerialized. *And I don't exactly sleep. Think nothing of it.*

Besides, I added to him as he reappeared, *you can always camp with me.*

Terj looked my way and grinned. *Might be cozy.*

And that would be too bad, wouldn't it?

He remained with me while I unpacked and freshened up, and though I didn't bother changing into a dress, I made sure to belt on my sword. Since Sanniah had given it to me in the first place, anything less would have been rude.

Aides came to collect us for dinner as the sun set, and we were shown into a private dining room set for six, with Sanniah already seated at the head. Thankfully, she'd chosen a tall table by local standards, meaning that I didn't have to sit with my knees splayed to either side. Drinks were poured, bowls of fragrant soup were passed around, and then, once the servants had stepped out, the queen said, "As pleased as I am to see you all, I know this isn't a social visit. What brings you here?"

I'd claimed the spot at the foot of the table opposite her, and as the rest of the crew turned to me, I took the lead. "Short version, I gave up my place in line for the throne of Daril, and my mother still tried to kill me. Managed to destroy most of my hometown and kill a bunch of innocent people instead. I want to make her pay."

Sanniah put down her spoon. "Why would your *mother* do that?"

I smirked. "How many courses is this dinner?"

"Five, but you have my attention. Tell me everything, Susan."

So I did. The rest of our party filled in the gaps, clarifying and backing me up.

And by the time the dessert dishes were carried away, Banilgh had joined the action.

CHAPTER 18

I hadn't hoped for much from Sanniah—beggars can't be choosers, after all, and I was asking her to take up arms in a matter that didn't concern her or her people. As far as the queen was concerned, however, the five of us had rendered a service to Banilgh that could never be repaid, and mobilizing five hundred soldiers on short notice was the least she could do. She could call for more, she assured us, as we watched the final preparations at the base outside Volng the next morning—double, treble, ten times the initial force, whatever was required. If we anticipated a siege, Banilgh could offer reinforcements and supplies. While I sincerely hoped it wouldn't come to that, the promise of aid without strings attached left me in better spirits than I'd been in since Janine's panicked phone call ten days before. The fact that Sanniah herself was coming along certainly didn't hurt.

Now it was just a matter of coordination.

We left from Volng and overnighted in Joh after about an eight-hour flight, which Terj admitted was a far better time than he could have managed. The following morning, after the depot's priests came out to give the departing troops a blessing of protection, we took off again, heading south. After a quick pit stop to pick up Anji's borrowed carriage, the convoy had to slow its pace—the dwarven vehicle was a reliable workhorse, but its top speed was less than half that of the Banilghish military craft. As noon approached and we made our final leg toward the tunnel, Sanniah passed the directions to the fleet. The hole we'd blown open was only large enough to permit single-file flight, so the pilots needed to line up and be ready to take their turn. Anji would go first, thereby demonstrating that passage into the Beyond was as easy as pressing on the far tunnel wall, and she would park in the Crossing's central cavern, where Mia would direct the incoming Unarans to the left and down the Kopaat tunnel with a pair of flares. We saw nothing to be gained by sending them to Ga'besh, only to have them turn around and navigate the Crossing again. While Mia handled traffic, Anji would monitor the tunnels for incoming vehicles unaware of the fleet moving through, while Terj would return to Ga'besh and tell those assembled in Ragatanu that the time had come. As for Fanakel and me, we rode in the lead with Sanniah, both to assist the pilot with the tunnels if needed and to guide him once we emerged into the Kopaati wasteland.

To my great relief, Anji passed back into the Crossing without a hiccup. By the time our pilot white-knuckled us straight into the brick wall, she had parked on the far side of the cavern, and Mia was standing in the middle with her yellow flares as a one-woman amateur ground crew, flagging us in the right direction. The pilot slipped down the tunnel and kept our pace slow and steady, and after a little more than an hour, we emerged into the bright light of a late Kopaati morning.

"The time zones at the tunnel exits aren't quite synchronized," I explained as Fanakel pointed the pilot toward a relatively flat area between two short hills. "It's a bit earlier here than it was in Banilgh."

"I see," said Sanniah, who squinted through the windows at the barren scrubland around us. "This…is your country?"

"Near the border—no one has an official claim to this area. If the tunnel weren't here, I doubt anyone would want it."

She nodded. "Rather dusty."

"Welcome to the dry season. A big chunk of this

continent is little more than desert." Pointing toward the east, I said, "The Falova River is the center of a north–south green belt, but it's a ways off."

As the Banilghish fleet slowly arrived, Sanniah ordered an encampment set up, and we waited out the heat of the clear spring day under whatever shade we could find. With twenty-five craft to pass through the Crossing, it was bound to be a bit of a wait; Anji and Mia were holding each newcomer for ten minutes or so, making a little distance in the line of ships so as to avoid a massive crash. By then, I assumed Terj had reached Ragatanu, though I had no way to communicate with him and nothing to do but watch the sand blow by.

The last of Sanniah's forces arrived midafternoon, and a soldier jumped out the side door and jogged toward the queen's tent as soon as her vehicle stopped moving. "Your Majesty," she panted, bowing as she approached. "I bring a message."

Sanniah nodded. "Which is?"

She pulled a piece of paper from within her jacket, and Sanniah frowned at the writing. "I believe this is for one of you," she said, handing it to me.

I recognized Mia's handwriting: *Ragatanu group starting through Ga'besh tunnel. We're staying to monitor traffic.*

"Looks like the rest of the party is en route," I told Sanniah. "We'll start seeing them before nightfall."

In truth, I expected the first of the dwarven carriages to arrive in about an hour, but as I had no clear sense of how Unarans demarcated time, I kept things vague.

Right on schedule, the first of Rokund's fleet appeared from the tunnel mouth and drew close, and a few of the Banilghish soldiers gestured toward a cleared spot in which it could park. The under-king himself wasn't aboard that carriage—he had, I learned, stayed toward the back of the pack to continue coordinating last-minute logistics—but Terj appeared shortly after the door opened and hurried through the crowd to join Fanakel and me. *We've got a veritable parade coming through,* he said proudly. *The nine dwarven carriages, plus twenty transport barges.*

Fanakel's brow knit. "What's a transport barge?"

Little more than a flying wagon with a windshield—there aren't even benches inside. Deep enough to transport chiquiws. They're Ragatanese craft of dwarven make.

"*Oh?*" I asked.

He grinned. *Yeah, Rokund's not thrilled to learn of their existence, but Parrian pointed out that if the dwarven guilds won't sell them vehicles, there's no reason that they can't buy from the local dwarves. I'm sure she paid a stiff premium for them if she got them from black market forgers, but they're at least as fast as Rokund's carriages, so perhaps she got her money's worth.* He shrugged. *If Anji and Mia stay together, maybe Rokund could be persuaded to sell to the in-laws.*

That was a concern for another day. The first batch of dwarves took over from the Banilghish troops in guiding the arriving carriages to parking spaces, and since they were coming through at roughly the same rate as the first wave, Rokund arrived less than two hours later. He proceeded straight to Sanniah's tent, and as the two nodded to each other, I was struck once again by how tall he was for a dwarf—he had nearly a foot on the Unaran queen.

Unsure of the protocol, I did my best. "Your Excellency," I said, turning to Rokund, "this is Her Majesty Sanniah oo'Kral sha'Volng of Banilgh. Your Majesty," I continued as Sanniah smiled, "allow me to present His Excellency Rokund, Under-King of Blackhorn Mountain…uh…third of his name?"

"That'll do, lass," said Rokund, and extended his arm to Sanniah.

She gripped it at the elbow. "A pleasure," she said. "Your daughter did a great service for my people."

"And I thank you for your hospitality toward her."

"The gods expect no less." Releasing him, she straightened her green jacket—a far cry from the dresses she seemed to prefer around Volng—and turned her head toward the tunnel as the first Ragatanese barge flew through. "I apologize in advance if I or my people inadvertently offend. This is our first time in the Beyond."

"Don't trouble yourself—you're doing us quite a favor," he replied.

"Our debt is considerably larger than this," she said with a soft chuckle, "but I'm happy to begin repayment."

Rokund grunted in acknowledgement, and his eyes narrowed. "You've no translators?"

"Like the one Anji wears? No. Such is beyond our capabilities. Are your people equipped in the same fashion?" she asked, gesturing toward the milling crowd of dwarves.

"Few among them, I would think, but we'll make do. Still..." He reached into a pocket within his vest and extracted a pendant, a piece of what seemed to be rose quartz set in silver. "Try this."

Her head tilted slightly as she considered the necklace, and I said, "Let me help you. It'll work once you're wearing it."

Sanniah stood still while I clasped it around her neck, and then Rokund removed a thick ring from his left hand and passed it to me. "Do you understand me?" he asked Sanniah.

She gasped, delighted. "Oh, this is wonderful! So cleverly made, and beautiful besides..." Her voice faded, and she turned to Terj, whose expression betrayed nothing. Though I couldn't hear him, I knew he was speaking to Sanniah, who soon murmured, "I see. Um...this is a most satisfactory piece," she told Rokund, "and it is accepted in the spirit in which it was given."

The under-king cut his eyes to Terj. "Mediating, are we?"

Assisting.

"Mm. You're very welcome, lass," he said to Sanniah, "and though that is a poor thing, I hope it serves you." He stepped back and folded his arms as he surveyed the growing cluster of vehicles. "You know, someone should probably start organizing dinner."

The last of our allies didn't arrive until long after the meal was served that evening. As the Cirivantis hitched rides on the Ragatanese barges, the vehicles were heavily laden and took all necessary precautions in the tunnels. Anji and Mia were the final ones out, and both gratefully accepted bowls of stew as they joined us at one of many campfires. "Long day," said Anji as she plopped into a dwarf-sized folding chair and groaned. "I don't care if all I have is a bedroll—I'll sleep well."

"And I'll be directing traffic in my dreams," said Mia, taking a seat beside her. "So if I smack you in the night, don't take it personally."

"Where's your dad?" I asked Mia. "I haven't seen him all day."

"There's a late barge coming in a bit," she replied. "Or so Grandmother says. Dad's bringing his equipment and Jerrcoa separately."

As the two tucked in, I noticed a willowy brunette in leather armor approaching and raised a hand. "Hi, there. Looking for someone? Need directions? The Cirivanti and Ragatanese encampments are that way," I said, pointing to my right, "and the kitchen tent is straight ahead."

"I have no need of the former," she replied, smiling as she approached, "but the latter is much appreciated."

By then, she was close enough that I could see the tips of her ears poking through her thick hair—an elf, to my surprise. While I thought she was speaking Common Elvish, her accent was notably different than Fanakel's. "Sorry, uh…where did you come from?"

"Oliem. We arrived in Ragatanu after you left." Pausing, she squinted at me, then nodded curtly. "As I thought. You're the Watcher, yes?"

"I was," I replied.

"A cruel arrangement, that. I'm glad to learn it has ended. Our maladeta showed us the recording of your fight Outside—remarkable work." Pointing toward the kitchen tent, she said, "I'm going to find rations. Might I join you?"

"Sure," said Mia. "If you can find a chair, bring that, too."

Once she'd left, I looked at Fanakel, only to find him staring after the departing elf like he'd been hit in the head. "Uh…are you okay?" I asked, nudging him in the shoulder.

He shook himself out of it and turned back to his stew. "Fine, thank you."

"Where's Oliem?"

"Oliem," he said slowly, "was founded after the war. It's on the north side of the Central Sea."

"Friends of yours?" Anji asked.

"Not exactly. Rebels and heretics. They left their kingdoms, claiming the old ways were misguided, and took control of some abandoned elven outposts in Ga'besh. We know of them, but Nokan'ti has no relationship with Oliem."

"Well, try to play nice, won't you?" I said. "If you can hang out here with Anji…"

He sighed and concentrated on his dinner.

By the time the elf returned, Sanniah had also joined our circle, and she and Mia scooted their chairs apart to make room. "My thanks," said the newcomer, taking a seat on the ground. "My people are weary, and I thought I should get acquainted while they rest…*ah*," she said, noticing Fanakel across the fire, "I was hoping to find you. Fanakel of Nokan'ti, yes? I'm Tavinnia of Oliem."

That she had so cavalierly introduced herself took me by surprise, but Fanakel seemed shocked. He fumbled briefly, then managed, "Good evening, Your Highness."

"Likewise," she replied with a smile, and laughed

nervously. "I can't believe you're all here. Really, that recording was *incredible*. I have so many questions…which are probably best saved for daylight, eh?"

She was, I thought, unusually friendly for an elf, but she seemed genuine in her enthusiasm. "Hey, as long as we're conscious…though I don't think Mia and Anji are going to be up late tonight," I said.

"Nor should the rest of us be, but since I spent most of the day waiting on that damn beach by the tunnel, I'm not quite ready for sleep." Turning back to Fanakel, she asked, "Will Nokan'ti be meeting us here or in Daril?"

"Nokan'ti isn't coming," he mumbled into his stew.

"Oh. Are the Twins not aware—"

"They're aware."

Tavinnia hesitated. "I'm sorry."

He grunted. "What's Oliem doing here?"

"Well, our maladeta informed us of Erianthe's deeds beyond the Crossing, and my mother and I decided that such could not be tolerated. So here we are," she said, gesturing with her spoon. "The soldiers and me, I mean. Mother remains at home for now. Someone has to keep the place running."

We ate in silence for a moment, but then Fanakel spoke up. "Nokan'ti might have come had I been True. Unfortunately…"

The other elf snorted with disdain. "Oh, yes, *True*. Such a big damn deal over nothing at all."

"Nothing?" he echoed, a note of challenge in his voice.

She didn't back down. "Nothing. Two of my captains here are half human, and they're eminently competent. We trade with a few dwarven artisans, and we're on good terms with all of the tekorish nations. I've yet to see proof that any deity is playing favorites. We have our differences, naturally, but I wouldn't call our allies *inferior*."

Fanakel considered that for a moment as he finished his meal, and then he met Tavinnia's eyes across the fire and smiled.

Just as I was about to turn in that night—though a tad undersized, the Banilghish tents were sturdy and plentiful—the last of the Ragatanese barges arrived with Cary at the controls. Pulling Mia from the fire, where Fanakel and Tavinnia had been chatting for half an hour straight, I threaded my way through the tents and vehicles to greet the latecomers.

Jerrcoa opened the door in the side of the barge and wheeled himself out, tired but all smiles. "Susan, Mia!" he called, and hurried closer. "Glad you're safely back."

"With *friends,*" I replied, and bent down to hug my brother. "How are you feeling?"

"Step aside."

I did as he asked, and he held out his hands, beckoning for mine. When I gripped his hands, he used me to pull himself upright, then barely wobbled as he sought his balance. "*Jerr,*" I said as he beamed, "this is great! When did you—"

"Last night. Makou worked with me once you left. He's here somewhere," he added, looking past me at the fleet, "but I haven't seen him all day."

"The growths haven't returned?"

"Not that I can feel. Here, let me sit down…"

I braced Jerrcoa until he was situated in his chair again, and he gripped his thighs to help him as he moved his feet back onto the rests. "A few more weeks of practice," I said, "and you'll be—"

"Dad, hi!" Mia interrupted as the cockpit door opened. "Did you get what you needed?"

"Hello, sweetheart," he replied—in English, I noticed with approval. "Yep, I got everything…and then some."

"Oh?"

He climbed down, revealing a figure beside him in the cockpit. As that person slid toward the open door, Mia's jaw dropped.

"*Mom?*" she cried. "What the hell are *you* doing here?"

"I can explain…" Cary began.

Mia stood aside and crossed her arms. "Oh, this should be good."

He stepped between mother and daughter as if to stave off a brawl. "Your mother has all the videos saved, and she's brought them with her. She wouldn't transfer them to my computer."

"Why?" Mia muttered, glaring past him at Janine.

"Because I'm worried about you!" her mother protested. "Because you've been running around on other worlds, fighting monsters and shit—"

That very un-Janine-like bit of profanity took me aback.

"—and I just want to protect you, okay?" she finished. "All I've ever wanted is to protect you, Mia."

"I don't need your protection," she snapped. "I *needed* you to understand me once, but you wouldn't, and I'm over it. Go home." Turning to Cary, she said, "Whatever happened to not forcing me to make nice, hmm?"

"He's not," said Janine. "Look, Mia…I'm sorry. Unequivocally, I'm sorry. I was wrong, and I hurt you and…and your dad…in ways that I can't fix. I can't ask you to forgive me. But I don't care if you hate me—if you're going to go marching into far-off lands with an army, you're not going alone."

"I'm *not* alone," Mia retorted. "Suze has always had my back, especially when you didn't, and I've got Anji now, too. I don't need you."

"I know." Even in the low light, I could tell that Janine was tearing up. "But I'm still your mom, and I want to protect you. Besides," she added, "I'm the only actual witness you have. I know where the recordings came from."

Mia looked back at Cary. "You really couldn't just *persuade* her to turn over the tapes?"

He shook his head. "I promised her that I would never use my talents against her, and I won't. Not even for this."

My friend didn't snap at him, but she huffed her evident displeasure with the situation. "And what does

Grandmother have to say about this arrangement?"

"She…is unaware," Cary admitted. "I told her I'd pick up some equipment at the Crossing once we were on the move, which wasn't *entirely* untrue—"

"Uh-huh."

"I couldn't very well show up in Enead with your mother," he protested. "That would have been unnecessarily awkward."

Janine frowned. "Why is your *mother* here, Cary? What's her involvement in all this?"

Mia looked between them, then snorted her laughter and turned away. "Oh, you didn't tell her everything, did you?"

"Tell me what?" Janine asked.

"I'll just let you two chat," Mia replied, and pointed toward the path back to the tents. "Come on, Jerr, it'll be easiest if we go this way. Suze?"

"Coming," I said, biting back my smile.

"Goodnight, you two," said Mia to her parents. "Oh, and Your Highness, the Ragatanese encampment is on the north side."

As we hurried off, I heard a warning tone I recalled well from childhood behind me: "Cary Smith, *what* is going on?"

"That's cold," I murmured to Mia.

"Don't fuck with me," she replied with a smirk in her voice.

"Noted. Jeez."

An elbow in my side was her response. "Hey, is Terj worn out, or do you think he'd be up to listening in on that mess?"

Terj was wise enough to keep the hell away from Janine and Cary, and anyone with sense avoided Parrian's tent until after breakfast, when those in charge of troops—and a few of us on the periphery—gathered to go over the plan.

Janine, I noticed, hadn't been invited, and Cary hung back sheepishly from the table, but Mia stood at her grandmother's right hand and carried on as if nothing were amiss.

With Sanniah's troops and the contingent from Oliem, our numbers had swelled to over twelve hundred, and more were on the way. Taliem and Junil had been in contact with their sisters in Taln'een, and they had news: a small contingent from the Meali Republic would be with us by midday, while Ti'cal, to our surprise, would meet us at the Falova near the Darili border. "So the plan, as I see it," said Rokund, leaning over a map of the continent, "is for us to travel due east once the Mealis arrive. We'll join Ti'cal at the river, and we can follow it straight to Deoni, with the Taln'een joining us from the northeast. They'll have an upriver trek, but theirs will be far shorter."

Peering down at the age-yellowed map, I tried to gauge the distance and turned to Terj. *How far are we talking?*

He made a face as he studied the hand-drawn terrain. *Say about seven hundred miles from here to the river, assuming we cut straight across the wasteland. We'll clip through the southernmost bit of Daril, but there's so little habitation out here that I don't see any trouble arising.*

I grimaced. *How long will it take to get everyone there?*

This is me estimating, but if I can hit sixty miles an hour, I doubt the dwarves' carriages can do better than forty. So unless we send the Banilghis as an advance force, we're stuck with our slowest vehicles...

Seventeen and a half hours, I replied, doing the quick math.

He nodded. *If no one calls a halt, and I would think that's a long time to be crammed into a barge. Say we stretch it out to a full day and night.*

Before I could respond to that, Rokund said, "Terj, my daughter tells me you've traversed this stretch. What are you thinking?

Do you have enough pilots to fly in shifts through the night?

"*We* do…" he said, and the other heads of state began to nod. "Yes, we can make that work."

Good. Plan for at least twenty hours—you'll want rest periods for, uh…bodily functions, yes?

"Good point," Fetull muttered.

Sanniah, it's a shorter distance than you think, he continued as her brow furrowed, *but if your group flies at full speed, you'll leave everyone else behind.*

"That might not be a terrible idea," said Parrian, turning to the younger queen. "You've got a massive force here. Why not take the lead, settle in, and wait to intercept Ti'cal?"

Sanniah spread her hands. "I can do as those who know this land see fit, but seeing as I alone of my people have one of these," she said, tapping her translator pendant, "perhaps someone who can better speak to your allies from Ti'cal could accompany us."

That was simple enough to accommodate. When the Meali group—another hundred strong, all riding chiquiws and very much outclassed by the Ragatanese fleet—arrived late that morning, Anji, Mia, Terj, and I set off with Sanniah. While Jerrcoa wanted to go with the advance party, the consensus was that he was safer with his uncle and cousins. As for Fanakel, he'd been primed to travel with us until Anji had pulled him aside and said, "Why don't you go with the Oliem group? It's their first time in Kopaat, is it not?"

Bemused, he'd frowned at that suggestion. "They're traveling with the others…"

"But don't you think Tavinnia would appreciate someone experienced by her side?"

"Would…oh. *Oh,*" he'd said, his eyes widening as the lightbulb turned on. "You think?"

Anji had stared up him with a look of deep disbelief. "*Men.* High Queen help me."

Thus nudged, Fanakel had volunteered his assistance to the elven princess, who'd accepted with perhaps more enthusiasm than was warranted. With the two of them getting better acquainted, the other four of us and Taliem set off with Sanniah and sped across the wasteland toward our rendezvous with Ti'cal.

It was fortunate that we left when we did, as Ti'cal was early. Though the sun was sinking behind us by the time we neared our destination, I could pick out the shapes of their tents and the lights of their fires along the riverbank—maybe another two hundred, I guessed, adding them to my mental tally. But more pressing to me was the tug of the river itself, the inexplicable feeling that I was homeward bound…and then, as we slowed for our final approach, I heard Falova's voice in my mind: *Susan?*

He sounded relieved, I thought, and reached out to him. *We're landing now, Father.*

Soul of my soul. He seemed to sigh. *You are safe? Unharmed?*

I'm fine. Terj is with me.

Yes, I sense him. She did not hurt you?

I knew I wasn't imagining the way his thoughts darkened when he referenced Erianthe.

No. We were nowhere near town when her men burned it. Mia's mother called us to let us know, and Terj and I cleared the opening to the Crossing. Had help, actually.

Oh?

Yeah…Watchers past, somehow. My uncle.

Falova grew suddenly cautious. *Did you speak with him?*

I did. It was good. Weird, but I'm grateful. I hesitated, then told him, *My dad's glad we've got each other. Uncle Malachi said so.*

Even from that distance, I could feel some of his tension melt. *That is good to hear.*

Yep. Hang on, we're coming down…

As the Ti'cali chiquiws reared in alarm, our pilot lowered us to the grass and cut the engine. "Will one of you make the introductions?" Sanniah asked. "I'm afraid I wouldn't know their leader if I were standing before them."

"Absolutely," I replied, "if you'll give me just one minute."

She waited in the vehicle while I pushed open the side door and hopped down. I ran toward the water as a figure rose in the shallows, and my father's wordless happiness washed over me as we hugged.

When we broke apart, I turned and found Merenel Palta, the queen of Ti'cal, standing a few feet away. She'd traded her bejeweled headwrap and gold gown for a simple green turban and leather-enhanced riding clothes, and her dark eyes had turned to saucers as she gaped.

"Your Majesty," I said, straightening my shirt, and bowed. "Thank you for coming. The Banilghish fleet is landing now, and the rest are on their way—"

"Is that...*that's* the elemental," she said, pointing at Falova. "I never...I mean, I..."

I glanced back at my father, then at the queen. "He's not hugely into manifesting like this, but he sort of makes an exception for me."

"I see." To my surprise, she offered him a deep nod. "I'm relieved that you have returned," she told him. "On behalf of my people, thank you. The years of your absence were...difficult."

Believe me, I did not choose to leave. He studied her briefly, then asked, *You go with Susan to confront Erianthe?*

"I do," Merenel replied.

Why?

"Why?" she echoed. "Well...an attack on the Crossing affects us all, and if Erianthe truly set off explosives, that's a matter of concern to us as much as anyone."

But you do not take up Susan's cause?

The queen paused before responding. "I...was told that a Darili force attacked a town beyond the Crossing, presumably while searching for the princess. That Erianthe would do such is, of course, troubling, but under the terms of the Peace, I have no right to advance Susan's claim, nor the prince's."

Then perhaps I can give you a claim of your own, my father replied. *You say the years of my absence were difficult?*

She smiled grimly. "Where shall I begin? The die-off in the river led to the collapse of our fishing industry, then starvation...I've paid exorbitant sums to Daril over the years to feed my people. And the fever seasons have been particularly brutal," she murmured. "I lost my husband nearly five years ago."

Do you know what happened to me?

"My understanding is that you were taken somehow and left in the wilderness, and Susan restored you. Is that not the case?"

That is accurate. His head tilted. *But do you know who had me ripped from the river in the first place?*

Merenel stared at him, and though her complexion was too dark to show the blood draining from her cheeks, I couldn't miss the sudden stiffness of her shoulders. "You're certain?"

Three human adepts did the deed, men armed with Aen crystals and protected by darkness. They worked outside the castle walls. And once they decided to abandon me in the desert instead of kill me outright, they fled for your lands rather than return to Daril.

Her voice dropped to a dangerous pitch. "Why were they afraid?"

They did not trust the one who had hired them. I found one of them within your borders yesterday, said Falova. *He works as a fisherman now under a new name. When I confronted him, he admitted that Erianthe had paid them to kill me.*

Though he spoke dispassionately, I picked up on an undercurrent of anger and hurt.

I could have ruined her marriage to the Cirivanti, you see, he continued. *She did not know that I had no knowledge of her pregnancy, and I suppose she decided to eliminate witnesses.*

"Merciful gods," Merenel whispered.

She tried to kill me. She left Susan to die, then planned to kill her when Susan came to her for assistance. Now she has destroyed the town beyond the Crossing, murdered innocents, and attempted once more to slay our daughter. His simmering anger began to rise to the surface. *If that is insufficient for you to confront her, then use what I have just given you. How many of your people might still live if not for Erianthe?*

She stared at him for a moment in silence, then murmured, "Thank you." After clearing her throat, she said, "Susan, perhaps you could introduce me to whomever is in charge of these...um..."

"They're like dwarven carriages, but twice as fast," I said, leading her from the water's edge. "If you're interested, I'm sure Sanniah wouldn't mind taking you up."

As we walked away, I said to my father, *You changed your mind about confronting Erianthe?*

I did.

Why?

She tried to kill you, soul of my soul. Again.

I smiled to myself. *Thanks. I appreciate it.*

Say the word, and I will flood the streets of Deoni.

Maybe not just yet. Let's try the political approach first, hmm? I replied.

As you like. I heard the splash behind me as he sank below the surface. *But know this: there will be a reckoning.*

After a very long day and night, the rest of our consolidated forces limped into camp the next morning, weary and cramped from their trip. "We need to rest," Parrian told Sanniah and Merenel as the offloading and tent pitching commenced in the fields. The other queens having erected pavilions and ordered breakfast prepared, they were willing to share, and Parrian gratefully accepted a cup of tea. "Rokund says we have a journey nearly as long as the last one to Deoni, and I can't ask my people to make that flight without sleep," she said between sips.

If I may make a proposal, Terj interrupted, *do it in two days. We'll have to camp in Darili territory, but what are a bunch of humans going to do about it? Throw rocks?*

Merenel looked at him askance. "We have *slightly* progressed beyond rock throwing, thank you."

Sure, but you're not the ones with the flying barges, and I know for a fact that Ragatanu can run rings around any human kingdom here when it comes to technology. I've yet to see firearms anywhere else in the four worlds.

She frowned at Parrian. "What's a…a fire arm?"

"Guns," I offered. "They shoot high-speed projectiles, more damaging than arrows. A little something poached from Earth, yeah?"

Parrian didn't deny it. "We're certainly not averse to adopting new tools. But I agree with Terj—I believe we can defend ourselves for one night if we avoid major settlements. That way, we'll be fresher when we reach Deoni."

As Parrian headed toward the buffet table, I approached her and murmured, "Is Janine still alive, by any chance?"

She cut her eyes my way, and I saw so much of Mia in the look she gave me. "For now."

"That's good, seeing as she's the one with the passwords."

"Yes, or so my son says. I suspect he's keeping her out of my sight."

I shrugged. "Love's weird."

"After everything that woman did to him and Mia, I cannot *imagine* what he sees in her, but…" She sighed and lifted the lid of a steaming chafing dish. "That's a matter for Cerian to resolve. He's a grown man." Glancing at me again, she said, "Be honest with me—did that woman abuse my granddaughter?"

I chose my words carefully. "Janine was hard on Mia, but I don't think she ever, like, beat her."

The queen snorted and helped herself to sausage—something identifiable to me, so I assumed Ti'cal had superintended the meal. "My son seems to have feelings for her."

"I don't know what she was like back when they met, but honestly, I think she had a rough time of it in Cole's Crossing. Not trying to excuse anything," I hastily added, "but maybe that's why Cary sees something in her that the rest of us don't."

"Perhaps." Closing the lid, she said, "Be that as it may, while I wish my son every happiness, I need to focus on my granddaughter. If that woman offends Mia, I'll have her packed off through the Crossing before she knows what's hit her."

"I...don't doubt that, Your Majesty," I replied, and left her to her meal.

We rested that day, either sleeping or taking stock of people and supplies. Dinner that night was a mélange of dishes, none fancy but all filling, and the oddly blue Banilghish savory pancakes were a surprise crowd favorite.

The next day, our departure was delayed by the inherent difficulty of coaxing skittish chiquiws into the barges and divvying up the Ti'calis in the limited empty space. By midmorning, we were on our way north, following the river through the southern reaches of Daril. On occasion, I'd look down from the windows of the Banilghish craft in which I'd snagged a seat and catch people running from their homes and shops to gawk at the fleet flying overhead.

The sun was setting when we stopped for the night, coming down in a pasture on either side of the widening Falova. Lights in the distance suggested farmers or ranchers, maybe a little town, but no one dared to investigate until after the tents were pitched, when a posse of about twenty men armed with farming implements marched on the left bank, following a balding old priest in a red robe. The red jewel in the center of the pendant he wore marked him as catch-all clergy, a mediator between the people in the hinterlands and whichever gods they sought to importune.

Fortunately, the modest mob had chosen the side of the river where the Ti'cali, Meali, and Cirivanti groups had camped. As the priest demanded an explanation and his followers grumbled, Fetull took the lead and stepped from his tent to answer them. "We seek an audience with your queen," he said simply. "We seek only justice."

The priest regarded him with suspicion. "And who might you be, then?"

"He's my uncle," said Jerrcoa, rolling out of the tent where we'd been playing cards. "My father's brother. His Majesty Fetull of Cirivant. And *you*?"

But the priest and his men laughed at Jerrcoa's proclamation. "A king, he says!" the priest declared, chortling. "What are you, then, boy, some sort of prince?"

There were certain drawbacks to living in a place without photography, chief among them the fact that the average Darili had no clue what the royal family looked like.

Before Jerrcoa could lose his temper, I flicked a finger, and the contents of a washing tub flew into the air and hovered above my head, a perfect sphere of soapy water that glittered in the light of the campfires. "Exactly," I said as the locals backed away. "And I'm Susan. Now, you can do the smart thing and go home, or this can get ugly in a hurry. Your choice."

The priest looked from the water above me to the sword at my waist, and recognition dawned. "You're the Watcher?" he asked, retreating another step.

"Uh-huh."

While the priest was smart enough to stand down, three of his muscle weren't so wise. "Come here, girlie," one of them said as they pushed past their fellows. "Let's see what you—"

That was as far as they got before I tossed the water straight at them, soaking them through and stopping them in their tracks.

Want a hand? Terj asked me.

If you're not busy.

A sudden wind swept the three off their feet and sent them sailing over their comrades' heads. "We'll be out of here in the morning," I told the spooked mob. "Might want to go on home, yes?"

As the villagers fled, I sighed and looked at Jerrcoa. "Right. Once Edes is king, it's your job to convince him to fund printing presses. I'll go home and get some books on photography—surely *someone* in this world can figure out a damn camera."

"Ragatanu may have done so already," Fetull muttered, glancing upriver toward their area. Unlike the human camps with their fires, the Ragatanese illuminated their tents with Aen-powered lanterns.

"A problem for later," my brother replied, and wheeled himself back into the tent. "Come on, Susan, it's your turn."

CHAPTER 19

The following afternoon, the fleet landed on the outskirts of Daril wherever the pilots could find room along the river. Traffic on the shore was low, as for the last ten days, Falova had been swamping any boat that dared to sail from the capital. He was, he informed me, making a point: to put it mildly, he was *pissed*.

I recalled Owir and Dewin, the dwarven guards Mia and I had encountered in Tightbend a seeming age ago, and how they'd warned us of the danger of antagonizing the elemental in the Blue River, who took offense to overfishing. Falova, by comparison, took offense to the whole *city*, and he repeatedly offered to flood it for me if that would help.

It was nice, I reasoned, to have a parent who cared, even if his methods were somewhat unorthodox.

Unsurprisingly, the general populace was in no hurry to confront us as we formed up and marched downriver toward the castle, and even the few guards on patrol stood aside. For a human city, an invading army of humans was bad enough; add in dwarves, a few elves, tekoraet, and the alien Unarans of Banilgh, and the wiser folks barred their doors. Those among our number who had chiquiws rode, but most of our forces were on foot, and my friends and I took turns pushing Jerrcoa's chair along, much to his consternation. While I understood his desire for independence, the area along the river was marshy, and his wheels weren't designed for mudding.

Our first impediment was the city wall, a forty-foot

stretch of gray stone that encircled much of the older part of the capital before joining with the outer walls of the castle. The arched gateway had been shut, but as I looked to the left, where the river curved around the city, I could make out the turrets and the blue and green banners of the royal seat far beyond the wall. We paused outside the closed gate, and a man in the watchtower above it leaned out a window to hail us. "What's the meaning of this?" he called down. "State your business."

For a lone watchman staring down an army, he had spunk, but I didn't feel like chitchat. Stepping forward and pushing Jerrcoa's chair, I said, "Your prince and princess have returned. Open the gate."

He squinted down at us, then quickly straightened as recognition hit. "Your Highnesses, I—"

"Open the damn gate," Jerrcoa demanded.

"But...but who comes with you?" he stammered, clearly torn.

I looked up at him, unsmiling. "The queen tried to kill us both. And our friends. She *did* kill a number of people I know and like, and then she managed to block part of the Crossing. So Jerrcoa and I have come home to have a *word* with our dear mother, while these fine folks with us would like answers. I'm going to ask you one more time: open the gate."

Whatever else the watchman might have been, he was no fool. I held my position until the heavy doors swung wide, then found a hastily assembled cordon of city guards waiting on the far side. "Your Highnesses," said their apparent leader, stepping forward, "we will escort you to—"

"That won't be necessary," I interrupted, and pushed Jerrcoa forward. "Let's go."

The guard tried to protest, but the army at my back was already surging, and the outnumbered men fell aside as we marched through the winding streets toward the castle.

On foot, it took about half an hour to navigate our way

to the bridge over the dry channel where the river had once run. I looked to the left and right ends of the ditch at the yellow bricks plugging the hole in the outer wall and the one in the inner wall that had once allowed the river to meander into the castle garden—yet another sign of the steps Erianthe had taken to hide her infidelity and my existence. My hands tightened on my brother's chair.

The gate on the far side of the bridge was much better guarded than the city gate had been, and I wondered how many of the men staring down at us from the wall had murdered my neighbors and incinerated my town. "Open the gate," I called up to them. "The prince and I command it."

"The queen orders that it remain shut," one of the guards called back. "You are to take your mob and leave, or there will be consequences."

A sudden strong gust pulled the man off the parapet and left him suspended over the ditch, shrieking and flailing for a handhold. I glanced at Terj, who cocked an eyebrow in query, and nodded before turning my attention back to the men on the gate. "And what consequences would those be?"

Terj flipped the guard head over heels a few times before returning him to the wall, a shaken mess.

"We're not here to hurt you," I said. "We've come for Erianthe. The people with me have grievances to be addressed."

Another guard took the lead while his commander recovered. "We could send a message to Her Majesty."

"That would be nice," I deadpanned, then felt a hand on my shoulder and looked back to see Merenel behind me.

"Tell Erianthe that Ti'cal has a claim against her," she called up, her voice echoing over the stone. "As do Meali, Cirivant, Blackhorn Mountain, Oliem, Ragatanu—"

"And Taln'een," shouted a familiar voice from the crowd, and I spotted Ganeel pushing her way to the front, leading a band of maladetan women. "Sorry we're late."

"Banilgh stands with the aggrieved," said Sanniah, stepping past the much taller Merenel to be seen. "Bring forth your queen. Let her explain herself."

"The Peace of Meali commands it," said Fetull, joining them. "Daril is a signatory and bound by its terms. If Erianthe refuses to concede that, perhaps my *brother* can persuade her."

The guard mumbled something vaguely affirmative and scurried off, and I looked at the tense faces around me. "So...this is my first siege..."

Rokund snorted. "It's not a proper siege until the flaming pitch comes out, lass. This is just the preliminaries."

Maybe I can speed it along.

I turned to Terj, recognizing the feel of a private communication. *What's your plan?*

A word with your siblings. I'll be back soon.

Gripping his wrist to stay him, I said, *If Erianthe catches you—*

She won't. As he kissed me, he added, *There aren't enough adepts in this damn city to keep me from you, understood?*

Be safe.

Likewise, he replied, then vanished. I was left holding air, and I felt him speeding away from me.

Rokund, still unaccustomed to life with a selectively corporeal being, gawked at the place where Terj had been. "Did...did he..."

"He'll be back," I replied, and hoped I was right.

The sun had set before we saw movement on the gate, and it was only a guard returning, torch in hand. "Her Majesty denies any wrongdoing," he called down to us, "and she orders that this unwarranted behavior cease immediately."

"That's not an option," Parrian called back. "Do go try again, won't you?"

"And inform your queen that we are here and not within only out of politeness," Sanniah added. "The least of my fleet could easily fly over your little wall. She would be wiser to discuss this with us rather than further try our patience."

When the guard disappeared, Parrian patted Sanniah on the back. "Nicely done," she murmured. "While we await an answer, perhaps you and I could become better acquainted. Have you any desire to trade in Ga'besh?"

The two queens walked off through the clusters of tents, a haphazardly constructed city within the city. Portable shelters covered the streets and sidewalks, and I overheard a few Unarans complain about the lack of sanitation as they passed by with lights. Anji and Mia were somewhere in that chaos, and presumably Fanakel was as well—I'd seen little of him that day, but I assumed he'd be wherever Tavinnia was making camp. Jerrcoa was safely ensconced in the bosom of his father's family, having been welcomed into the Terol tents. Fetull had offered me a spot as well, but I kept vigil by the gate, and soon enough, Jerrcoa emerged to join me.

As I sat on the bridge, he practiced moving his legs and wiggling his feet. "Don't wear yourself out," I cautioned.

He scowled at me. "The only way I'll ever walk is if I work at this."

"Yeah, but it doesn't have to all be done in one night."

"If my sister is strong enough to slay Outsiders," he muttered, raising his knees one at a time, "then I can do a few measly exercises."

I sighed. "Jerr, that's completely different."

"Really? How many Outsiders had you killed before you got the sword, hmm?"

"None," I admitted, "but Mia and I had our share of trial and error. You *have* noticed my face, yes?"

"What about it?" he said, straining to keep his leg aloft.

"I wasn't born with the big scar."

He paused and stared at me for a few seconds, then

said, "Oh, that," and went back to work.

"Yeah, *that*," I mumbled.

"Honestly, I'd forgotten about it."

I laughed in disbelief. "How did you *forget* it? It's right there, and it's huge!"

"Eh." He switched to bending his knee to raise his lower leg and gritted his teeth as he tried to hold it in place. "Maybe it's always noticeable to you, but I've never known you to look otherwise, and it's just...*Susan*, you know? I mean, yes, I noticed it at first, but now, you might as well ask me about imperfections in your nose."

I hesitated while he changed legs. "Really?"

"Yes," he replied, then grunted as his weaker left leg fell. "You're not some hideous monstrosity, if that's what you were worried about."

"That may be the nicest thing you've ever said to me."

He chuckled. "That's what little brothers are—oh, look!" he said, pointing toward the wall in sudden agitation.

I turned in time to see Edes and Zadi float over the top and sink toward us. Our brother appeared troubled, even in the low light, but our baby sister seemed absolutely delighted to be airborne. As they landed on our side of the bridge, Terj switched forms and grinned when I approached to kiss him. *Guess who I found?*

"Terj told us everything," said Edes, pushing himself off the cobblestones. "Mother has lost her *mind*, I can't believe she would...*no*. Jerr, how are you..."

I smiled as Jerrcoa proudly lifted his right leg. "Leaving the Aen was the cure," he replied. "I can't walk yet, but I'm getting—"

Whatever else he meant to say was lost as Edes pulled him out of his chair and into a bear hug. Not one to be left out, Zadi joined them, and Jerrcoa showed off by supporting himself against Edes's shoulders for a moment before he folded himself back into his seat.

"I'm glad you're both alive," said Edes, sobering as

Jerrcoa adjusted his feet. "You're *certain* it was a Darili force that attacked that town?"

"Come with me," I said, and set off into the tents.

After a ten-minute walk, a few tight squeezes, and some apologies, we reached the Ragatanese group, and I asked directions to Cary. I found him on the outskirts with Janine, who looked up anxiously through the open flap as I rapped against a support pole. "Hi, Ms. Randolph," I said, slipping back into English—I had no idea whether Cary had found a translator for her yet. "We need to see the videos."

She eyed the group behind me. "Uh…sure, Susan. Who are—"

"The rest of my siblings. Could you pull up one that shows the armor, please?"

As she worked on her phone, Cary frowned. "How did you two get out of there? Hidden exit?"

Elemental.

"Ah." Noticing Terj at the back of the group, he nodded. "Could you airlift the rest of us in there?"

In batches? Sure. Say the word. We could do it tonight…

"We could," Cary muttered, "but my mother informs me that the consensus is to wait at least until dawn."

"So you two are speaking?" I asked.

He grunted. "She's not happy, but yes, we are."

"And Mia?"

"Mia," said Janine, tapping at the screen, "is with her girlfriend tonight, and that's for the best. Here we go."

She passed me the phone, and I held it and played the video for Edes and Zadi, which showed several Darili guards gliding by on their hovering boards in the light of a streetlamp. Once the clip ended, I backed up until I could freeze it on a clear shot of the wavy blue and green flag on a guard's chest. "Any questions?" I murmured.

"Maybe it's someone pretending to be from Daril," Zadi mumbled.

"But who else would have a motive? Much less access

to *that* equipment," Edes countered, and glowered at the phone as I passed it back to Janine. "And not just you, but Jerrcoa…"

"I'm expendable," he quipped. "More trouble than I'm worth. You know that."

"I know nothing of the kind," Edes snapped, and squeezed Jerrcoa's shoulder. "But I do know this: if Mother attacks one of us, she attacks *all* of us. Right, Zadi?"

My little sister hugged herself miserably. "If Mother really did that…"

"Then there's no reason why she couldn't do the same to any of us," said Edes, stooping to look her in the eye. "Anyone inconvenient. Me, you, Father…"

"Falova," I said softly.

My siblings turned to me, stunned, and I nodded. "Who else do you think would have the resources to rip him away from the river? She hired some adepts to kill him. They dumped him instead and fled the country."

"But…but…" Edes stammered, "but the river, it's been dead…"

"Oh, yeah. She wrecked that whole ecosystem, hurt her own people, and *starved* Ti'cal, on top of the torture my father went through. But hey, as long as no one knew that she'd had a fling with someone other than Narod…"

My brothers looked sick, and Zadi seemed to shrink into herself.

"Noticed how Falova's been a little peeved in recent days?" I asked. "He was willing to let bygones be bygones with Mother, but she went too far."

Edes held Jerrcoa's stare for a moment, then turned to me. "What can I do to help? I can't offer you an army."

"I'd be happy to have a brother," I replied.

"And a sister," Zadi protested.

"Absolutely." I hugged her. "Let's get you three to your uncle. You'll be safe there. Goodnight, Ms. Randolph…uh, Cary."

"Who are they?" Edes whispered as we walked off. "And Uncle Fetull is here?"

"There's a whole force from Cirivant," said Jerrcoa, wheeling himself along behind us. "He's *not* pleased."

"And to answer your other question, the guy back there is the crown prince of Ragatanu, and the woman is someone I know from Cole's Crossing. They're Mia's parents."

"Ragata..." Edes pulled me to a halt, gaping. "*How* many tekoraet are in this city right now?"

About two hundred, and you're not on the menu, Terj interjected, giving him a little shove forward. *More walking, less gawking. This could be a long night.*

The paranoid among us had anticipated an attack in the dark, but the castle remained locked fast all night—watched, yes, but not on the outer gate. Perhaps the guard who'd experienced Terj's idea of fun had warned his colleagues of what could happen if they provoked us. Perhaps Erianthe had recalled everyone into the innermost rooms, where she could hole up and hope we'd go away.

I wondered if she'd noticed her missing children yet.

Morning broke quietly, and rations from the kitchen tents at the back of the awkward encampment made their way to those of us waiting at the front. I was picking at a Banilghish dish—tasty but too green for that time of day—when I heard the sounds of bumping wood and creaking metal heralding the opening of the gate. To my surprise, however, we weren't immediately confronted with armed guards, but rather with Narod, who didn't sport so much as armor. Well-dressed but haggard, the prince consort obviously hadn't slept, and his mouth moved into a grim line as his brother approached.

"Where is she, Narod?" asked Fetull.

"Within. I've come to treat."

Fetull looked back at the assembled—the tents, the

bustling soldiers, the saddled chiquiws, the growing cluster of his peers gathered behind him—then turned to Narod again. "We're not here to kill Erianthe. This isn't a full-scale invasion. But there have been *serious* accusations leveled against her, and I've seen the proof for myself—"

"As have I," said Edes, stepping out of the crowd.

Narod's eyes widened. "*Son?* How did you—"

"That doesn't matter. They have recordings, Father—much like the one the maladetas showed us from Susan's trip Outside—and those clearly show the royal guard putting a town to the torch."

"Narod," I said, and he looked my way, his expression haunted and torn. "She had my hometown destroyed. People who've never so much as heard of Daril are dead, injured, or homeless because of Erianthe. And if Jerrcoa and I had still been there, then we'd be dead, too. I left these in my safe, and someone must have tracked them," I continued, pulling my Aen crystals from my pocket. "Look, I get it—you owe me nothing. But come on, man, that's your *son* she was going to kill."

"And my granddaughter," said Parrian.

"My daughter as well," Rokund piped up beside her. "Plus the Nokan'ti boy. It would be egregious enough if she'd assaulted our people, but for her to endanger *our children...*" He shook his head and stared up at Narod, whose hunched posture seemed to worsen by the minute. "Not to mention the damage her men did to the Crossing. Once this business here is concluded, I'm sending a team to evaluate it for structural damage."

"And let's not forget what she did to my father," I said. When Narod turned to me again, silently questioning, I nodded. "Falova didn't just wander off. She dumped me in the woods—why not silence the one other person who could blow her cover?"

I felt for the man. He seemed sick, and I had to wonder what was going through his mind—fear for his children? For himself? He must have been asking himself for the last eight months who he'd married, but maybe he'd been able to rationalize Erianthe's actions to that point, explaining them away as youthful indiscretions, the desperate actions of a girl following her mother's orders. But to then be faced with accusations of murder and attempted murder...I couldn't help but pity him.

"Erianthe's attack on the elemental has led to starvation, disease, and death in Ti'cal," said Merenel, who fixed Narod with a steely stare. "We've been beholden to Daril for our survival for my entire reign, and only now do I learn that this disaster is of *Erianthe's* making?"

"This isn't your fault," said Ganeel, stepping in before Merenel's rising temper could explode. "We have no quarrel with you, Narod. But Daril signed the Peace, and Erianthe needs to account for herself."

He stood alone for a moment, a broken man, then quietly sighed. "Show me these recordings."

Parrian sent word to her son, who hurried through the press with Janine and her phone. "We have better projection equipment," Cary told him, "but this might be simpler for now—it's Narod, correct?"

He nodded.

"Sorry, I've been away since before your marriage. Cerian Venel—I *think* I remember you from a visit to Perem, but gosh, you would have been a boy. Yeah," he mused as Janine queued up the videos, "let's see, Fetull was about ten, so you..."

"About three," Narod mumbled.

"Ah. Well, I would say it's nice to meet you properly but for the fact that your wife tried to kill my daughter." When Narod's brow furrowed in confusion, Cary smirked. "Mia, yes? Now, Ragatanu has long had a neighborly relationship with Cirivant. I would hate for that to change. Here you go," he said as Janine passed him the phone. "Let's start with this one. Just tap the big circle there, that's a good fellow..."

To his credit, Narod must have watched a dozen videos

before he handed the phone back to Cary and murmured, "No more." He raised his head as if hoping to spot a friendly face in the crowd, but his myopic gaze landed on me.

"My childhood home is ashes," I said. "If we'd been there, it's doubtful we would have all made it out alive."

"This chair helps," Jerrcoa interjected, rolling up beside me, "but it's not so great on stairs."

Narod's eyes began to film. "Jerrcoa…"

"I realize I've never been your easiest child," he continued, casually crossing his legs, "and perhaps Mother is tired of the disappointment, but I *am* getting better."

"All that time he spent with his sister beyond the Aen killed off the growths causing the paralysis," Cary explained as Narod gaped at his son. "It's a known treatment in Ragatanu—I wish someone had made you aware for your boy's sake."

Finally, something in Narod snapped. "Erianthe will not come out," he told us. "You'll have to come in and get her."

Fetull gripped his shoulder as Narod clung to his composure. "How do we do this? Break down the main gate? Go over the wall?"

I can help there, Terj offered.

But as I considered the assembled and the aggrieved, I thought of Falova, who had a claim as real as any of ours but couldn't join the deliberations. "I've got an idea," I said. "Terj, could you give me a lift, please?"

He picked me up and carried me over the outer wall, and I landed on the bank beside the river, a few steps away from the patch Erianthe had built to keep it out. Gripping the largest of the Aen crystals in my fist, I said, *Father?*

Yes, soul of my soul?

Mind if I borrow the river for a minute?

Take whatever you need.

I walked back a few paces, hoping to avoid both the spray and any debris, then gestured with my fist until a thick stream of water rose into the air as if it were being sucked up an enormous pipe.

You've got this, Terj whispered to me.

I compressed the stream to the width of a thick screw, a highly pressurized drill, then flung it into the yellow bricks. The mortar was far too weak to withstand the assault, and within minutes, I'd penetrated the patch. I called up a second stream, then a third, hitting the bricks in multiple locations, until finally, a whole chunk of the wall fell away. As Terj removed the debris, I aimed lower, breaking up the bricks…

And then a *wave* slammed against what was left, dislodging the last of the patch and sweeping it into the depths before the water came flooding in.

That wasn't my doing, and I glanced back with a smirk. *Showoff.*

I felt Falova's pleasure as the river poured back into the long-dry channel, unimpeded by so much as a grate. The ditch below the bridge quickly filled, leaving only the second patch to block the river's access to the garden.

I stepped onto the moving water, willing it to solidify beneath me, and rode it inside the castle while the waiting mob gawked. Ignoring them, I jumped to the stone bank and followed the river until I reached the other yellow patch, the barrier between us and the inner reaches of the complex. Once more, I raised my fist, squeezing the crystal until its facets seemed to meld with my flesh, then threw the river at the bricks until I pierced them. That patch fell more quickly than the other had, and within minutes, the river was pouring into the garden. With its former course filled in by gravel, it had nowhere to go but out, and the ground was soon inundated.

I nodded to Narod, then walked back onto the river, ducked through the arched hole, and emerged in the garden. Standing atop the flooded grass, I yelled, "Mother! I'm home! Let's *chat*."

A moment later, Erianthe emerged onto a balcony,

disheveled and wide-eyed, not even wearing a tiara.

"You've got a lot to explain," I said, folding my arms as I held her stare. "Come down."

She shook her head.

Before I could ask again, my father emerged from the flooded garden, sucking the available water into himself as he rose to the balcony's height. As Erianthe started to retreat, he surged over the railing, grabbed her, and pulled her screaming to the ground, then out through the hole in the wall. By the time I followed, he'd tossed her onto the cobblestones by the bridge, where she huddled in a terrified ball, staring up at her husband, her children, and a ring of her impassive peers.

It was Merenel who stepped forward first, head high and turbaned in gold that morning. "The gods demand truth, Erianthe," she said in a voice like iron. "What have you *done*?"

There was, we soon realized, a slight problem: no one had ever invoked the Peace of Meali's grievance protocol.

Unsure what to do, the assorted sovereigns pored over the copy of the treaty in the castle library, then decided a course forward. Obviously, none of them were fit to sit in judgment, nor did they trust the Darili highborn to be neutral, so Ganeel asked the other maladetan clans to send representatives to comprise a jury. Assembling them would take time, as many lived considerable distances from tunnels, so our forces were garrisoned in a fortress on the outskirts of Deoni while anyone titled was accommodated in the castle. Narod saw to everything, ensuring that guest chambers were set up and meals laid, and Erianthe reluctantly went along with it. She had little choice in the matter; her husband and children had turned against her, the priest who ministered to her in the palace was appalled at the accusations, and she found no support among the nobles closest to the city. They might look the other way when it came to murder, but the death of the river had cost several prominent families much of their fortunes. As such, Erianthe remained in her quarters with guards at the door, tacitly on house arrest.

It took the better part of two weeks for the maladetas to trickle in, clan mothers all. I recognized some of them from Ganeel's long-distance conference the previous year, the leaders of the Erefuri and Yrton of Ildon, the D'pll and Gerian of Honslia, the Furnig of Kopaat, and the Murieg of Ga'besh. The women and their attendants kept to themselves in a wing of the castle set aside for them, where they could eat, sleep, and debate without undue influence.

At last, the day arrived. Narod arranged for the proceedings to be held in the large room where they'd hosted my wedding banquet, with the maladetas seated at the high table, the complainants to the left, and Erianthe to the right. One by one, those with claims or evidence approached the jury, taking turns as needed. I told them of Erianthe's plan to marry me off to Makou and of my decision to forfeit my claim to the throne so as to avoid further conflict with my mother. Cary helped Janine set up the equipment and play every recording for the maladetas, showing them the extent of the damage to Cole's Crossing through video and still photos. I returned to talk about the blocked Crossing and the efforts it had taken to clear the opening, which Terj reiterated in turn. Then came the actual parties: Parrian, Rokund, Fetull, and Merenel. Meali declined to speak, Tavinnia was unauthorized to do so, and as for Sanniah, she observed the proceedings with interest, answering the curious maladetas' questions but not attempting to insert herself into the trial. "I came to help my friends receive justice," she said, "but here, I cannot fairly offer them assistance."

The final scheduled witness required a slight change of venue to the castle walls, and as the jury looked down at the river, Falova manifested to give his account of his tryst with Erianthe and his subsequent abduction. *But you need not accept only my word*, he concluded as a small boat floated downstream and stopped beside him. The boat's lone occupant appeared to be a human man, gray-haired and wiry, who looked like he wanted to sink into the river and disappear.

He was, the man confessed, an adept, one of the trio Erianthe had hired to eliminate her lover. It was he who had suggested abandoning Falova in the desert, and he had fled from there to Ti'cal, where he witnessed the devastation caused by the dead river but held his silence. Judging by Merenel's expression of disgust, I gathered that Ti'cal was no longer safe for him, but I couldn't bring myself to scrounge up any pity.

With that, the jury retired to discuss their impressions. They locked themselves away for only two hours before they returned to announce a decision.

Erianthe had clearly tried to kill Jerrcoa and me. She had ordered that a human town far beyond Daril's borders be destroyed, and she had authorized the attack on the town and her children with no regard for Anji, Fanakel, or Mia. (*Or Terj*, I wanted to interject, though he had no sovereign to claim him.) Her actions had led to death, injury, and extensive property loss, and she had caused damage to the Crossing to cover her tracks.

But equally egregious in the jury's eyes was Erianthe's treatment of Falova. Not only had her would-be assassins nearly succeeded in killing him, but her actions in removing him from the river had hurt her people's livelihoods and left Ti'cal to starve and suffer with raging disease.

Clearly, said the jury, Erianthe could not walk away unpunished. The question, then, was how to do so.

Merenel wanted her life, and Parrian wasn't opposed, while Rokund and Fetull pushed for something a little more merciful. Narod said nothing in his wife's defense, and as for the Darili highborn, none would raise a hand to assist the queen who'd harmed her people to hide her secret. Finally, some of the jurors made a suggestion: strip Erianthe of her title, banish her from Daril, and let her make her own way through the four worlds.

This plan proved acceptable even to Merenel, but it required the participation of Daril's new sovereign to be carried out. Thus, the following day, the parties, the local nobles, and the jury gathered in the palace's throne room for Edes to do the honors.

Standing beside Jerrcoa's wheelchair with Terj, I watched as my brother mounted the dais and contemplated the pair of gilded thrones, the larger one for the sovereign and the smaller for the consort. He studied them for a long moment, then turned to the room and cleared his throat for silence. "This is not my throne," he said simply. "I am not our mother's eldest child."

Amid the mutterings around the room, I stepped forward and said, "You're the eldest who hasn't renounced their claim, Edes."

He cut his eyes to me, then beckoned for me to join him. I felt a light push in my mid-back—Jerrcoa, no doubt—and hesitantly climbed the dais to stand beside him.

"What are you doing?" I whispered.

Edes leaned close to me, then murmured, "Payback, dear sister."

When he straightened, he winked at me, then turned to face the room once more. "Susan is the rightful heir. She renounced because our mother pressured her into doing so after Susan exposed her as a liar. Again," he muttered. "And even after Susan renounced, Mother tried to kill her. That's hardly fair." Looking at the assembled Darili nobility, he said, "*Susan* is the heir, and if she lacks some of the education, training…polish…that we assume a queen should possess, the fault lies entirely with Erianthe. Susan defended our worlds—and yours," he added as Sanniah vehemently nodded. "I can't imagine that she would do less for Daril."

"Edes—" I began, but before I could protest, he took a knee.

Maybe it was the presence of so many foreign powers in that room with an army close at hand and a flying fleet now parked across the river. Maybe it was the fact that Falova was still sufficiently peeved as to prevent use of said river until Erianthe was dealt with. Maybe the Banilghish sword I wore made me look vaguely competent, even if it wasn't nearly as fancy as the Watcher's weapon had been.

Whatever it was, they knelt. Nobles. Priests. Zadi. I caught Jerrcoa's eye, and while he couldn't easily leave his chair, he deeply bowed his head.

"Hail, Susan Fulquir, queen of Daril and all its territories," said Edes. "Long may she reign."

I offered him my hand and pulled him back to his feet, and we shared a look.

You're sure? I asked, speaking only to his mind.

His eyes widened at the mental communication, but he nodded.

Why?

Unable to answer me in kind, he leaned close once more to whisper in my ear. "Because it's yours. It's always been yours. And because this way, I don't have to marry some damn princess."

I snorted but hugged him, and the crowd began to applaud.

Once the noise died away and Edes stepped off the dais, I looked at Fetull, who stood nearby with my siblings and their cousins. "Well, I'm afraid we're back in the position we were in before I called off the wedding in terms of that pesky treaty Erianthe can't uphold."

He chuckled. "It seems we are. What does Daril propose?"

"What I did last time." I pulled my largest Aen crystal from my pocket and showed it to him. "For Cirivant's protection."

Fetull stroked his short beard. "You have smaller ones, do you not?"

"I do," I replied, digging them out as well. Together, the pair weren't half the size of the pommel crystal.

"A counter-proposal, then," he said with a little smile. "As these are not merely crystals, but also pieces of historical import...the pair for five hundred years of protection."

"That's...very generous," I said, surprised. "And you have yourself a deal."

As I stepped to the edge of the dais to put the crystals in his hand, Fetull murmured, "The family of my family is close enough for certain considerations to be made, is it not?"

I smiled at him as I returned to my position, then sobered as I looked to Erianthe, who stared at me sullenly from the front row, flanked by guards—*my* guards now, I realized, which made me feel a teensy bit more secure in my new role. She was still a pretty woman, despite it all. Her brown waves had been pinned back by her maids that morning, and she sported a green dress with a deep neckline and pinched bodice—fashionable but highly impractical. While she hadn't dared to wear a tiara that day, her necklace flashed against her skin, the blue-green Aen crystal prominent in its gold setting.

The necklace Fetull had requested, and for which she had offered me instead.

"Erianthe Fulquir, for your crimes, I banish you," I said, raising my voice until the vaulted hall rang with it. "You may have the clothes on your back. If I catch you within Darili lands after five days' time, your life will be forfeit." She glared in silence, and I allowed myself a faint smile. "To help you on your way, I will allow you to take the necklace you wear. Sell it wisely."

Head held high, she started to follow the guards as a path through the crowd opened before her, but she paused and turned to Narod, frowning in confusion. "Do you mean for me to go alone?" she asked. "After all of this, will you abandon me, too?"

"We're finished, Erianthe," he replied. "I'm going home...and if you're wise, you won't follow me."

The look Fetull shot her was unmistakably a warning.

I almost pitied Erianthe as her shoulders slumped, her bravado faltered, and she was led away to her fate. But she never looked back, and even if she'd seen compassion in my eyes, I doubt she would have wanted it.

CHAPTER 20

Coronations are not simple matters. There are logistics to plan, invitations to send, flowers to arrange, priests and officials to consult, dresses to make, food to prepare...in other words, a party planner's nightmare, as coronations tend to pop up on short notice. Mine was no exception, but with an added wrinkle: I'd asked Terj to make our relationship official, and so the poor royal event coordinators were faced with the prospect of a wedding two months later.

I was crowned with all due ceremony five days after Erianthe's banishment, with the titled and the wealthy in attendance. Though the part of me that appreciated fairness wanted to open the event to all comers, Edes explained that this would simply not *work*. Not only was the throne room insufficiently large for all of Deoni, but security would be a nightmare, and the well-heeled would end up in a massive snit. Meali was a republic, Daril was not, and unless I wanted an uprising among the aristocracy, I needed to keep them somewhat pacified.

Little as I liked it, my brother had a point. I settled for following the coronation with a parade through the capital, giving anyone who wanted it a glimpse of their new queen. I *did* start a few tongues wagging with my attire for the occasion, a sheath gown in green and blue more reminiscent of Ti'cali fashion than Darili, but my dress was non-negotiable. The seamstress begged me to reconsider and choose something with a corset, but I never wanted to see one of those miserable torture devices again.

And I *was* queen, damn it. Susan Cole Fulquir, first of my name.

The heads of state took their armies and went home before I was crowned. My friends stuck around for the big event, but they departed far too quickly thereafter. Fanakel, who'd rapidly grown chummy with Tavinnia, accompanied her back to Oliem, the two of them having bummed rides as far as Ragatanu with Mia and Anji. While Parrian had been anxious for her granddaughter to come home, Mia wasn't about to miss my coronation, and Anji offered to fly her back after the ceremony. Rokund, who was wise enough to accept that his daughter wouldn't be spending much time in Heartfast while her girlfriend was stuck in Enead, had left one of his carriages with her for use as needed, along with instructions to check in via maladeta at least once a week. Parrian just smiled and assured him that his little girl would be safe in her care, then went home with Cary and Janine. Neither the queen nor Mia was as yet on decent terms with Janine, but they seemed to have decided for the moment that her presence in Enead wasn't the end of the world.

Sanniah wanted to stay for my coronation, but considering the expense and hassle of garrisoning her army, she bowed out. Plus, seeing as she needed maladetas to open the way back to Unara, she opted to fly along with the fleet bound for Ga'besh. I invited her to the wedding before she left, and she promised to return, albeit with a smaller party.

As for Narod, he left with Fetull and the rest of the Cirivanti delegation. Edes promised to stay with me through my wedding, an advisor in matters of protocol, and Zadi certainly had no plans to go, but Jerrcoa also managed to snag a place in Anji's carriage, bound as he was for Enead with her and Mia. Since the Ragatanese seemed to have a decent understanding of his condition, he was eager to compare notes with their medical scholars, and Parrian assured him that he could stay as her guest until they returned for my wedding.

The coronation went off without a hitch—I even managed to say my lines in passable New Kopaati—but as I changed dresses in my expansive apartment that night, Anji knocked. "I've been thinking," she said as I pulled a dark purple gown from its hanger on the privacy screen.

"About what?" I asked.

"I have an idea of what to give you for your wedding—"

"Anji," I protested, "your presence is gift enough. Seriously."

"You haven't heard my proposal yet. Loan me your Aen crystal."

I stuck my head out from around the screen. "Can I ask why?"

She smiled. "Because, to use Mia's words, I'm a damn good forger. Obviously, *I* would not say as much, but to keep things simple…"

"And since you're going to Ga'besh…" I said.

"Yes, where tragically, there is no guild oversight. Loan me the crystal, lass, and I'll do what I can with my skill, poor as it may be, to ensure that you don't regret it."

I trusted Anji with my life—of course I'd trust her with a rock. Slipping my new dress on, I emerged and handed her the crystal.

She regarded my ensemble dubiously and gave her short beard a tug. "You've been carrying it all day?"

"Pockets," I said, pulling the hidden ones out of the folds of my dress. "I insisted."

Travel in the Kopaati dry season was far from ideal, but our wedding guests made the most of it. I received a few enquiries from invited dignitaries in the weeks before the event, only half in jest: would *this* wedding actually transpire? I assured them it would, as Terj showed no inclination to leave my side.

Between my brother and my fiancé, I couldn't have asked for a better support team in the first unsettled weeks of my reign. Edes knew virtually every soul on the palace staff and within the guards closest to the throne, and after a few replays of Janine's tapes, he'd been able to name everyone involved on the attack on Cole's Crossing. I called them to me, gave them a chance to insist that they were just following orders, then tossed them from the guards and told them to get the fuck out of Deoni before I stopped feeling merciful.

They believed me.

Edes selected my new guards, and we got along swimmingly except on those occasions when I insisted upon privacy, particularly when I visited my father. Falova worried about me, but I suspected that was going to be a constant.

My brother helped me vet advisors, guided me through the finer points of not offending the local priests, and showed me all the good hiding spots in the castle that I'd missed in my few months there. As for Terj, he lived up to his name, my unflagging shadow. If I needed a message delivered, or someone to deal with the wedding planners, or just a bouncer at the door while I caught a nap, he proved willing and almost tireless. I coaxed him to bed with me after realizing he'd been physical and on his feet for five days straight—Terj appreciated that he should take occasional rest, though he didn't understand how much better it made him feel until after the fact—but his stamina far surpassed my own, and I often woke to find that he'd been snuffing little fires for hours while I recharged.

I told him not to kill himself. I'd inherited this particular circus, these were my monkeys, and it wasn't his responsibility to keep things running behind the scenes.

"Love," he murmured, then kissed my forehead and went on about his self-appointed tasks.

While the palace shakeup was underway, the best change for me was in the in-house maladeta. Tonnera was a nice woman, but I was thrilled when Ms. Quince announced she'd be staying, at least for a while. She was experienced in Deoni, she knew the players…and if anyone tried anything, she wanted to be on hand. While the odds of an uprising seemed lower by the day, I certainly didn't mind having an unusually protective maladeta around.

Thus, by the time the first of our guests started to arrive, the palace was operating smoothly, the wedding events were planned to the last detail, and I wasn't haggard from weeks of all-nighters.

Nobles began to trickle in from across Daril, followed by dignitaries from our nearest neighbors. The Taln'een delegation arrived a week ahead of time—perhaps just to spy, though I liked to imagine that Ganeel wanted to serve as a quiet but firm warning against disruption. Packs of maladetas were useful like that. Sanniah and her retinue arrived the following day, and once we'd found a safe place to leave their vehicles, I was eager to show her around the city without threat of war.

I heard through Ms. Quince that Ragatanu, Cirivant, and Oliem were, for lack of a better term, carpooling. The Ragatanese transport barges seldom saw use, and their existence was a shock to most of their neighbors. Parrian ordered one to be retrofitted for passenger comfort, and she extended offers of a lift to those who had supported our claim.

Mia and Anji arrived early and on their own steam, however; Mia wouldn't be denied, and Anji was eager to present me with her work, which she did in my apartment that night. She'd set my crystal in a gorgeous necklace, complementing the blue-green centerpiece with a few smaller gemstones she'd found lying around. Given the wealth of the Ragatanese mines—hell, the Amethyst Throne was carved from a massive chunk of the stuff—I suspected that Parrian hadn't begrudged her the materials.

"It's forged so that you don't need to grip the stone to

use it," Anji explained as I goggled at the piece. "Wearing it will be sufficient—"

"This is *stunning*," I interrupted, carefully pulling the necklace from the presentation box. "Anji…"

She blushed above her beard, which had finally grown long enough for braids again. "It's a poor thing—"

"Yes, yes," I said impatiently, "adequate at best, but if I may be slightly blasphemous for a second?"

Grinning, she waved me on.

"Holy *shit*, woman, I love it. Could you help me with the clasp, please?"

As Mia and I admired her work, Anji said, "There *is* one thing I should warn you about."

"What's that?" I asked, settling back into a chair.

Anji shared a look with Mia, then turned my way again. "So…I realize that our religious backgrounds are rather different…"

"We're not going to war, are we?"

"High Queen forbid," she replied, chuckling. "No, it concerns the wedding and my father's gift to you both."

"It's not horrible," Mia hastily assured me.

"The Great Temple in Heartfast is home to the oracle," Anji continued. Seeing my confusion, she explained, "I mentioned her, yes? When we were at the aquarium?"

"Right…" I murmured.

"If the gods ever choose to speak, they do so through the oracle," she explained. "It doesn't happen often—certainly hasn't in my lifetime—but every now and then, They make Themselves known." After pausing to ensure that I followed, she said, "People are only allowed to pose questions to the oracle on special occasions—major festivals and such. Again, they're seldom answered, but just having the chance to ask is rare."

"I see."

Anji nodded. "So typically, for something like a royal wedding, my father's gift is the opportunity to speak with the oracle. He brought her last time but didn't mention it once your wedding fell apart. He's again bringing her in his retinue—I've already asked."

"That's…very generous," I replied, unsure of the proper response.

"Yes, well, some of my siblings have suggested to him that non-dwarves might appreciate something else, particularly as the oracle never responds at weddings, but he can be stubborn."

"Look, I meant what I said the last time you were here: your presence is gift enough," I insisted. "I appreciate the gesture."

Mia looked at Anji, smirking. "I told you Suze wouldn't be offended."

"And I believed you," Anji protested, "but there's still a *tiny* matter to address. I know you two understand how we give and receive, even if you laugh—"

"We don't mean to be insensitive, Anji," I interrupted. "We just really like your work."

She spread her hands. "Which is why Mia has tried to help me learn to appreciate well-meant compliments. But what I'm telling you is that this is the sort of gift you *should not* downplay. This is not a 'most adequate' situation. For a dwarf, it might be a once-in-a-lifetime chance to hear directly from the gods, so…I mean, no one expects outsiders to be quite as thrilled, but—"

"I'll do my best not to embarrass you or spark another religious conflict," I assured her. "Out of curiosity, what *does* one ask an oracle?"

Anji shrugged. "Anything you like. If it's interesting enough, maybe you'll get an answer."

Most of our guests made their way to the castle and were received by servants, assured that they would have a moment with us before or after the ceremony, but Terj and I wanted to be on hand when the converted Ragatanese barge landed in our makeshift airstrip on the far side of the river. They touched down the day after Mia and Anji arrived, a few hours ahead of the evening reception for foreign dignitaries, and Parrian laughed when she saw Terj and me waving at them in the grass. "Aren't you supposed to be *dressing*, dear?" she asked as she disembarked. "You're hosting tonight, are you not?"

"We'll make it," I assured her, and grinned. "Thank you for coming back so soon."

"It's no hardship," she replied. "And assuming my granddaughter will be frequenting this place, I should acquaint myself with it."

Cary followed his mother out of the back, followed by Janine. Mia had warned us the night before that her mother would be attending. "I wouldn't say things are great yet," she'd admitted over drinks with Anji, Terj, Edes, and me, "but Mom's trying, and Dad's trying, and Grandmother is sort of ignoring them both."

"Are they...*together*?" Edes had asked.

Mia had nodded at that. "She looks more like his mom than his girlfriend, but he doesn't seem to give a damn, and...frankly, I've never seen her so happy. Mom *laughs* these days. She never used to do that."

It was, I thought, too much to hope that Janine and Mia would be best friends after years of hurt and half-truths and two months of quasi-reconciliation, but they were speaking again, and Anji had yet to see the need to kneecap anyone. I counted that as progress.

As Cary helped Janine down, Fanakel emerged, grinning as he waved to us. He'd kept the short beard, I noticed with approval—really, it worked for him—and I felt Terj's twinge of amusement as Fanakel offered a hand to Tavinnia. The princess had come in a long, embroidered tunic and leggings instead of her armor, and the look she gave Fanakel as she let him assist her out of the barge was anything but platonic. Another brunette elf followed her down—the queen of Oliem, I assumed—and Fanakel helped her as well.

Through Ms. Quince and the Oliem-based maladeta, Terj and I had already heard the gossip. Oliem being a rogue kingdom by elven standards, they had little contact with others of their kind, and finding a prince of *Nokan'ti*—even a half-blooded one—in their midst had been a bit of excitement. Oliem had a university in its capital, not nearly as renowned as the prestigious Schools of Nokan'ti but growing, and Fanakel had been persuaded to offer a few guest lectures about elven culture and relations beyond Oliem's borders. To his surprise, he enjoyed teaching. He didn't need to worry about finding a lucrative career—the queen had gladly hosted him, as Tavinnia was smitten, and whatever the princess wanted, her doting mother provided. Still, it pleased Fanakel that he could offer something of value, and I had it on good authority that he would be teaching a full class within a few months.

When I thought about the reception that night and how the Twins would see their renegade prince with a beautiful elf on his arm, I couldn't help but smile.

Following them came the Cirivanti delegation—Fetull and Cofali, of course, and all eight of their children and their sons- and daughters-in-law. Makou left the disembarking pack to give me a hug, then clasped Terj's hand with mock solemnity and thanked him for doing him a favor. Cofali rolled her eyes at her son's antics, but Terj wished him better luck next time, and Makou retreated in good spirits.

After the last of Makou's siblings climbed out, Narod appeared in the doorway, a little more tanned than I'd last seen him and certainly far better rested. I started to approach to welcome him back—the situation was awkward enough—but he raised a finger to stay me and stuck his hand into the barge.

And out walked Jerrcoa.

He used his father's arm to steady himself as he slowly descended the steps, and he leaned on a cane in consideration of his weaker left side, but he was ambulatory, and I almost cried to see the pride in his eyes. I hugged him, careful not to throw him off balance, and stepped back to find Narod beaming.

They'd had a pact with Junil and Taliem, the maladetas stationed in the courts of Ragatanu and Cirivant, to keep Jerrcoa's progress a surprise. The Ragatanese medical scholars had done wonders for him in terms of physical therapy, and he'd been training with weights for weeks, insisting that he'd attend the wedding on his feet. He might always need a cane, he said that afternoon while Terj and I sneaked a quick meal with my siblings before the long reception, and he'd brought his wheelchair in case he tired, but his team was convinced that he would continue to improve.

And what will you do now? Terj asked. *Remain in Ragatanu? Come home?*

At that, Jerrcoa smiled and lifted his glass. "I'll be home eventually, but you know, I've much to see first."

The following day, after a night spent making small talk with the dignitaries—some of whom were *very* surprised to find certain others in their midst—I once again greeted the long line of well-wishers who'd come to the castle to see the happy couple. This time, however, I almost enjoyed the experience. Having donned another lacing-free gown for the day, I sat not in a little chair at the front of the dais, pinned under my mother's watchful eye, but enthroned with Terj at my side. It was amazing how much more pleasant the experience was when I was actually looking forward to marrying my intended. For his part, Terj knew damn well that he was a curiosity, but he bore it in stride and mostly let me make the conversation unless asked a direct question. As the number of Darilis who had ever been in communication with an elemental was nearly nil, hearing his voice in their heads came as a shock. Still, people were at least polite, and several with whom I'd spoken at my first such reception commented that I seemed so much *happier* this time around.

After a rehearsal and dinner that night, Terj and I retired, me to my bed and him to parts unknown. I teased him that he was getting cold feet, but he assured me that that night was too nice not to enjoy, and he would return.

And he did. I awoke at first light to find myself spooned with my back to his chest and his arm draped over me, and I rolled over as he smiled. "You know," I whispered, "it's supposed to be bad luck for the groom to see the bride on their wedding day until the main event."

Is it, now? His pale eyes twinkled. *Would you like me to go?*

I kissed him and snuggled closer. *Nope.*

I was hoping you'd say that.

As I closed my eyes to steal a few more minutes of sleep, I told him, *I'm so glad you chose me.*

Likewise, he replied, and adjusted the blankets to cover my shoulders. *You're not sick of me yet?*

Ask me again in a hundred years' time, and I'm pretty sure it'll still be a no.

Mm. In that case, want to do something crazy and get married today?

Maybe in a few hours.

His chest rumbled as he laughed. *This is nice, too.*

On the other hand, there is a banquet to follow the wedding.

Oh, I'm invited this time?

I'm going to be cross if you don't show up.

Well, then, Your Majesty, he said, kissing me again, *I'll clear my schedule.*

For tonight?

How about forever?

I like the sound of that, I told him, and prayed my maids would stay away just a little longer.

Tradition held that royal marriages in Daril took place in

the temple in Deoni, but we weren't a traditional couple, and I needed an outdoor venue. Fortunately, the dry season was on my side, and not a drop of rain fell upon the massive pavilion we'd had erected in a field by the river. Some of our guests grumbled at the inconvenience of having to leave the city walls for the ceremony, but I wasn't about to exclude my father from the festivities. Falova didn't seem particularly bothered by the spectacle—the grand procession of priests, the instrumentalists, the dozens of floral sprays bedecking any flat surface that wasn't a chair—but I felt his flash of happiness as I prepared to walk to the altar, and when I turned to the river, I found him risen above the surface, watching. I grinned and waved, and he lifted a hand in greeting before motioning me onward.

The only time I teared up that afternoon was when Ms. Quince, adjusting my pale blue train, whispered, "Barnaby and Malachi would be so proud of you."

"I know they are," I whispered back, and hugged her before I started toward Terj.

I spoke my vows before our guests and the gods, carefully enunciating my New Kopaati. Terj, who didn't have to worry about minutiae like pronunciation, made his vows in his fashion. If the high priest was unnerved to hear the voice in his mind, he didn't show it. Flashing and clicking in the audience told me that Mia and Janine had come with cameras.

And when all was said and done, Terj kissed me like he would never let me go.

Once again, I sat at the high table for a wedding banquet, but I sat at the center with my husband that time, feeling more carefree than I had in months. Though I'd changed dresses, I still wore the necklace Anji had given me, and Terj and I laughed about our his-and-hers Aen crystal jewelry. His was buried beneath his shirt, but mine sat on full display, the subject of many a compliment during the night.

As the meal wound down and tables were moved aside for dancing, Rokund approached and smiled up at us. "One of the finest I've yet attended," he said, giving his belly a slap, "and no one knows feasting like dwarves."

"Thank you so much for coming," I replied. "It means a lot that you're here, especially considering your *last* visit to Daril."

"Of course, lass." Stepping closer to lower his voice, he added, "You think I'd let Nokan'ti show us up?"

I glanced at the elves, who kept to themselves at a table midway down the hall, watching as Fanakel twirled laughing Tavinnia. "I don't think you have anything to worry about, Your Excellency."

He chuckled, then gestured toward a door into an anteroom. "Would you two mind joining me? I have a wedding gift."

Terj and I rose and followed him out, where we found the entire Blackhorn Mountain delegation assembled, along with Anji and Mia. At the center of their group, seated among a cluster of priests, was a white-bearded figure, thin with age but bright-eyed.

"This," said Rokund, leading us closer, "is Ganivan, our oracle. She alone among all dwarves receives direct communication from the gods."

"Very impressive," I said, and nodded to Ganivan. "Thank you for coming to our wedding, ma'am. I hope the travel wasn't overly taxing."

Frail though she was, she reached for my hand and gave it a firm squeeze as she smiled. "Not at all," she replied, her voice faint and wobbly. "Blessings to you both."

"It has become tradition in circumstances like these to offer the gift of a question to the gods," said Rokund as Ganivan released me. "I made the same gift to your mother and Narod. Unfortunately, I can't guarantee an *answer,*" he added, rubbing the back of his neck, "but if you would ask, Ganivan is willing to try."

Having already discussed the matter with Terj, I said, "This is a far greater gift than we merit, Your Excellency. But since this is our wedding day…"

I looked at Terj, who nodded.

"Anji has been a wonderful friend to us," I continued. "She put herself in harm's way for two *very* inept strangers to whom she owed nothing, and I don't think Mia will disagree when I say there's a decent chance we wouldn't be alive today if not for her."

"Amen," Mia chimed in, while Anji regarded us bemusedly.

"And we know Anji is devout," I said to her father. "Which is why Terj and I would be terrible friends if we didn't ask her to accept this incredible gift in our stead."

"*Susan,*" Anji started to protest, but Rokund lifted a hand to silence her.

"You do not wish this opportunity?" he asked us.

I quickly studied his expression, hoping I hadn't caused grievous insult, but I saw his tiny smile of pride. "Oh, no, it's a wonderful gift," I replied, "but we fear that we would waste it on something beneath the gods' notice. It would give us great pleasure if Anji would ask instead."

His smile widened briefly, and then he turned to his daughter. "Well, my dear?"

Mia nudged her forward, and Anji, saucer-eyed, shuffled toward the oracle. "I don't deserve this," she mumbled as she approached.

Ganivan reached for her. "None of us do, child. Ask what you would know."

As Anji took her hand, the priests readied themselves, just in case.

Anji hesitated, then glanced over her shoulder at Mia before turning back to the oracle and releasing a small sigh. "I know that the gods' creations are perfect and flawless, but…if I could ask the High Queen…why am I the way I am?"

I didn't know what I was expecting from the oracle—maybe a pause to listen for a word from on high and a comforting word to the supplicant. What I was *not* expecting was for her back to snap straight like she'd just grabbed a high-voltage line and her face to flip toward the ceiling. While the startled priests backed off and scrambled for the pencils they'd dropped, Ganivan gasped, then slowly lowered her head until she was looking at Anji again.

Her eyes, I saw with alarm, now shone white.

When Ganivan spoke, the voice that emerged from her was not her own—female, yes, but lower-pitched and ageless. "You are as you were intended to be, Anjikora."

Anji, still held tightly in Ganivan's grip, had gone pale, but she didn't pull away. "I have always tried to follow the laws," she said in a rush. "I've done my best, worthless though it is, but I...why do I..."

"Why do you love her?" the voice that wasn't Ganivan's finished.

She nodded mutely.

"Because you were meant to. Because you will find happiness with each other."

"But the laws say—"

The oracle snorted. "We *said* that marriage was a union of two souls brought together and bound to each other. We made no mention of gender, little daughter. You know that."

Anji's dark eyes widened in the glow of the oracle's stare. "Then...but the priests..."

"They interpreted poorly." The being possessing Ganivan turned to her trembling entourage and said, "Have I made Myself clear?"

The bravest of the lot nodded and clutched his notebook. The rest fell on their faces.

"Does that answer your question, Anjikora?" she asked with a little smile.

Anji went to one knee and kissed the oracle's gnarled hand.

"Be well, little daughter. And though you did not ask, know that your mother is very proud of you."

Rokund stiffened, and Anji's head shot up again, but the light had gone out, and the old woman blinked as blearily as if she'd been shaken from deep sleep. "She answered?" Ganivan asked in her wavering voice.

Anji rose and gave her a hug. "Thank you."

"Of course," replied the surprised oracle. "She hasn't spoken in years. The last time...when was that?"

But Anji didn't wait to consult with the priests. Turning from Ganivan, she marched past her father and took Mia's hands. "You heard the High Queen, lass. Marry me?"

Common wisdom holds that it's rude to propose marriage at someone else's wedding, but as Terj pulled me close, the assorted clergy of Blackhorn Mountain tried to figure out what the hell had just happened, and Anji wrapped her legs around Mia's waist, the better to hold on as the two embraced, I smiled.

EPILOGUE

Five years later

I went to bed with the usual pre-travel checklist running through my mind. We were bound for Ragatanu in the morning, heading to Enead for the third annual international tech conference, and I *thought* I had everything packed and in order, but my brain churned as I tried to turn it off.

The four worlds had never seen anything like the conference, and it might never have come about had Mia not spent one too many nights with us and finally snapped with the lack of plumbing. Working with Cary, and draining his bank account, Janine's, and mine, the three of them had made dozens of visits back to Earth to buy books on every subject they could imagine: mathematics, physics, engineering, circuitry, electrical systems, architecture, urban planning, and yes, plumbing. Parrian had endowed a center at Enead's university for the massive research project, and the finest scholars in Ragatanu had descended, armed with translators, to begin the long task of educating themselves in human technology. Cirivant had wanted in on the action, I'd sent a team from Daril, and soon, the center was full of the four worlds' best and brightest—all but the traditional elves, who refused to lower themselves. Oliem had no such reservations, making them the only elves at the table but most welcome nonetheless.

The annual conference was a ten-day stretch of

presentations, roundtables, panel discussions, and proposals for implementable change. I'd scheduled meetings with the best engineers at the center, who had sent word via maladeta that a true sewer system was possible in Daril, though it would be a costly undertaking. They were more optimistic about water conservation projects to defend us against the dry season, and I knew from Falova that similar projects were already underway in Ti'cal. While it still annoyed me to no end that the maladetas refused to share the secret to their communication devices, I'd heard whispers that a group within the center was toying with a workaround, a hybrid piece of Aen-powered technology that could revolutionize communication across the four worlds. If it was anything like a phone, I'd take it.

Terj and I had built in time to make the social rounds as well. We'd see Mia and Anji, of course, who periodically switched between Heartfast and Enead to satisfy both women's parents. Fanakel and Tavinnia were coming in with the Oliem delegation; the queen felt out of her depth at the conference, but her daughter and son-in-law took careful notes. Even Sanniah would be there, since some of Banilgh's scholars had joined in. I didn't know who from Cirivant would be in attendance, but I'd scheduled a visit out to our Ga'beshi territories for a sibling reunion. Zadi was traveling with us, Jerrcoa had joined the center two years prior, and Edes was, by all accounts, still very much enjoying his role as local governor. While I'd been sorry to see Edes go, I knew he wanted a change of pace, and he'd flourished in Ga'besh. His actual responsibilities were few, he had plenty of time for hunting and sailing, and he lived within easy reach of his uncle and father...and Makou, who had broken up with his boyfriend about a year after our aborted wedding. I wasn't entirely sure how I felt about the quiet relationship between my brother and his cousin, my ex-fiancé, but they seemed happy, and I really wasn't one to talk.

Besides, Makou *was* handsome. Edes could have done far worse.

Eventually, I drifted off to sleep that night, but I awoke in the darkness to the percussion of pounding rain and Terj's hand on my shoulder. "Love," he murmured. "She's out again."

I groaned, knowing too well that he was right, and rolled over to face him. "Do we need to go now?"

"Falova is watching her. We can collect her in the morning."

Peeved but reassured by Terj's confidence, I settled against him and closed my eyes, struck once again by how strongly his eventual accent had developed. Granted, he didn't sound like he was from Cole's Crossing, but he'd picked up enough of its patterns to mark his time there. Neither of us sounded Darili, no matter how hard I tried, but that mattered little day to day. No one had yet arisen to challenge me for the throne, and if I brought basic sanitation to the kingdom, then maybe they never would.

I tried to sleep, but worry wouldn't let me, and so Terj and I rose before dawn and headed onto an open walkway in the drizzle, which I shielded away. "Ready?" he asked.

"Sure."

He dematerialized and picked me up, and we set off toward the north, following the river toward its outlet into the northern sea. This wasn't our first such excursion, and I knew it'd be about a two-hour trip each way if Terj wasn't fighting a headwind.

What are our options? I asked him as he flew over the sodden fields outside the city. *We can't nail the windows shut. She'll just sneak out a door.*

She can't slip through cracks, he replied. *She's a physical being—*

To this point. We don't know that she'll stay this way. What if she hits puberty and... I let the thought fizzle, as the coloration of Terj's thoughts told me that continuation was unnecessary. *I don't want to be cruel to her, but if something happened to her out here, alone...*

She's not alone, Terj reminded me. *No one would leave a child her age unattended.*

You say that, but that's my baby, and she keeps running away from me. God, I feel like the most inadequate mother.

Love flowed through our mental connection. *You're not. Tying her to the bed would be cruel. You're giving her room.*

You're really not worried?

I worry, he admitted, *but I also do the same thing. This is natural.*

He had a point. I slept well on rainy nights, and so I seldom stirred when my husband vanished to go wandering in the seasonal gales. It was invigorating, he said, to be in the midst of so much potential, and considering the number of air elementals who rode through the city with every storm, I didn't doubt him.

But Terj was several hundred years old, and Canami was barely four.

She'd been born on a miserably rainy night a few months after our first anniversary, a perfectly normal-looking baby with dark hair, a scrunched red face, and the traditional number of fingers and toes. When she opened her eyes, however, they were the impossibly pale gray of her father's, and she quickly figured out how to fly from her crib whenever she didn't want to be left alone. We'd thought that she favored him until she discovered the fun of making giant bubbles of bathwater float out of the tub and pop on the floor, and then we realized what we had on our hands: a rogue with *dual* elemental abilities.

We'd named her Canami at Jerrcoa's suggestion, going for a traditional Darili name with positive connotations, but those of us who loved her just called her Stormy.

I can hear her, came Falova's voice from below us. *She is approaching.*

I sighed with relief. *How far out?*

Oh, you know...

Father.

Far enough, he said, keeping it nice and vague. *The storm was strong. She handled herself well—only two falls.*

I groaned, imagining my little girl landing on a rock beyond my father's reach.

I caught her, he quickly reassured me. *You know I would not leave her unwatched, soul of my soul.*

And I appreciate that, I told him, *but the kid's going to give me gray hair.*

His amusement filtered into my mind. *How do you think I feel every time you leave Kopaat?*

That's different!

How?

She's four! I'm grown!

By whose standards? he teased. *I watched Deoni rise from the dirt. You have far to go, little one.*

I rolled my eyes and looked toward the northern horizon, waiting to spot the glimmering line of the sea.

The drizzle petered out just before the sun rose, and daylight broke through the patchy clouds in pinks and oranges as Terj neared the ocean. I squinted down at the waves as we sailed over the ships docked around the harbor, then heard a voice that had become familiar in recent months, that of one of the sea's nameless elementals: *Little sister is safe.*

Where? Terj asked.

We will meet you at the mouth of the river.

He put us down on the bank and solidified, and moments later, a wave came speeding the wrong way through the harbor and up the river, carrying atop it our laughing daughter. Seeing us, she grinned and leapt into the air. "Mommy! Daddy!"

I caught her and squeezed her close, holding her chilled little body against mine, and Terj sandwiched her between us.

Thank you so much, I said to the elemental, then kissed Stormy's forehead and looked down at her. "What do you have to say for yourself, young lady?"

"We're meant to be leaving soon," Terj added. "Remember? We're going to Ragatanu today."

Stormy stared up at us both, all big-eyed innocence. "I couldn't sleep," she protested. "The sky was dancing last night."

"And what have we said about going out alone?" I replied.

She huffed. "Tell Daddy first?"

"Uh-huh." I kissed her again. "So why didn't we tell Daddy?"

"I tried! He was gone!"

I turned to Terj, who smiled sheepishly. "She's...not wrong."

"Seriously?"

"I was just gone for a few hours! You were comfortable."

There were definite allowances that had to be made when one was married to an elemental born to air...though the perks weren't too shabby.

"Want to go home before Zadi freaks out that we've left her?" I said.

I will tell her when she wakes, Falova offered.

Thank you, I replied as Terj lifted us off the ground.

Grandfather! Stormy called down, reaching toward the river. *Carry me?*

Another time, he promised her, and a hand emerged from the water to wave as Terj sped us toward Deoni.

We hadn't been airborne twenty minutes before Stormy was asleep in my lap with her thumb in her mouth. *She's a cute little mess*, I said to Terj.

She's the best of us both, love.

In the last five years, I'd acquired a handful of regnal monikers: the Rogue of Daril, the Scarred Queen, the Last Watcher. The Usurper, technically true but not my favorite. The Godslayer, a bit much.

But of all the names I was called, the one Terj used was my favorite.

The sun rose, and the soaked grasses sparkled like diamonds beneath us, potential I could reach out and seize as easily as breathing. Instead, I cradled our sleeping daughter and leaned back against the invisible cushion holding us aloft.

Rest, love. We'll be there soon, Terj coaxed.

Not for long. Soon, we would start for Ragatanu, my sister, my husband, and me, along with a child born of air and water whose powers were yet to be fully revealed. We would make our way between the worlds through the great cavern, avoiding the tunnel that led up to the woods by the ruins of Cole's Crossing. Someday, I would take my daughter to Earth and show her the locations of places that now existed only in memory, and I would help her understand why she, like her mother, bore two last names. Though the Coles had left the Crossing, our family endured.

But that was for the future. That morning, as the clouds drifted away and the world below came alive, I closed my eyes and sensed the water all around us, then let the tug of the river guide me home.

ACKNOWLEDGEMENTS

Thank you for coming along with me on this long, strange trip through the Crossing. I hope you've enjoyed the ride!

As always, my thanks go to the Novel Chicks, who've put up with my flights of fancy for quite some time.

And yes, here's to you, Mom and Dad.

ABOUT THE AUTHOR

When not writing fiction, Ash Fitzsimmons is an appellate attorney and an unrepentant car singer.

Find her online:
www.ashfitzsimmons.com